EYES

OF

ELISHA

D0879619

BRANDILYN COLLINS

EYES OF ELISHA

Cover Photo by Michael29
Author Name Logo by DogEared Design
Author photo by Angela Hunt

Challow Press
212 W. Ironwood Dr., Suite D
#316
Coeur d'Alene, ID 83814

ISBN: 0692502858
ISBN 13: 978-0692502853

"A taut, heartbreaking thriller … Collins is a fine writer who knows to both horrify readers and keep them turning pages."
--*Publishers Weekly, Over the Edge*

"Solidly constructed. One of the Top 10 Inspirational Novels of 2010." --*Booklist, Deceit*

"Intense. Engaging. Whiplash-inducing plot twists."
--*Thrill Writer, Dark Pursuit*

"A harrowing hostage drama." --*Library Journal, Amber Morn*

"One of the Best Books of 2007 … Top Christian suspense of the year." --*Library Journal Starred Review, Crimson Eve*

"A chilling mystery … not one to be read alone at night."
--*RT BOOKclub, Coral Moon*

"A sympathetic heroine … effective flashbacks … Collins knows how to weave faith into a rich tale." --*Library Journal, Violet Dawn*

"A master storyteller … Collins deftly finesses the accelerator on this knuckle-chomping ride." --*RT BOOKclub, Web of Lies*

"Finely crafted … vivid … another masterpiece that keeps the reader utterly engrossed." --*RT BOOKclub, Dread Champion*

"Chilling … a confusing, twisting trail that keeps pages turning."
--*Publishers Weekly, Eyes of Elisha*

BOOKS BY BRANDILYN COLLINS

Southern Contemporary

Bradleyville Series

Cast a Road Before Me
Color the Sidewalk for Me
Capture the Wind for Me

Dearing Family Series

That Dog Won't Hunt
Pitchin' a Fit

Suspense

Stand Alone Novels

Sidetracked
Dark Justice
Gone to Ground
Over the Edge
Deceit
Exposure
Dark Pursuit

Rayne Tour YA Series
(co-written with Amberly Collins)

Always Watching
Last Breath
Final Touch

Kanner Lake Series

Violet Dawn
Coral Moon
Crimson Eve
Amber Morn

Hidden Faces Series

Brink of Death
Stain of Guilt
Dead of Night
Web of Lies

Chelsea Adams Series

Eyes of Elisha
Dread Champion

Non-Fiction

Getting Into Character:
Seven Secrets a Novelist Can Learn From Actors

Now the king of Aram was at war with Israel.
After conferring with his officers, he said,
"I will set up my camp in such and such a place."
The man of God [Elisha] sent word to the king of Israel:
"Beware of passing that place, because the Arameans
are going down there." So the king of Israel
checked on the place indicated by the man of God.
Time and again Elisha warned the king,
so that he was on his guard in such places.
This enraged the king of Aram. He summoned his officers
and demanded of them, "Will you not tell me which of us
is on the side of the king of Israel?"
"None of us, my lord the king," said one of his officers,
"but Elisha, the prophet who is in Israel, tells the king of Israel
the very words you speak in your bedroom."

2 Kings 6:8-12

Prologue

Beep-beep, beep-beep.

Her eyes flew open at the sound from her jogger's watch. Twenty times its alarm resounded through the bedroom, washed gray with the nascent day's light. A shrill awakening on an otherwise still summer morning. She fixed the textured ceiling with a glassy stare, willing her body to catch up with her mind, already whirling.

On any other day, she would steal a moment or two as the white luminous hand on her clock radio marched toward 5:35 A.M. But as lazy as she might feel in those few minutes, inevitably the pavement would beckon. Jogging had proved the one regimented step in her loosely choreographed life.

But today she would allow herself no slack. And her four-mile run would be particularly necessary. Instead of spending the day in front of a computer, she would soon be in the low-slung bucket seat of her burgundy Camaro, zipping toward the state line at a pace that meant business.

Haverlon, California, to Chicago, Illinois. A three-day journey by car, four hours by plane, flying out of San Francisco. In rational thought, the numbers would win. But she was scared to death of flying. She'd done it once on a summer vacation with her family when she was in high school. Memories of the experience still sent a tic of fear down her spine. The plane had hit hard rain and winds, and the five-hundred-ton piece of machinery had bucked like a scared filly. Even the stately flight attendant with her hair in a French twist had worn a pinched look on her face.

Far safer to feel the rubber hit the road. Besides, starting her vacation midweek, she had time to bow to her fears.

She rubbed her eyes, smiling at the thought. Hoisting herself from bed, she made for the bathroom. The daily routine followed — contacts, T-shirt, jogging shorts. Thick white sport socks. A quick brush through her long blond hair. She dressed automatically, her mind on seeing the man she loved again. She'd missed him *so much.* He was The One — she knew it this time, the short-lived tryst with her neighbor notwithstanding. Maybe, *maybe* this trip, he'd give her a ring.

"Oops, strap those shoes on tight," she chided herself aloud. "Stopping to retie is bad luck." She paused to squeeze the small blue fabric pack attached to the top of her right shoe. Force of habit, learned the hard way. Her house key lay inside. She removed it only to unlock her front door at the end of her run every morning. She had trained herself to replace the key before stepping over the threshold, even in cold weather. Locking yourself out of the house early in the morning, sweaty from a run, was a lousy way to start a day.

Humming a little tune, she slipped through her front door, pulled it shut, and eased into a jog.

~ ~ ~

Through his living room window, he watched her jog down the street, blond hair bouncing, lithe body held with ease. Her elbows were slightly bent, arms loose at her sides. An experienced jogger. Her route, he knew, would be the same as every morning. A beeline to Trent Park.

In his mind's eye he scanned the park's wildly sprawling acres. No Sunday-afternoon-picnic-in-the-grass park, that one. A one-lane gravel road cut through the corner of Trent, twisting into the forest and turning back again to join up with Wickens Road about a half mile north of the first entrance. It was a popular route for joggers and walkers who enjoyed raw, woodsy surroundings. The rest of the park lay uncultivated, some parts barely passable. Boy Scouts used Trent Park for camping and rock climbing, thanks to

12

its exposed crags and one particularly large gully, which a hiker would find only by following one of the narrow paths beaten by troops over the years.

Ah, Trent Park. He knew it well. Its beckoning fringes and its silent, seldom trod core.

He drank in the sight of her and swayed, goose pimples popping down his arms. He could not fight the pull any longer. It wrapped tentacles around his ankles, threatening to suck him beneath the waves of his childhood memories. Throwing out his hands, he caught the back of an armchair and hung on.

The drunken voice of his rich, widowed mother — heavily mascaraed and bleach-haired — ricocheted through his head. It was "Come here, baby, come hug your mommy" one minute, blows of rage the next. Hands of silk and fire, trailing enticement and revulsion. His hatred of those hands had sizzled into a bonfire as he'd grown.

He choked out a breath, summoning his reserve strength, his basic instinct for survival. That instinct had served him well at nineteen, when his mother died of cancer. After her death, he'd promised himself that his inheritance would make up for the damage she'd caused. One warped soul, paid in full.

And so he had fought the fire within, throwing oceans of repression over the flames until they abated to a flicker. Then *she* had come along, with her roving eye and raised brow, her glances heat-soaked and inviting ... only to turn on him, just like his mother.

He straightened up, steadied himself, took a long, deep breath. A strange calm descended as he moved toward the entryway of the townhouse. Stealthily he opened the door and stepped outside, pulling the door shut. A quiet morning, with a promise of warmth. A bird warbled from a trio of lanky birch trees in a neighbor's yard. His thoughts accelerated, rolling along dual tracks of murderous intent and cunning self-protection. He glanced left. Right. Scanned the curtained windows of townhouses across the drive. Not a soul to be seen. He kicked into a long-strided run, intent on his mission as he bounded from his sidewalk onto the street. After a few pumps, he skidded suddenly and turned. There. Lying on the front stoop. Why hadn't he thought of using something like that? He stared hard, eyes narrowed, as if willing it to tell him what to do.

In a split-second decision, he trotted down the sidewalk, snatched his find from the porch, and stuffed it into the waistband of his shorts, eyes flicking from side to side. The sidewalk rolled under his feet again, leading to the entrance of the townhouse development. He concentrated on gliding his feet smoothly, almost soundlessly, over the pavement. As he turned left onto Wickens, he slid a hand into his shorts' inner pocket to feel the reassuring bulk of a switchblade — small, but deadly.

He exhaled in even gusts as he ran, trees and an occasional house bouncing by. Eight minutes later, he turned into the north entrance of Trent Park, then veered onto a narrow trail, a shortcut that crossed the main gravel road after a quarter mile. His eyes widened as he disappeared into the trees, straining for sight of the trail in the still-dark forest. A heavy mist hovered over the path, flinging beads of moisture onto his hair.

Be alone, please be alone.

Light began to filter through the trees ahead. He dropped to a crouch just off the gravel and waited, muscles tense. After all his planning, some other jogger coming along could ruin everything. He shuddered to think what would become of him if he could not fulfill his task. He had to accomplish this. He *had* to.

At a sound, he jerked up his head, ears cocked, legs quivering. He heard the rhythmic *crunch, crunch* of a ten-minute-mile pace but saw no one. His heart turned into an erratic pump. *Crunch, crunch.* Soles on gravel. *Crunch, crunch.* The fire grew in his belly. His hand felt again for the switchblade and tightened around it. *Crunch, crunch.* Air rattled down his throat.

14

With ultimate clarity he saw her, outlined against the early morning sky as if bounding toward him on three-dimensional film. The sudden sight of her blond hair bouncing, her easily held body, sucked away his breath. Elbows slightly bent, hands low, she rounded what would be her last bend in Trent Park.

~ ~ ~

Revulsion. Relief. An energized exhaustion.

It was done.

Panting, he stood over her bruised body, bathing himself in the sudden, soul-wrenching calm. Sweat plinked into his eyes and flicked salt on his lips. He wiped his forehead with a sleeve, looking dispassionately at the crumpled form at his feet. The symbol of his drunken mother. She was dead. And her despised hands had never touched him.

He was free.

For a moment he savored the memory of her terror, then blinked as his thoughts turned to logistics. What should he do with what he'd picked up from the porch? Neck straining, he made his examination. No blood on the front. No blood on the back. He rotated it for an omniscient view. No blood anywhere. Only dirt. Good. He again secured it in the waistband of his shorts.

Now for her.

With a final victorious glance at the object of his affliction, he nudged a foot underneath her and shoved her body to the edge of the gully, then watched it fall, rolling, crashing. He gazed almost idly at the sprays of dust and dirt that puffed into the air as the body tumbled downward to its final resting place.

Silence.

He backed up, using a small branch to scruff out any footprints in the soft dirt. When he reached the leaf-covered trail, he paused, allowing his eyes to again grow used to the forest's dimness, then set off down the trail, carrying the branch for a few minutes before throwing it into dense underbrush. His jog back to the road was serene, melodic bird calls trilling above his head. Near the end of the trail, he halted, listening for any telltale *crunch, crunch* on the road. He heard nothing but lurked in the half shadow of the last bend to be sure. Just before jumping onto the road, he reassured himself that the knife was still in his pocket. That had been his threat, the reflection of the rising sun hitting steel fast extinguishing the light in her eyes. A flash of that knife, and she had done everything he'd demanded, disbelief etching ragged lines into her face.

He hit the gravel and accelerated into a steady jog toward the north entrance of the park. Left the gravel road, hit pavement, turned right. The muted *crunch* of his strides gave way to soundlessness. Down a mile and into the complex, eyes flicking. Still no one to be seen. Passing the townhouses on Dapple, arrayed neatly side by side, he wondered again what to do with his find from the porch, forecasting possible consequences.

Ah, yes. How deceptively simple.

PART I
WITNESS

"I know it and am a witness to it,"
declares the L*ORD.*

Jeremiah 29:23

2000

Wednesday, June 7

Chapter 1

"We need to get going, Chels."

Chelsea felt her husband's gentle hand against her back as she lingered to watch the final moment of evening news. Paul had just arrived home from work. His finely woven ecru shirt, 100 percent cotton, light starch, was etched with the cares and stresses of twelve hours at the office. Chelsea's black dress belied her jeans-clad day at home, ferrying two boys to school and back, doing laundry, going to the dentist.

"Okay." Chelsea punched off the TV and turned to smile at Paul, taking in his square jaw, the intense blue of his eyes. "You make a mighty fine date tonight, Mr. Adams."

"Not half as fine as you." He pulled her close, lips lingering against her neck.

"Thought you said we had to leave."

"That we do." He sighed. "Business awaits."

Downstairs, the babysitter sat at the kitchen table, head bent over a textbook. The boys — Michael, twelve, and Scott, ten — were sprawled on the family room carpet in front of the TV. "I want hugs, both of you." Chelsea smiled at them. She had to grab hugs whenever she could. The boys considered themselves far too mature to allow anything of the sort in public. "Bye. I love you." She pushed Michael's hair out of his eyes.

Fifteen minutes later, Paul's Lexus sedan wound its way up Skyline Boulevard toward Bayhill, one of their favorite coat-and-tie restaurants overlooking the San Francisco Peninsula. "Remind me of your candidate's name again?" Chelsea rested a hand on her husband's knee. "It's something different."

"Gavil Harrison. He's the one who lives in Haverlon."

Chelsea pictured Gavil Harrison taking the 280 Freeway to Highway 92 and turning west toward Skyline Boulevard. Haverlon was only a ten-minute drive up 280 from their town of Woodside, and just north of Redwood City. "Amazing, isn't it, finding a candidate right here in the Bay Area. A lot cheaper than moving someone across the country."

Vice president of sales was a new position at AP Systems, created because of increasing demands upon the four regional sales managers as the company continued to grow. Chelsea knew Gavil had made it through the initial meeting and call-backs with Paul. He'd also passed muster under the meticulous questioning of Henry Morrow, founder of Morrow and Associates, the well-heeled investment firm in Silicon Valley that backed the six-year-old company.

"Well, we're not sure we've found him yet. You've got to pass him first."

Chelsea patted Paul's knee, masking her disbelief. Paul wanted her to feel as though her opinion counted, and she was grateful for that. But what was left for her to say when he'd practically made up his mind?

"Gavil does seem right for us," Paul said. "But I wonder how well he'll transition to a start-up company after fifteen years with a large firm."

Chelsea was silent. She knew Paul could answer this kind of question better than she. Paul understood the needs of AP Systems better than anyone. He'd built the software company from the ground up.

"I think you'll like the guy, Chels. Though I have heard two things that gave me pause. He did have something about ten years ago—a near breakdown due to job stress and personal matters, he says. But I don't see any signs of a problem now, and his references indicate that it hasn't happened since. And one person mentioned he saw Gavil get really angry at someone over the phone. But it sounded like a personal conversation."

Chelsea reflected on this. "So what does that mean? Does he show a tendency to get mad easily at work?"

"Couldn't find anyone who'd say so."

"Then why would this person who mentioned it bring it up? I mean, everyone gets angry once in a while. There must be something more to it."

Paul shook his head. "Don't know."

Chelsea focused on the darkened trees along the winding road. "How old is Gavil?"

"Around forty."

"Married?"

"No. He's been dating someone for about a year, and I think he just moved in with her. I don't think he's ever been married." The car bounced as they rolled across the entrance into Bayhill. "She's divorced, but I don't think she has kids. Look." Paul pointed with his chin toward the restaurant. "That's him going in now."

The car's headlights washed through fog to light the lean figure of a salt-and-pepper-haired man entering the restaurant. Chelsea caught a glimpse of an angular jaw with a stately Grecian nose. "Nice looking." She reached for her purse.

~ ~ ~

Over dinner Chelsea learned that Gavil was an only child, his parents deceased. He'd moved to Haverlon from San Jose about a month ago to live with Marian, the woman he hoped to marry someday, putting his own townhouse up for rent. Chelsea sensed from the oblique reference to "someday" that Marian wasn't ready to commit yet, much to Gavil's frustration. It lay in the slant of his head, the dropping of his eyes as he made the remark. What was the issue—money, kids, values? Fear?

The conversation soon turned to business—new software, sales trends of various Silicon Valley competitors up or down, five-year strategies. The possibilities and pitfalls of going public. Gavil mentioned how busy the next few weeks would be for him as he closed out annual sales figures at his current company.

"... in my meeting with them Friday morning," Paul said, cutting his steak. "They've been dragging their feet, but this just might close the deal."

"What about the glitches in the beta test? The people in Atlanta don't sound very patient."

"I know. We've done two things. First, we revamped the program to ..."

Chelsea's mind wandered as she leaned back to let the maître d' take her plate. "Your server is needed by a large party that has just been seated," he explained to her in a low voice. "I'll be serving your dessert." Chelsea nodded. Their soufflé, a specialty of Bayhill's, had been ordered with their entrée because of the time needed to prepare it.

A chill stole over Chelsea, and she rubbed her arms. She took a drink of coffee, found it lukewarm, and asked for a refill. The maître d' nodded, slipped away, and returned with a silver coffeepot. Conversation at the table continued, unabated, as he lifted her cup and filled it, eyes checking Paul's and Gavil's cups. Smiling at a comment from Gavil, Chelsea watched steam rise from the dark liquid and gratefully encircled the cup with her hands.

Chelsea's eyes danced from her husband to Gavil, comparing qualities. Gavil seemed articulate and creative, his insights bespeaking a solid understanding of the whys and wherefores of the software business. Chelsea interjected questions that focused more on his personal life. Gavil's open answers told Chelsea that he understood why she and Paul were interested in this aspect of his life. Theirs proved a common philosophy: a person who lacked integrity in his personal affairs may lack it in business as well. A couple of times, Chelsea sensed the slightest edge in Gavil's tone as he spoke with her, and she wondered if it hinted at a tendency to anger easily. Or perhaps it came from nervousness over wanting to make a good impression. Still, watching Paul's animation as they finished dinner, Chelsea knew that, after a long, often disheartening search, her husband believed he'd finally found the right person to hire. Any candidate would have some kind of fault. Even if Gavil did have a tendency toward anger at times, his work experience and knowledge far outweighed it.

The soufflé arrived.

Paul excused himself as dessert was being served, asking the maître d' for directions to the rest room. Chelsea smiled at him as he rose, then lifted both eyebrows in a silent "ooooh" at Gavil as they watched the soufflé being spooned onto their plates.

"I've never had one of these before," Gavil said. "Great suggestion."

Chelsea opened her mouth to reply. Instead her teeth started chattering. She blinked. "I'm sorry. I must be coming down with …" Her voice trailed away, and she shook her head.

Her sight clouded.

Oh, no. Not here, not now.

"What is it?"

Gavil's voice was there but not there. It echoed in a tunnel, retreating, far away. The sound waves twisted and turned, encasing her in a muffled cocoon, then gradually metamorphosed into another place, another time. Gradually, Chelsea began to hear a different tone, at first faint, then increasing in strength. A harsh, choked whisper.

"I hate you! I've always hated you! *Look* what you made me do!"

Disoriented, Chelsea stretched out her hands and waved them before her. They prickled with heat. Other sensations began to form. She lay on cold, hard ground. Her bare legs throbbed as if they'd been scratched by thorns. Her face hurt. Something trickled into her eyes. She squeezed them shut in terror.

The image of a forest faded in. Chelsea sensed trees and wild brush around her. The sweet, aromatic smell of eucalyptus penetrated the air, and a light breeze ruffled the tops of towering sequoias.

Sobs shuddered through her lungs as the voice, inches away from her face, spat out again, "I *hate* you!"

"No!" Chelsea fought against her tormentor. But he was too strong. Hands grabbed her shoulders, lifted her upper body off the ground, then threw her back with violent force. *Crack!* Her neck snapped back like a newborn baby's. Pain seared through her skull.

"Nnno." Weaker this time.

She struggled to open blood-filled eyes, seeing only the fuzzy features of a man with dark hair. Again the hands lifted and dashed her head against the ground. She could feel her arms falling, falling, until at last they lay useless across her chest.

A third lifting. A third *crack*. And a fourth. She could do nothing. Couldn't fight. Couldn't move. With each blow the world grew darker. She felt her body shutting down.

I'm dying.

This final thought wrapped itself around her.

The forest started to fade. The smell of eucalyptus waned. She lay trapped again in the fuzzy walls of the cocoon, then found herself back in the tunnel. She saw only darkness except for a vague flicker that mesmerized her as it slowly danced into focus, kicking shadows onto a background of white.

A candle.

Linen on a table. A restaurant. Low lights thrown across polished wood and chintz.

The tunnel disappeared. In its place, Bayhill. But the unmistakable sense of evil still clung to her.

Chelsea found her eyes locked with Gavil's. He gawked at her, as if willing her to move. *Jesus, help me.* Her thoughts jumbled. God had sent her a vision, far more chilling than all the others put together. But this one felt different. She couldn't explain why but knew with certainty that this event had already taken place. Still, the others had been much more clear. This time she didn't know details.

What *was* this?

"Are you all right, ma'am?" The maître d' looked ill at ease, as if not certain whether to offer help or withdraw his intruding presence.

Chelsea felt her chest close and sucked in a breath. Beads of sweat sprang to her skin. She could hear her heart pumping. Her fingers gripped the table.

"What is it, Chelsea?" Gavil asked. "What's wrong?"

Gritty words scraped her throat. "I'm so sorry. Sometimes I ... see things."

Why had she said that? It would sound so crazy to him.

The maître d' quietly disappeared.

Gavil frowned, shook his head. Then the creases in his forehead smoothed away and his pupils enlarged. He drew back, eyes still locked with hers. Horror flicked across his face, as if he'd caught her gasping at secret revelations in his diary.

The moment hung in the air.

Chelsea jerked her gaze away. "I ... I really am sorry." She pried her fingers open. "I think I'm coming down with something. Just felt a chill. Got dizzy for a minute."

Gavil gathered himself. "Maybe we should go soon. When Paul gets back." His voice held an edge.

She nodded, eyes averted. Chelsea couldn't look at him again.

When Paul returned they were hovering silently over their chocolate soufflés. Neither had touched a bite.

Chapter 2

Paul sat in the car with his arms around his sobbing wife. What in the world had made her so hysterical?

"It was so *real!* So *awful!*" Chelsea's body shook. "Why is God doing this to me? I don't want these visions, I *never* asked for them. They make you think I'm crazy. I didn't even want to tell you, but this one was so strong!"

Oh, no, another one of her weird visions—in front of Gavil? Great. What if she'd scared him away? "Tell me what happened, Chels."

She pulled a tissue from the glove compartment and wiped her nose. Sank back against the seat rest.

A knock sounded on Paul's window. He jumped. Turned the car on and hit the window button. Cool air filtered in.

"Sorry to bother you, sir. Your wife left this in the restaurant." The maître d', his face half in shadow, passed a purse through the window.

"Oh. Thank you." Paul tossed it in the backseat.

"I hope your wife is all right, sir."

The guy was no doubt worried his customer had gotten sick on the food and would soon be suing him. "She'll be fine. I think she's just coming down with something."

"Yes, sir. Good night."

The face withdrew.

Paul closed the window and turned back to Chelsea. "Good thing he found it before somebody else did."

Silence.

"Come on, Chelsea. Tell me what happened."

She shuddered in a long breath. "You won't believe me."

He sighed. If this was about one of those visions of hers, she was right. "I'll believe you."

"No you won't. But here goes anyway."

Chelsea launched into an outlandish tale that only got worse. A woman murdered in a forest. How Chelsea had been inside the woman's body, feeling it all. How she'd come out of her trance to see Gavil watching her. "I told him I see things sometimes, and you should have seen the guilt on his face!"

"Guilt? About what?"

"About—. Oh, Paul." She reached for him. "I know you think I'm crazy. But I really need you to listen to me. I didn't see the man's face clearly in the vision, but when I came out of it, I still *felt* the evil. I stared at Gavil and I saw the guilt in his eyes. He is clearly, absolutely hiding something. I *know* what I'm saying. The man in the vision had dark hair and looked to be the same size. It was Gavil, Paul. I'm sure of it."

Paul stared at her, speechless. Suddenly the car felt hot. He opened his window again. Refreshing night air swirled across his face. If only it would clear his mind.

"Chels, this is insane!" He spread his hands. "I bring you to dinner to look over a candidate, and you end up telling me he's some crazed killer? Gavil comes with great references. He's got *all kinds* of credentials."

She dropped her head in her hands. "I know how it sounds. I also know what I felt was totally, absolutely real. You know every time this has happened to me, I've always been right. What if God sent this vision to warn us away from Gavil? Just think how awful it would be if everything I said was true and you hired him! No matter what you believe, I *know* what I'm saying. I'm not going to change my mind."

No, she wouldn't. Not his stubborn Chelsea. She was warm and loving, always willing to compromise. Until she got religion. On that subject she would not budge.

Paul focused on the dashboard. Twelve years of marriage without this God stuff. Both of them had been centered on getting ahead, making money through his company. Then a year ago Chelsea became a Christian. Boy, had she changed. Weekly Bible studies and church every Sunday. But that was just the beginning. Then came the visions. She said they were sent by God. He would have belittled all of that—except the "visions" kept coming true.

One time, Chelsea said she'd "seen" a freak accident on the highway, a couple of teenagers throwing a two-by-four off an overpass and splitting open a car windshield, hitting the driver. The driver she'd "seen" was a woman from church who Chelsea knew planned to attend a baby shower for her granddaughter down the Peninsula. Chelsea called her, warning her to take side streets rather than Highway 101, and she listened. The next day the newspaper ran a story about two teenagers being caught throwing a two-by-four off an overpass, narrowly missing a car. The incident occurred around the time Chelsea's friend would have been on that highway. Chelsea had been convinced God sent the vision to protect her friend, who'd been under "spiritual attack," whatever that was.

Crazy coincidence. That's all it was.

Paul pressed a hand against his forehead—and out of nowhere, he laughed.

Chelsea eyed him.

"I'm sorry, Chels. I know you're upset, but it's almost funny. I've been worrying about structuring a benefit package and salary Gavil would accept. We've talked about his experience and his sales techniques, and I've asked him all kinds of questions. Except, 'By the way, Gavil, have you ever *murdered* anybody?'"

Chelsea looked away. "I know how it sounds. But I know what I saw. Like I did the other times. True, this one has some holes in it. But I'll ... have to pray about it."

Wonderful. Chelsea would pray, all right. And no doubt run to Gladys Dell, who "mentored" her. Gladys was in her sixties, bright, with years of experience in office management. She'd come to dinner one night, and she and Paul had talked about business. Paul respected her keen mind. But Gladys believed all the stuff about church and prayer. She'd listened to Chelsea's stories about her visions without an ounce of disbelief.

How could rational people *do* that?

Chelsea started crying again.

"Oh, come on, Chels." Paul pulled her close. "I'm sorry for laughing. What you felt must have been so scary. Let's go home, and I'll get you to bed."

~ ~ ~

The ride home was quiet. Chelsea didn't press Paul about hiring Gavil, afraid of what he might say. She prayed for God to lead Paul, even if he didn't ask for divine guidance. There was no easy answer. How would she feel if Paul ignored her and hired Gavil? But if he *didn't* only for her sake, he'd resent her. Especially if nothing happened to prove she'd been right.

God, please tell me more. Why did you send this vision if I don't know what to do with it?

For the rest of the ride home, while she paid the baby-sitter, as she took off her makeup, and throughout the night, Chelsea relived those last five minutes in another woman's life. The smell, the rustle of leaves, the hard ground, her bare legs. The furious whispers. Hands lifting her up, throwing her down. Excruciating pain. Darkness. Death. Always, the face of Gavil Harrison floated before her. Try as she might, she couldn't separate him from the man in her vision.

The *guilt* on his face! Gavil Harrison murdered that woman.

Thursday, June 8

Chapter 3

Who was she? Who was she? The words echoed in Chelsea's head. She rolled over and threw an arm across her eyes to block out the bedroom light. The new day's sun remained faint.

Paul was already up, his travel bag spread across his side of their king-size bed. He smiled at her. "Morning. How do you feel?"

"Fine."

"Did you sleep?"

"Some."

Paul nodded.

"Where are you off to?" Not that he hadn't told her. Chelsea remembered bits of conversation on the way to the restaurant about a trip. Now it seemed so long ago.

"Atlanta. I've got to talk to the coalition there about our new software." Paul folded the travel bag over on itself and pulled the zipper shut. "It's a pain for just overnight." He lifted the case off the bed and set it on the floor. "This is the kind of trip I'll be able to send our new V.P. of sales on."

She felt his regret as soon as the words were out of his mouth. Clearly he did not want to broach the subject now. *That* could take all day, and he had a plane to catch.

She sat up and leaned against the headboard, hugging the covers over her chest. "You still want to hire him, don't you?"

"Look, Chels." Paul sat on the foot of the bed. "You're putting me in a very tough position. Gavil's a great candidate, and I can't just turn him away when I have nothing concrete. What in the world would I tell Morrow?"

Chelsea dropped her gaze. "What I saw is concrete enough for me, Paul. I know God sent that vision. Believe me, it would be very easy to forget the whole thing, particularly after your reaction. But I can't. And when I came out of the vision and looked at Gavil, he *knew*. If you'd only seen the look on his face!"

"Chelsea, come on. He just knew you were acting pretty weird. He probably was afraid he'd bombed out at dinner." Paul stood with a sigh. "Sorry, but I gotta go." He planted a quick kiss on her forehead. "See you tomorrow."

Suddenly, she didn't like the thought of being alone in the house.

After Paul left, she sat for some time in bed, arms wrapped around her knees, praying. At seven she got up to roust the boys. As soon as they were off to school, she would call Gladys.

~ ~ ~

Pancakes and bacon. Scott liked his pancakes soft. Michael liked crispy edges. They both expected their bacon to crunch.

"Scott! Where's my Oakland A's T-shirt?" Michael leaned over the stairs, yelling at his younger brother.

"Uh-oh." Scott slid across the kitchen hardwood floor in sock feet, grabbed his backpack, and made for the door.

"Scott, where do you think you're going with no shoes and no breakfast?" Chelsea caught him by the elbow. "And what have you done with your brother's shirt?"

"Nothing. I just need to show it to a friend. I'll bring it back tonight."

"You put that shirt right back where it belongs."

"But Danny Harris doesn't believe Michael has a signed T-shirt, and he bet me two bucks. I have to get my money today."

It wasn't fair that Michael had the T-shirt anyway, Scott complained. Michael had gotten to meet some of the starting

33

players at the Oakland A's first home game of the season while Scott had been at some stupid Scout camp in Trent Park. How totally unfair. Michael got the T-shirt, and what did he have? A dead salamander from a creek in the forest. Big deal.

"Scott, that shirt belongs to Michael, and besides, I don't want you betting. Take it upstairs right now, then get your shoes on and come to breakfast. And bring Michael with you." Chelsea moved to the stove to turn a pancake.

Scott kicked his way out of the kitchen, mumbling. "I didn't wanna go to that stupid old camp anyway. All's we did was mark a new trail through the dumb gulch."

Chelsea froze.

Eucalyptus.

Sequoias.

Her heart danced, and the hair rose on her arms. In an instant the tunnel in her vision surrounded her. She braced herself.

The spatula and pancake clattered to the floor.

The sensations disappeared.

Chelsea hung there, staring sightlessly at the stove.

Trent Park.

Trent Park was in Haverlon, where Gavil lived. Trent Park had eucalyptus trees and giant sequoias.

She flashed to the previous summer, when she and Paul had attended a parents' program there after Scott's weeklong camp. They'd walked down the gravel road to the "arena" to watch campers put on skits and sing crazy songs. That afternoon the forested park had seemed so safe, so open. But step off the road, and you could easily be lost in the trees and brambles.

Lord, is this from you?

No question it was. This sensation felt so like the one last night.

Clutching the tile counter, she closed her eyes. *Thank you, Lord. What should I do now?*

"Aw, Mom, that better be Michael's pancake!"

34

Chelsea's eyes flew open. Scott was leaning over the mess on the floor, disgust on his face.

"Oh. Yes, it's Michael's." Distracted, she scooped the half-cooked pancake off the hardwood floor and flopped it onto a plate.

Her son stared as if she'd gone batty.

Chelsea bit her lip, mind racing. Trent Park, just a short distance north. Surely the Haverlon police knew about the murder.

Why hadn't God sent the vision *before* this happened? Maybe she could have helped prevent it.

Why had He sent it at all? What was she supposed to do now?

Surely the police were working on the case. They'd find evidence to lead them to Gavil. She couldn't just march into the Haverlon police station and tell them her story. They'd think she was crazy. And Paul would be furious.

She needed to talk to Gladys about this.

"*Yuck,* Mom! That's *Scott's* pancake!"

Chelsea jumped. She focused on the plate she was offering Michael. A pancake lay on it, crispy at the edges, oozing in the middle.

Like a cracked, leaking head.

Chapter 4

"I'm so glad you could see me right away." Chelsea sank onto the couch in Gladys' living room.

"How could I say no?" The woman's green eyes twinkled behind her fashionable glasses. "You know I'm always up for a new adventure." She set a mug of coffee on the glass table before Chelsea, then scooted into an armchair. "Okay. Tell me."

Gladys had a zest for life that could make Chelsea's head spin. Seeing her dressed for church, Chelsea could hardly picture Gladys decked out in black leather, taking the ocean side curves of Highway 1 on her motorcycle. "Bikin' Grandma," Gladys called herself. But she was also the most caring person Chelsea knew.

"Well, I've had a whopper this time."

Gladys listened in amazement as Chelsea spilled her story—and Paul's reaction.

"Wow." Gladys set down her coffee mug, nearly missing the table. "What a *horrible* thing to go through." She spread her hands. "We'd better pray first. I haven't a *clue* how to help you with this."

For the next few minutes they took turns praying for God's wisdom.

"So." Gladys shifted in her seat. "What do *you* think you should do next?"

Chelsea sighed. "I think I'm supposed to go to the police, but what could I tell them? They're not going to believe me. And Paul—you know how hard I've been praying for him. But these visions are just driving us further apart. I don't understand what God is doing."

"You may not understand that for some time."

"But why is this one so full of questions?" Chelsea asked. "All the others were clear. I knew exactly what to do!"

"Perhaps God wants to hone your skills. You've not been at this very long. In fact, it's pretty unusual for someone so young in the faith to already possess such a strong gift. God's ultimate goal is to draw us nearer to him. I can see now that every time I've had to wait for an answer, I've learned to hear His voice a little more clearly."

Chelsea winced. "The problem is, I'm half afraid of what God will say. I really wish He'd just give these visions to someone else."

"Oh, no." Gladys shook her head, smiling, "You're stuck with 'em! God gave this gift to *you* for a good reason. Maybe simply because you're willing to listen." She mushed her lips. "I know it sounds trite, but I have to believe if God sent you this vision in the first place, He'll reveal more of it when He's ready."

"But I need to know *now*. What if Paul hires Gavil? Then it'll be too late."

"Chelsea, the Lord's going to take care of you. *Believe* it. As for this man's guilt or innocence, I think you should tread very carefully there. It would be no small thing to accuse a person of such a horrible crime."

Chelsea looked at the floor, confusion flowing within her.

"If you do go to the police," Gladys added, "see Sergeant Dan Reiger. He's a Christian. And perhaps he's already working on the case. Which must be brand new, by the way, because I've seen nothing on the news. Anyway, I don't know Dan myself, but some of my friends at Haverlon Baptist do. He's a member of that church."

"Really?" Chelsea's head came up. "Then maybe he wouldn't think I'm totally off my rocker." She searched her friend's face. "Do you think I should see him now?"

Gladys raised her shoulders. "I honestly don't know. I'll continue to pray that God will lead you. But again, if you go now, I don't think you should mention Gavil Harrison's name yet. Pray more about that. Be very sure. Remember, Chelsea, God will reveal everything in His time. I know you're in an uncomfortable position with Paul, but don't let fear of Gavil — or anything, for that matter — influence your thinking."

"What's left to tell the police then?"

Gladys thought it over. "The details of the murder as you saw them. Every little piece of information may help them in solving the case. Especially what you heard — 'I hate you,' for instance. It sounds like maybe the two people knew each other. That could mean a lot."

Driving home, Chelsea prayed so hard she almost missed her exit. She sensed she should go to the police, even though the thought scared her to death. Okay, so Dan Reiger was a Christian. He was also a policeman. She'd be making a formal statement. She'd be involved. Paul would be furious.

All the same, the closer she drew to home, the more strongly she felt that she should go. Seeing the familiar entrance to her long driveway in the distance, Chelsea experienced a rush of relief, as if she were turning away from danger. And that relief told her that once inside the safety of her own home, she'd find it hard to leave again.

Chelsea pulled into the driveway. Then braked to a stop, fighting within herself.

She should go.

She *did not want* to go.

Lord, if I do this, You'll really need to help me with Paul.

Chelsea heaved a sigh. Then, breathing a prayer, she backed out of the driveway.

Chapter 5

"Congratulations to Sergeant Dan Reiger, Haverlon's Man of the Year."

The large gold-lettered plaque hung across from the sergeant's desk, where he could see it whether he wanted to or not. Not that he had hung it there. It had been Pat Turnbow, the brown-haired, fresh-faced detective down the hall, who'd held the hammer that drove the nail that hung the plaque that Dan won. And Reiger had left it up because, well, heck, there would be an ugly nail hole in the wall without it.

Frustrated with his paperwork, Sergeant Reiger leaned back in his chair, hands behind his head, and surveyed the plaque for the thousandth time. Thirty years on the Haverlon police force and what had it gotten him? A trip down El Camino in last year's Fourth of July parade, perched atop the backseat of a limousine with "Mr. Haverlon" in large silver lettering on the doors. And that garish plaque.

He shrugged his shoulders and sniffed. The plaque was no reflection on his city.

It was a nice place to live, Haverlon. Population about 20,000 thirty years ago; now closer to 30,000. In the middle of the San Francisco Peninsula, where the weather proved fine, indeed. Not that anyone new to the area would necessarily know Haverlon from any of the surrounding towns. You could drive down the main drag of El Camino from South San Francisco clear to Sunnyvale and beyond, and all the towns just ran together — one great mass of humanity. More than six million people lived in the Greater Bay Area, which ran from San Francisco to San Jose and

39

included the Peninsula and East Bay. And of course, the famous Silicon Valley, whose northern border Haverlon straddled. But the people who'd lived in the area for some time, they knew the difference. Each town had a feel, a certain aura.

Haverlon citizens were mostly middle class. The population used to be older, but yuppies had started moving in, especially to the new houses and townhouses in the hills. Get a great view of the Bay that way, if you didn't mind the drop-off in your backyard. Most of Haverlon was residential, but it did have a small downtown area. Camilla Street remained particularly popular, with its quaint stores and banks and coffee shops. Reiger's wife, Edith, ran her own florist shop on Mayfield, one block off Camilla. Reiger and Edith had raised two daughters in Haverlon, Reiger watching his hair turn from brown to gray over the years. Now he was fifty-five, his baby girls were long grown — one with babies of her own — and his gray hair was thinning on top.

In a town the size of Haverlon, policemen tended to rotate duties from patrol to detective every two to three years. Thirty years on the force would afford an officer the unofficial title of "informed generalist" — possessing knowledge about a wide range of police work, but requiring years on the force to glean experience in any one particular field. Reiger handled about a hundred cases a month, covering the gamut of crimes. Many were burglaries — cars, homes, offices. Reiger had seen only three homicides in Haverlon — one during patrol duty and two in which he'd served as detective on the case.

Pushing back from his paperwork with a sigh, Reiger headed for a cup of the barely drinkable coffee he'd learned to stomach over the years.

"Hey, Reiger, we've got a live one." Monica Hudson's pixie face held a look of intense curiosity. She motioned toward the dispatch counter — around the corner and across the green carpet of the waiting area. "There's a woman out there says she wants to

40

see someone about the 'murder in Trent Park.'" Monica spoke the last four words succinctly.

Reiger's eyebrows rose, and he pushed up his lower lip, puckering his chin. "The murder in Trent Park?"

"That's what she said."

"Hm. Okay. I'll be right out."

He headed back to his office and set the coffee cup on his desk. From the top right drawer he pulled out a yellow legal pad and placed it on his desk with a pen on top. Then the sergeant walked down the hall, mumbling greetings to three officers hustling by, and rounded the corner into the lobby.

He took in his potential informant with a glance. Thick reddish-gold hair set off by an olive-green blouse and matching pants. Large eyes of a unique golden color. A delicately molded face, makeup moderate. She wore a fine gold chain. A wedding ring on her left hand. Then he registered her body language. She perched on the edge of a wooden chair, hands clutched in her lap.

"I'm Sergeant Reiger." He extended a hand. "I heard you wanted to see me about a homicide."

She flinched at the word. "Yes." She shook his hand, then hesitated, looking to him for the next move.

The woman looked as wound up as a rubber band on a toy airplane. "Come on back to my office."

~ ~ ~

Chelsea followed the sergeant down a hallway of beige walls and gray carpeting. He extended an arm, allowing her to enter his office before him. It held sparse furniture — a beat-up desk and swivel chair; two extra chairs, one of which he pulled up to the desk for her; and a metal filing cabinet. The one window, topped by dusty Venetian blinds, looked across the street toward Haverlon's City Hall.

"Please, ma'am, sit down."

Chelsea placed her purse on the floor and sat.

41

The sergeant eased himself into the worn brown swivel armchair behind his desk.

"Coffee?" He motioned to his cup.

"No. Thank you."

The sergeant puckered his chin. "You haven't told me your name." He spoke easily, as if he'd read her discomfort.

She inhaled, swept her eyes upward in a gesture of embarrassment. "I'm sorry. It's Chelsea Adams. I live in Woodside."

She watched as he wrote her name, address, and phone number, and the name of her husband. He would recognize Woodside as a small, affluent town southwest of Haverlon, with large, rural lots and plenty of horses. Due to its size, it had no police department of its own, instead contracting services with the county sheriff's department.

"Woodside. But you came up here to see me."

"Yes, because ... it's about what happened here."

He nodded. "You told Monica it was about Trent Park."

"Yes."

"Okay. If you know something about a murder, better fill me in." Reiger looked expectant, his pen poised.

She shifted in her seat, unsure where to begin. "I go to church in Menlo Park, and I heard your name from a friend of mine. She thought that maybe because of your faith, you'd understand my rather unusual story."

Reiger reassured her with a smile, but did not pursue the subject of her church. Chelsea sensed that he was private about his beliefs, at least while on duty. "I'm listening."

Chelsea took in a deep breath. "I need to tell you a little background information first." Gathering her confidence, she told him of her conversion the previous year and her subsequent visions from God. "The first ones were about 'seeing' an aspect of a person's life that God wanted given over to Him. The knowledge helped me pray for people. But then I had two that

42

were different, because they were about physical harm." Chelsea told the sergeant about the one that had affected her most. She and Paul had been at a baseball game for Scott. A boy from the opposing team caught her attention after the game. She noticed his shoulders moving as if his shirt chafed. Suddenly she "saw" the shirt being lifted to reveal scars and fresh, red welts. Chelsea had been horrified, the pain she felt over the young boy's trauma weakening her knees. Spurred by compassion, she'd made her way to the boy's coach and boldly told him to take the boy aside and check his back. "I knew as a coach he'd have to report any signs of abuse," Chelsea continued. "Later, I heard the boy and a brother were taken out of the home and are now safe with an uncle and aunt. Apparently, his mother had left the family years ago. The father is now in jail for abuse."

Sergeant Reiger jotted notes while barely breaking eye contact. "Sounds like you have a real gift."

"Well, it's not me, you know. It's God choosing to speak through me to help others. To tell you the truth, it's not fun for me. I mean, I'm very glad that I've been able to make a difference in people's lives. That amazes me and is very humbling. But sometimes I wish God had chosen someone else. The visions are very draining because I feel others' emotional pain. The mental picture of that poor boy's back still haunts me."

Sergeant Reiger processed her words. "So now you've 'seen' something in Trent Park?"

Chelsea swallowed. "I saw the whole murder. It felt like I was actually in the body of the woman who was killed."

The sergeant's stare was piercing. "Tell me what you saw."

In painstaking detail, Chelsea reported everything she could remember about her vision. She told of the sequoia trees and the smell of eucalyptus. How she'd been lying on hard, cold ground. Her face and forehead hurt. Her legs had been bare and stinging, her hands hot and prickly. She told of the man above her — the words of his throaty whisper and the way he had killed. She did not mention Gavil.

When she finished, she watched the sergeant decide which question to ask first. "Exactly where in the park?"

She shrugged. "I think it's some remote trail. I didn't recognize it."

"Then how do you know it's Trent Park?"

She thought of a pancake flipping in midair. "It's hard to explain. I just know."

"Did you recognize the killer?"

Chelsea hesitated. "I couldn't see his face. Because, as I said, my eyes were closed most of the time, and when they were open, everything looked blurry."

Reiger set down his pen. "Mrs. Adams, have you ever in one of your visions seen something that hadn't happened yet? That you were able to prevent?"

"Yes." Chelsea told him about the teenagers throwing wood off an overpass.

Sergeant Reiger nodded. "How can you know this vision isn't also about the future?"

Chelsea searched in vain for the words. "I can't explain that either. I just know."

"You're sure."

Why was he asking her this? "I'm positive. I *saw* the murder. It's already happened. Maybe you're not that familiar with the case?"

Reiger rested an elbow on the armchair and rubbed his jaw. "I need to ask you—have you ever been wrong?"

"No." She felt her confidence drain away.

He tapped a knuckle against his pad of paper. "Trent Park has been around a long time, you know. We've had amazingly little trouble out there."

"I know. My son has been there for Scout camps."

Reiger grunted. "Right. So you must realize that a murder in Trent Park would be pretty big news. Have you wondered why you haven't read about it in the papers?"

"Well, actually, yes. I thought you were just ... keeping it quiet for some reason."

He shook his head. "There's no way to keep something like that quiet." Leaning forward, he put both elbows on his desk. "Mrs. Adams, I believe your stories about your past visions. I know God can work in mysterious ways. But I don't know what to do with this one. I certainly thank you for coming. I'm sure it wasn't easy for you. But I need to tell you the truth." He spread his hands. "There hasn't been a murder in Trent Park. As a matter of fact, we haven't had a homicide in Haverlon for over eight years. And no woman is even missing, as far as I know."

Chapter 6

How had she gotten into her car? Chelsea could hardly remember. Somehow, after Sergeant Reiger's statement, she'd pushed back her chair, lifted a hand, and said with as much calm as she could muster, "Sorry to waste your time." Was that before or after he'd commented that sequoia and eucalyptus trees "grow all over this part of California"? Perhaps she'd been wrong about the location.

Despite the officer's politeness, Chelsea knew he'd been placating her. Sergeant Reiger must think her some fanatic who danced with snakes in her backyard.

Chelsea gripped the steering wheel of her Range Rover as she drove down Junipero Serra, 280 — "the world's most beautiful freeway." She stayed in the right lane, barely noticing cars whizzing by. Her foot didn't have the energy to push the accelerator past fifty. Was it just last night she and Paul had gone north to Bayhill?

"Oh, God, what have I done, how could I be so *wrong?*" she said aloud. "I was so sure! I *still* am sure. How can that *be,* what am I supposed to *do?*"

Could she be wrong about the location? Maybe Scott's mention of Trent Park had pushed her to that conclusion. Chelsea narrowed her eyes, considering. Sergeant Reiger was right, sequoia and eucalyptus trees did grow throughout the Bay Area. And there were forested areas all around 280. Still, a murder anywhere in the area would have made the news. She'd been dumb to think otherwise. And besides, she could not shake her certainty that it was Trent Park. That belief obliterated all known facts as surely as fog could obliterate the San Francisco skyline.

Chelsea signaled her exit and veered off the highway, bearing toward home. A half mile later, she turned onto Pennhill Lane. "I just don't understand this, Lord. If you sent this vision, where did I go wrong? Am I not listening hard enough? Praying hard enough?" Winding to the end of her long driveway, she pushed her garage remote button and watched the door slide open.

She pulled into the garage and turned off the motor. The Rover's suspension system shut down, lowering the car with a series of sighs.

Shutting down.

Chelsea's thoughts flashed to the scene in Trent Park — the feeling of her bodily systems closing down one by one. She caught her breath.

God was telling her something.

Yes, came a confident voice inside her head. *What you felt was real*.

Chelsea stared unseeing through the windshield. "Then how …?" she whispered.

She remained transfixed, waiting. The car grew hot. Still she did not move.

Until she understood.

Chapter 7

Thursday was not going well for Gavil Harrison.

The morning had begun badly enough when an anxious Marian questioned him about dinner with the Adamses. Luckily, she'd been asleep when he'd gotten in the previous evening. One look at his face would have been enough to keep her awake all night. "Yes," he'd told her, "the dinner went great. I'm probably in the top running for the job."

She grinned and threw her arms around him. "How wonderful! We'll go out and celebrate when you're hired."

He hated lying to Marian. It was necessary at times, but a lousy thing to do all the same.

Gavil reflected, as he hunched over the computer keyboard in his office, that he really did love Marian. Planned to marry her, never wanted to hurt her. But the constant half-truths ...

The phone on his desk buzzed, and he jumped. "Gavil Harrison."

"Hey, Gav! How'd it go last night?"

Stuart Hocking, Gavil's mentor and closest friend. Fifteen years Gavil's senior, Stuart Hocking was largely responsible for Gavil's being hired at Titan Electronics due to his personal recommendation. Stuart remained the only person Gavil had trusted with the news of his recruitment by AP Systems.

"Oh, hi." Gavil cleared his throat. "It was ... interesting."

"What does that mean?"

Gavil sighed. "We talked some more about a few of the issues that Adams is concerned about. I think he wants to hire me, and it's clear that my experience, particularly here, is the sort of expertise he's looking for. However," Gavil drew out the word, "he seems somewhat nervous about my having worked here for so many years. Different atmosphere at a start-up company and all that, plus the added responsibility of being a vice president, which I haven't done before."

Stuart snorted. "Tell me about it." Stuart Hocking had left a well-paying job years ago to forge out on his own, like hundreds of other entrepreneurs in Silicon Valley. Some had made it, some had gone broke. Stuart had made it in a big way, building a company that designed and manufactured computer-based special effects systems used in television and movies.

"Right. At any rate, I think I managed to resolve that issue in his mind."

"So what's the problem?"

Gavil hesitated. "I don't think his wife liked me."

"Oh. Think that carries much weight?"

Gavil drummed his fingers on the desk. Stuart understood the potential power of a savvy wife. He had one of his own. Sonya Hocking, two years younger than Gavil, was Stuart's second wife, the prize he'd caught after his first wife died of breast cancer the day after their twenty-seventh anniversary. Sonya was intelligent, beautiful, and ambitious. The daughter of poor immigrants, she'd worked as a bank teller until Stuart discovered her and catapulted her into his influential and wealthy social circle. Now, just four years later, a growing cadre of prominent citizens had encouraged Sonya to enter politics, with a future race for state assembly as the goal. Gavil knew she was systematically "putting her ducks in a row," as Stuart would say, but publicly, she demurred from any such decision. Her current project, Sonya insisted, was far too important, leaving her with little time to spend planning a political career. In truth, Sonya *had* spent countless hours raising money through the Sonya Hocking Foundation to build the most advanced children's oncology center in the nation. The center, part of the West Bay Hospital complex in Sunnyvale, would bear her name in large block letters over its entrance. She and Stuart had contributed one-fourth of the funds themselves. The rest had been donated by successful friends and businesses as a result of her passionate pleading.

Sonya was a complex person. Many knew her only as the tireless activist for the young victims of cancer who adorned the posters she used in her efforts. But Gavil knew her better than most. Sonya Hocking had very quickly become used to "having it all." Underneath her humanistic posturing dwelt a woman of calculating mind who understood that her social standing and reputation for integrity were absolutely essential for her future ambitions.

"Yeah," Gavil said, "I do think it carries weight." Sarcasm crept into his voice. "You know how it is. Paul Adams has worked fourteen hours a day building the company, leaving her to raise the kids, so she figures she's got a personal investment in the business."

"I get it. So what happened? She sense something slimy about you?"

Stuart was just teasing, but Gavil felt a flutter in his stomach all the same. "Everything went great until she started acting really strange. She said she felt sick, and maybe that's true. Anyway— probably nothing to worry about."

"Well, I hope you get the job if you want it. Even if you don't, you've got a good thing going at Titan. If you sell well, you'll make another great bonus next year. Plus you've got a lot of room to grow right where you are."

The bottom line — that was Hocking. "Ah, but it's the entrepreneurial spirit, man." Gavil lightened his tone. "Gotta go, gotta build, gotta make that private stock worth millions!" More importantly, it would prove his worth to Marian. "Say, how was golf yesterday?"

"The weather was perfect, and I played lousy." Stuart sounded disgusted. "Sonya played great, though. You should have been there. Maybe you'd have won for once."

"Ha! If I'd won, you'd have to hang up your clubs." An old joke. Stuart had declared that if Gavil ever beat him at golf, he'd know it was time to take up a new sport.

"Well, keep me posted, Gav." Stuart suddenly sounded pressed for time.

"I'll do that." Gavil began to pull the phone from his ear, then stopped. "Hey, you around this weekend? Maybe we can scare up a golf foursome for Saturday."

"Nope, you get another reprieve. I've got a convention in Seattle starting Saturday morning. I'm flying out tomorrow after work. Sonya's staying here, though. Maybe she'd join you."

"That's all right." Gavil kept his voice light. "I've got too much work anyway. Thanks for calling, Stuart."

The line clicked off. Gavil turned back to his computer, staring at the spreadsheet on the screen. A ton of work awaited him before the end of the month — which also was the end of the fiscal year at Titan Electronics. Pressure, pressure, pressure. For him and the entire sales force. Right now every salesperson was running in ten directions at once, trying to bump up their sales figures. Final numbers were big stuff. Commissions depended on them, company-paid tour packages — this year to Hawaii — depended on them. In addition to staying on top of his own sales, Gavil had to refine next year's projected revenues for the Western Region, for which he was responsible.

Lots of luck today. Anger rose in his chest. He couldn't begin to keep his mind on work.

His foot tapped the floor.

The numbers before him blurred, refocusing into the expression on Chelsea Adams' face when she had frozen, trance-like, in her seat at Bayhill. Gavil remembered her accusing eyes as she'd stared at him a few seconds later. He remembered the immediate, implacable knowledge that she'd seen something deep within him. Gavil drew in a breath and hunched over his desk. He was determined to get the job at AP Systems. For himself and for Marian. Rubbing his neck, he wondered exactly how much Chelsea Adams knew — and what it was going to cost him.

Chapter 8

Eleven-thirty.

Chelsea ran through a mental check as she tied her walking shoes. She had exchanged her green slacks and blouse for jeans and a cotton knit shirt. The boys got out of school at 2:30. Starting next week, they would be out for summer vacation. But today, Michael would take the bus home and arrive by 3:10. Scott had band practice on Thursdays. She'd have to pick him up at 4:00.

She had over three and a half hours. Plenty of time.

Chelsea bounced down the stairs, crossed the kitchen, and strode into the garage. As she slid into her car, she prayed for courage. Fear snatched at her, but she ignored it.

She was on a mission. She would pray and focus only on the mission, nothing more.

Despite her resolve, questions flooded her mind. Trent Park was huge. No way could she hike through it all. What if she found nothing? What if she did? What in the world would she say to Paul? He'd think it bad enough that she'd gone to the police. But to pursue it this far? For once, Chelsea was glad he was out of town until tomorrow evening.

On the other hand, maybe finding some evidence would convince Paul of God's power. Maybe Paul was the reason God was putting her through this.

But more important than Chelsea's own problems was her compassion for a family she didn't know. Someone out there would soon begin worrying about a missing wife, a daughter, a sister. Chelsea could only imagine the despair. How could she just go home and forget what God had shown her?

~ ~ ~

Chelsea's shoes crunched on the gravel parking lot at the north entrance to Trent Park. She carried nothing with her except a pair of binoculars. Her car keys were in her pocket. She'd hidden her purse in the back of the Rover.

The park was quiet. A few other cars dotted the lot, most of them in various areas of shade. Joggers, or perhaps retired folks out for a walk. Chelsea also noticed a dusty county park ranger's car close to where the lot funneled into the beginning of Trent Park's gravel road.

The sun warmed her as she set off, not a clue as to where she would go. Mentally, she played back the tape of her vision. She'd smelled eucalyptus. And felt hard ground — not gravel — at her back. Chelsea looked around. She saw plenty of tall, lean sequoias, but no eucalyptus, with its peeling white bark.

One thing she knew — she'd have to leave the main road.

A bird cackled through her thoughts, and she raised her face toward the bright sun. She blinked hard, lowering her gaze to the loose rocks beneath her feet. Rays bounced off their whiteness. Sunglasses would help. She dallied with returning to her car for a pair, then discarded the idea. Once she entered the forest, the light would be dimmer.

Thinking of the shadows, the quiet of the forest, she found her footsteps faltering.

Maybe this was a bad idea.

Lord, help me. Show me where to go.

A sudden rhythmic stride behind her snapped Chelsea to a halt. Her scalp prickled. She whirled around.

It was only a jogger, mouth open in the steady inhale, exhale of a run, sweat trickling down his temples. He looked at her oddly as he passed.

Oh, good grief. Barely out of the parking lot and she was terrified already.

She stood still after he ran by, regaining her nerve. The binoculars felt heavy around her neck. Then she set out again, looking for any path veering off the road. She'd take the first one she came to.

Before long she saw one off to her left, winding narrowly through dense trees. She stepped onto it, feeling immediate coolness. The bright sunlight faded.

For no reason, goose pimples skittered down her arms.

The path was easy to follow, well marked by many a Scout. Chelsea managed a smile at the thought of Scouts traipsing through the trees, arguing over who would tie the next yellow tag around a scratchy trunk. After a slight downhill grade, the path cut left again, then dipped down a hillside and wandered to the right.

A growing chill hovered as she walked. What if she were to see Gavil Harrison right now? What if he'd come back to hide evidence?

Well, that was just crazy.

Still, the thought persisted.

You know what was really crazy? What *she* was doing. She should be at home right now. Just forget all this ...

Listen!

She cocked her head.

Nothing.

Okay, this was really dumb. Every little sound was getting to her. To calm herself, she began mentally reciting verses from the Psalms.

Chelsea pushed forward.

The foliage thickened, sunlight fading. After five minutes, she came to a fork in the path. The right fork traveled up a short barren hill, then vanished into the trees. The left one ambled around a large fallen trunk and also disappeared.

Which way?

She veered right.

The trail beckoned her up another hill and around a small grove of trees. Smells of rich dirt filtered up between gnarled roots. The trail grew brighter. Rounding the last trunk, she gazed ahead expectantly, only to see the gravel road again.

Relief mixed with irritation. Now what? She stepped onto the road, squinting, and felt the hardness of rocks under her feet. What about the other fork in the trail? She stared back at the path. Then she pivoted, retracing her steps around the trees.

At the fork she took the alternate route around the fallen trunk into a thick grove. Here it became darker still, and cooler. The chill soon returned, settling over her shoulders. Pinpricks bounced down her body. Her breathing grew shaky. Her heart began to beat quickly, hard.

Lord, help me keep going.

On through the trees.

No one out here but her now. No other walkers or joggers.

Chelsea pushed on, even though her legs began to tremble. Each breath sounded loud in her ears. Fear coiled in her chest. Chelsea clutched the binoculars, feeling their hard, round surface.

Slowing, she eyed the next bend.

The stillness was deafening.

Tall trees lined the path. The soil smelled damp, its dew untouched by the sun. Invisible fingers rasped down her spine.

Down yet another hill and through an area of fine, sand-like dirt.

A thorny branch scratched her ankle.

"Ouch!" She jerked her leg away. Shuffled backward into some brush. It rustled.

Chelsea's eyes darted. So quiet here. So … raw. She could almost imagine a furtive step, the swish of a striking hand.

The back of her neck tingled.

The forest seemed to grow alive, taunting her with whispers. Chelsea turned in a circle, eyes straining to look ahead. No matter where she turned, she felt someone behind her. She sidestepped to the right, caught her heel on a root, and fell.

"Ooof." Air whooshed out of her lungs. She scrambled up again and pressed her back against a tree, breathing hard. She tried to pray, but the words wouldn't come.

Come on, Chelsea, don't be an idiot. She wasn't in danger. The place was just ... spooky, that's all.

A smell blew across her face.

Sweet, aromatic. Wild. Chelsea swiveled her head. Where was it coming from? She turned, slapping a hand against the tree for support. The trunk scratched her palm.

Peeling bark.

Chelsea snatched back her hand. Slowly, she tipped her head to rake a gaze up and up the tall white trunk.

Eucalyptus.

She jumped away from the tree, back onto the trail. Then stood shaking, willing herself to move.

She was almost there now.

The knowledge pulled at her. Chelsea moved forward.

She spotted a second eucalyptus, and a third. More lay beyond, lined up like sentinels along the path. Anxiety pinged through her veins.

Chelsea willed herself to walk, first with hesitation, then gaining speed. She moved faster, faster until she nearly ran. *Just do this thing, just finish it.* Once she saw what she'd come to find, her part would be over. The police would handle everything from there.

Past the trees, over a little hill. Chelsea fought for calm, sucking in oxygen. Her lungs creaked like old leather.

A light began to glow ahead, sun rays breaking through the trees. A flashlight from heaven to show her the way.

Chelsea broke into a full run and rounded a bend.

The path spilled out of the trees.

Chelsea carved to a stop. Shielded her eyes from the glaring sunlight. She stood near the edge of a deep gully that ran from right to left. The sky canopied a brilliant blue. A lone hawk glided over the gully. A picture of peace.

Her heart hammered.

Nothing here. Nothing at all.

How could that be?

She'd passed the eucalyptus. Come to the end of the trail. And—*nothing*.

She'd been wrong. The whole time. She'd imagined all of this. Now she could just go home. *Forget* it.

Relief washed over Chelsea. She dropped to the ground, panting. The packed dirt lay warm beneath her hands. She rested there, waiting for her mind to stop spinning. It was so nice and warm. She didn't want to return to that dark forest.

After a few minutes she shifted her weight and looked around. Her gaze fell on a large rock a few feet away, embedded in the ground. Streaked red-brown.

She blinked.

What was that? Some weird reflection from the sun?

Chelsea took in the shape of the rock, the jutting ridge at one end. Before she knew it, she'd stood up, drawn toward it like a moth to flame. She leaned over to touch it. At the last minute her hand pulled back.

Dried blood.

"Oh!"

Her cry echoed through the gully. Underbrush crackled down in the gully. Chelsea spun toward the sound. She grabbed the binoculars, raised them to her eyes. The gully floor leaped into magnification. More sound. What *was* that?

There. Movement. She peered harder.

A coyote. Worrying at something. She moved the binoculars—and saw a body.

Her heart stopped.

The body lay on its back, bare legs sticking out of bright yellow running shorts. One arm was bent to the side, the other thrown straight out. It had no face. Just blood, hair, and a mass of buzzing flies. The coyote's snout was buried in what remained of the torso.

A shock ran through Chelsea. She froze, then dropped the binoculars against her chest. Staggered backwards.

Get out of here!

She whirled and began a frenzied dash back down the path.

Chelsea had never been a jogger. But she ran now, raging with adrenaline. Her mind rose in a surreal float above her body as her legs pulled her past the eucalyptus trees, over the sand-like dirt, through dense trees. The binoculars bumped against her ribs, bruising her skin. Every tree she ran past, every snaking root, seemed to squirm to life. Branches reached out with gnarled fingers, stones jutted up to trip her.

On she pounded, arms flailing. The farther she ran, the more her terror grew, until she *knew* someone was chasing her.

Where was the fork in the path, *where was it?*

Tears blurred her vision. A fallen tree lay in the path. Chelsea hurled herself over it. Her foot caught on a branch. She tumbled to the dirt.

Please, God, protect me!

Chelsea scrabbled to her feet and pushed on. In a white-lightning burst of clarity, she veered left at the fork, taking the trail that would lead more quickly to the gravel road. Gasping for breath, sobbing, she pulled up the last hill and through the final grove of trees. Sun-dappled light beckoned in the distance. She lunged toward it. Her final gush of energy sent her crashing out of the underbrush into the piercing whiteness of the sun-drenched gravel road.

And straight into clutching arms.

The man struggled to pin her arms. Chelsea squeezed her eyes shut and screamed. Her attacker pulled back. Chelsea freed her arms and double-barreled the man in the chest.

He grunted.

She slammed another punch.

"Whoa, lady! Hold on!" He worked to pin her arms again. "I heard you coming, you made so much noise." He panted aloud, finally gripping both her wrists in a bear hold. "What is the *matter?*"

Chelsea threw her head back, eyes wide with terror. The image of her assailant blurred, then wrenched into stark focus. A stranger. Young. County park service uniform.

"Come on, now, calm down. I'm trying to help you!"

Chelsea opened her mouth, but no words came. Her body melted. Mouth gaping, she uttered a croak. Dimly, she felt her eyes roll back in her head and her knees cave. The world darkened, and she collapsed against the man's chest.

Her last conscious awareness was of the binoculars digging into her ribs.

PART II
PURSUIT

So do not fear, for I am with you;
do not be dismayed, for I am your God.
I will strengthen you and help you;
I will uphold you with my righteous right hand.

Isaiah 41:10

Chapter 9

Sergeant Reiger sighed as he wiped sweat from his forehead. Crazy Bay Area days. Fog made things cool in the mornings, then by noon it grew too hot. Seventy-eight degrees may be perfect for some people, but not for him. Probably had something to do with that extra twenty pounds he'd never gotten around to losing. He stopped to take off his jacket before getting into the car. Could be worse. He could be stuck in black leather, like back in his motorcycle days.

Reiger swung his mind back to business as he drove away from the Williams' house. He had a load of reports to write. This burglary wouldn't help matters any. And he could only push the pencil between calls from dispatch.

His thoughts strayed to Chelsea Adams. He hadn't been able to get her out of his mind since she'd fled his office shaken and embarrassed, obviously unused to being wrong. But if she thought he questioned her sanity, she was wrong about that too. In truth, he admired her.

Reiger had a deep faith in God, and for the last twenty years he'd built his life around that faith. Before then, he drank too much and had been in danger of losing his job. His marriage was on the rocks. Something pulled him to church one Sunday morning. There his life was changed. He went back the following week, taking Edith with him. They'd been attending faithfully ever since.

Every day while on duty, Reiger prayed. For victims. For perpetrators. For the bored teenagers who fell into drug use or made bad choices. For his colleagues. He wondered now how he'd ever managed this line of work without Christ's help. All the same, he was a private man and found it hard to discuss Christianity outside the accepting bounds of church friends. He shouldn't be like that, of course. He was as bold and aggressive as necessary in his job. Why couldn't he be bold about his faith?

Chelsea Adams — now that was one bold lady. Probably twenty years younger than he, yet already strong enough to look a stranger in the eye and tell him about her visions from God, never knowing whether that stranger might call her a lunatic.

If Chelsea Adams hadn't been a Christian, Reiger would have been uncomfortable with her abilities. His study of the Old Testament had afforded him all the information he needed about "psychics." Bottom line: all supernatural powers came either from God or from Satan. No gray area. The laws of Israel made God's hatred of séances, fortune-telling, palm reading, and the like very clear. Yet God had used his own prophets many, many times to foretell occurrences or to warn people of evil.

Would God do such a thing today?

If Chelsea Adams' visions came from God, why was this one wrong? Reiger sighed. God was perfect, but his servants here on earth certainly weren't. Maybe she'd grown too sure of herself and had interpreted too hastily. What a problem to work through. At least his own talents were more concrete.

Reiger pulled into the police station parking lot, only then remembering he'd forgotten to get something to eat. Well, too late now. He'd pick up a candy bar from the machine inside. Eating on the run was one of his job hazards. No wonder he had a paunch.

Wiping sweat from his brow, he pushed through the station's double glass doors. Thank goodness for air conditioning.

"Reiger!" Monica goggled at him from dispatch. "I was just about to beep you."

The door swooshed behind him. "Are you bothering me again? I just got here."

"Yeah, you're here and you'll *hear,* but you ain't gonna believe it. Remember the woman who wanted to talk to you about the 'murder in Trent Park'?"

Something shimmered up Reiger's spine. "What about her?"

"The county ranger over at Trent Park just called." Monica gazed hard at Reiger. "Seems that lady took herself a hike and found a body in the gully."

A moment passed before he reacted. "Monica, you joker, you pulling my leg again?"

"No, sir, not about something like this." She held up her right hand.

She was serious. A whirligig of thoughts spun through Reiger's mind.

"Okay. Call forensics and have 'em meet me over there." He swung back toward the door. "Call the coroner's office too. Ask for an hour's lead. Better ask 10 Charles 55 for another hour or so. And make sure Detective Turnbow's on his way." Ten Charles 55 was the code for the county unit that removed a body from a scene. Reiger stopped with one foot out the door and looked back. "Mrs. Adams still over there?"

"Yeah." Monica pursed her lips. "She's waiting for you."

"Good." Reiger whisked out the door.

Chapter 10

Trent Park was no Scout roundup at the moment. Squad cars checkered the gravel, with Haverlon police scurrying to control rubberneckers and secure the scene. Radios cackled and red lights flashed, throwing a blanket of disarray over the typically sleepy area.

Reiger slammed his Chevy door and surveyed the commotion. Four backups. Road into the park sealed off. Two county park rangers. The older man, he knew. And Chelsea Adams, jeans clad, with binoculars around her neck. She leaned against a ranger's car, looking shell-shocked. Her face looked pale, makeup smeared.

The county rangers crossed the lot toward Reiger, meeting him halfway.

"Jim."

"Hi, Dan." They shook hands. "This is Troy Jenkins. He was here when this lady ran out from one of the dirt trails like a scared rabbit."

The kid looked a little green. "Why don't you fill me in," Reiger said.

Troy swallowed. "About forty minutes ago, I heard a crashing coming off a trail a ways up the road. She ran right into me, crying and gasping. Before I could find out what was wrong, she fainted. When she came to, she started moaning about a body she'd seen down in the gully. I finally got her calmed down and came out here to radio Jim. She was so scared I didn't want to leave her alone while I went down the trail to investigate. So I waited till he arrived."

66

"I ended up going down the trail," Jim cut in. "Troy was getting along with the lady and, well, I've had to do this kind of thing a time or two."

Jim Sykes was near retirement age and had served in many a park over the years, including Golden Gate in San Francisco. He'd most likely seen it all.

"It's an awful sight down there, Dan." Jim lowered his voice. "It's a woman. Been down there not long enough to smell from afar, but long enough for the animals to get to her. Looks like the back of her head's bashed in. There's a large rock at the top of the gully with blood on it — looks like that may have been where it was done. 'Course, I didn't touch anything."

A rock, with blood on it. It fit with what Chelsea Adams had described. "Did you notice if a car's been left here overnight?" Reiger asked.

Troy shook his head. "Not a one. The lot was empty when I arrived this morning. Those here now can be accounted for by a few people still being cleared out. And one of 'em belongs to Mrs. Adams."

"Okay. Thanks, both of you, for your work. I'll talk to her now while I wait for forensics." The criminalist would be coming from the county lab and had a longer drive than Reiger. "You'll need to keep out of their way." Reiger nodded at the bustle of policemen. "But we'll want one of you to take us down the trail. The other one should wait for the coroner's investigator and removal specialists, and point them the way down."

The park rangers nodded.

Reiger glanced at Chelsea Adams and breathed a prayer for wisdom. This would be an interesting balancing act. Ironically, it had been easy enough to believe her sincerity when he'd thought her vision false. Now that there *had* been a murder, things were quite different. Thanks to Monica's big mouth, word had already drifted around the station about his meeting with Chelsea Adams.

Now the station would really be buzzing. The Chief would be all over Reiger on this one. He'd have to handle it just right.

Best thing to do for now, he figured, was to let Detective Turnbow handle Mrs. Adams until he could get back to the station. Turnbow had a way with women. Thirty-five years old and divorced, with a smooth mixture of tough cop and boyish charm that positively glowed around females. Pat could put Chelsea Adams at ease while grilling her like a charbroiled steak.

Sweat trickled between Reiger's shoulder blades as he ambled across the parking lot.

~ ~ ~

Chelsea tensed as she watched the sergeant approach.

"Hello, Mrs. Adams." Dust kicked around Reiger's feet as he drew to a stop before her. "I hear you've been through a pretty emotional ordeal."

She searched for an adequate explanation. "You must think I'm crazy for coming out here alone."

"No, I — "

"I just couldn't let it be! It wasn't 'til I got home that I understood that the ... woman was here, and you just didn't know it yet."

"I see. Why didn't you call me back?"

She glanced at her feet. "I really didn't think you'd send men to scour this whole park on my word."

Reiger studied her face. "You were pretty lucky — if that's the word to use — to find the right trail so quickly. It's a big park."

"True. I guess God had a hand in it."

"Maybe. Well, let me tell you what needs to happen now. I'll be going down the trail soon. I'll send you back to the station with my partner, Pat Turnbow, who'll be here any minute."

Across the parking lot an officer yelled at an onlooker to "Move back, sir!" Reiger glanced over his shoulder, then turned back to Chelsea. "He'll be asking you questions in detail about the vision you claim to have seen. Where you were, was anyone with you, etc. Plus he'll need more information about you personally."

Chelsea's stomach tightened. *Claim to have seen.* "Are you saying you don't believe me now?"

Reiger held up a hand. "This isn't about what I believe. It's just standard procedure. Anyone who found a body would be questioned. But you must understand, Mrs. Adams. You told me details about this murder that so far sound pretty accurate. I'll know more about that after I examine the scene. I do share your faith in the Lord. And I know He can do mighty things. But my colleagues, and most importantly my superiors, are going to be very suspicious. That just comes with being a cop. So anything you can tell us that can help verify your story will be important. Of course, if you want, you're entitled to have an attorney present."

Chelsea's jaw hinged open. Why hadn't she thought of this? Why hadn't she realized how it would look? Would she actually be a *suspect?* The idea was crazy. And what about the newspapers? She looked around. Were reporters already here? What about her boys? Paul would be so upset with her. Had she acted too fast? Gladys had warned her to be sure.

Well, she *was* sure. Just look what she'd found. She'd done the right thing.

Lord, where are you? Help me!

"I don't need an attorney. I have nothing to hide. But I need to get home. My sons get out of school soon."

Reiger tilted his head. "This may take a while. Do you have a friend who could help?"

Gladys would do it. If she wasn't available, there were others from church. "Yes."

"Good. Detective Turnbow will let you call from the station." The popping of tires on gravel turned his head. Two cars were rolling in at once. "There he is. And there's the investigator. I'll

69

turn you over to Detective Turnbow now. You'll be in good hands."

Chelsea stared at the officer getting out of his car, fear dancing down her nerves. He looked about her age, with wavy, light brown hair and a strong jaw, mouth turned up at the corners. He was strikingly handsome, but she could only focus on his authority as her questioner. She *had* to prove her innocence to this man.

She would have to tell him about Gavil Harrison.

Introductions were made quickly. Reiger seemed uneasy, preoccupied by reporters arriving. The man from the second car approached. He looked to be in his late twenties, with strawberry-blond hair.

"Hal, this is Chelsea Adams," Reiger said. "She found the body. Mrs. Adams, Hal Weiss from the county forensics lab."

"Hi." Her voice sounded weak.

Then before she knew it, Detective Turnbow was escorting her to his car. "You'll need to ride with me, Mrs. Adams. We'll get your car later."

Walls were closing in around her. Now she couldn't even have her car?

A commotion beyond the yellow tape caught her attention. Reporters raised their cameras. "Oh, no!" She turned her head away, hiding her face with a hand. Turnbow opened the back door of his car and she clambered inside, ducking down.

"Sorry about that." He started the engine. "No way to keep this kind of thing quiet, I'm afraid."

She kept her head down all the way to the station. Had she just landed on another planet? She tried to pray, but her mind could only form two words.

Why, God? Why?

Chapter 11

Reiger followed Troy through the forest, stepping only where the young park ranger stepped. Reiger knew Hal, an experienced criminalist, was doing the same behind him. Evidence could be anywhere along the route. They should disturb as little as possible. But they found nothing of value along the trail. No footprints good enough for casting. Nothing dropped.

As they walked, Reiger prayed. No matter how long he'd been on the force, he'd never gotten used to examining a body. Fortunately, he hadn't seen many. He had friends from county homicide who'd seen it all, and they agreed it never became easy.

The path broke into sunlight near the edge of a gully.

"The body's down there." The young ranger pointed. "And here's the rock."

"All right. Thanks." Hal surveyed the ground for footprints.

Reiger knew Hal was in his element. He would be very thorough with the puzzle pieces of evidence.

Reiger pulled out his camera, spiral notebook, and pencil. "Look, Hal." He stooped down. "Looks like a branch has been scraped through here."

They both leaned over for a closer look while Troy stepped back. "You're right."

Hal followed the undulating trail in the sand with his eyes. "The killer must have backed up and swept his own footprints away. These smaller ones look like they could belong to Mrs. Adams. Looks like these others, crossing over hers, could be Jim's."

"Not much likelihood of any good castings. But I'm not surprised." Reiger took the lens cap off his camera, sidling his eyes toward the bottom of the gully. Even from where he stood, the sight was gut-wrenching. He looked away. "Let's get to it."

For the next forty-five minutes the two men worked side by side, methodically collecting evidence. Reiger photographed the rock and surrounding ground, the trailhead, and the gully below. He'd learned over the years in covering burglaries and other crimes to do his own camera work. He also took meticulous notes.

Hal scraped blood and hair samples off the rock into separate paper bags and labeled them. He also discovered a tiny fragment of what looked like skin — possible strong DNA evidence, if it didn't belong to the victim. That, too, went into a bag. He dusted the rock for fingerprints. Nothing. He'd have liked to take the entire rock back with him, but it was much too big and lay embedded in the ground.

Overlook nothing — the detective's creed. Reiger noted the position of the rock — how far it lay from the trail, how far from the gully. He and Hal searched the ground for palm prints, although they didn't expect to find any. They discussed how the body must have been rolled into the ravine. Only when they had exhausted their findings at the top did they begin to make their way down the side of the gully. There was no trail to follow, and they had to weave their way around rocks and bushes, hanging on to branches as they zigzagged down to the floor.

"She must have been here at least twenty-four hours." Hal peered at the stage of fly larvae on the body's face, then leaned back. "Obviously a jogger. Shorts and running shoes."

Not a good sign. Joggers rarely carried identification. "Look at the right shoe." Reiger pointed. "She's got one of those little fabric cases on it. Maybe we'll find something there."

They continued their survey of the body and surrounding area, being careful not to touch the corpse itself. Legally, a coroner's investigator had to be present.

"I gave the coroner's office an hour's lead." Reiger bent for a closer look at a broken twig. "I don't know who they're sending."

"Mm." Hal wrinkled his nose as a breeze tousled a strand of the victim's blond hair. "Probably find lividity stains on her backside. Must have been killed up there and then sent rolling. I doubt she's been moved since, other than by animals." His voice was grim.

Lividity — the flow of blood to the lowest point in a body, due to gravity — caused brownish-red stains on the skin. It was a clear indication of a body's resting position soon after death.

"Man." He shook his head. "There's not gonna be much to autopsy here."

Certainly no chance for a liver temperature probe. Sometimes it took a while for creatures to smell remains, but they hadn't seemed to waste any time here. Most of the tissue between her neck and groin had been eaten. That meant no proper weight for either the body or major organs.

Dear Lord, help this poor woman's family.

A shout filtered down from above. Reiger tilted back his head to view Jake O'Brien, the coroner's investigator, on his way down. Troy stayed out of sight.

"Dan, Hal." Jake nodded to his colleagues when he reached the bottom, glancing at the corpse. "Mm. Nice nails. My teenage daughter's always messing around with her nails. Probably kill for a set like that."

Hal managed a wan smile. Reiger understood their need for comic relief. They lived with this gruesome stuff every day. Some things the heart had to turn off for the sake of sheer emotional survival. Knowledge was assembled, registered, then dumped in a holding tank, laughter clinking on the lid.

Jake moved toward the body. "Let's see what we've got."

The three of them examined the victim, Jake pointing out all contusions and bruises. He was disappointed in the manicure after all. A lot of dirt was embedded under the nails, and one had been broken just above the quick.

"Probably occurred on the trip down, or maybe during a struggle. Bright red. Didn't see it around, huh?"

Hal shook his head. "Some bird probably made off with it by now."

"I'll make sure this bit is clipped during the autopsy, just in case." Jake held up the hand and leaned over to examine the fingertips.

Hal peered under a dirty nail. "Here's something." Using tweezers he plucked some fibers of golden material caught under the second and third fingernails, then sealed and labeled them in a bag. "Let's hope these aren't from some fabric found in half the homes in Haverlon."

Reiger peeled back the top of the small pack attached to the victim's shoe—and found a house key. He pulled it out with a handkerchief. "Bingo." Better yet, it was attached to a ring with "MEG" in gold letters.

"Well, you can hardly beat that," Jake said.

The sergeant shot him a look. "You're gonna let me take this now, aren't you?" Reiger would lose valuable time if he had to wait until it was logged at autopsy. The longer a victim's identification took, the colder the suspect's trail would become.

Jake nodded. "Go ahead."

"Hang on, I'll print it," Hal said. A good fingerprint could be their chance of identifying the victim if she'd ever been fingerprinted for a job or any other reason. Reiger waited while Hal dusted for a print on the key. "Hey, not bad." He showed the result.

"Great. Let's hope we find a match." Reiger took the key from Hal and placed it in his pocket.

Jake chuckled. "I've heard of some pretty wild ID leads in my day. One time the victim had a set of dentures from the army, and the military conveniently stamped her name on the inside of the teeth." He fell silent as he opened an eyelid to extract a sample of vitreous humor from the blue eye that stared in glazed emptiness. "Another time San Francisco homicide tracked down an identity from a dry cleaning receipt in the dead man's pocket."

It became quiet again, save for the crackle of brush under their feet.

"Well, that's about it." Jake stood up to stretch his legs. "Here's what I can tell you so far." He pointed toward the victim's head. "Beaten on the face, head smashed, probably on that rock up there. No bullet or knife wounds, at least in what's left of her. No visible signs of rape. I'd say the smashing killed her, but I'll reserve the official statement until after autopsy."

Hal shook his head. "I didn't get much. No fingerprints on her, no footprints, no foreign objects. Four or five strands of gold fiber. That's it."

They waited for about ten minutes until the removal unit arrived with a stokes — an orange basket-like affair used to drag bodies from hard-to-reach areas. By the time the two specialists had removed the victim, and Reiger, Hal, and Jake had carried their equipment up the gully and through the woods, led by a squeamish Troy, it was almost 4:30. Hal's car, with Reiger and Troy inside, followed the white removal van down the gravel road toward the parking lot, its row of yellow lights flashing.

Onlookers and reporters rushed toward the vehicles. *Click. Whir.* A TV camera rolled.

Haverlon would lock its doors tonight.

"Sergeant Reiger!" A microphone was shoved in his face as he stepped from the car. "Do you know who the victim is?"

"How long has the body been there?"

"Someone said it's half eaten!"

They buzzed around Reiger like bees. "No statement at this time, folks. There's not much we can tell you yet."

The white removal van drove out of the park first, rolling slowly through the parted crowd to take "Meg" to the morgue. Hal headed with his evidence toward the county lab, and Jake prepared to return to the coroner's office.

"Buckman!" Reiger yelled at a policeman as he pushed past reporters. "Gather all the officers you can." He patted the pocket with the house key. "We have a door to find."

The officers were to call dispatch if they uncovered any information on a young blond jogger named Meg. Reiger held on to the key. If any prints on file matched those taken from the house key, he would be notified at once.

As he drove through the crowd to head down Wickens, Reiger realized he hadn't eaten since breakfast. No matter. After what he'd seen, he didn't want to eat. Besides, he had a more immediate concern.

He needed to interrogate Mrs. Adams.

Chapter 12

Reiger pulled open the door to Haverlon's police station at 4:45 that afternoon. Monica raised thinly plucked eyebrows at him as he crossed the green carpet. Without saying a word, she pointed in the direction of Turnbow's office.

"Let me know if the investigating officers find anything about the victim." Heading down the hall, Reiger stopped first in his office to make a phone call.

"Edith's Flowers."

"Hi, love."

"Dan!" His wife sounded surprised. "Uh-oh. It can't be good if you're calling me from work."

"You're right. We've had a homicide. I don't know when I'll be home."

She drew in a breath. "Somebody was killed in Haverlon? Who?"

"We don't know yet. A woman jogger in Trent Park. Edith, you better prepare yourself. This case has an element to it that the reporters are gonna love. The town'll be in chaos for a while."

"What happened?"

He sighed. "It's a long story. I'll tell you when I see you." Opening a drawer, he pulled out a tape recorder as he spoke, laid it on his desk, and checked that a fresh tape was wound and ready to use. "I gotta go now. Listen, we were supposed to go to that Giants game Saturday. You'd better find a friend to take."

Edith sighed. "Okay, Dan. I'll be praying for you."

"Thanks." Reiger placed the phone back on its base, then headed for Turnbow's office.

~ ~ ~

Turnbow had done his homework.

"She's on the level, as far as I can see," he said in low tones outside his office door.

"I've talked to a couple of her references. One of them is a woman watching her kids right now. Gladys Dell. They confirmed some of Mrs. Adams' previous visions. Especially this Gladys. Apparently, there have been a couple interesting ones. And I ran a make on Mrs. Adams' license. Nothing, not even a moving violation." Turnbow related Chelsea's information about her husband's company, the dinner of the previous night at Bayhill, and the timing of her vision. "Everything checks out. Plus, she has confirmed alibis for the better part of yesterday. I didn't go back any further than that for now." He handed Reiger a large three-ring binder — the beginnings of what would be the "murder book," holding all reports on the case. "Here's what she did Wednesday."

Reiger scanned his partner's scrawled letters. Normal day. Up at seven, hubby and kids to work, school. Aerobics class at BB's, 8:30 to 9:30. Home, dressed, went to grocery store. Home, noon. Housework, laundry 'til 2:30. Pick up kids, to dentist. Home, 5:00. Laundry, dress, dinner at Bayhill. He handed the binder back.

"The restaurant confirmed that the Adams had reservations for a party of three at 7:45. Their server wasn't at work yet, but I talked to the owner. A ..." He consulted his notes. "Fred Night. He remembered them. He said the third person was a man. And, how's this, the reason he remembered them so well is because of what happened at their table. He said the lady wigged out at the end of the meal."

Reiger raised his eyebrows.

"He couldn't really explain it. He was across the restaurant and noticed that the woman at the Adams' table was acting like she

78

was ready to faint or something. One man had gotten up for a moment, so she was left with the other guy, who seemed concerned about her. Then the first man came back. The maître d' was nearby, but they didn't seem to want his help. Later, the maître d' told Night that the woman had almost gone into a trance. Anyway, the three of them left soon after that." Turnbow lifted a shoulder. "Night said he really knew something had happened when he saw that they hadn't touched dessert."

"Dessert?"

"Soufflé. Apparently, Bayhill is famous for it. Claims nobody's ever left their soufflé before."

"Oh."

Turnbow shut the notebook. "One more thing. Something she didn't tell you."

Reiger locked eyes with his partner. For some reason, his skin crawled. "What?"

"The guy they went to dinner with? She says he did it."

~ ~ ~

Once more Chelsea went over every detail of her vision, this time with Reiger capturing it on tape. Now and then he interrupted with a question and she would clarify. The details, he told her, could be very significant, since so far her vision seemed accurate. Chelsea sensed that Sergeant Reiger believed her, while his partner remained skeptical. The part about Gavil Harrison, though, seemed to make them both uneasy.

"Let me understand this." Reiger sat to the right of Turnbow's desk. "You didn't see his face in your vision, but saw guilt in his expression afterwards?"

Chelsea hesitated, her morning's conversation with Gladys chafing her thoughts. "This is so hard to explain. Remember, I let the words 'Sometimes I see things' slip. Almost immediately, he looked frightened. We said no more about it. But you know what I'm talking about. Surely it happens to you when you interview

79

people. You can sense whether they're telling the truth or not, or when they're hiding something. He looked at me with guilt. He probably doesn't realize the extent of what I know. But I think he at least senses that I glimpsed something inside him. And there's another thing that leads me to think it's him. When I came out of that vision, I *knew* evil was present. I've never felt that before. But then in my past visions, I've never been in the actual presence of the people causing harm."

Reiger let the subject drop, probing further about her other visions. When an hour had passed, Chelsea was surprised to hear her stomach growl. She hadn't thought she could ever eat again. The sergeant smiled.

"Me too. I suppose we both missed lunch." He glanced at the notebook in his lap. "We're almost done here and then Detective Turnbow can take you back to your car."

"What then?" Chelsea asked. "I mean, what do I do now?"

Reiger nodded. "For now, your part is done. We may need to contact you if we have any further questions or if we find any discrepancies between the information you've given us and our own follow-up. Two things I want to make clear, Mrs. Adams. One is that I'm tending to believe all you've said, unusual as it is. Two, that belief will mean little to our investigation. In other words, everything has to be verified. As far as Mr. Harrison, we can look into that, see if he has any ties to the victim, for example. Once we find out who she is. But you must understand that a vision would never stand up in court. Or even in this station or with my superiors, for that matter. What my partner and I need now is solid evidence of who committed this crime. And evidence is built on detective work, which can take time. So just because you're not hearing from us, don't think we're not working on this with everything we've got."

Relief trickled through Chelsea. "Okay."

Reiger looked at his partner. "Anything else you can think of?"

"Yeah. The media."

Reiger's eyes flicked heavenward. "Have you done anything about that out front yet?"

"It's taken care of. Apparently Mrs. Adams never gave her name. The Chief's already saying heads will roll if 'rumors' come out of here. And this report," Turnbow indicated the notebook, "is for our eyes and the Chief's only."

Chelsea's gaze jumped back and forth between the two men. What was this?

"We're talking about when you came in this morning," Reiger said. "Our receptionist was apparently in such a dither over your statement, she forgot to ask your name. So no one's heard it but us. As I'm sure you can guess, the word's already running through the station about the ... strangeness of this case."

Chelsea cast him a penetrating look. With his partner in the room, he apparently wouldn't speak about God.

Reiger shifted in his seat. "The media's going to be all over us, Mrs. Adams. They're going to be talking to officers and officers' wives and girlfriends and anybody they can think of who might know some inside news on this story. We're going to do everything we can to button up the station, and that includes our dispatcher. We'll probably succeed for a while and after that, we'll see. You know how it is, reporters eventually go to other things. But some details will most likely get out. We'll try to keep your name from getting out there. If it does, the next thing you know, you'll have reporters camping on your front lawn."

Sickness rolled through Chelsea. Her gaze slipped to the floor. Imagine being hounded by the media. Her sons at school, Paul, his company, her church, their friends. All of them could be affected. She swallowed. "Believe me, I'll do everything I can too. I won't be telling anyone else. Only my friend Gladys knows. And of course my husband will have to —"

A horrible realization hit. Chelsea's eyes rounded. She lifted her head to Sergeant Reiger.

"Gavil Harrison. If he hears I discovered the body, he'll know for sure what I saw in the restaurant. He'll understand everything."

Chapter 13

Reiger could hear the clock ticking. With every minute, the murderer's trail grew colder. An hour could spell disaster; a day, defeat.

He fidgeted in his seat as Turnbow drove down yet another street in the Trent Park area. After returning Chelsea Adams to her car at the park, they'd joined in the search to identify the owner of the key that was burning a hole in his pocket. No matches to the fingerprint from the key had been found. An hour later, they'd knocked on lots of doors, but no "Meg." Nothing from the officers either. It didn't make sense. Joggers were not transients. They tended to have families or friends or at least a job. Why hadn't someone missed this woman?

He glanced at his watch. Seven o'clock.

"Dapple Street." Turnbow's voice cut through Reiger's thoughts. "I used to ride a neighbor's horse named Dapple when I was a kid. While my dad was still alive."

Reiger swung a look at his partner. He had nervous excitement written all over him — not unexpected on his first homicide. Most of the time, police work was just plain boring. Reiger muttered a response, then swiveled his head back toward the road.

Dapple Street was a narrow cul-de-sac with twenty-four townhouses of beige stucco and brown shingle roofs. Neighboring houses shared a common wall, with covered porches grouped in close pairs jutting into small front yards. Within each pair of houses, each home appeared to be a mirror image of the other, at least from the outside. Detached garages were in a clump toward the end of the street along with a circular turnaround for visitor parking, its center landscaped with grass and small trees. The place was attractive and quiet.

"Townhouses usually mean a homeowners' association," Reiger said. "And that means a president who would have a list of residents. If we can find that person, we'll get through here in a hurry."

The first door they tried near the parking area, number seventeen, yielded a young couple new to the Bay Area who didn't know anyone named Meg, but did know where the association president lived. "That would be Alice Geary." The woman pointed across the way to a house with three silver birches out front. "Watch out," she whispered as Turnbow and Reiger turned to go, "she's a talker."

No matter. They had no time for small talk.

"I saw you coming," sang the diminutive woman who opened her front door before they had a chance to knock. Her gray hair lay in a loose bun at the nape of her neck, her cotton pants and shirt a shocking pink, reflecting a circle of blusher on each cheek. "I noticed the emblem on your car, and of course I was already keyed up from hearing that bunch of sirens this afternoon. So I thought to myself, something must be going on in the neighborhood. And if that's so, I need to know about it, because I keep watch over these homes, you know."

Reiger introduced himself and Turnbow, fighting impatience. They were conducting an investigation, he told her, and they needed help. Did she have a list of residents? At her questions, Reiger held up a hand. "Sorry, ma'am, we can't tell you any more right now."

Alice Geary joggled her head. "Humph. I may be an old widow, but I know when something's going on." Turnbow opened his mouth, but she cut him off. "Don't worry, don't worry, I got just what you want." She assumed a look of superiority. "Follow me into my office."

84

Reiger and Turnbow exchanged glances and did as they were told. As soon as Alice Geary opened her front door, the rich smell of homemade vegetable soup surrounded them. The audience of a television game show cheered loudly from her living room. She trotted over to turn down the volume. In front of the TV was an armchair and matching footrest, balls of yarn and knitting needles stuffed into an oversize basket beside the chair. She herded them past the living room and into her office.

"Here it is." She opened the drawer of a gray steel filing cabinet and extracted a small black book. "I keep this list updated — always change it whenever somebody comes or goes. And I note the date that they move in or out. That way," she leaned closer to Reiger in a conciliatory manner, "they can't complain they've been overcharged when dues time rolls around."

Reiger took the list from her hands. He skimmed the first page, noting that names were listed in street address order, beginning with number one. He saw no "Meg." But he did see something else.

Marian Baker and Gavil Harrison. Number four.

Reiger flipped over the first page and skimmed the second, half expecting to find what they'd come for. His eyes stopped again, this time at the last listing. Number twenty-four. Owner, Michael Ward. Renter, Meg Jessler.

Oh, boy.

He looked to Mrs. Geary. The woman was practically leaning on his shoulder. "Would you excuse us a moment?"

She stepped back with overabundant dignity. "Of course."

Reiger extended the book to show Turnbow, pointing from one name to the other. Turnbow's face went slack.

"Mrs. Geary." Reiger turned. "Could you describe Meg Jessler?"

Alice Geary waved a hand. "Oh, you wouldn't have any trouble with Meg. Nice girl. Little flighty, but she's young yet.

She's out of town right now." A frown creased her forehead. "Oh, dear. She never gave me her house key to water her plants."

"Where was she headed?"

Mrs. Geary took two minutes to answer, rambling on about how Meg had met some boy in Chicago and how she was driving "all the way across country" to visit him. "She's just crazy about him, you know. She told me—"

"When did she leave?"

"Yesterday morning."

Reiger's mind flashed to the grim scene in the gully. "You never said what she looks like."

Apprehension crossing Mrs. Geary's face. "Why?"

Turnbow touched her elbow. "Ma'am, please."

"Okay." Her eyes wandered to the ceiling. "She's about twenty-five, blond hair. I don't think it's real, you know. About five-foot-seven. Slim. Jogs a lot. Every morning, she says, though I'm not up early enough to see for myself."

Reiger absorbed the information. "Would her front door key also open her garage?"

Yes, Mrs. Geary responded, either the key or the remote control.

Reiger moved into the hallway. "Could you tell us which garage is hers?"

She wagged her head, leading them out to the porch. "Over there." She waved an arm. "Same number as the unit. But if it's a car you're looking for, you won't find it. Girl's probably halfway to Chicago by now."

Reiger had already reached the bottom step. Turnbow stopped halfway down. "She lives alone, right?" A second resident would cost them time, forcing them to seek permission to try their key.

"Yes. But she doesn't own the place. She rents from Mr. Ward who lives out in Concord. Her parents pay most of the rent. It's expensive, you know."

Turnbow nodded a thanks, then hurried to catch up with his partner.

~ ~ ~

"Let's see if this is our girl." Reiger stopped in front of the garage.

Turnbow didn't know what to make of it all. Where would Chelsea Adams' "vision from God" lead them next? It was just too weird.

Reiger took the key out of his pocket and turned it over once, staring at the gold letters on its chain. "MEG." He fit the key into the lock. Turnbow held his breath.

It slid home.

Reiger grabbed the garage door handle, pulling it up with a quiet rumble. They peered inside. There were boxes along the walls, a bicycle hanging from a large hook in the rear. And a burgundy Camaro.

They inspected the car, saying little, opening doors with the gingered touch of a handkerchief from Reiger's pocket. On the floor of the front seat lay a clothing store bag containing a man's sweater, the receipt dated June 4. A map of the western United States, going as far east as Wyoming, was spread across the passenger seat. Another map, still folded, of the eastern states, lay beneath it. Cassette tapes, a hairbrush, and a couple pairs of sunglasses littered the back seat, as well as a visor and a fast-food bag, scrunched and holding a few stale fries.

When they'd finished, they stepped out of the garage, rolling the door closed, and walked the short distance to unit twenty-four. Reiger knocked on the door, waited, then knocked again. No answer. He slid the key into the lock. The metal key chain clanked softly.

Eeriness crept up the back of Turnbow's neck as they stepped into the silent house. It felt like stepping into a mausoleum, the air inside oppressive, stuffy. They walked a few feet down the hall, their shoes resounding against a bare hardwood floor. To their left lay the living room, its windows shut. A shaft of light from the setting sun glimmered through a double window on the front wall. Dust danced in its path. Books and magazines, a few pieces of clothing, a glass half full of water lent an aura of easy familiarity, as if someone had gone out for an errand and would return any moment. Across the hall, the kitchen was tidy without being clean. Like someone had rustled through it in a hurry, her mind on other things.

The bedroom at the back of the townhouse lay in disarray, bed unmade, clothes, costume jewelry, and shoes scattered around. A large suitcase yawned on the floor in the far corner, one side holding lingerie in lacy black and ice blue, panty hose, bikini underwear, a green taffeta dress.

"She was going somewhere, all right." Turnbow's voice grated his own ears. He squatted on his heels beside the suitcase.

Reiger approached a long oak dresser to Turnbow's right and picked up a gold-framed eight-by-ten photograph. Turnbow hoisted himself to his feet and closed in for a look. She was blond, her hair straight and long. She leaned on the shoulder of a man in his mid-twenties, one arm behind him, another across her stomach, stretching a hand to hold his. Her nails were manicured, long and red. She smiled widely, almost possessively. There was a sensuality about her that lacked refinement. Although she wore a flowery sundress, Turnbow could picture her in cutoff shorts and a tank top, slinky legs crossed, hanging over a margarita in a bar on El Camino. The thought flicked across his mind that this would be a young woman impressed by money, not in moderation, because her own lifestyle reflected that, but in large amounts. Say, the annual bonus of a successful salesman. Or the glitter of promising company stock.

"Can you tell if that's her?"

Reiger remained focused on the photograph. "She's not much younger than my second daughter." His voice sounded gruff. He cleared his throat and replaced the picture with both hands, almost reverently. When he turned around, Turnbow saw that his face was gray, his jaw working.

"Let's get to it."

Chapter 14

Gladys was waiting when Chelsea pulled into the garage. "How *are* you, dear?" She hugged Chelsea hard.

Chelsea's eyes filled with tears. "Okay."

"It'll be all right." Gladys held on until Chelsea was ready to pull away.

"Where are the boys?" She wiped her eyes.

"Watching a movie. I got them two at the video store. High adventure, naturally." Gladys grinned, as if she hoped her own energy would cheer her friend. "Their homework's done, and I figured the movies would keep them busy."

Gratefulness flooded through Chelsea. "Bless you."

"Ah, nothin' to it." Gladys waved a hand.

"Do they know anything?"

"Nope. I told them you were at a meeting, that's all."

"Good." Chelsea sighed. She felt so tired. "I don't want to tell them anything unless I have to."

They headed for the door. "Hey, you hungry?" Gladys asked. "I made some homemade mushroom soup and rolls. Fine and dandy, if I do say so myself. You know I'm as mean in the kitchen as I am on my motorcycle." She bustled into the kitchen toward the stove.

"Gladys." Chelsea almost laughed. "You really are something."

~ ~ ~

90

By 9:30 both boys were in bed and Gladys had gone home. "Want me to stay with you tonight?" she'd offered. "Be happy to."

Chelsea knew that meant going back home to pick up her things. Gladys had already done enough. "I'll be fine, really. Besides, Paul will be calling, and I'll need to tell him everything. It could be a long conversation."

Gladys nodded. "I'll be praying about that God will use these events to soften Paul's heart."

"Thanks, I'll need it. Paul may think he really has reason to be mad at God now. Not only is He sending me crazy visions, but now He's taken Paul's main candidate away."

Gladys tilted her head. "I wonder about that."

"What do you mean?"

She hesitated. "I know everything else you 'saw' has come true. Just don't be too surprised if Paul still doesn't believe you about Gavil."

Chelsea stared at Gladys. Was she disappointed that Chelsea had mentioned Gavil to the police so soon? "I guess I ... hadn't thought of that."

Great. Just great. Chelsea dreaded talking to her husband even more.

~ ~ ~

Paul called at ten o'clock.

How to begin?

Chelsea half listened to the events of his day before talking about her own. She spoke for over ten minutes. Paul never said a word. Not a good sign. When it came time to tell him about giving Gavil's name to the police, she couldn't do it. He would be *so mad.*

Maybe when he got home, after he'd had a chance to settle with all this, it would be easier.

Chelsea finished her story. Paul remained silent. "Paul?" She perched on the edge of their bed, praying for his acceptance. If ever she needed his understanding, it was now. "*Say* something. Are you mad at me?"

He made a sound in his throat. "No. I'm not *mad* at you. How can I be, after what you've been through? I just wish you'd waited until I got home. We should have talked about this first. We usually make decisions together. Seems like ever since you got into this Christianity stuff, you're doing more and more on your own. Going to church, having these visions. I'm out in left field somewhere."

"That's not true at all! I need you now more than ever. I'm *scared*. You don't know how awful this day has been."

"Then why couldn't you wait? Maybe I wouldn't have wanted you to get involved in this."

Chelsea's eyes drifted to their wedding picture on the bedroom wall. "I already *was* involved. If *you* knew this information, could you keep it to yourself? Somewhere out there, people are missing a member of their family. Don't you think they at least deserve to know what happened? I know the whole thing's terrible, and I would never have chosen to be a part of it. But maybe God's going to use this to help catch whoever did it. That man needs to be off the streets."

A pause. "And you think that's Gavil."

Exhaustion washed through Chelsea. Thank goodness she hadn't told Paul everything. She didn't even want to finish this conversation. Nor did she want to face him when he came home. What if he thought to ask her if she'd told the police about Gavil? She couldn't lie. Chelsea almost laughed. The only reason he hadn't asked is because he assumed she wouldn't be so stupid.

"Paul." Her throat tightened. "I know you think I'm crazy. Maybe I am. But I'm going to need you through all this. I can't get the picture of that body out of my mind. And whether you believe Gavil was involved or not, I'm scared of him. So believe me, I'm not pulling away from you."

"Oh, Chelsea, I'm sorry." Paul sighed. "You've had a terrible day. And here I am going on about my own worries."

Chelsea's eyes closed in relief.

"Don't be afraid tonight. You're perfectly safe. Turn the alarm on if it makes you feel better."

Their house was protected against fire and burglary by an alarm linked to a security company in Redwood City. They usually didn't activate the alarm when they were home, using it mostly when they were away on vacation. There were two control panels, one in the kitchen and one in the master bedroom.

"I'll do that."

"Good. I get in around four tomorrow. I'll try to come home rather than stopping at the office. Okay?"

"Okay."

"We'll talk more then. And if you need me for any reason tonight, you call."

"I will."

Chelsea hung up the phone and walked to the control pad to turn on the house alarm.

Chapter 15

"Let's start our questioning with Gavil Harrison," Reiger told Turnbow as they crossed the townhouse parking area.

Even with the incredible coincidence, Turnbow felt leery. "Why start with *him*? We've got *all* these townhouses to cover."

Reiger strode down a short sidewalk toward unit number four. Red and yellow flowers dotted the path. "Why not? Look, Turnbow, it's all we've got. Don't worry, we'll hit every door."

With the help of Mrs. Geary's files, Turnbow and Reiger had found the address of Meg Jessler's parents. They called local police to visit the couple and inform them of their daughter's death. At least one of the parents would be escorted by an officer to the morgue to identify the body. In the meantime, Reiger and Turnbow needed to press on with their investigation.

Reiger rang Harrison's doorbell and waited. Turnbow heard the chime. The door was opened by a woman who looked to be around his age, with light-brown hair, cut short and very curly. She stood about five-foot-seven. Probably wanted to lose ten pounds. Her face was round, with large, deep-set hazel eyes. Business suit, little jewelry, conservative makeup.

"Marian Baker?"

"Yes?"

Reiger introduced himself and Turnbow, holding up his badge. Her eyes flashed wider. "May we talk to you a moment?"

She raked a look across visitor parking. "Where's your car?"

"Over there." Reiger pointed. "It's unmarked."

She insisted they wait on the porch, closing her door while she verified their identities with the police station. When she returned, she apologized for the delay.

The kitchen was on their left as they entered, tiled in light green. A large eating area lay at the back of the room, near a sliding-glass door leading out to a patio. On their right was a living room, tailored in basic beige and browns. Down the hall, Turnbow saw two doors, the first to an apparent office. He assumed the back one was to a bedroom.

In the living room, Marian Baker sat on the edge of an armchair, motioning for them to take the couch. Reiger set his tape recorder on the coffee table in front of them. "Sorry, Ms. Baker, to have this thing running. It takes notes faster than I can."

They asked if Mr. Harrison was home. No, she replied, he was still at work. It wasn't unusual for him to arrive home as late as 9:00.

Marian reacted with shock at the news of her neighbor's death.

She'd met Meg shortly after moving to Dapple Street the previous year. Meg had noticed the moving truck and come over a few days later, wanting to show Marian a line of cosmetics she sold. Marian soon became a regular client.

"How often would you see her?" Reiger's voice sounded casual as he flicked a piece of lint off his shirt, but Turnbow could tell he was in high gear.

"I don't know. Maybe every three months or so. Even then, I'd usually just call her to order, and when the products came in, she'd drop them by and I'd write her a check."

Turnbow filed the information away in his mind. Meg Jessler could have had contacts with every home in the complex. "Did you ever see her around here with friends, driving out or coming home?"

Marian shook her head. "No. Dapple Street's really quiet. We live close, but we don't really know each other." She shrugged. "Everyone's busy. Even the people right next door to us, we don't see much. The ones over there," she pointed in the direction of Wickens Road, "own a bakery. They hire bakers, but they're out real early in the morning to open up. And the guy on this side," she nodded her head toward number six, "has been here a few months. I've introduced myself, but I don't think Gavil's even met him."

She'd last had contact with Meg Jessler about two weeks ago, when she bought some nail polish and lipstick. "But I didn't really see her then. Like I mentioned, I ordered the items over the phone, and when she brought them by a few days later, I was out of town. Gavil was home. He paid her."

Turnbow kept a poker face. "Would he have seen her any other time?"

Comprehension flicked across her features, trailed by the firm muscles of certainty. "I don't think so." She seemed to want to explain. "He's here even less than I am because of his work hours. And he travels a lot more than I do. Plus he's only lived here about three weeks."

Reiger thanked her for her time but left the tape running. "Where do you work, by the way?"

She'd been a consultant with Barry & Barry in Haverlon for five years, she said. She helped businesses manage employees, designing ways to run an office, writing job descriptions, that sort of thing. Reiger chatted with her, extracting the name of a "particularly dependent" client in southern California. Two nights ago she'd flown there to work with him, staying in a hotel overnight.

Interesting.

Reiger clicked off the tape, muttering that he'd almost forgotten it.

They trailed Marian to the front door, Turnbow still fixed on the fact that Gavil Harrison was alone Tuesday night. Reiger kept up an affable chattiness, commenting on the weather, complimenting her on the townhouse's decor, pointing to a pair of worn leather garden gloves on the kitchen counter and asking if she was the gardener. She was. His wife loved gardening too, he rattled on. And Edith's gloves were in just as bad a shape as hers.

The two men stepped out onto the porch, repeating their thanks. Reiger fell silent as the door clicked shut behind them.

~ ~ ~

They split up then, Reiger going to the door of unit two—the bakery owners. Turnbow knocked on number six and got no answer. He moved on to number eight. It was occupied by a couple with a new baby girl, the wife feeding her in a bedroom while the husband spoke with Turnbow. No, they didn't really know Meg Jessler. She'd come to the door one evening, displaying her cosmetics, but his wife wasn't interested. No, they hadn't seen anything unusual in the last forty-eight hours. Turnbow took a few notes and thanked them.

He stepped out their door as Reiger came up the same side of the street.

They met in the middle, near unit six, to exchange information. The bakery owners, Reiger reported, had told him that until the last month, they would pull out of their garage at 5:45 A.M. to open up shop in San Mateo, and often saw a blond woman jogging through the complex at that time. Lately they'd been leaving at 5:30 A.M. and hadn't seen her since the time change.

"Five forty-five is fairly early." Turnbow pictured Dapple Street in the stillness of the summer's just-risen sun. Wickens Road, the straight route to Trent Park, was rural, with few homes. "We may not find anybody who saw her."

The front door of number six clicked open, and Turnbow turned to see a young man, tall with thick, dark hair and clad in a black suit with bow tie, hurry outside. His hair was damp.

"Excuse me." Turnbow stopped the man as he approached the sidewalk, pulling out his small notebook and pen. He introduced himself and Reiger. "We need a moment of your time, sir. Could you just answer a few questions?"

Turnbow first asked for his name. "Jackson Doniger," the young man replied, eyeing the detectives curiously. Doniger informed Turnbow that he'd moved to Sequoia Townhomes fairly recently. They had rung his doorbell? Sorry, he'd probably been in the shower. When Turnbow explained what had happened, Doniger registered the wide-eyed surprise of a neighbor.

"No, I didn't know her." He ran a hand through his hair, his agitation to be on his way reflected in the movement. Catching the recognition in Turnbow's eyes, he seemed embarrassed. "Sorry. Here we are talking about a neighbor's death, and I'm worried about getting to work on time."

Reiger's gaze fell to the suit, the standard uniform for dozens of upscale restaurants on the Peninsula. "Did you happen to see anything or anyone in the last few mornings that seemed unusual?" He noted that Meg was known to jog early.

"No, afraid not. I don't get up until about noon. I work at the restaurant evenings, then I usually go out afterwards, so I don't get to bed until late. I was supposed to have tonight off or I'd have been at work much sooner, but they just called me in for a couple hours."

Turnbow made a note. "So you're not up that early."

He shrugged. "Not unless I can't sleep, for some reason. But that's not often." He checked his watch. "Look, I need to do one of two things. Either go on to work and talk to you later or, if you want to ask me some more questions now, I should call the owner and let him know what's going on."

Turning to Reiger, Turnbow saw his partner focusing on something across the parking lot. He looked over his shoulder. A man was edging his BMW toward garage number four.

Gavil Harrison.

Doniger was waiting. Turnbow swung back toward the young man. "We'll be in the area for the next few days. We'll catch up with you again. Probably tomorrow."

Doniger said that was fine, offered them his phone number, then scurried toward his garage.

~ ~ ~

Turnbow watched Harrison get out of his car, pulling a briefcase and suit coat from the backseat. He exited the garage and hit the button on a remote in his left hand, the briefcase and jacket in his right. The whirring grind of the door filtered across the cement.

"Mr. Harrison?"

They intercepted him on the sidewalk, explained the situation, and asked if they could ask a few questions. Turnbow saw tired surprise cross his face, then resignation, as if their presence lent an unpleasant ending to an already taxing day. Once inside the townhouse, they maneuvered him to the office and closed the door. Turnbow stopped first to tell Marian they needed to interview him alone. Changed from her business suit to jeans and a T-shirt, she looked almost childlike to Turnbow. For her sake, he hoped Harrison proved clean.

The office held a large oak desk with computer, a swivel chair on rollers, built-in shelving, an oak file, another chair, and a five-foot leather couch. Reiger claimed the swivel chair, placing his tape recorder on the desk. Turnbow took the couch.

Harrison hesitated, then stood before the chair in the corner. Reiger motioned for him to sit and flicked on the tape recorder. The sergeant first asked when he'd last seen Meg Jessler. He told them it was a few weeks ago, when she'd stopped by with some products for Marian. He paid her, and she left.

"How long did you talk to her?"

Gavil shrugged. "Not very long. A minute or two."

"Did she come inside?"

99

"No."

"You had to get some money, didn't you? What did she do during that time?"

"Actually, I went to get a check. She stood at the door and waited."

"You didn't invite her in?"

Gavil hesitated. "Sounds kind of rude, huh." He gave a short laugh. "Maybe I did, but I can't remember her coming inside."

"So you're not sure."

"I guess not. I really can't remember."

"Have you seen her since then?"

Harrison pressed his eyes with the thumb and fingers of one hand. "I don't think so."

"Okay." Reiger thought a moment. "Have you ever been in Trent Park?"

"Yes. Marian and I walked through it one Saturday a couple months ago."

"Did you hike some of the trails?"

"No. We walked down the gravel road."

"Never jogged there?"

"I'm not a jogger."

"So you never jogged there."

"That's right."

"All right." Reiger paused. "Could you tell us how you spent yesterday?"

Gavil shot Reiger a look. "Why?"

"Just routine, sir," Turnbow put in. "It's the same question we're asking everyone."

Gavil closed his eyes and sighed. "Not much to tell. I worked all day and then went to a business dinner. I didn't get home until almost 10:30."

"What time did you go to work?"

For a split second, he hesitated. "I usually get up around 5:30. I leave around 7:00 and arrive at work about 7:30."

"And where do you work?"

"At Titan Electronics in Sunnyvale. I'm in charge of Western Region sales."

Reiger scratched his cheek. "So you usually get to work around 7:30. What time did you get to work *yesterday?*"

"Hey, what is this?" Harrison lifted a hand.

A stillness settled in Turnbow's chest. The man was acting like he had something to hide. It was in the arch of his back, the narrowing of his eyes.

"Standard question, sir." Reiger shrugged.

Harrison swallowed. "Like I said, I usually get there about 7:30."

"What about *yesterday?*"

A soft answer, eyes on the floor. "Around 7:30."

A bony finger trailed down Turnbow's spine. The guy was lying.

"Seven-thirty," Reiger repeated.

"Yes. Seven-thirty."

"And you didn't leave your house until you went to work?"

"That's right."

"And what time did you come back home?"

"I told you." The answer was immediate. "I stayed until about 7:00 in the evening. Then I went to dinner 'til about 10:30."

"Did you go out for lunch or attend any meetings that day?"

Harrison shook his head. "No, only in my office. I ate in the deli on the first floor."

Reiger leaned over to turn off the tape recorder. "Well, that's about it. Thank you very much, Mr. Harrison. Sorry to be such a bother at the end of a long day. If we have any further questions, mind if we come back?"

Gavil Harrison stood, smiling woodenly. "No, no, not at all. Meg seemed like a nice person. Be happy to do whatever I can to help."

Really. They'd see about that.

101

Chapter 16

Nerves sparking, Chelsea waited for the late evening news to begin. For the third time, she'd checked that all doors downstairs were locked, all window shades closed. She'd spent many an evening in the house with Paul away and had never been frightened. Not so tonight.

Chelsea lay back against pillows on her bed and punched the TV remote. She didn't have to wait long to see the story. Milt Waking, the reporter who covered Peninsula news for Channel 7, was standing outside the Haverlon police station.

"… in Haverlon today. According to police sources, an unidentified woman hiking through the park stumbled upon the body." Chelsea watched herself on the news, ducking her head from cameras at Trent Park. How weird, watching herself like that. Would people recognize her? Would *Gavil* recognize her? Pinpricks danced across her neck.

"Earlier this evening, the victim was identified by her father. She is twenty-five-year-old Meg Jessler, a resident of Sequoia Townhomes near the park. Police have no motive or suspects at this time."

The information rooted Chelsea to her bed. She could not begin to imagine a father having to identify such remains. *Oh, dear Jesus, help that family.*

"Meg Jessler." She whispered the name. What kind of person had Meg been? Where had she worked, who were her friends? She was so *young*.

"Police would not comment on the case, Chief Wilburn saying only that they have 'immediately gone to work to solve this horrible crime and bring the perpetrator to justice.' We will keep you updated as this case develops."

Chelsea turned off the television. How would she ever sleep? She glanced at the phone. Maybe she should call Gladys after all, have her stay the night. But it was too late. Besides, what could Gladys do?

Chelsea rose from the bed and headed for the bathroom. She would leave the light on in there tonight. Back by the bed, she gazed at the red light on the alarm pad, signifying activation. If any door or window was opened, it would whoop loud enough to wake the dead. The security company would immediately call to check it out. If no one answered the phone, they'd notify police.

Muscles tense, Chelsea slid into bed. No matter how much she prayed, the darkness seemed to have eyes, and every rustle of the trees outside the window whispered. For a long time, her gaze remained fixed on the reassuring glow of light from the bathroom. Gradually, exhaustion from the long day's events overtook her.

She slept.

~ ~ ~

In the middle of the night, a sound awoke Chelsea. The room was pitch black. Her thoughts raced. Why was the bathroom light off?

She couldn't see anything until her eyes grew accustomed to the darkness. She heard another sound. Someone coming up the stairs. A tread. Pause. Another tread. The muffled squeak of a hand sliding over a polished railing.

Get up! Chelsea screamed to herself. *Lock the door!* Then she remembered her children, with rooms closer to the stairs than her own. *God, help us!* Her body grew rigid with horror. How could she protect the boys? She saw herself throwing back the covers, hitting the panic button on the alarm, running down the hall to protect her sons. But she could not move.

How did he get in the house? Blood pounded through her head, leaving her giddy. Panic choked her.

He must have cut the alarm wires.

The air in her bedroom was suffocating. Her throat felt tight. In those long, drawn-out seconds, she heard the steps reach the landing and turn right toward her room. One tread. Another. She visualized the thick beige carpet crushing slowly under the pressure of each footfall. Closer. The scuffed toe of a running shoe. Closer still. A hand scudded along the wall, smearing a trail of blood.

Stop, stop! Chelsea screamed, but no sound came out.

Skin touching metal. The click of a knob turning, a silent push as the door inched open. Chelsea's mouth dropped open in a scream, but the sound gurgled in her throat. Another step, and Gavil was in the room, crossing the floor toward her bed. As he loomed larger, she was overpowered by the smell of eucalyptus. A sudden breeze swept through the room, rustling sequoia trees in the corner. The bed beneath her grew rock hard, and the ground felt cold. *No, no, this can't be!* Through the darkness she saw two hands, locked at the thumbs, lowering themselves toward her throat. She fought vainly to scream again, but her tongue thickened and her throat locked tight.

At the first brush of his fingertips, a coyote howled beneath her window.

Chelsea squeezed her eyes shut and tried again to scream, her larynx rattling. She burst out of her skin then, like a terrorized spirit seeking sanity. In that instant, the hands disappeared. The breeze rustled no more. The coyote was silent.

Her eyes flew open. Five seconds passed. The bedroom was quiet. Still. Lit softly by a bathroom light. Her own form lay underneath the covers of her bed.

A moan escaped her lips, and she sucked in oxygen. Her heart hammered. Twisting her head, Chelsea looked at the clock by her bed. Four-thirty. Dawn was still almost an hour away. She fought to control her breathing.

She'd had a horrible nightmare. That was all. Just a dream. She let that sink in.

Just a dream.

After a few minutes, she felt able to stand. Creeping into the bathroom, she guzzled a glass of water. Before she fell back into bed, she flicked on every light in the room.

She would sleep no more that night.

Friday, June 9

Chapter 17

The autopsy took place at 10:00 on Friday morning. Reiger was present, along with Hal Weiss, from the county forensics lab. The coroner, Gene Mowery, was a sixty-year-old veteran. His investigator was Jake O'Brien. Turnbow was busy checking the information he and Reiger had gleaned the night before and piecing together a profile of the victim.

Reiger was tired. He'd spent a long time talking to Edith after he finally arrived home. They prayed together—for Meg Jessler's family and for justice to be done. "And, dear Lord, even through this awful event," Reiger asked, "bring glory to Your name. Through me, through Chelsea Adams, through the others involved."

Silently, he prayed those words again as he cast reluctant eyes on the gruesome remains of Meg Jessler. He'd had little to eat for breakfast, and at the moment was glad of it.

"We've got contrecoup trauma here." Mowery was examining the brain. "See the tearing that's occurred and the protrusion here." He pointed to the frontal lobe. "Obvious battering in the occipital. She must have been hit three, maybe four, times in the back of the head." He turned to Hal. "You mentioned you found blood on a rock embedded in the ground there." Hal nodded. "That'll be the cause of death, unless toxicology comes up with a surprise."

The toxicology report would state findings from analyses of the brain and other organs, and Mowery wouldn't state with certainty the cause of death until receiving it. Obviously Meg had been hit on the back of the head. But what if she had been drugged or even poisoned first? Unlikely, but the toxicology report would provide definite answers.

"Contrecoup?" Reiger kept himself a few feet from the table. "That's new to me."

"Has to do with tearing of the membranes. When you have a blow to the back of the head, for instance, you can have as much, sometimes even more, trauma to the opposite side of the brain. That's what we've got here."

Reiger nodded.

Mowery analyzed the remains of the organs, and the body was X-rayed for any broken bones or projectiles. Completing a rape kit was standard procedure, as well as fingerprinting, although the victim had already been identified. Weiss collected dirt scrapings from underneath the fingernails and took a clipping from the broken nail. He combed Meg's hair, searching for any foreign material. Each bit of evidence would be bagged separately and marked.

Little evidence was found.

Reiger walked out of the morgue shortly before noon, pulling his spiral notebook out of his pocket as he squinted in the bright sunlight. Time for a case accounting. Mowery had made his own notes during the autopsy, sometimes referred to as the "protocol," which would form the basis of the coroner's report. Reiger's notes of the autopsy were for his personal use until he received the report. Leaning against his car, he wrote on top of a new page, "Autopsy." Then he listed the facts that had been gathered that morning, barring any "surprises from toxicology."

One, cause of death: three or four blows to back of head. Two, only other trauma to body was beaten face. No broken bones, no stab wounds noticeable in remains of body. Three, estimated time of death: between sunrise and noon Wednesday. Four. no signs of rape. Five, only evidence to analyze was gold fibers from underneath fingernails and dirt from same.

"God, please let the DNA work." Reiger pocketed the notebook.

If they could match that tiny piece of skin found on the rock to a suspect rather than the victim, it would be their ace in the hole. Without that, they had little to go on.

~ ~ ~

Turnbow knocked on the door of number six Dapple Street. He had driven over to Sequoia Townhomes to talk again with Mrs. Geary and thought, while he was there, he may as well finish interviewing Jackson Doniger. Surveying the complex from Doniger's front stoop, he waited for a response, then knocked again.

"Coming." Doniger's voice sounded thick. The door opened to frame him in a white cotton robe, hair mussed, face unshaven. "Oh. Sorry. I was still asleep."

He invited Turnbow into a unit with the same layout as Marian Baker's, but in reverse image. Turnbow had seen many units just like it, having become far more intimate with the architecture of Sequoia Townhomes than he'd ever cared to be. They sat at a black chrome kitchen table. "You want some coffee?"

Turnbow had drunk his quota for the day, trying to wake up that morning. It hadn't worked. He nodded.

Doniger had little to add to their previous conversation. "After I'd been here maybe a month," he noted, refilling their quickly drained cups, "I might have seen Meg Jessler. I noticed a blond who fit her description driving out of the complex. But I really don't know." Neither could he tell Turnbow much about his neighbors. "From the glimpses I've had of them, most are older than me. And most work during the day, I think. Sometimes I see people coming home about the time I'm leaving for work. I say 'hello,' they say 'hello.' That's about it."

Turnbow itched with frustration. This interview, like so many others, was going on fifteen minutes, yet getting him nowhere.

He had other stops to make, plus a long list of phone calls. He concluded his questioning, apologizing for rousting Doniger out of bed.

"Don't worry about it." Doniger waved a hand as he placed their cups in the sink.

Driving out of the complex, Turnbow passed a local TV news van turning in. "Here we go." Tonight's news would undoubtedly show footage of the townhouses and Meg Jessler's front door. One of the reporters, Milt Waking, had been particularly obnoxious, trying to question officers around the station, wanting to know when autopsy results would be in.

How long before the information about Chelsea Adams leaked?

Turnbow kneaded the back of his neck. His muscles were tense. A good night's sleep would sure help, but he probably wouldn't enjoy one anytime soon. No time to think of that now. At the moment, he had a long shot to pursue on Wickens, and as he rounded the bend, his destination came into sight.

~ ~ ~

The house was small, a crackerjack box, as Turnbow's grandmother would have labeled it back in Kansas. Plain, white, and rectangular, it reminded him of the neighborhood he'd grown up in, where men with etched faces left early in the morning, metal lunch boxes under their arms, to work the wheat-ribbed farms of the town's more prestigious. At night, they dragged themselves home again, worn and smelling of sweat and manure. As a small boy, he'd marveled at his father's callused hands, the wide, thick fingers whose strength directed two-ton farm equipment as easily as little Pat rolled his toy dump truck. Those same hands were gentle in a quick hug, firm in discipline, hard-clasped around a bat during Sunday baseball games.

The first bullet fired, the startled reflex of a robber surprised, had pierced the winter night's stillness and one of those hands, thrown up in defense.

110

Turnbow rolled to a stop. A car passed on Wickens, headed toward Trent Park, just a quarter mile down, its tires singing against asphalt. In the ensuing quiet, Turnbow's slammed door seemed loud enough to alert anyone who might be inside. No one had been home here Thursday, when other residents in the area had been questioned in hopes of turning up a witness. Upon checking, Turnbow had learned from a neighbor that an elderly man lived alone in the house and often went to visit his daughter across the Bay. No, the neighbor didn't know the daughter's name.

Probably nothing here, but Turnbow had to be sure.

As he started up the narrow sidewalk, its broken cement dotted with weeds, the front door clicked open.

The man looked to be in his mid-seventies, short, almost gaunt, with rounded shoulders and thinning white hair. He moved slowly, but his deep gray eyes fairly danced.

His name was Jenkin Tommason, he said after inviting Turnbow inside to a small living room darkened with clutter. Been to visit his daughter, yes, sir, just like the neighbor said. Left Wednesday morning about 11:00 when his daughter, along with her two young children, his grandkids, you know, came to pick him up. Yes, he'd seen the news from over there about the girl murdered in Trent Park. Just got home earlier this morning, he did, his daughter having to bring him back early so she could take one of the kids to the doctor for a cough. Tommason hadn't wanted to catch any bug, so had opted to return a day earlier than he intended.

Turnbow dutifully admired a wood-framed photo of Tommason's daughter and her children. "The girl who was killed, Mr. Tommason, we think she jogged by here sometime Wednesday morning. I wonder if you saw anything."

Tommason screwed up his face. "Well, I did see a gal early in the morning when I got up with my backache. 'Bout 5:55 it was."

"How do you know? About the time, I mean."

In a rambling discourse, Turnbow learned that Tommason had been plagued with low back pain for the last year or so, had been unable to sleep early Wednesday morning, and so got up to take two aspirins. He glanced at the clock, calculating how much longer he could sleep before preparing for his daughter to pick him up. The digital clock radio by his bed, a Christmas present from his daughter, read 5:55. He took the aspirins and returned to bed. They'd helped.

"What did she look like?" Turnbow cut in.

"Well, pretty, what I saw of her. Long blond hair, slim."

Hope welled within Turnbow. He was almost afraid to ask the next question for fear he'd ruin a good thing. "Do you remember what she wore?"

"Sure do." Tommason grinned, showing crooked teeth. "It was their brightness, you know. I remember thinking they looked like the sun. Her shorts, that is. They was yellow."

~ ~ ~

Turnbow looked up, his mouth around the side of a taco, when Reiger entered his office. "Want some?" He shoved a colorfully printed cardboard box at his partner.

Ugh.

Reiger held up both hands. "I'll pass." He slumped into a chair across from Turnbow's desk, wiping sweat from his forehead. "Getting hot out there. Sure miss the morning fog."

"Yeah. News said we'd have a heat wave for a few days." Turnbow slashed at his mouth with a paper napkin. "What did you find?"

A quick relating of Reiger's list. "The only good news is I got a promise from Weiss to look at our evidence this afternoon. If we're lucky, we might even hear from him today. 'Course, the DNA's gonna take a couple of weeks. So what did you get?"

"A few interesting things." Turnbow dumped his trash and pulled a yellow legal pad forward. "First, Meg Jessler. Here's a profile of her last twenty-four hours, as best I can reconstruct. She worked as a typesetter at Ford Printing in San Mateo, hours 8:30 to 4:00. She usually left the premises for lunch. Tuesday she went to a nearby deli with one of her coworkers. Seems three girls at Ford hung around together a lot. One of them, Candy Seifer, said she went shopping at Hillsdale Mall with Meg for about an hour after work on Tuesday. Meg bought a present for her boyfriend. That would be the sweater we found in her car. Then Meg told Candy she was going home to do her nails and start packing. That's the last time Candy saw her.

"I also talked to the owner of Meg's townhouse. He confirmed that she'd rented from him for about a year. Basically a good renter. He said she was a little flaky at times."

Reiger drummed his fingers on the desk. What relevance, if any, could "flakiness" have? Unpredictable? Compulsive? Easily forced off Trent Park's main road? He and Turnbow batted around ideas. An assertive woman, knowing she probably wouldn't get out of the situation alive, most likely would not cave in easily, Reiger noted. He could think of two other possibilities. Maybe she knew the perpetrator and wasn't afraid to go with him. Or maybe she'd planned that hike to the gully. A rendezvous with a lover, perhaps. Although it seemed a mighty strange hour.

Turnbow said he'd called on Alice Geary. "She didn't have much else to tell. No men lurking around the Jessler place, no wild parties. According to her, it's like we thought. Meg hit on everybody in the complex sometime or other for her cosmetics. I asked if she'd seen Meg hanging around any neighbors in particular, but the question got me nowhere. Alice Geary seemed to think Meg's friends lived other places."

"Did you talk to her boyfriend?" They'd been able to obtain information about Meg's boyfriend from her parents.

"I tried but haven't been able to get through to him yet. He's apparently at a convention in Atlanta. I left a message for him. I did confirm that he's been there every day. I talked to someone who helped organize the convention, who said she'd seen him at meetings Tuesday and Wednesday, starting at 9:00 A.M."

Reiger nodded. "Okay. Keep checking on that, but it sounds like he may be off the hook." Husbands and boyfriends tended to be high on the immediate suspect list when a woman was killed.

"I will. Now the next major thing. I know when Meg went jogging." Turnbow told Reiger about Tommason. "He just happened to glance out his window. She was alone, and he didn't see anyone following her."

Reiger calculated the time line. "She could've been dead by 6:30."

Turnbow threw him a meaningful look. "That's right." He flipped to the next page of his notes. "Which brings us to townhouse number four."

Reiger lifted his eyebrows.

"I checked out Marian Baker's story, and everything fits. I called that company she said she visited down south, Raynor's Spring, and she was there, all right. It's one of those companies that bottle water. I checked on flights out of the area and found her booking. She was on the plane."

"And Harrison?"

"That's just it. I checked with his work." Turnbow leaned forward. "On Wednesday, he didn't arrive until *10:00.*"

"Ten o'clock?"

A nod. "I spoke with his receptionist first, then his secretary. They both agreed."

"What do you know." Reiger gazed out the window. Like Turnbow, he'd sensed Harrison was lying. All the same, this was nothing short of amazing. "We'll have to pay him another visit. Mrs. Adams may just prove to be right again. That would really be incredible." He gazed out the window. "Man. She'd have to have the eyes of Elisha."

"Elisha?"

Reiger blinked. "Yeah. A prophet of Israel in the Old Testament. God gave him special knowledge about lots of things. One of the stories tells how Elisha knew again and again where the enemy king of Aram was going to make camp, and he warned the king of Israel not to go there, which of course saved his life. The king of Aram was furious, yelling at his servants to tell him who was leaking the information. One servant said, 'It's not us, it's Elisha. That guy knows what you say in your bedroom.'"

Turnbow made a face. "You believe that stuff? I know you're a churchgoer and all, but ... Do you think Chelsea Adams *is* right? Don't you think she's just not giving us the real story?"

Reiger winced. His own partner should know him as more than just a churchgoer. "Let me ask you a question, Turnbow. Do you believe in God?"

"Well, yeah. I was raised in church. I just haven't gone in a long time."

"Do you believe God created the earth and the sun and us?"

"Sure."

"Then why couldn't such a powerful God give someone a little supernatural knowledge?"

Turnbow shrugged. "Why would He want to?"

The question hit Reiger hard. This was the view of a lost world—a God who lit it, then quit it. But he'd already said enough to his partner.

He took a deep breath and smacked his palm on Turnbow's desk. "Anything else in those eye-opening notes of yours?"

Chapter 18

Chelsea hummed along with the radio. She stood in the kitchen, preparing an early dinner. Anytime before eight in their house was early, due to Paul's work schedule. He'd already called from the airport to say he was on his way home, no stopping at the office.

"Good," Chelsea had replied. "Guess what, both boys are gone tonight. Scott's already over at Tim's, and I'm about to take Michael to Brandon's. So it's you and me."

"Great. We need to talk anyway. Want to go out?"

"No. I want to stay home. With you."

Chelsea dropped vegetables into a pan on the stove. What a difference a day could make. After a horrendous night, she'd dragged herself from bed to get the boys to school, then fell asleep on the couch for an hour. When she awoke, she felt much better. Sitting in her favorite armchair with her Bible, she read the book of Ephesians, concentrating on chapter six. The words of the apostle Paul calmed and encouraged her. "For our struggle is not against flesh and blood," read verse twelve, "but against the rulers, against the authorities, against the powers of this dark world and against the spiritual forces of evil in the heavenly realms." As verse eleven said, she was therefore to "put on the full armor of God" that she may be able to "stand against the devil's schemes."

Chelsea laid the Bible in her lap and gazed idly out the family room window. A gentle breeze ruffled the leaves of the trees lining the long driveway. The day was warm and peaceful, far removed from the previous night, when every rustle of the trees had struck fear in her heart. How wrong she'd been to wallow in that fear.

The thought struck her, then, that the trees hadn't changed. The only difference between last night and now was light.

Wasn't it the same with Christians? God's people lived in a world of darkness, where evil reigned. But they carried God's light. As Paul said, with the "full armor of God" they could stand firm in that darkness, and they did not need to fear. Peace descended on Chelsea as she read the verses again, letting God's promise settle over her, enfold her. She had to trust Him. She had to rest on the fact that He'd chosen to give her the gift of visions to help build her own faith and that of others. She remembered the first one she'd experienced, just one month after becoming a Christian. During a church service, numerous people had gone to the altar to pray. Chelsea noticed a young woman kneeling at the very end of the altar, and she couldn't take her eyes away. She stared at the young woman's back, transfixed. And while she stared, Chelsea "saw" in her mind with perfect clarity the young woman hugging her mother after a long, painful separation. *Go tell her,* a voice inside Chelsea said, and before she knew it, she was on her way down the aisle. Kneeling by the young woman, Chelsea found herself saying, "God wants you to know he's heard your prayers. Your relationship with your mother will be healed." To this day, she did not know the reason for the two women's estrangement. She did know, however, that the relationship was slowly healing, and all because the daughter had begun reaching out to her mother in love.

Standing now at the stove, Chelsea prayed for everyone involved in this murder case. And she thanked God even for the vision that had frightened her so much. "You are in control, Lord. I trust you for guidance."

She did not need to fear. God's will would prevail.

No matter what, she would cling to that promise.

Chapter 19

Hal Weiss' rubber-soled shoes squeaked as he crossed the tile floor in the county forensics lab late Friday afternoon. If normal days were whirlwinds, this one had been a hurricane. A particularly gruesome autopsy that morning had been followed by about ten hours of work crammed into five. The crime lab always seemed overloaded these days. Everything from analyzing blood (was or was not the suspect high when traffic cops pulled him over?) to vial upon vial of drugs from one narcotics case or another. Hour after hour, millions of dollars' worth of high-tech machinery in the lab spun, heated up, vaporized, computed, and analyzed bits of evidence that could make or break a case.

The machines were wonders, but weren't the stars of the crime lab. In the end, Hal knew that any piece of equipment was only as good as the person behind it. Criminology was an exciting, intense field that attracted folks from all kinds of backgrounds. Here they hoarded what in the outside world would be everyday objects—a cigarette butt, a clothing fiber, a used coffee mug. In the crime lab, those same materials could become the cornerstone that supported the prosecution's case against an arsonist, a drug dealer, a killer.

Hal entered the small spectrometer room and closed the door. Here, the detail work took place. From the first bag of evidence, he'd already checked out the gold fibers through one of the microscopes. That had been an easy call. They were definitely soft, almost suede-like leather, which wasn't bad. At least they weren't from some Brand X carpet used in most of the homes on the Peninsula. Occasionally, a fiber would stump the lab. The fallback then was the FBI, which had on file samples from just about every piece of material in the world. Those guys could take any bit of cloth and tell whether it was animal, natural, domestic, imported, dyed, or woven. Great information, but it took time. Fortunately, Reiger's evidence wasn't in that category.

Hal opened his second bag of evidence from Trent Park, pulling out a small pointed wooden stick that had been used to scrape underneath the victim's fingernails. He shook his head. Fingernail scrapings, the most overrated evidence in the business. And this was just dirt. What could they expect from a woman who had died on the ground, probably clawing the soil in sheer panic? But he wouldn't let it rest until he'd determined that just plain dirt was all it amounted to. Evidence in this case was too scarce for assumptions.

Hal scraped the dirt particles from the stick onto the large scanning electron microscope hooked up to an X-ray defraction unit. The microscope would enlarge an object to 250,000 times its normal size, then zoom in on one particle with its X-ray defraction, resulting in a display of the elemental composition of that particle on the computer screen. The computer came complete with a built-in library to search for the identities of a specimen's components.

Hal saw the results—and blinked.

It was dirt all right, but why so rich? He frowned at the screen. The graph indicated a high nitrogen content, followed by traces of phosphoric acid, calcium, sulfur, iron, and zinc. Hal asked the computer for a list of possibilities from its library, already knowing the answer. *Organic material.* He almost expected the screen to add, "You dummy."

Pulling his chair closer, he stared at the graph as if trying to wrench an explanation from the computer. He could think of only two possibilities. One, the dirt in that area of Trent Park was supreme enough for the most reticent of seeds. Or two, those particles weren't from there at all.

Come on, this was probably just chasing moonbeams. Likely not worth the trouble of pursuing. Even if the dirt was foreign material, what then? It could have come from anywhere.

Let it go, Hal. At least he had the fibers.

Hal stared at the screen a moment longer. Then he skidded back his chair and rose. Before turning off the computer, he bent over the keyboard to save his "rich" dirt's graph in the library for future comparison, labeling it "Trent." He'd need it again on Monday, because he'd already decided what he had to do. Sometime during the weekend, he'd take himself a hike through Trent Park and collect a sample of dirt, whether he relished the thought of that walk again or not.

Oh, well. He could use the exercise.

~ ~ ~

Reiger hung up the phone with a sinking feeling in his stomach. So little to go on. Sure, the dirt was surprising. But he'd have to wait until Monday to see if it came from Trent. And even if it didn't, so what?

Frustrated, the sergeant reread the notes he'd scrawled during his conversation with Hal, then flipped back to the notebook's first page and wrote under his list made earlier that day. Six, Harrison lied re: whereabouts Wednesday morning. Seven, gold-colored fibers = soft leather, like a suede jacket. Eight, fingernail scrapings are organic compound, "rich."

Closing the notebook, Reiger leaned back in his chair. Sleepiness filtered through his veins.

His mind drifted to the previous night, when he and Turnbow had worked late, questioning the residents of Sequoia Townhomes. They'd split up, Reiger taking the units with even numbers, Turnbow starting across the street with the odd. Reiger's questions had been curt, recording names, places of business, addresses, and phone numbers, asking if they'd seen Meg Jessler with anyone in the last few days and what their

120

relationship with the victim had been. Overall, they'd talked to people at each unit except for numbers three and twenty-one. Mrs. Geary thought those folks were on vacation. Nothing had come of any interview. Many claimed they'd been in bed at the time Meg was known to jog. Must have been a lazy morning in Haverlon.

Come to think of it, wasn't that the day Turnbow came dragging in, saying he'd overslept?

Reiger rocked slowly, chair creaking in protest. Turnbow's interview with the old man had given them a narrow window of time for the murder. Early morning alibis were now far more important. The "I was asleep" claims were difficult to check. Single residents had no one to back them up, and couples may cover for each other. Reiger had checked employment alibis this afternoon, trying to determine if any of Meg's neighbors had arrived at work later than usual on Wednesday morning. Only one had.

Gavil Harrison.

Reiger's phone rang. He snatched it up. "Sergeant Reiger."

"Good afternoon, sir, this is Milt Waking, Channel Seven News. I need to verify the rather unusual information I've been hearing about the Trent Park case."

Reiger repressed a groan. Somebody was already leaking. This was all they needed right now. "Sorry, Mr. Waking, I'm afraid I can't comment at this time."

"I've heard the woman who discovered the body had already come to you about the murder, saying she'd had a vision about it. One source even said she claims the vision was from God."

Oh, *terrific.* "Like I said, I can't comment."

"Then you don't deny this information."

"I'm not denying and I'm not verifying."

"In all fairness, sir, you're not going to keep something like this quiet. Wouldn't you rather I get the story right?"

"I'd *rather,* Mr. Waking, that you not call me again. I'm extremely busy."

Reiger hung up the phone and rubbed his forehead. He and Turnbow had better come up with something concrete, and fast. The leaks were already bad enough, but in the absence of any real progress on the case, the leaks would be all the media had.

And wouldn't reporters just lap them up.

~ ~ ~

Gavil spotted the detectives as he walked toward the house shortly after 6:00 P.M. The sight was enough to draw him up short. Apprehension filled his chest.

"Mr. Harrison." The older cop nodded but did not smile. "Reiger and Turnbow here. We need to take you down to the station and ask a few more questions."

Gavil stared at Reiger. He'd been haunted all afternoon, ever since his secretary told him of her conversation with the younger detective. Gavil knew he'd made a bad mistake, one that could cost him dearly. Too sure of himself last night, he'd assumed his word to the police would be enough. He should have made up something plausible. Told them he'd worked on his laptop at home for a few hours Wednesday morning. Now it was too late for that.

"What's going on?" Gavil asked. "I already told you everything I know."

"Yes, and we appreciate your cooperation. Now we've got just a few more things."

Gavil's feet cemented to the sidewalk. The younger cop leaned toward him. "I'm sure you don't want to talk here, in sight of your neighbors. Let's just get in the car, and we'll have you back home soon."

What to do? He could refuse to go, say he needed an attorney. As he played out that scenario, Gavil realized his left fingers were curling with tension—and forced them open. The stress at work was bad enough. Now this. In the last forty-eight hours, nothing had gone right. The years of building his life, the job he so wanted, Marian, *everything* looked doomed to unravel. Fear clutched at his gut. He'd have to hold himself together. He'd gone through depression and a near breakdown ten years ago due to stress, and it had been awful. He never wanted to live through that again.

Gavil stared at the cement, the weight of two pairs of eyes on him. His briefcase felt heavy in his hand. Not until he heard a car approaching and realized Marian could come home at any moment did his mind clear.

"Let me just put my things in the house."

~ ~ ~

Gavil looked out the car window without seeing as Turnbow drove the short distance to Haverlon's police station. The trip seemed like some out-of-body experience. He could almost see the two sides of himself threatening to converge. All because of Meg Jessler. Stupid girl.

Throat tight, he took a seat in Reiger's office. The humiliation of being escorted past the watchful eyes of the woman behind the front desk had left a sour taste in Gavil's mouth. He pushed his heels against the floor, afraid his legs might shake.

Reiger placed a tape recorder on the desk and clicked it on. Turnbow drew up a chair next to Reiger's.

"Mr. Harrison, we just need you to clear something up for us," Reiger said. "We have a tape of you telling us that you were at work by 7:30 Wednesday morning. However, we talked to the receptionist at your company and your secretary, and they both said you got to work about 10:00. You want to tell us where you were?"

Gavil averted his eyes. His throat felt like a desert. Licking his lips, he rearranged himself in the chair. He did *not* want to do what they were forcing him into. "Look, what difference does it

123

make? I didn't have anything to do with that girl's death, if that's what you're worried about."

"I'm glad to hear that. However, when we find that someone has lied to us, we get a little concerned. I'm sure you can understand."

"But I don't know anything about it. I haven't even watched the news about it. I've been too busy."

"All right. Fine. But I'll let you in on a little secret. We now know what time Meg Jessler was killed. And out of all the people we've talked to so far, including most of her neighbors, you're the only one whose story doesn't check out. That's a significant thing to us. Now, we'd love to move on, but we can't do that until we can verify where you were at that time."

Gavil's mind raced. He couldn't imagine their having any other reason to suspect him. He ought to just ride it out.

Reiger leaned over the desk, his chair squeaking. "Maybe we should go back to Marian. Ask *her* where you were."

"No." Gavil pushed down his panic. "Leave her out of this."

"All right then." The detectives waited.

Gavil longed for more time to think. How to walk the line between them and Marian?

"Mr. Harrison?"

Cornered, he calculated his risks. Maybe he should get a lawyer.

"Mr. Harrison."

His hands flew up. "Okay, okay! I'll tell you where I was. But I don't want Marian to know. *No one* else can know this."

"We're listening."

A knot grew in Gavil's stomach over what he was about to do. He swallowed hard. "It indirectly involves my closest friend. He's done a lot for me, and I don't want to hurt him. I spent Tuesday night at his house and went to work from there the next morning. I left there about," Gavil thought a moment, "9:30." He couldn't look Reiger in the eye.

124

"His name?"

"Stuart Hocking."

"Address, phone? Place of business?"

In monotone, Gavil gave them the information.

"What time did you leave your place Tuesday night?"

"Uh, probably around 10:00."

Gavil dared a glance at Turnbow. The detective's arms were crossed as he stared. "Why didn't you tell us this before?" he demanded.

"I didn't want anyone to know. There's too much at stake."

"Why?"

At the last moment, Gavil almost lost his nerve. But where else could he go from here? "Because Stuart was out of town that night. I was with his wife. Sonya."

A flicker of surprise, then recognition, crossed Reiger's face. "Sonya Hocking? The woman raising money for that children's hospital?"

Gavil's voice was low. "An oncology center, yes. Now maybe you can understand why I didn't tell you. I've got too much to lose and so does she. And if something happens to her and the center isn't built, those sick kids lose too."

Turnbow exhaled aloud. Disgust? Or from disappointment in losing a suspect? Gavil could imagine their judgment against him—a man who'd betray both the woman he lived with and his closest friend. A man who'd allow his own lust to jeopardize a project that could save dying children.

Yeah, well. Better that than a murderer.

But it didn't matter what they thought. He'd crossed his Rubicon.

The detectives pressed for background information and details, committing Gavil to his alibi. Their questions were an ever-tightening noose around his neck. He told himself it would all work out. Sonya would back up his story, even if she never forgave him for what he'd done. And Stuart and Marian didn't need to find out.

This sudden stress would go away. Would not sink him back into depression.

By the time he found himself once again in the back of Reiger's car, Gavil was drenched in sweat. Somehow he had to face Marian. And he had to call Sonya immediately.

In front of his home, he pulled himself out of the detective's car on weak legs and made his way up the sidewalk. As he stepped inside the townhouse he remembered Marian was out to dinner with a friend. Disbelief at his own stupidity washed over him. He could have taken time to think this through!

Gavil sagged against the wall, sick over what he'd done.

Then, through sheer willpower, he pulled himself together. Everything could still be okay. He just had to convince Sonya that he'd been given no choice. And that no one but the two of them and the detectives would ever hear of his alibi.

Chapter 20

"What do you make of all that?" Turnbow buckled his seat belt as he rode with Reiger out the grilled gate of the Hockings' driveway. Rolling up the private road in Atherton an hour earlier, he'd emitted a low whistle at the posh estate grounds complete with tennis court, huge house, and swimming pool. Apparently expecting them, Sonya Hocking answered their ring and buzzed open the gate.

Reiger tried to sort his thoughts. "When Harrison first gave us his alibi, I told myself 'maybe so.' I could see why he hadn't told us before. Even though trying to keep it from us was incredibly *stupid*. But now ..." Reiger shook his head. "She sure was a mixture of shock and righteous indignation, wasn't she?"

Turnbow rubbed his eyes. "So now you're not sure which one to believe."

No, he didn't. Sonya Hocking had adamantly denied having an affair with Gavil Harrison, or anyone else, for that matter. Cheeks flushed and dark eyes snapping, she agonized aloud over why Gavil would claim such a thing. "How could he *say* this?" she cried. "How could he do this to his best friend, after all Stuart's done for him? Why would he want to destroy me and all I'm working for?" She wheeled on Reiger, trembling. "Look. I don't know what's going on. I don't know why he needs me for an alibi or where he really was. All I know is, Gavil called before you came and begged me to back him up." Tears filled her eyes. "I'm just glad Stuart's not home to hear this. He'd be *devastated!*" She took a ragged breath. "Please, for Stuart's sake and mine, don't spread this story. People trust me. That's the only reason I've been able to raise so much money for the oncology center. And *nobody's* helping me. It's *my* project. The longer I take to raise the money, the longer it'll take for the center to be built. Meanwhile, children are *dying,* do you understand?!" She flung out both hands, then dropped like a broken doll onto her couch. "And, please." Her voice went thick. "Leave Gavil alone. He's still a friend, even after this, and I don't want to see anything bad happen to him. Besides, he's not a murderer, I can assure you of that. Whatever he's not telling you, I *know* he couldn't have had anything to do with killing that girl. Please just let him get back to his life."

Reiger and Turnbow had exchanged weary glances. As if it were that simple.

"If *she's* lying," Reiger said to Turnbow as they drove, "she put on one terrific act. If *Harrison's* lying, my question is, how could he expect to get away with it? Does he really think she'd cover for him, no questions asked? That's bizarre."

Then there was Chelsea Adams' belief that Harrison killed Meg Jessler. Reiger couldn't deny the weight of her word in his own mind. All the same, they had to stick to the facts. They needed evidence that would supply proof in court beyond a reasonable doubt and to a moral certainty. They were nowhere near that with Harrison.

Maybe the man *had* told the truth, Turnbow offered as Reiger headed up El Camino toward Haverlon. And Sonya Hocking simply had too much to lose in admitting it.

"So she'd leave him hanging out to dry?"

Turnbow shrugged. "She probably doesn't realize how serious the situation is. If she knows for a fact he's innocent, she's figuring we can't possibly nail him for the murder anyway. So she might as well save her reputation."

Reiger stopped at a red light at the Broadway intersection in Redwood City. To his left loomed the darkened grounds of Sequoia High School, named, as numerous other local institutions and businesses, including Sequoia Townhomes, after the ubiquitous evergreen trees. "What if Harrison purposely gave us an alibi scandalous enough to make it plausible that he'd first try to hide it? Plus, just in case Sonya Hocking refused to back him up, he could then accuse her of lying to save herself." Reiger had to admit that would be pretty smart thinking for a perp. Most of them were not very bright, which is why they got caught. But Harrison was different. Reiger could almost feel his cunning.

Lord, show us what is right.

Reiger sighed. "At the moment we've still got an alibi that's not checking out. That's enough reason for a search warrant."

Turnbow glanced at the dashboard clock. "It's pretty late."

"I'll manage it." So he'd lose a little more sleep. "Let's get to Harrison's place early tomorrow morning. Before any reporters are out and about. Maybe we'll get lucky and turn up some gold leather clothing." A second check at Meg's home had eliminated the chance of the fibers under her nails coming from her own clothes. "I'll come down hard on Harrison, see if he cracks. If not, we'll have to check out Sonya Hocking, see if anybody else knows about this claimed affair."

He glanced at Turnbow, shrugging. "This isn't rocket science, you know. One of 'em's gotta be lying."

Chapter 21

"Have you heard anything from the police today?" Paul asked Chelsea as they drew their chairs up to the table. They were having dinner on their backyard deck, the table's large umbrella shielding Chelsea's eyes from the sun.

"No. They said they wouldn't contact me unless they had more questions."

"The paper sure gave it a big spread."

Chelsea had hoped he wouldn't see the story. "It's not surprising. Trent Park's a popular place. Now people will be afraid to use it."

A dark look flitted across Paul's face. With a twinge of apprehension, Chelsea concentrated on eating her chicken.

"I'm still not happy about you going out there alone."

"I know."

He surveyed her. "Are you having any different thoughts about all this, now that you've had a good night's sleep?"

She almost smiled. If he only knew what her night had been like. "Not really."

"Oh."

Here it came. She might as well tackle it. "Did you expect me to change my mind or something?"

He studied his plate. "I've been thinking a lot about everything, Chelsea. Last night and on the plane coming home. And the more I thought about it, the more I realized that what I said on the phone is true. Ever since you started going to church, you've been different. It's separated us. I don't want to feel separated from you, Chels. I love you too much. And these visions of yours make me very uncomfortable. I haven't said much about the others. But this one is really bad news. I don't like you being involved in a murder. I don't like the way it's made you act without talking to me first. And I don't like the way it's affecting me at work, because now I don't know what to do about this man I want to hire."

Chelsea searched for words. How could she explain that the vision had been God's doing, not hers? "You still want to hire Gavil?" Her voice was small.

"He's perfect for the job."

Her eyes closed. Perfect?

"It's not that I don't believe your sincerity. And I know everything else you said has turned out to be right. But, Chelsea, you were with him for less than two hours. And your vision lasted, what, seconds? I've interviewed him four times now. I've had other people at the office meet him. Our investment firm's interviewed him. We've talked to his references. I just can't believe that Gavil could do this. It doesn't fit."

This could not be happening. "So what are you going to do?"

Paul sighed. "I don't know. I don't want to lose Gavil, and I don't want to upset you either. I've got to get back to him, though. I've been putting that off. He probably figures I'll call him at home this weekend. We have each other's phone numbers. If I don't, he'll be wondering why."

"He won't be wondering."

Paul gave her an exasperated look. "I have to call him Monday at the latest. Maybe you'll feel differently by then. I can tell him I need to check on a few more references, buy a day or two. But then I've got to give him an answer. Besides, the board's ready to go with him, so what am I supposed to tell them?"

Chelsea's heart sank. She'd felt so strong that morning. Now what? *How* could Paul say this? Didn't he realize all she'd been through? Couldn't he at least try to understand how hard this was for her?

He wasn't going to listen. No matter what she said.

Please, God, do something!

"Okay." Her voice sounded flat. "Do what you need to."

"Good." Paul inhaled with satisfaction. "Now I need to tell you something else. While I'm on a roll. I know you're not going to like it, but I think it's for your own good and for our good."

She raised her eyes to his and waited.

"I don't want you to go to church anymore."

Her chest turned to lead.

"Like I said, all this business about visions is getting out of control. I don't like what it's doing to you or us. And I think the church and your friends there are just feeding the frenzy. Gladys too. I know she's a smart woman and all that, but if she's encouraging this stuff, I don't want you seeing her anymore."

"Paul, I need those friends now more than ever! I need to pray with them."

"No, you don't. Chels, listen to me. How often have I asked you not to do something you wanted? You know I always support you and want you to be happy. But I'm really worried about what this is doing to you. It's frightening you and coming between us, and I *don't* want any more of it. So I'm asking you to do this for me. For us. Besides, doesn't the Bible say something about 'wives, listen to your husbands'?"

Ephesians chapter five. She'd read the chapter just that morning. Chelsea nodded.

"Well, then, there you have it. If you want to do what God says, you need to listen to me."

Paul leaned back, proud of himself, as if he'd just beat her at her own game.

Saturday, June 10

Chapter 22

A ringing doorbell pulled Marian from sleep.

She rolled toward her clock radio, her mind groggy. Six-thirty. Who could it be at this hour? She raised her head, listening to Gavil's footsteps on the hallway's hardwood floor. She hadn't heard him get up, but that wasn't unusual. Gavil was an early riser, often wide awake at 5:30, even on weekends. He'd start the coffee and enjoy a few cups of fresh-ground French roast while reading the newspaper.

The footsteps stopped. She heard a vaguely familiar voice and Gavil's angry answer. Then more voices and footfalls. Throwing back the covers, she grabbed her robe from the floor. By the time she reached the bedroom door, she recognized the voice.

Sergeant Reiger.

Marian opened the door and stopped short. Reiger and two uniformed policemen were headed in different directions in the townhouse. The sergeant was arguing with Gavil, backing him toward the kitchen. A short policeman with thinning hair strode into the living room. The other one disappeared into the office.

"What's going on?" Anxiety pinched her voice.

Gavil leaned around the sergeant. "They say they want to search the house!"

Marian looked around in a daze. "What for?"

Reiger talked over his shoulder at her. "I'll be with you in just a minute to explain. And you," he pointed to Gavil, "I'm gonna ask you again, nicely, to sit in that chair over there until we're through."

"What do you want now?" Gavil demanded. "Why do you keep bothering me?"

Reiger held up a hand. "I'm not *asking* you anymore. I'm telling you we're going to search this place, and you need to sit *right there* while we do. Any more interference from you, and you'll be taking another ride down to the station. Do you understand?"

Gavil stared at the sergeant with frightened eyes. Marian saw the look and felt the pressure of unknown terror in her chest. *Another* ride to the station? She watched, frozen. Gavil swiveled and disappeared into the kitchen. Marian fluttered down the hall toward him. He sank into a kitchen chair.

"Thank you. Now, Ms. Baker," Reiger's tone softened, "I'll need to talk with you one moment."

She didn't answer, her attention diverted by the man in her living room pulling open a coffee table drawer. She couldn't see the policeman in her office but heard his shuffling.

"Ma'am. Please."

A distracted nod.

He edged her down the hall away from the kitchen, apologizing that she had to be put through this, saying they had good reason to search. That they'd be as careful with her belongings as possible. She was to go with Detective Turnbow down to the station. He'd give her coffee. They could talk.

To the police station! Marian could barely make her tongue work. "Why? I don't know anything about Meg's death!"

"Turnbow will fill you in," the sergeant said. "Just please cooperate. It'll make this easier for all of us."

Like a frightened child, Marian obeyed. In five minutes she was dressed in cotton pants and a knit shirt and had run trembling fingers through her hair. She threw a longing glance at Gavil when she passed the kitchen, but his head was down. Reaching the front door, she wavered at the *creak* of furniture being pushed across her bedroom floor. Then she fled.

Turnbow ushered her into his car. He did not speak until they had pulled out of the townhouse complex onto Wickens Road. "Ms. Baker—"

"Call me Marian." Her tone turned bitter. "You and your partner must know all about me, with all the checking up you've done at my work. And now you're ransacking my home. You may as well call me by my first name."

He threw her a glance. "Marian. It's a special name to me. My mom's name."

Well, good for her.

They stopped at a red light. Turnbow turned toward her, the picture of sincerity. "I hope I can put you somewhat at ease. I know this is hard for you, and dragging you through it is not exactly my idea of a good time."

The light turned green and the detective's eyes were back on the road. Marian remained silent.

"I grew up in a little town in Kansas," Turnbow said, "before I moved out here to seek my fame and fortune. The three most important people in my life were my mom, baby sister, and grandmother. My grandfather died before I was born, and I lost my dad when I was nine. He was shot in the chest by a robber holding up a store. My dad was a customer and tried to help the clerk. He took the bullets. My sister was only four. That's when I decided to become a cop."

Marian dropped her eyes. "I'm sorry."

His smile was brief. "That was long ago. The point is, I learned to respect women's strength after that." He exhaled. "Now I'm on a homicide case, and the victim is the age of my sister on her wedding day. I want to find the guy who did this. I want it real bad. And I think you may be able to help. And that's why you're in this car right now, heading for my office."

She felt herself soften. "I'll try. I just don't see what this has to do with me."

~ ~ ~

136

Marian declined Turnbow's offer of coffee. He put off having a cup until later. They sat across from each other, his beat-up desk between them, his office door closed, shutting out the shift-change greetings of officers in the hall. Without makeup, Marian looked white and drawn, younger. She had a lost look about her, like a lone puppy on a city street.

Gently, Turnbow broke the news that he knew would shatter her life. Whoever was lying, Sonya Hocking or Harrison, Marian lost. The way it looked right now, either she lived with a man who would betray her with his best friend's wife, or she lived with a murderer. The lesser of those two was still devastating.

Without mentioning the Hockings, Turnbow related Gavil's first and second alibis, saying only they "had reason" to doubt the second one also, although they were "still checking." He also hoped to learn if Harrison owned a gold leather shirt or coat, in case it had already been destroyed.

Turnbow was aware, as he watched Marian's face turn white, that he was using her pain. That her anguish would inevitably lead to fury at Gavil, and that her fury could sharpen some memory of events, previously deemed insignificant. He did not like himself for it, but told himself it was for Meg. At least Marian would still be alive.

Marian did not take her eyes off him as he spoke, pressing three fingers to a trembling mouth, blinking through tears. Turnbow sensed that she wanted, needed, to believe his compassion was genuine. He excused himself to grab a bunch of tissues. She received them gratefully.

"I'm sorry. I just … I can't believe this." She worked to regain her composure. "I don't know why you think Gavil is responsible for this crime. I do know him well enough to assure you that he's not capable of such a thing. He gets mad sometimes, but who doesn't? Even with what you've just told me, I'd never believe he'd hurt anyone. But maybe I can see how …" She gazed at the ceiling, searching for the words. "Gavil's been wonderful. He brought me out of depression after my husband left me. For another woman." She pressed her lips together. "He's been through depression himself, so he understands. But there's always been something about him that I couldn't quite place. It's a side of him that I can't seem to reach. And I don't know what it is."

"Have you told him?"

A nod. "It's why I've hesitated to marry him. Sometimes I've thought, 'Maybe he has another woman, too.' It's hard to trust a man so soon after one betrays you. But Gavil has always insisted he'd never do that to me."

Turnbow thought about what she had just said. "There's one more thing I need to tell you. You probably know the woman Gavil said he was with Wednesday morning. Sonya Hocking."

"Sonya Hocking?" Marian's eyes widened. "No! I'll never believe that!" She stared at Turnbow, as if waiting for him to change his story. "Stuart Hocking is Gavil's best friend! Gavil wouldn't *do* that to him, or to me. We've been with the Hockings many times, and there was never *any* indication that—" She pressed a hand to her forehead. "I can't believe this. Gavil wouldn't do that. He just *wouldn't*. It's not *true*."

Turnbow leaned across his desk. "I know this is difficult for you. But sometimes people aren't what we think they are. I was married too, for over seven years. And then eighteen months ago the woman who vowed she'd stick with me forever took off with one of our neighbors, a guy I always thought was a total jerk. Just like that." His voice softened. "Marian, people can fool us. Sometimes the closest person in life turns out to be a complete 180 from what we thought. And we don't want to see it. Usually there are signs before the whole thing blows up, but we hide our heads in the sand because we don't want to know. And then one day, we find out. The proof hits us in the face so hard there's no way to deny it.

"As the days pass after that, days where you think you can't go on, you remember all those times when you felt that little twinge, that 'something,' as you called it. And then you think, 'I knew all along, didn't I?'" Briefly, he touched Marian's hand. "What is it that you know, Marian? I mean, if you looked deep inside and didn't deny any of the suspicions that you've been pushing away, what would you know?"

His hand remained near hers on the desk. Turnbow thought she would draw away. She didn't.

Marion swallowed. "I really know that Gavil is not a murderer. So given the choice, I'd have to believe he spent the night with another woman, if that's what he says. With Sonya Hocking. I never would have thought it possible. But then," her voice was barely audible, "I'd have said the same about all of this."

~ ~ ~

"All right, Harrison." Reiger thumped his tape recorder on the kitchen table and pushed the record button. Pulling out a chair, he sat opposite his suspect. "I have a scenario for you."

He'd already taken a look through the house and had not found what he was looking for. The two policemen were still searching. If Harrison had owned gold clothing, it probably was long gone.

"You said you leave for work about 7:00 every morning, so I assume you get up fairly early. Let's say around 5:30, 6:00. One morning you look out your living room window and see a cute little blonde jogging down the street. You don't think too much about it, but then you see her again the next day. And the next. And pretty soon, you find yourself waiting to watch her run by your house each morning. She's attractive. You'd like to meet her. Then by sheer luck you find out she sells makeup to Marian." Reiger puckered his chin. "One night she delivers an order while Marian's out of town, and you two find yourselves together. You make a move."

Gavil glared in silence.

"Then things go wrong. Maybe she wants more than you can give. Maybe she threatens to tell your girlfriend. Or maybe you

139

want more and she's backing off. You're furious. When Marian is gone again, you follow Meg as she jogs by one morning, all the way to Trent Park. Somehow you persuade her to leave the main road and take a hike with you. You try to talk to her. You argue. Things get out of hand."

Reiger tapped his teeth with a fingernail. "Did you know, Harrison," he bluffed, "that leaving hairs and fingerprints on a victim is like signing your own death warrant?"

Gavil Harrison's eyes grew wide, then hardened. His teeth clenched. "I told you where I was Wednesday morning. What do you want from me?"

"The truth, Harrison!" Reiger hit the table, rattling the recorder.

"I *gave* you the truth! Why don't you go ask Sonya herself?"

"Oh, didn't I tell you?" Reiger cocked his head. "She was incensed at your claims of an affair. Said they were totally false. And that she never saw you that morning."

Gavil's face drained white. His mouth hung open. "She's lying!" He gripped the table with both hands. "She's lying and you're lying!"

Reiger leaned over, his voice like ice. "I'm telling you, we talked to Mrs. Hocking. And she says you weren't with her. So if you weren't *there,* and you weren't in Trent Park, *just where were you?"*

Gavil's mouth hung open, but no words came. He slid a trembling hand across his face. "This is crazy. I just ..." His voice died away.

Reiger watched him twist in the wind.

~ ~ ~

That afternoon, a frustrated and exhausted Reiger played the taped conversations of his interviews to date. He and Turnbow had been busy running down leads all day. At present, Turnbow was checking up on Sonya Hocking. So far, all her friends had insisted they knew nothing of her ever having an affair. With every report from Turnbow, Reiger found himself believing more in Harrison's guilt. But they needed proof. So far, all they had were questions. Little about the case made sense. Doggedly, Reiger wrote notes in his small spiral book and tried to reason it through.

Meg's hands bothered him most.

Chelsea Adams had made a strange comment about those hands in her vision. She'd described them as "hot and prickly." Should he believe she was right? If so, what did it mean?

What if? A detective's inevitable pastime. What if the dirt under Meg's fingernails came from somewhere else? Hal had surmised that she picked it up around her own house or off her running shoes. Reiger doubted it. It didn't fit with the fact that she'd done her nails the night before. A woman with a new manicure was going to be fussy about getting dirt on her hands.

They may never find the source of the dirt, and it could be of little consequence anyway. Matching the gold fibers, however, was critical. Marion had insisted to Turnbow that Gavil did not own any clothes from which they could have come. Reiger sensed that a part of the puzzle lay just beyond his reach. Somewhere there was a leather shirt or jacket, a case-breaking piece of evidence.

Swiveling in his chair, Reiger wondered whether Marian Baker had told Turnbow the truth.

Chapter 23

Gavil tossed three pairs of underwear and socks into his suitcase. Next came a couple shirts and pants, landing in disarray, followed by toiletries. Should he take a suit? Gavil hesitated. He considered returning the following night, then told himself he was grasping at straws. He chose a suit and tie, hanging them in a slick black bag for protection. Brown dress shoes and socks. A pin-striped shirt.

The appearance of calm, Gavil felt like stone inside. His every movement seemed slow. Both arms and legs were heavy, and a crushing weight filled his chest. He could hear Marian in the next room, throwing her energy into straightening the office. He pictured her arranging the tumbled contents of each drawer.

He snapped the case shut and picked up his hanging bag. "I'm leaving now." He stood in the office doorway.

Marian swung around to face him, hands full of pens and papers. Her eyes were swollen from crying. "You'd better call when you find a hotel and leave your number. In case the police want to get hold of you again."

"Right." His response dripped in sarcasm. "Wouldn't want to disappoint them, would we."

"Gavil, this is hardly their fault." Her voice was thick. "How *could* you expect to hide it from me?"

He supposed he should be thankful that she believed Sonya was lying. Better to be an adulterous cheat than a killer.

"Oh, never *mind*." She sighed. "We've been through this already. Just go for now. I need a few days to think."

~ ~ ~

Marian stared at the desk as Gavil's footsteps took him down the hallway and out the door. Out the door and perhaps out of her life. *Please, God, not out of my life.* But how could she live with him now?

She finished straightening her office, then wandered into the hallway and stood gazing at the emptiness around her. She hadn't felt this lonely in a long time. The silence was so loud. She wanted to *think*, but her mind jerked from one thing to the next. What to do now?

Here she was, thirty-six years old, a career woman once again facing life without a man. Her time for having children would run out before she knew it. What if she'd just sent what could be her last chance through the door?

The one silver lining was that Gavil could be cleared of any involvement in Meg Jessler's murder. The police had found nothing. They'd suspected Gavil only because he'd lied to them. Once they proved his alibi was true she wouldn't be seeing them again. She should be glad about that. They'd pried at her work, left her house a shambles. She should be bidding them good riddance. But there was something about Detective Turnbow ...

Marian made a face. There she went again, soaking in whatever a man threw in her direction. He'd only done it to gain her cooperation.

Grief threatened to sweep Marian away, and she leaned against the wall to steady herself. She would *not* cry again. She had to *do* something, push the thoughts away. Her eyes closed and she let out a moan that filled the house. Then she gathered her strength, pushed away from the wall. She would force herself into her bedroom, change clothes, and do some gardening. Her old escape. Working in the soil, smelling its richness, often brought relief beyond her understanding. She had taken up the hobby in the throes of her divorce. Her backyard was fairly small, but it and the front walk had been tended with the best of care.

Marian changed into loose-fitting jeans and a T-shirt, then stepped onto her brick patio and opened the storage closet to her right. The closet was one of the features that had sold her on the townhouse, a convenient space for her garden paraphernalia. She selected her gloves and a few tools from their shelves, fighting to keep her mind focused. Before tackling the backyard, Marian checked the multi-colored snapdragons lining the front porch. A few weeds needed pulling. She dropped to her haunches, put on her garden gloves, and reached toward a pink-blossomed plant.

The sound of the door opening in unit six brought her hands to a halt. Scuffling about on her knees, Marian hunched over the flowers, head down. She tensed at the muffled contact of a soft-soled shoe with pavement. Then silence. She could feel her neighbor's eyes on her, sensed in his hesitation the imaginings of a mind fraught with curiosity. He had to have seen the police cars this morning. Spotting a tiny weed, she pulled it out. She heard a heavier step, as from porch stoop to sidewalk. A second step followed.

"Hi." He sounded almost apologetic.

Reluctantly, Marian looked over her shoulder. "Hello."

Jack Doniger stood on his sidewalk, sliding both hands into his pants pockets. Marian heard the jingle of car keys and loose change. "Haven't seen you for a while."

He was casually dressed in a blue knit shirt and khaki pants. His dark hair framed a strikingly chiseled face, one that would set a younger woman's heart throbbing. An air of reticence hung about him, sensitivity in his eyes. She forced a brief smile. "I guess we've both been busy."

He nodded. Marian watched him gather his nerve. "Did I see the police here this morning?"

Her eyes closed.

"I'm sorry. I shouldn't have asked."

"No, no, it's okay." How polite she sounded. "They were here."

"Yeah. Well. They're talking to everybody, you know. They've asked me questions too. don't think they've singled you out."

Marian laughed bitterly. "It's not *me* they've singled out, it's Gavil." Immediate humiliation stung her face. *Why* had she said that?

Jack puffed out his cheeks and blew. "Look, it'll be okay, all he's got to do is talk to them, tell them where he was that day. He probably was with you anyway, right?"

She stared at him. The explanation to that question was a lifetime's response. "I wasn't here."

"Oh."

Marian turned away. "I'm sorry, I need to get back to work."

"Yeah, sure."

She sensed him wavering.

"Look, is there something I can do for you?"

Not daring to look back, Marian shook her head. "Thanks. They'll just ... have to work it out."

Another jingle of change. "I'm sure they will. Well, see you later."

"Bye."

Jack moved down the sidewalk toward his garage. Marian fled through the house to the backyard. If curiosity had gotten the best of this shy new neighbor, others were sure to follow. Doubtless, Mrs. Geary would head the pack. No way could she handle that right now.

Marian stood on her back patio, scanning the yard. One orange tree still hadn't been fertilized. She'd done the others a few weeks ago, but ran out of time. Gavil wanted to make a matinee that day. The remembrance brought fresh tears to her eyes. She gave into them, then wrenched her mind back to the garden. All the trees needed extra watering, the roses needed tending, and there were weeds in the left corner.

Good. Enough to keep her busy for awhile.

Marian fetched a bag of fertilizer from her closet, then headed for the fence that she shared with Jack. Dropping to her knees, she began to weed.

The sun glowed hot on her back, and a trickle of sweat ran down her arms. She could smell her own warm skin, mixed with the hint of roses.

The fourth finger on her right hand began to itch as she worked. Felt like something digging into its tip. At first she ignored it. But the feeling grew worse. She scratched it with her other hand. It wouldn't go away.

How irritating.

Marian yanked off the glove and shook it. Nothing. Sighing, she sat back on her haunches and reached into the palm. She felt around inside the glove's fourth finger until she got hold of the burr. Marian tugged, expecting it to be stuck, but it came away easily. She glanced down, ready to toss it aside, when a flash of color caught her eye. Turning over the object, she brought it closer to her face, realized what it was, and blinked. What was *that* doing here?

On a normal day, she'd have thought more about it. She'd have run to Gavil to ask him just where the thing came from. But today he was gone. She and Gavil had spent two hours arguing after Detective Turnbow had brought her home. She'd cried, she'd accused, she'd screamed and cursed and pummeled him on the chest. Gavil had cried too, begging for forgiveness as he tried to explain a part of himself that she could never understand.

A sludge of emotion flooded her once more. Betrayal, anger, hurt. The tears began to flow. Once begun, she couldn't stop them. Landing back on her knees, Marian bowed her head, watching the drops fall to form dark blue spots on her jeans. Heaving a sob, she flicked the thing aside, crossing her arms across her chest and rocking as she cried.

~ ~ ~

146

Alone again.

Those two words shot fear through Gavil, followed by an anger that stunned him. The solid world he'd built was caving in, and he didn't deserve it. He sat down hard on the bed and grimaced at the feel of a firm mattress. Another hotel. How many had he slept in during his hundreds of business trips? Today, Saturday, he should be home with Marian.

Gavil punched the bed.

At least the detectives should disappear. They hadn't found a thing in the house. Surprise, surprise. There was nothing they *could* find.

If they bothered him again, if they harassed him *at all*, Gavil would sue.

And then there was Sonya. Some friend, leaving him an open target for police. He should have known Sonya would protect her own reputation above all else, no matter how much he'd pleaded with her over the phone. Gavil had called her three times in the last hour. Sonya's only response was to slam down the receiver. And, finally, there was Marian. She loved him, Gavil knew that, but she'd been skittish enough of marriage before.

How *dare* those two detectives force him into an alibi, then tell her about it!

Gavil snatched up the phone again. After four rings, the answering machine whirred on, and he listened to the message Marian had taped after he'd moved in. "Hello, you've reached the residence of Marian Baker and Gavil Harrison. Please leave a message, and we'll get back to you."

How long would his name survive on the tape?

"Hi, Marian. I'm at the Welthing Hotel in San Carlos. Here's the number." He read it off the phone. "Call me if you need me. I love you." Replacing the receiver, he sat motionless, staring at a cheap watercolor on the wall. So much had happened in the last three days. He tried to settle his mind, figure out what had gone wrong.

It started with dinner Wednesday night.

He remembered his welling panic as Paul Adams' wife looked right *through* him. *Sometimes I see things* ... He'd never experienced anything like that before. She laid him open and examined his soul. He drove home from that dinner like a zombie.

One thing for sure—Gavil never wanted to see Chelsea Adams again. How could he face her? Gavil could see her now. That expression. Her accusation. The more he thought about her, the madder he got. Who was she to judge? How could she know what he felt inside? Then he thought about the job at AP Systems. How could he work closely with Paul while hating the man's wife? What about company parties, or the days she'd happen by the office? He was bound to run into her sometime.

It probably didn't matter now. Things had been going great until that dinner. But he hadn't even heard from Paul Adams since then. Gavil tried to imagine the conversation between Paul and Chelsea after they'd left the restaurant. Exactly what had she told him? *How much* had she told him? Would he believe her? Why should Paul Adams care?

Gavil stared at the wall, thoughts churning. Now this nightmare with the police. And Marian. Gavil had to make things right with Marian. He *needed* her. Maybe, just maybe, landing the job at AP Systems would restore a little of her respect for him. Thanks to two meddling, stupid cops, that respect was now gone. And thanks to Chelsea Adams, his chance for the job was likely gone.

Gavil felt like strangling all three of them.

Chapter 24

"Turnbow!" The weekend dispatcher caught him late that afternoon as he swung through the station's glass doors. He threw her an exasperated look. "I know you're busy, but this woman's called three times. Says she's got to talk to you."

"Who is it?"

"Marian Baker."

He looked at her in surprise. "She on the line right now?" A nod. "Send it back to my office, I'm on my way."

Give me something good. Turnbow jerked up the phone. "Marian?"

"Hi." Her voice shook. "I didn't want to call you, but I don't know what to do. Reporters are everywhere, and they keep coming. They keep calling. I'm not even answering the phone anymore. I just hear the messages they leave. And they're knocking on the door. How could you *tell* them you were here when you didn't find anything?"

Turnbow sank into his chair. "We haven't told them anything. We're trying to keep information from getting out, but in a big case, people talk. We don't like it any more than you do."

"But you should hear their messages! They know you searched the house! They also know you didn't find what you were looking for, but they don't seem to even *care* about that!"

Turnbow's heart went out to her. She sounded so distraught. Then he thought of Harrison. How was *he* going to react? "Where's Gavil?"

"He's gone." She sniffed. "I asked him to leave for a few days."

"Leave! Where did he go?"

149

-"Don't worry, I can tell you where he's staying." She sounded bitter.

"Marian, I — " Turnbow took a breath. "You're right, it is important that we know where he is. And before I hang up the phone, I'll need that information from you. But I'm also worried about your safety."

"He's not going to hurt me. I *told* you he couldn't hurt anybody! The problem is these reporters. One of them left this long message about some woman's 'vision' of the murder happening and what did I think about you going through our house just because she said Gavil was the murderer? What is he *talking* about?"

Turnbow's stomach turned sour. Unless Chelsea Adams was talking, and he doubted that, there were only two sources for that information. Their murder book or the tape of her interview. Somebody around the station had gotten hold of one of them. Oh, were his and Reiger's heads gonna roll. If the media accused them of harassing an upstanding businessman only because of some woman's crazy story ...

Turnbow could only hope Harrison's alibi would never check out.

"Marian, I'm really sorry. Don't listen to the reporters. They'll spout any rumor they hear. I'm not free to tell you all the facts of this case. But I can tell you we searched your house with good reason."

"But you didn't *find* anything!"

"That's true, but— "

"Then announce that! Tell them Gavil didn't *do* this. They have no *right* to ruin a man's life!"

"Listen to me." Turnbow forced calm into his voice. Too bad he wasn't with Marian in person. She sounded very shaky. "Marian? I need to tell you something. Can you hold up right now?"

"I'll try."

She didn't sound very convincing. "Okay. What you need to know is that we haven't been able to verify Gavil's alibi. Remember how I mentioned we were checking on that? That's because Sonya Hocking said Gavil wasn't with her, and she vehemently denies having an affair with Gavil."

Silence.

"Marian?"

"You mean Gavil *lied?*"

"We've been checking with other friends of Sonya. But they all think she's been faithful to her husband."

"He *lied?*"

"So far it looks that way."

"How could he lie about something like *that?*" Marian's voice broke. "Why would he *do* that to me?"

Turnbow searched for words of comfort and found none. She wouldn't face the obvious reason until she was ready.

"This is why you think Gavil's guilty, isn't it?" Her voice tightened. "Because Sonya's denying it. Let me tell you something. I know Sonya well enough to know she'd do *anything* before she let her reputation be ruined. Of *course* she's denying it." Sobs rolled through the phone. "Oh, what am I *saying!* As if I want it to be true! I'm going *crazy!*"

Helplessness washed over Turnbow, followed by anger. Stupid Harrison, didn't know what he had.

"Marian, listen to me. Please try." He waited for her crying to subside. "I'm going to keep in touch with you, maybe even come by tomorrow or Monday if I can manage it without going through reporters. I'll tell you all I can as we learn things, all right?"

"Okay." Marian gulped. "But what's this thing about a vision?"

Turnbow hesitated. He couldn't tell her any more. But what if he denied it, then she heard it on the news? "I can't really talk about that, Marian. It doesn't matter anyway, no matter what reporters say. Please believe that. What matters is evidence that we find. Nothing else."

Marian begged him to tell her, but he stayed firm. Turnbow felt about two inches high.

"Fine then. I don't know if I can trust you, either."

He winced. "You can trust me."

She was silent.

"Look, Marian, I've got to get back to things here. I want to ask you one thing, though. Are you *sure* Gavil doesn't own a gold leather or suede jacket? Or shirt? Or even a rag or piece of cloth?"

"I *told* you. I'm sure."

He repressed a sigh. "Okay. One more thing. Does he have a key to your place?"

"I made him give it back."

"Good. It's probably best if you don't see him for a while."

If Harrison was guilty, and the police and now reporters were breathing down his neck, no telling what he'd do.

Chapter 25

Chelsea was none too happy as she cooked dinner. Paul and the boys were out on the driveway, washing both cars. She could hear their yelps and the harsh spray of water against cement. Apparently, the task had turned into a water fight. At least their day sounded fun. Hers had been terrible. God seemed to have abandoned her. One minute she'd pray, pleading with Him to make everything all right. The next minute she'd wonder why she was praying, because it didn't seem to be doing any good.

Earlier that afternoon, she'd sneaked a call to Gladys, who told Chelsea she was doing the right thing, abiding by Paul's wishes to stay away from church and her church friends. "It's only for now," Gladys said. "God will deal with Paul, and when He does, we'll see you *both* at church. But for now, you'll be no witness to Paul by fighting with him. And you're *not* being weak in this decision, believe me."

Chelsea knew Gladys was anything but a weak woman herself.

"You're being strong, leaving this in God's hands. Plus it's just not practical for you to be fighting with your husband, with all that's going on. You two need each other. Just know that I and others will be praying for you."

"Thanks, Gladys. I know God will work through this."

Wasn't that what Gladys had wanted to hear? But Chelsea found herself railing at God. If He *ever* sent her another vision, she'd ignore it.

The kitchen phone rang. Chelsea wiped her wet hands and picked up the receiver. "Hello?"

"Mrs. Adams, this is reporter Milt Waking, Channel 7 News."

Chelsea stilled.

Waking hurried on, as if afraid she'd hang up on him. He knew everything. Her vision, how she'd gone to the police, how she'd found the body. And her suspicion of Gavil Harrison. Chelsea listened, blood draining from her face. "Did you really not know the suspect before, Mrs. Adams? Or was this claimed vision of yours a way to tell police what you knew while removing yourself from the crime?"

Chelsea could not speak.

"Mrs. Adams?"

She slammed down the phone.

Before she could remove her hand, it rang again. Chelsea picked up the receiver and slammed it down a second time. Then jerked the phone wire out of its jack.

She clutched the tile counter for support. What *now*?

Was all this going to be on the news? Would reporters start banging on her door? How had they found out? What about Paul? What would he say? She'd never told him she'd given Gavil's name to the police.

Chelsea pulled herself to a kitchen chair and sank into it, resting her head on both hands. Vaguely, she registered the sounds of Paul's water fight with the boys. Then it grew quiet. Footsteps sounded through the garage. At the opening of the kitchen door, her head jerked up.

"Boy, did they get me!" Paul stopped. Water dripped in a puddle at his feet. "What's wrong?"

Lord, please help me!

Chelsea didn't know which she feared most—her name being on the news or Paul's reaction when he heard what she'd said about Gavil. What had she *done*? Paul would be so mad he'd *never* let her return to church. How was God going to reach him now?

Her insides were cold. "I just got a call from a reporter. He knows everything."

Fear flicked across Paul's face. "Oh, no."

154

Chelsea turned her eyes away.

"How'd they find out?"

She shook her head.

He didn't move. She could hear the drip, drip of water on the hardwood floor. She took a deep breath. "It'll probably be on the late news tonight. He wanted my comments before he ran the story."

"What'd you say?"

"I hung up on him. Twice."

As if on cue, the phone rang again from a distant room. Rang and rang without the kitchen extension's answering machine to pick it up.

Chelsea couldn't lift her eyes from the table. "There's something else I need to tell you."

His voice tensed. "What."

Maybe she shouldn't say anything. Just wait for the news story. Hope it never aired. Or maybe by some miracle they wouldn't talk about Gavil.

Maybe the moon would turn green.

Chelsea steeled herself. "After I found the body, I ... the policemen first acted suspicious of *me*, like I had something to do with it. And so I ..."

"You told them about Gavil." The words dropped like bullets on wood.

She managed a nod.

"Oh, I can't *believe* it!" Paul pressed a hand to his eyes. "How could you *do* that? How could you point a finger at somebody for no reason?" He swung away from her, then swung back. "Don't you know he could sue us for everything we have? You can't just tell the police somebody committed a crime as terrible as this! And now it's going to be all over the news! What're people going to *think*? What's *Gavil* going to think? What are Morrow at the investment firm and my board going to think? And what *on earth*

155

are we going to tell the boys? That their mother's some kind of lunatic?"

"I—"

"Oh, *forget* it." Paul thrust out his hand. "I don't even want to hear it."

He strode out of the kitchen, smacking his fist against a doorpost on his way out.

Chapter 26

By dinnertime, Turnbow and Reiger had holed up in Reiger's office, Turnbow's stomach growling. But they would not eat until they'd reviewed the day's events with each other. Reiger had brought a large metal lockable box from home to keep the murder book and tapes in from now on. Although it probably was too late. Once any news station decided to run the leaked information about Chelsea Adams and Gavil Harrison, the rest would follow.

Reiger groaned. "The Chief's about to bust a gut. Fortunately, he's just as unhappy over the leak itself as he is over the content."

Still, that did little to lift the heat. Turnbow knew they had to come up with some answers fast. Either find enough on Gavil to warrant an arrest, or find another suspect.

"We *had* reason to search," Turnbow protested for the third time. "We wouldn't have gotten a warrant if his alibi checked out."

"Yeah, but we didn't come up with anything."

"I know, I know." Turnbow flicked through his notes. "So where were we?"

After their search that morning, the two detectives had chased down every possible angle on Gavil Harrison. Turnbow began with a call to the jurisdiction in which he'd previously lived. Any unsolved murders there with a similar M.O.? They had no reason to believe their suspect was a serial killer, but the possibility should be checked.

Answer: no.

Turnbow questioned more of Sonya Hocking's friends. No one knew anything about an affair with Gavil.

Then came a second round of questioning homeowners between Dapple Street and Trent Park, including those townhouse residents who had not been home before. They, too, said they were asleep and saw nothing. Reiger and Turnbow also planned second and third "stakeouts" for Sunday and Monday mornings at Trent Park, during which two policemen would position themselves at either end of the gravel road to question runners. The first stakeout had rendered no witnesses. No one other than Jenkin Tommason had seen Meg jog by, and no one at all had seen anyone who could have been her killer. Reiger spent time with Meg's coworkers and her distraught boyfriend, Brent, who'd flown into town to attend the funeral. But none of them had any answers as to why Meg would have been killed.

After all their work, Gavil Harrison was still the only suspect. He knew the victim and he'd lied to them about an alibi—apparently twice. Turnbow felt his stomach twist at the thought of the man still on the streets. "Harrison's slick. A successful businessman with a dark side. Makes you wonder how he's hid it this long. Did he just snap? Will he do it again?"

Reiger raised a shoulder. "He's lost a lot in three days. New job opportunity, girlfriend, home. Now he's about to hear his name on the news. Plenty of reason for him to snap."

"We'd better keep a close eye on him. He could try to skip town."

Or far worse—take it out on Marian.

Chapter 27

Night fell. Chelsea and Paul were still barely talking.

Chelsea put the boys to bed, hiding her despair. She and Paul loved each other so much. She couldn't stand to be in conflict with him. She shrank from his anger—only to find *herself* angry. Did he think she'd asked for what had happened? Did he think it was fun for her? What right did he have, in the midst of her needs, to take away her fellowship with Christian friends? It was hard for her to picture getting up the following morning and not going to church. Half of her expected Paul to relent by then. The other half was afraid he never would.

She turned out the light in Scott's room. "Good night, Scott."

"'Night, Mom. Hope you feel better."

She paused. How did he know something was wrong?

"Oh, I'm fine." She closed the door.

Shortly before 11:00 Chelsea found Paul on the family room couch, flicking TV channels. The news was minutes away. She sank into an armchair and waited. He ignored her. *Flick.* A couple kissing jarred into a chase scene. *Flick.* A Spanish-speaking station. *Flick.* A comedy. Chelsea watched the scenes jolt by.

That's what her life had felt like the last few days.

Eleven o'clock arrived. Paul flicked to Channel 7. The anchorman led with a teaser for the story. "Shocking new revelations in the murder of a female jogger in Haverlon's Trent Park. Stay tuned for our exclusive report on this bizarre case and the incredible story of a woman who knew all the details before the body was discovered, claiming she'd had a 'vision from God.'"

~ ~ ~

159

The news story concluded. Paul clicked off the TV and stared at the empty screen. Chelsea sat in the armchair, silent. He could feel her anxiety over his reaction.

Paul didn't know *how* to react. Yes, he was still mad at her for going to the police. Upset that her name was spread across the news. And Gavil's name. Harrison would be furious about this. The man could sue them for everything they were worth.

But as bad as all that was, Paul couldn't focus on any of it. He could only struggle to absorb the unbelievable information he'd just heard.

Gavil Harrison—the man he'd been so impressed with—a murder suspect. Surely the man could not be guilty. Yet Gavil knew the victim. He was her neighbor. And he'd lied to police about an alibi. *Lied!* Why would he do that?

Paul tapped his finger against the remote. Why *else* would he do that?

No. There had to be some other explanation.

Maybe Gavil just panicked. Maybe the woman he claimed to be with was lying. Maybe the media had made too much out of a routine search. And how much of the detectives' actions, by the way, had been a direct result of Chelsea's finger-pointing? Did they focus on Gavil just because of her?

Surely not. If anything, the police probably thought Chelsea a little crazy.

Maybe the reporter didn't have all the facts. Gavil's alibi would prove solid after all.

Problem was, the details were fitting with everything Chelsea had said. Everything.

How could that be?

Paul turned to his wife and sighed. "Look, Chels. I don't know what's happening here. And I surely don't like it. But ... I'm sorry for not listening to you." She started to speak, but he held up a hand. "Understand me, I'm not changing my viewpoint. I don't like these visions of yours. And now more than ever, I don't want you going to church. But I will certainly reconsider about hiring Gavil." Accusation crept into his tone. "I'll *have* to, now that his name's been plastered across television."

Chelsea's eyes filled with tears. "I'm scared," she whispered.

Empathy pulled Paul from the couch. He held his arms out, and Chelsea rose to press against his chest. "I'm sorry I got us into this." Her words muffled into his neck. "I'm so sorry."

He stroked her hair. "We'll find a way through it."

~ ~ ~

Gavil spent the evening in his hotel room, trying to concentrate on papers from work. Anything to divert his thoughts. By 10:45 he couldn't take the sight of one more blurred sales figure. Disgusted, he pushed the files to one side of the small writing table and dropped his head in his hands.

He hated what was happening to his life. *Hated it.* He wanted to crawl into bed, pull the covers up, and sleep for days. Which scared him to death, because the thought pointed to depression. His therapist had warned him once he'd come through depression, it would be easier to fall back into it, given the right circumstances.

And if ever the circumstances were right, it was now.

Gavil leaned back in the chair and ran a hand over his eyes. He refused to give in to that feeling of hopelessness, powerlessness. He would fight it. Do anything to keep from living through that again.

For the hundredth time Gavil relived his humiliation in front of that sergeant—was it just this morning? Marian's eyes on Gavil, her disdain at his alibi. He *would* get her back. And the Haverlon Police Department would pay.

Gavil pushed back the chair with sudden force, snatched up the TV remote, and fell on the bed, punching pillows into place so he could sit up. He snapped the television on, flipping through local channels for the news. If there were any new developments about the case, he wanted to know. He landed on Channel 7—and a familiar name froze his hand.

His own.

"... Gavil Harrison's alibi that he'd been with the wife of a good friend at the time of the murder does not appear to be holding," a reporter was saying as he stood in the parking lot of Sequoia Townhomes. "According to our sources, that woman, yet unnamed, said she was not with Harrison at the time. Police would not comment on this exclusive information, nor would they say what they were looking for when they searched this townhouse that the suspect shares with his girlfriend, Marian Baker." The reporter pointed over his shoulder at the door of Marian's house.

Violation washed through Gavil. How *dare* they camp out in front of Marian's door! Did she know they were there?

"But apparently they did not find it because no arrest has been made. Phone calls to Ms. Baker have not been answered. But the case becomes even stranger. Channel 7 has obtained exclusive information about a woman who claims she had a vision from God about the murder before the body was even discovered ..."

Gavil listened to the rest of the story, transfixed. Horror crept up his neck, down his arms and legs. His heart went numb until he could barely breathe.

Long after Milt Waking's image left the screen, through advertisements on detergent, telephone services, and a foreign car, Gavil Harrison sat like stone. Staring at the TV, hearing nothing, seeing nothing. He could only think of one thing.

Chelsea Adams.

Sometimes I see things ...

He couldn't believe it.

162

At the restaurant, she'd seen—all this? The murder. The details. *Him?* How could that be? How could this happen? Were Paul Adams and his wife some kind of religious freaks?

And what in the world was going to happen to *him*, now that he'd been publicly accused of murder? What would happen to Marian? His job? His *life*?

He'd lose everything he'd worked for. All because of one woman and her so-called vision.

Speaking of that "vision"—no wonder the police had singled him out so quickly. Did they know his name before they even knew about the body?

Gavil choked out a stunned, angry laugh. They had nothing on him. *Nothing*.

Yet look what had happened.

Gavil could barely take it in.

Because of Chelsea Adams, he'd been forced to bring Sonya into this. Because of Chelsea Adams, he'd lost the job at AP Systems. Marian. His home.

Now he'd lost his reputation.

As Gavil hung there, mind spinning, his numbness slowly turned to a rage that fired his veins. His fingers curled into the bedcovers. The cords on his neck strained. Gavil welcomed the rage, embraced it. With it came power over the powerlessness.

Blackness descended over him, humming through his brain. In the midst of that blackness, something in Gavil snapped, as cleanly as an ice-encased branch in winter.

So they thought him a murderer, did they? Dangerous, did they?

Fine. He'd show them. He'd show them all.

Gavil Harrison was *not* going to take this. He wasn't going to stay in a hotel room, scared of two detectives who'd harassed him for *no reason*. He wasn't going to let Marian go or allow his life to be ruined.

The news ended.

A talk show came on, its host greeting guest after guest.

Gavil barely heard any of it. He was thinking, *obsessing* about what to do.

He'd take back his alibi about Sonya. Tell Marian he'd panicked under pressure. After all, the detectives had nothing on him. He didn't *need* an alibi.

He could sue the police department, make them clear his name. But that would take time. He wanted them to stop bothering him *now*. And for some inexplicable reason, they were hanging on to Chelsea Adams' every word.

How do you fight a "vision from God"? Gavil almost laughed.

One thing was very clear. Since she so obviously was running the show.

Gavil would have to change Chelsea Adams' mind.

Chapter 28

Paul sat on the couch with his arm around Chelsea. She'd finally stopped crying, but still lay against his shoulder as if clinging to him for strength.

"Maybe we ought to go on a family outing tomorrow, get the boys out of town and away from the phone," he suggested. "It'll probably be ringing off the hook all day."

"Sounds good to me."

As if on cue, the phone rang once again from their bedroom upstairs. It had hardly stopped since the newscast. The kitchen extension was still unplugged. Weariness flicked across Chelsea's face, and she sat up. "You probably ought to answer it. It might be important."

Paul shook his head in defeat. Crossing into the kitchen, he plugged in the phone and picked up the receiver. If this was some curious friend of Chelsea's, he'd cut her off with no qualms. "Hello."

"Paul. Gavil Harrison." The voice was clipped, unfriendly.

Paul's stomach turned to lead. He took a moment to regroup. What on earth could he say to this man? "Hi."

"I'll get right to the point. I'm very disappointed in the newscast. I don't know what's going on here. I thought it was pretty much decided that I'd be a good addition to your work team. Now I hear I'm being called a murderer—publicly. By your wife."

"Wait, Gavil, she never said anything public. She never talked to any reporters. This is not her doing."

"Are you denying that she told the police I'm responsible for that murder?"

Keep calm, Paul, keep your head. "I … no."

"Then let me tell you something." Gavil's tone hardened. "I think your wife had better watch herself. I think she'd better stop throwing around God's name when she lies about someone. 'A vision from God.' Come *on*. If there *is* a God up there, He may be a bit disappointed at the way she's tarnishing His reputation. Not to mention mine."

"Hey, wait a minute. You don't have to talk to me like that."

"Talk to *you*? After what she's said about *me*? Who do you think you *are?*"

"Stop it, Harrison." Paul took a deep breath. "Look. I don't know everything that's going on, either. Most of the stuff I heard tonight was news to me too. I'm sure—"

"You're not 'sure' of anything. You can't even control your own wife."

"Gavil, you—"

"Don't 'Gavil' me, Paul. I'm in no mood. You have no *idea* what my life has been like the last three days. All because of your wife. So you tell her something for me, hear? Tell her to back off. *Now*. Tell her to call those cops and tell them the truth. She obviously knew about this murder before anyone else. Ask her who *really* did it. Maybe *you* even know."

Paul stiffened. "Shut *up*, Harrison! You don't know what you're talking about!"

"Oh, hit a nerve, did I?"

"That's it. Don't call this house again."

"I'll keep calling!" Gavil yelled. "I'll call, I'll do anything I have to do to shut your wife up!"

Paul dug his fingers into the phone. His voice fell to deadly quiet. "What's that supposed to mean?"

Silence.

"Are you *threatening* my wife, Harrison? Is *that* what you're doing?"

166

"Did I say that?" Gavil's tone thickened with sarcasm. "Just goes to show which one of us has violence on his mind."

Paul's throat felt so tight he could barely spit out the words. "Don't call here again, Gavil. *Ever*. And don't come anywhere near my wife. Or you just might *see* me violent. Is that clear?"

Paul smashed down the phone.

Chapter 29

Reiger tossed and turned in bed, envious of Edith's sleep-laden breathing. He'd gotten home in time to hear the news. He and Turnbow discussed it on the phone afterward. Somebody had leaked a lot of information, all right. "Better practice saying 'no comment,'" Reiger growled. "We'll soon be saying it in our sleep."

If he ever slept again.

He stared at the ceiling, dimly lit by the orange glow of a street lamp. They had to come up with some answers soon. Only solid evidence would displace the sensationalism of Chelsea Adams' vision.

The woman really did have an extraordinary gift from God. Where would they be right now without Chelsea's vision? Meg Jessler's body could still be undiscovered. Even if she'd been found, he and Turnbow might not have gotten around to interviewing Harrison so quickly. As much as Reiger hated the news leak, he had to admit that at least the public was now hearing of God's power. If they believed it. Most wouldn't.

That was the world for you. It cried for a miracle from God in times of trouble, yet refused to grasp it when one occurred. In this rationally minded society, there was no room for a divine word from the Lord. Law enforcement certainly wasn't prepared to handle it. If this case ever got to court, what would the criminal justice system do with Chelsea's vision?

Reiger knew one thing. Officers at the station would sure be buzzing about all this. What would he say? Would he stand up for his faith—or throw Chelsea Adams under the bus?

The phone shrilled. Edith jumped. He snatched up the receiver. "Reiger."

"It's dispatch, sir. A man just called about the homicide, saying he wouldn't talk to anybody but you."

"Who is it?"

"Paul Adams. Said he's Chelsea Adams' husband."

Reiger jumped from bed, reaching for pen and paper in the nightstand drawer. He flicked on a lamp, squinting in the sudden light. "Number." Dispatch read it off. "Thanks."

He punched in the digits. The phone was answered on the first ring.

"Mr. Adams? Sergeant Reiger."

He listened to the man's recounting of a phone conversation with Harrison. Reiger felt his toes curl.

"Did he threaten her?" He jotted a note. "Tell me again exactly what he said." He cradled the phone with his shoulder, writing. "All right. Thank you for calling. I'm sorry about this. How's Mrs. Adams?"

"She's scared. She's been scared of Gavil all along. I just wouldn't listen until now. So what are you going to do?"

Reiger blew out air. Paul Adams sounded like a man who was used to making people jump. "I can assure you we'll do all we can. I'll call my partner right now. We'll pay Harrison a visit at his hotel room. And it won't be friendly. But I've got to tell you, I don't think we can arrest him based on what he said."

"He's threatening my wife!"

"It sounds like he didn't make it clear."

"But I heard it in his tone! I tell you, the man's not all there. We were with him just three nights ago. Now he sounds like a totally different person."

"I understand. We'll go talk to him. If he says anything more concrete to you, we'll bring him in. But we're already being watched closely on this one. By our own superiors and now by the media. If we bring him in without a solid reason that could stand up in court, we'll have even more trouble on our hands. In the meantime, we can at least tell him he can't go anywhere near your property or any member of your family. If he breaks that, he *will* be arrested."

"If he breaks that—I'll break his *head*."

~ ~ ~

Two rapid-fire knocks on the hotel door. Turnbow's nerves were already humming. One woman dead, now the guy was threatening somebody else. The detective itched to see this man behind bars. He did not like his own feeling of helplessness as long as Gavil Harrison was on the streets. At least Chelsea Adams had a husband to look out for her. Marian Baker had no one.

"Haverlon police. Open up, Harrison!" Turnbow's command rebounded through the hallway.

No response. Turnbow pounded again. "Now, Harrison!"

"I don't have to talk to you." A muffled voice just beyond the door.

"You've got two choices," Reiger cut in, "here or down at the station."

"You have no reason to arrest me."

"Open the door, Harrison," Reiger said. "We have to get a key, we won't be happy."

"So get one."

Turnbow seethed at the man's belligerence. He and Reiger had already obtained a key from the front desk, just in case. Turnbow shoved it in the lock and threw open the door. Gavil flew backwards with an awkward three-step. Turnbow pushed him into a chair. He landed with a thud.

"Easy." Reiger stood over him.

Turnbow spread his left hand across Gavil's chest. "You stay *right there*. I'm gonna do some talking and you're gonna listen." Gavil's face was stone. "We know about your conversation with Paul Adams. We know you threatened his wife."

"I never——"

"Shut up!" Turnbow pressed his hand harder against Gavil. "I'm going to tell you this once. You are *not* to call the Adams again, is that clear? You are to stay away from that whole family. You will not go near Chelsea Adams, or her husband, or her kids, or her home. You will find yourself no closer to any of those people than the length of a football field. If you *do* go near any one of those them, we'll haul you in immediately. *Do you understand?*"

Fury rolled across Gavil's face. "Why are you still harassing me? I'll have you both fired. I'll sue you for everything you've got."

"Watch yourself, Harrison." Reiger glared down at him. "You're hardly in a position to be threatening us."

"You're in no position to be threatening me! If you had anything on me, you'd have arrested me by now. You both know I didn't kill that girl! You just want a scapegoat to cover your own incompetence!"

Turnbow's blood sizzled. "I don't take kindly to innocent women being hurt. It's a soft spot with me. I've got a sister and mother of my own. So believe me, I'm being as *nice* as I can be with you right now. *Don't* push it."

Gavil sneered. "Go ahead, get meaner than you already are. See what happens then. See how fast you lose your badge."

The detective clenched his teeth.

"Where were *you* when that sweet young thing was getting battered, anyway? Making eyes at Girl Scouts?"

Turnbow's vision blurred. His right hand balled into a fist.

"Pat, stop." Reiger grabbed his arm.

"Go ahead," Gavil spat, "hit me!"

"Pat, no, that's just what he wants!"

Turnbow drew his fist back. Gavil ducked.

"Turnbow, *stop!*"

The fear in Reiger's voice brought Turnbow to his senses. His fist froze in midair. Nobody moved. Turnbow breathed double-time, jaw working. Trying to clear his head. He swallowed hard, forcing down anger. Gavil remained a statue. Slowly, Turnbow's fist relaxed, fell away. He flicked his eyes to Reiger, straightened his shoulders. Glared again at Gavil. Stepped back. Reiger moved between them.

"Harrison," Reiger said, "watch yourself. Don't even *think* about leaving town. Do I make myself clear?"

Silence.

"Do I?"

"Yes, okay!"

"Good."

Reiger looked at Turnbow and gestured with his head toward the hall. Turnbow slid a look of pure contempt at Gavil, then followed his partner out the door.

Sunday, June 11

Chapter 30

Reiger poured himself a second cup of coffee, then slumped back into his kitchen chair. Four aspirins hadn't touched his headache. It was seven in the morning. He'd had two hours of sleep, max. Soon he'd be dragging himself back to the station to go over all his notes one more time. Something was there, something he'd missed. It nagged at him. But his mind was so thick, he could hardly think. And when he thought of the reporters he'd have to wade through, the answers he'd have to give, both to the media and his superiors, he just wanted to go back to bed.

"Sorry I groused at you this morning, Edith." He squeezed his wife's hand as she headed to work in her garden for a few hours before church.

She patted his arm. "Don't worry, dear, this one will work out. God's behind it."

Reiger sighed as he gazed through the kitchen's sliding screen door. Edith's garden gloves and thick knee pads lay on the patio. He'd given her the knee pads last Christmas, and they'd saved many a pair of pants since then. The sun pierced through his skull, and he averted his eyes to the coffee mug. The caffeine probably wasn't doing a whole lot for his head, either. He grunted at that consideration, then took another slurp.

Edith rolled back the screen door and stepped into the yard, closing the door behind her. "Whoo! It's hot out here already."

Reiger watched as she pulled on her gloves and knee pads. He set down the coffee mug and arched his back, spine popping. Eyes closed, he twisted his neck from side to side.

The thought hit him like a brick.

Gloves.

His eyes snapped open, pulled to Edith like metal to magnet.

"Are you the gardener?"

He froze, forcing the memory. He'd been on his way out Marian Baker's door, chatting her up in hopes of an unguarded slip of information. *"My wife gardens too ..."*

Gold leather fibers. Rich dirt. Meg's "prickly" hands.

From warding off an attacker wearing garden gloves?

"Ah!"

If those fibers were from gloves, this was no crime of impulse. Gloves meant malice aforethought—willful planning and intent. Their killer was even more dangerous than they'd realized ...

Reiger shoved back his chair. Pushed open the screen door and strode across the lawn, grabbing his surprised wife's hand.

"What is it?" Her eyes searched his face.

He snatched the glove from her hand, turned it over. Could this be it?

Three policemen had searched Marian's house. Where were her gloves? Either Gavil had gotten rid of them in time, or they'd flat out missed them. Reiger wasn't sure which was worse.

"Dan, what is it?"

He held out the glove. "This!" He balled it in his fist and squeezed, as if trying to shake out answers. Then he pushed it back into her hand and jogged toward the kitchen.

~ ~ ~

"Reiger," Turnbow said for the third time, "I *don't* want to use the search warrant."

"We can't warn her, Pat, where's your head? You expect her to just turn the gloves over to us with no question—if she has them at all?"

"Yes, I do. Let me do the talking, I'll handle it." Reiger gave him a reminding look. "Okay, so I got a little heated last night. That was ... different."

"What's gotten into you, Turnbow? You almost knock out a suspect, now you refuse to search his home?"

"This isn't Harrison, it's his poor girlfriend. She's already been through enough. I don't want to tear apart her house again."

"I feel sorry for her, too, but we've got a job to do!"

"We can do our job, but ... Tell you what. Let's take the search warrant. But I'll talk to her first, see if she'll cooperate. Then if we have to use it, we will."

Reiger studied him. "All right. We'll do it your way." He slid the warrant into his pocket. "But you're sure acting funny lately."

~ ~ ~

"Who is it?" Marian leaned her head against the front door. *Please let it be Gavil.* Maybe he'd beg her forgiveness again, and she would give it. Less than twenty-four hours had passed since he'd walked out of the townhouse, and already the loneliness seemed overwhelming. And after last night's newscast, she didn't know what to think. Maybe he had been targeted only because of some crazy woman. One minute she shook with fury at him and the next she trembled with grief.

"It's Pat Turnbow."

Disappointment surged through Marian, trailed by inexplicable relief. "Just a minute." She opened the door and stepped back. That's when she caught sight of Sergeant Reiger.

She eyed them both. "What now?"

"Marian," Turnbow spoke quickly, as if afraid she'd shut the door, "something's come up. We need to talk to you."

176

Marian let them in, not bothering to hide her reticence. Turnbow gazed at her, and she saw his recognition of her swollen eyes. She looked away.

"Come on in." She led the two men into the living room and invited them to sit.

Turnbow perched across from her. "It's about your garden gloves. Remember how Sergeant Reiger noticed them on your kitchen counter last Thursday?"

Marian's mind flicked across the memory. "Yes."

"Do you still have them?" Turnbow was clearly on edge.

"Uh-huh."

Reiger exhaled. "Where are they?"

"In the patio closet out back."

Reiger exchanged a revelatory look with Turnbow. "We must not have checked it." He stood up.

Gold leather fibers. In a nauseating flash, Marian guessed the gloves' significance. But it made no sense. "Garden gloves?" She lifted a hand. "Surely you don't think ... Why would anybody wear garden gloves?"

The detectives exchanged a glance, as if deciding whether to answer. Turnbow finally spoke. "Any kind of gloves hide fingerprints, Marian."

"Fingerprints? In a park?"

He shook his head. "On the body."

Marian dropped her gaze, swallowing hard. Fingerprints on a dead woman. *Her* gloves. A knot formed in her throat. This couldn't be happening. She saw herself kneeling yesterday in the garden, wearing the gloves. Could those same gloves have been used to kill—

Marion's blood froze. What she'd found. In the glove.

She couldn't breathe.

Maybe it meant nothing. It couldn't. If what they were saying was true, it made no sense.

But it *had* to mean something. That thing hadn't come from her.

Marian felt the detectives' eyes on her.

She had to move. They would get no more from her than they already knew.

Someone else's legs stood her up. Someone else's body floated her toward the kitchen. Stepping onto the patio, she opened the closet. There lay the gloves, easily visible on a shelf.

Reiger pulled a black felt-tip pen from his shirt pocket and wrote his initials on each glove. Slid them into a paper bag. Then he rummaged around the closet, peering at various bags of fertilizer. "Have you used the gloves since last Wednesday?" He pushed aside a watering can.

She hesitated. "Yes. Yesterday afternoon."

He didn't appear happy at that. "Use any fertilizer?"

"Yes, this one." She pulled out a near-empty bag of citrus feed and handed it to him.

Reiger glanced at the brand name, then turned over the bag, searching for its list of contents. He mumbled through the fine print. "Nitrogen, phosphoric acid, calcium, sulfur, iron, zinc." He shoved the bag at his partner. "Hold this a minute." Pulling a small spiral notebook from his pocket, he flipped through pages.

His expression told her he'd found the page he was looking for.

"Did you also use this fertilizer recently *before* yesterday?" he asked.

"I think so."

"I'll need to take it too."

Marian's hand lifted in assent. What else could she do?

Reiger marked the fertilizer bag with his initials.

This couldn't be happening.

Revulsion swept over Marian. She turned away. Was it only moments ago she'd wanted Gavil back? She couldn't begin to imagine what to do now. She wandered into the kitchen. It was dark, fading, spots blocking her vision. Her knees wobbled. From nowhere, Turnbow appeared at her side, easing her into a chair. He started to speak, but she waved him off.

"Please go. I can't ... I just need to be alone right now."

He hesitated.

"Please."

"Okay." He put a hand on her shoulder. "But, Marian, I want you to call if you need me." He waited for a reply. She looked away.

Reiger came in then, carrying the gloves and fertilizer as though they were diamonds. Turnbow pulled his hand from Marian's shoulder. His partner didn't seem to notice. Reiger gave her a slight nod. "Thank you, Ms. Baker. We'll be in touch with you."

Marian's eyes slid to Turnbow. The empathy in his gaze pierced her heart.

In the next moment, he was gone.

She could not find the energy to move.

The front door opened, then shut.

~ ~ ~

Marian slumped in the kitchen chair, thoughts churning. How long had she been there?

Was time still moving?

Part of her wanted to scream that Gavil was innocent, protect him from the two policemen who seemed bent on destroying him. Another part longed to hit him, kick him, make him bleed for the pain he'd caused her.

A third part just wanted to die.

She told herself that none of it was true. She argued with the imagined figures of the two detectives, Turnbow's face before her. What he must think of her!

But what she'd found in that glove ...

Marian's head came up.

Some inner force shoved her out of the chair, through the sliding door. Across the patio and into her garden. The sun was hot on her shoulders, the air oppressive. Marian stopped and swiveled her head from side to side. Where had she been?

Bits and pieces of confused reality marched before her. Orange trees. Weeding ...

She closed her eyes, visualized herself kneeling, saw the fence at her right shoulder.

Scurrying feet took her toward the tree overhanging her fence. She dropped to her knees. The richly colored fertilizer shot an acrid smell into her nostrils. With bare hands she began raking through the soft black dirt, throwing it aside like a furious puppy. Her breathing grew ragged.

Minutes ticked by. The breaths turned into sobs.

It wasn't there. She'd imagined it.

Marian ignored the dirt stains spreading on her pants and the fetid soil on her hands. She dug all around the tree.

Nothing.

She crawled to one side, checking where she had weeded. She grabbed handfuls of grass and yanked them out by the roots. Pieces of the lawn she'd so carefully tended flew in all directions, smashing into the fence.

Still nothing.

See! It's not true!

Marian's eyes stung from tears. Her knees ached and her back hurt. But she continued raking, digging, pulling. Clawing next around the rosebushes of yellow, pink, red, white, she ignored the thorns that bit into her hands, drawing blood. The roses were so vivid, as vivid as what she'd found.

That was it! That's what she had seen! A petal, nothing more. A petal inside her glove. She'd been so upset, she'd thought it was something else, but it wasn't. It *wasn't*.

One by one Marian began snapping each petal off its stem and flinging it into the dirt. *There, and there, roses! That's what you get for tricking me, for making me crazy!* Soon she was tearing away whole flowers at a time, sobbing louder with the death of each one. When all her roses were gone, she thrashed around the bare bushes to draw abused hands through her marigolds. Tears blinded her eyes and salty mucus ran over her lips.

It wasn't there. She had dreamt it.

Marian was tiring. Her cries became jagged, and the scratches on her hands throbbed.

But she pressed on, pulling out every last one of the golden flowers, pound-pounding them into the dirt until their delicate petals lay crushed and broken. Not until there was nothing left to destroy did her frenzy begin to ease, then drain away.

A moment passed.

Stunned, she gazed around her, surveying the damage. A moan rose to her lips. What had she *done?*

Regret surged, making her sick. Her eyes swept full circle and came to rest once more on the marigolds, now a total waste. A dirty, mustard-brown waste.

Except for a glisten of color beneath one mashed bloom.

With a cry, Marian reached for it. It would be nothing—just another rose petal. But the instant her fingers closed around it, she knew. She squeezed her eyes shut, praying to see something else, *anything* else when she opened them. Five. Ten. Twenty seconds.

Heart thudding, Marian straightened all five fingers and peeked through clumped lashes at what lay in her palm.

~ ~ ~

Jack Doniger stood in his bathrobe on his back patio, one hand rubbing his groggy head. What was going on next door? A woman's cries had filtered through his open bedroom window, dragging him from much-needed sleep. He made his way barefoot across his small lawn to peek over the fence. The sight widened his eyes. Marian Baker knelt, sobbing, her yard trashed.

A dozen thoughts flashed through Jack's mind. He pulled back before she could catch sight of him. What had happened now? The police? Had they arrested his neighbor?

His sleepiness forgotten, Jack hurried back into his house to peek out the front window.

Nothing. No police car.

He turned and leaned against the wall, thinking.

Poor Marian. She seemed so sweet. Could he do something to help?

Easing toward the kitchen to make coffee, Jack Doniger determined to find out what was going on.

Monday, June 12

Chapter 31

"Michael, where's my mitt?" Scott yelled up the stairs to his older brother as he tied his shoe.

"How should I know?" Michael pounded down the stairs and raked at his brother's head as he hit the landing.

"Ooww! Mom!"

"Go ahead, baby, run to Mama. But if I were you, I'd look in the living room."

A flicker of recognition crossed Scott's mind. They'd been tossing the baseball across the long formal living room. Mom would have a fit if she ever caught them, which is why they ducked out the sliding door onto the back deck when they heard her coming.

"Oh, yeah, I bet it's in the yard!" Scott raced with one shoe down the hall to the living room and slid on his sock foot across the hardwood floor to the sliding door. He struggled with the lock, which always got stuck, since it wasn't used very often. The living room was just for dinner parties and guests.

"Ughh!" Scott leaned against the lock with both fists until he heard it *click*. Pushing back the large door, he bounded outside and across the patio. His mitt lay in the grass.

"Michael! Scott! Come to breakfast!" Mom's voice filtered through the kitchen window at the far end of the house.

"Uh-oh." Scott swept up the mitt. He hopped on the shoed foot back across the deck and jumped over the threshold into the living room. Moms were nosy, and the sight of one dirty sock could result in some difficult questions.

"Scott, where are you?" Mom sounded irritated.

"Coming!" Scott pushed the door closed, slid across the living room, and ran down the hall, slowing just enough to scoop up his other shoe as he passed the stairway. He ground to a halt before entering the kitchen and popped his foot into the shoe. Then he walked through the door with a frustrated air, as if to say, "Mom, I did everything I could to get here on time and it *wasn't* my fault."

~ ~ ~

"Five more days, five more days, five more days of scho-ool," Michael chanted between bites of cereal. Scott took up the cheer, their voices fraying Chelsea's nerves. She hadn't gotten much sleep last night. Chelsea threw them a look.

"You've got about three minutes, guys. Then your father will be down and ready to go. And you don't want to hold him up."

"Why's he taking us today?" Scott asked. Paul was usually out the door long before they left for school. "Is it because you were on the news?"

Paul entered the kitchen, straightening his tie. "Because I want to check you two out and make sure you're behaving. So up and at 'em, we're history."

"Brush your teeth first," Chelsea told the boys.

They clattered out of the kitchen, leaving sudden calm in their wake.

Paul ran a finger across her cheek. "You sure you're going to be all right?"

She nodded. "I'm not going anywhere. Thanks to you, I don't even have to take them to school. Besides, it's only a couple hours, right?"

"Right. I promise I'll be home as soon as this investor meeting is over. Believe me, if I could have rescheduled it ..."

"I know, I know." Chelsea smiled. "It doesn't matter. I'll be fine until you get back. Really."

Paul studied her. "Okay. And maybe by the time the boys are out of school, it will all be over."

Chelsea, Paul, and the boys had spent Sunday in San Francisco, trying to get away from all the chaos. When they got home they discovered a phone message from Sergeant Reiger. Paul returned the call. Reiger apologized that he could not specify details, but did say they'd found new, specific evidence linking Gavil Harrison to the murder. Lab tests would be run that morning, and if results were as expected, Harrison would be arrested.

"This is so incredible," Paul told Chelsea after the boys were in bed. "Looks like Gavil really did it. He really killed that girl. And I was going to *hire* the guy."

Paul must have apologized five times to Chelsea before he finally fell asleep.

Chelsea had lain awake, thanking God for the evidence—and praying for her husband. Surely Paul could no longer deny God's power.

"And another thing." Paul now wagged a finger at Chelsea. "I'll be calling to check up on you. Somehow I'll sneak in a call during the meeting. You hear that phone ring, you jump."

"You got it."

"And turn on the alarm as soon as we leave."

"Okay."

Four pounding feet entered the kitchen.

Chelsea shook her head at her sons. "That couldn't have been much of a brush."

"They're zippy clean, Mom." Michael gave her an exaggerated smile. "See?"

Chelsea leaned in for a look. "Oh, all right then."

The boys raced out the door leading to the garage, slamming it behind them.

"You remember Reiger's phone number?" Paul asked.

"Yes. But I'll be fine." Gavil Harrison would be at work anyway." Don't worry. I'll see you soon."

Paul raised his eyebrows. "Yes, you will." He gave her a quick kiss and stepped into the garage. "All right, boys! Head 'em up and move 'em out!"

As soon as they were gone, the house felt so silent. A chill snaked down Chelsea's spine, but she ignored it.

At the alarm pad in the kitchen she punched in the code to activate the alarm.

~ ~ ~

Striding into the county crime lab two minutes after nine, Reiger found Hal Weiss leaning toward a fine-looking blonde near the coffee machine.

"Hey, Weiss. Got something important. Can you look at it right now?"

Hal broke up his tête-à-tête with obvious reluctance. "Sure."

"Take me to your fancy microscope." Reiger held out the bag containing Marian's gloves. "They're gold and they're leather."

Hal raised an eyebrow. "Let's do it. I'll go get the fibers."

Reiger prayed hard as he waited. He'd been praying ever since they seized the gloves. He and Turnbow badly needed this match. The police chief had been furious that morning about the newscast, pulling them both into his office to rail about the leak all over again. "It wasn't us!" they both insisted.

"Well, whoever it was, this station's looking as secure as a fishnet!" Wilburn yelled. "With Gavil Harrison's name now plastered all over the news, we'd *better* come up with something in a hurry." Stress lined the Chief's forehead. "This psychic stuff is stirring the media into a total frenzy!"

"It's not psychic," Reiger said.

"Then just what would you call it?"

Reiger could have kicked himself. Why had he opened his mouth? Then thoughts from his sleepless Saturday night flicked across his mind. How long would he be such a coward? "She said it was a vision from God."

"What*ever.*" Chief Wilburn waved a hand. "The bottom line is, those gloves better match. And it better be enough for an arrest. Because if you don't get something solid on this guy and get it soon, we're headed for trouble."

"Hey, Reiger, you with me?" Hal motioned him down the hall.

Reiger blinked. "Yeah. Coming."

In a small room, Hal opened Reiger's bag and removed a glove. With one snip of a scissors, he cut away a fiber sample and positioned it gently under the microscope. Then he selected one of the fibers found under Meg's fingernails and laid it alongside the first. Reiger stood rooted to the floor, praying.

Hal leaned over and gazed through the microscope for what seemed an interminable amount of time. "Well, what do you know." He straightened. "Take a look."

Reiger bent to peer through the microscope. The fibers below looked like two large tubes, crisscrossed many times over. They also looked very much alike.

"It's twins." Hal put out a hand. "Congratulations, man."

~ ~ ~

Gavil drove along the winding road, a map on the seat beside him. Good thing Paul Adams was listed in the phone book. Chasing down his home address would not have been easy under the circumstances.

After Adams smashed down the phone in Gavil's ear Saturday night, he'd sat frozen in his hotel room. He couldn't believe what he'd done. He never intended to be so hostile when he called, but the anger just frothed out of him.

Then the detectives showed up. Turnbow's near punch put an end to any of Gavil's self-incriminating thoughts.

He had all the right in the world to be furious.

Now, in spite of what he was about to do, he felt calm. And he was rested. He'd actually slept all night. The weekend had been beyond belief, but now that his rage and fear had settled, he knew

188

what he had to do. He didn't care about the cops' warnings. A week ago, he'd never have imagined planning such a thing. But then, look where he'd been a week ago.

What did he have to lose now?

Number 1284. Gavil slowed to peek up a curved driveway that disappeared into redwoods. Through the trees he glimpsed the outline of a large contemporary house. He drove a little farther until he came to an old gravel road.

Perfect.

Turning onto the gravel, he followed it a short distance until his bumper rested against a thick chain hung across the road, bearing a "No Trespassing" sign. He turned off the engine, slid out of his BMW, and tapped shut the door. He paused a moment and looked around, listening.

All quiet.

Satisfied, he pocketed his keys and began the short journey to the Adams' home.

~ ~ ~

Reiger exhaled in relief. "There's more." Reaching into a brown paper sack, he pulled out the fertilizer. "I think this is your 'rich' dirt."

Hal made a face. "You mean I walked all the way to that gully this weekend for no reason?"

"You get a dirt sample?"

"Yeah. I haven't run it yet. If your stuff matches, we'll need to run my sample to make sure it doesn't." Hal's shoes squeaked as they walked into the spectrometer room. "There's my baby." He indicated the row of machinery. "So what is this stuff?"

"This all came to me while I was watching my wife garden." Reiger handed over the bag. "We went back to our suspect's house and found the gloves and this. Look at the ingredients. They're exactly the ones you came up with when you ran the dirt sample."

Hal read the contents and scratched his chin. "You're right about that. But how would she get the stuff under her fingernails?"

Reiger shrugged. "She fought back, Hal. If the perp was wearing the gloves, those long nails of hers probably scraped off some stuff."

"I saw way too much dirt under her fingernails for that, Reiger. It doesn't sound right to me." Hal hesitated. "Well, anyway, let's see what we've got."

~ ~ ~

Chelsea was in the upstairs laundry room sorting clothes when her hand stopped, midair.

What was that?

It sounded like the quiet hiss of metal on metal as a sliding glass door opened. Her breath caught.

She dropped a pair of socks and tiptoed out to the hall, where she could gaze down the stairway to the main floor below. All was still. She stood listening for a minute, heart skipping. Her eyes scanned the length of the entryway hardwood floor, back and forth, back and forth.

Nothing.

Chelsea, you've got the alarm on, remember? And the two sliding doors are locked.

She took a deep breath. Wow. She was definitely on edge.

With a final downward glance, she retraced her steps to the laundry room.

~ ~ ~

Hal spooned some fertilizer onto a plate to view under the electron microscope and waited for results on the screen. These he compared to the graph he'd stored under the file labeled "Trent." The computer showed identical peaks.

"Look at that!" Reiger jabbed at the screen. "I knew it!"

"Hm." Hal went through the process again, this time with the dirt he'd collected from Trent Park. It was nowhere near a match.

190

He pushed his chair away from the computer and stared at Reiger, contemplating their discovery.

"What is it?"

Hal thought another moment, then reached for the paper bag containing Marian's gloves. "Now how do you suppose all that fertilizer got under your victim's fingernails?" He tapped the bag. "Say the perp did wear these gloves, and she clawed at them. I still say that wouldn't do it."

Reiger frowned. "So ..."

"You said your wife's a gardener, right?" Hal opened the bag and pulled out a glove. "Let's check something out."

Hal pushed each finger of the glove in on itself until he could turn the entire thing inside out. Particles of dirt fell onto the table. These he collected and positioned under an electron microscope for examination. Then once more, he consulted his computer.

First results were inconclusive. They looked somewhat like the dirt collected from under Meg's fingernails but didn't match completely. Thinking aloud, Hal said the dirt from inside the glove probably had particles from various dirt sources—the fertilizer and a garden. He tried again, scraping more bits off the table to examine. The third time it worked. The screen showed a perfect match.

"There you go, Reiger."

The sergeant shook his head. "So you're thinking ..."

"Ever notice how your wife's nails get dirty when she gardens even though she always wears a pair of these?" Hal indicated the gloves. "That's because the fingers get worn. These things get old enough and, after a while, just about as much dirt finds its way inside as there is in the garden. So you wear them and your hands still get filthy."

Reiger gave a slow nod. "I get where you're going."

Hal shrugged. "Yup. Looks like it. The murderer wasn't wearing these gloves. The *victim* was."

Chapter 32

Chelsea closed the washing machine lid and pushed in the silver dial.

She heard another noise. A footfall on a hardwood floor?

The machine whooshed into action. She yanked the starter back out and waited, nerves tingling, while the spray of water gave way to drips. After an eternity, it trickled to a stop.

Chelsea cocked her head to listen.

Nothing. Just her own breathing.

She sighed. One imagined sound she could ignore. But two ... What to do?

She could slip into the master bedroom and lock the door, call Sergeant Reiger. And tell him ... what exactly?

This was ridiculous. What she needed to do was go downstairs, look around, and put her mind to rest. While there, she'd check all the doors, just to appease her imagination.

Chelsea turned toward the stairs.

Fear slithered around her shoulders.

She crept across the hall carpet to the top of the steps. Stopped to listen again. Down in the living room the grandfather clock ticked. With one hand on the banister and the other sliding down the wall, she lowered herself one step at a time.

Her recent nightmare flashed across her mind. *A tread. Another. Blood trailing across the wall.* Chelsea tried to shake the thought away.

Halfway down, she froze, eyes sweeping all she could view. She was being stupid. A minute from now she'd see everything was fine. But her body wouldn't believe that. Her heart thumped in her ears.

Three more stairs. Her tongue dried out, stuck to the roof of her mouth.

Two.

Both ankles shook with each deliberate step. *Beige carpet beneath a running shoe.* One. She eased off the last stair onto the parquet floor of the entrance.

Which way should she go? The sliding glass doors were in the kitchen and living room. The living room was closest.

Chelsea turned left toward it, her sock feet silent on the thick Persian runner that ended at the doorway. Her lungs begged for more oxygen. She pulled in air.

A breeze through sequoias.

Almost there. Five steps and she could lean around the corner to see the whole room. It would be empty, of course. Four steps. Three. *The smell of eucalyptus.* She shuddered at the thought of straining her neck around the doorway. What if he *was* there? What could she possibly do?

Run like mad.

Hands reaching for her throat.

Two steps. She could touch the doorpost. One, and she was almost even with it. Another gulp of air. With a final shuffle, she placed a hand against the wall and hunched forward, every sinew snapping with tension. *A coyote howling.* She leaned in until one eye could see around the doorway. Her gaze swept the long room. The chair nearby. Across the fireplace. The piano at the far end.

Gavil moved beside the couch at that end, eyes on his feet.

Chelsea's brain exploded. She scrambled backwards and slipped on the hardwood.

Gavil's head jerked up. He ran toward her, banged his shoulder against the doorway. Chelsea screamed and lunged for the stairs. She hit the first step. Tripped. Scrabbled on all fours. The top was so far away! She could hear Gavil, feel his breath on her feet. She neared the top and wrapped her hand around the banister. *Pull!*

Gavil caught hold of her foot and yanked.

Chelsea hung on and flailed both legs. She kicked Gavil in the head, the face.

He fought to hold her legs down. "Stop! I won't hurt you!"

Sweat lathered her hands. They slipped from the post. Gavil yanked again. She rolled over to face him, punched with both fists. Her right fist caught him in the eye. He growled, then threw himself on top of her. She screamed. He pinned her arms, her legs.

She strained to free herself, lunged up to bite him. He jerked backwards. They slid down one stair. She tried to scream again. Gavil slapped a palm over her mouth, his breath hot on her face.

Chelsea wrenched her jaw loose and bucked under his weight. They slid down another step, then another. She fought until they had tumbled down every stair. By the time they reached the bottom, every ligament burned. She stared at Gavil wide-eyed, gasping for breath between his bruising fingers.

She lay still.

"That's better." His voice was low. "Now, I'm going to take my hand away from your mouth, and you will not scream. Understand?"

Chelsea snorted, nodding once.

Slowly, Gavil unwound his fingers. "That's good. Good girl." He breathed raggedly. "Now we're going to get up. And we'll walk into the kitchen. Then we're going to sit down and talk. That's all. Just talk."

He extricated his arms and legs from Chelsea's and stood, pulling her up. Her whole body shook. She should run again—but where? He'd only catch her. Gavil stood a good seven inches taller and outweighed her by at least fifty pounds. She didn't stand a chance.

All she could do now was ... whatever he wanted. Anything to stay alive.

~ ~ ~

Henry Morrow spread his hands. "We're in the middle of a discussion here, can't it wait?"

"No. I just need to check on home." Paul pushed his chair away from the conference table and hurried out of the room before his lead investor could protest further.

In his office he picked up the phone and dialed home.

Busy.

He frowned. They had call waiting. The only way to get a busy signal was if Chelsea was talking on one line with a caller holding on the second.

Paul tapped his desk. Chelsea knew he'd be calling to make sure she was all right. She shouldn't be tying up both lines.

Maybe he dialed the wrong number.

He clicked the receiver and repunched seven digits.

Still busy.

"Hey, Paul."

He jumped at the sound of his administrative assistant's voice. Paul hung up the phone and blinked at her distractedly. "Huh?"

"Are you out of the meeting already? I didn't see anyone leave." She hustled toward his desk. "I've been trying to find that letter—"

"Not now." He wagged a hand at her. "I'm still in the meeting."

"Oh. But you're here."

"Just let me make this call, okay?"

Janet eyed him, then left.

Paul picked up the phone again.

~ ~ ~

Chelsea slumped in a kitchen chair, her back to the counter where their phone lay off its hook. A *beep-beep* sounded from the receiver. After a few minutes, it stopped.

195

Gavil scraped his chair close and grasped her jaw, forcing her eyes to his. "Now we're going to talk. And you're going to listen. When it's all over, you'll think differently about me. And if you don't, we'll start at the beginning until you do."

Chelsea's chin quivered. *Help me, Lord!* Her heart banged double-time. Her face burned. She couldn't stand to look at Gavil.

"I don't know why you say I killed that girl. I don't know how you knew about this murder or who you're trying to protect. But you picked the wrong guy to scapegoat."

Lies. Chelsea tore her face away. Gavil snatched her chin again and shook it. Her head rattled.

"*Look* at me when I'm talking to you!"

Tears scratched her eyes. She forced her gaze to his face.

"Now I'm going to tell you everything. And then you're going to tell those crazy cops you've had yourself a new 'vision.' Understand?"

She managed a nod.

Gavil began his story slowly, as though talking to a small child. He left Marian's townhouse on Tuesday night, he said, after she phoned him, something she always did when she traveled. He drove to Atherton, to the home of a close friend, who was also out of town. His wife was home alone. Gavil and this woman had been having an affair for over six months. With Marian gone, and the woman's husband gone, it was a chance to spend a night together. Wednesday morning, Gavil and the woman lingered in bed, even though he had plenty to do at the office. He left for work about 9:30.

Infidelity was his weakness, Gavil said. Because of it, he'd managed to ruin every serious relationship he'd ever had.

Gavil told Chelsea about Sonya Hocking, a woman who'd married into money. A woman whose public persona of generosity covered her searing ambition. For all her charitable work, she was self-centered. He just hadn't realized how much.

Now it was too late. She'd panicked and lied to the police, and she wouldn't turn back. She would protect herself, whatever the cost. Even if the cost was Gavil Harrison's hide.

"I know the cops are talking to her friends. But they won't find anyone who knows about the affair. We hid it too well. That's why, right now, it's just her word against mine."

Chelsea's throat felt so dry. "What do you want from me?"

"What do I *want* from you?" Gavil's face twisted. He pushed to his feet. "*Look* what you've done to me! You've turned my life upside down! I didn't kill that girl! You *know* that."

Odd sounds spilled from Chelsea's lips. She slipped off her chair to the floor and cowered against the wall, hands raised to her face.

Knives.

The thought whirled through her head. Gavil was only a few steps away from her wooden block of cutlery.

He lurched toward her, shoving her chair aside.

"No, *please!*"

He towered over her, fisting his hands. Then his face cleared. He held out a palm.

"Come on. Get up."

Chelsea peered at him. His hand hung in the air.

"Come on. I'm not here to hurt you."

Shaking, she placed a hand in his and pulled herself up.

Gavil sat down. Motioned for her to do the same.

She obeyed.

He glared at her. "Tell me the truth. *Why* are you doing this?"

How to answer? "You know I did have a vision. You were with me. At the restaurant."

His face blackened.

"But maybe I was wrong." She jerked her head in a nod. "That's it. I was wrong."

Gavil's expression smoothed. "That's more like it." He nodded. "Now. Let's go over it again."

~ ~ ~

Paul dialed his home phone a third time. Still busy. He punched the number again.

Beep-beep, beep-beep.

He banged down the receiver.

One more thing to try.

He snatched up the telephone and hit zero. Four rings. Where was the operator?

"Thank you for calling Pacific Bell."

"This is an emergency. I'm dialing 555-0440 and the line's busy. I need you to break through for me."

"Just a moment, sir."

Paul shifted on his feet. He *would* hear his wife's voice. She would be all right.

"Sir? I'm sorry, that phone is off the hook."

Dread stuck a finger in Paul's chest. "Thanks." He smashed down the receiver.

Off the hook? She wouldn't do that. Not today.

A horrible thought filtered across his brain.

With clumsy hands Paul flipped through his Rolodex. C, M, P, T—Titan Electronics. He jabbed the digits on the phone. After two rings, a receptionist answered. "Gavil Harrison, please." His voice was tight.

"I'm sorry, Mr. Harrison hasn't come in yet today."

"*What?* Where is he?"

"I don't know. He was supposed to be here for a sales meeting, but he hasn't shown up."

No, no!

"You're *sure* he's not there?"

"Yes. Do you want to leave a mes—?"

Paul threw down the phone and ran out of his office, crashing into Janet. "Call 911!" He grabbed her by the shoulders. "You hear? Call 911 and give them my home address. I think Chelsea's in trouble!"

Before she could respond Paul shoved her aside, pushed through the double doors, and pounded down the building stairwell, two steps at a time.

Chapter 33

"No!" Gavil banged the table with his fist. "I left her house at 9:30, not 8:30. Why can't you get it?"

"Okay, okay!" Tears ran down Chelsea's face. Gavil had made her repeat every detail of his alibi again and again. Her frayed nerves were worn thin. How long had this gone on?

How had he gotten through that sliding door? She'd checked it just last night, knowing she'd find it locked. They hadn't used that door in weeks. Why hadn't it tripped the burglar alarm?

And *why* did it make any difference now what she believed? Couldn't Gavil see the police were beyond that?

Chelsea needed to go to the bathroom, needed water. But she didn't dare ask.

If she could just get to the control pad of the burglar alarm, she could hit the panic button—the star and pound signs pressed together. That alarm was silent, sending a flash to the computers of the security company.

But would that happen? Or was the whole system not working?

Chelsea forced her eyes not to drift to the control pad. It was on the wall, on the other side of the table.

"Yes. I hear you." She forced herself to calm. "It was 9:30."

Her mind ticked through possibilities.

~ ~ ~

Paul hit the highway and revved the Lexus to seventy, eighty, ninety. He evened off at one hundred, careening up the fast lane, honking at cars in his path. He took one hand off the steering wheel to reach for his cell phone. Holding the phone up high, he darted his eyes from the road to the buttons and back as he punched in Sergeant Reiger's number. Twice his hand slipped. Twice he redialed.

He was closing in on two cars.

"Aahh!" Paul dropped the phone and clutched the steering wheel with both hands to shoot around them. They blurred white and blue as he sped past.

He fumbled for the phone again.

On the fourth dial, he got a ring.

~ ~ ~

Reiger slid into his car, his mind on the gloves. All worries about the media and Chief Wilburn were gone. Along with his theories of why the gloves had been used. Reiger snapped on the seat belt in his hot vehicle and opened a window. He pulled out of the parking lot, driving by rote.

Maybe Meg had borrowed the gloves. But Marian would have told them that. Besides, Meg had a fresh manicure. Girls with long red fingernails weren't likely to garden.

Reiger pictured Harrison carrying the gloves to the park, luring Meg down a trail, forcing her to put on the gloves, smashing her head against a rock. Taking the gloves off the corpse. Pushing her down the gully. Carrying the gloves home. Putting them away.

Why?

To keep her from touching him? Scratching him? If he'd been worried about evidence, like his skin under her nails, he'd have disposed of the gloves, which carried evidence of their own.

Were they part of some dark ritual?

Wouldn't a killer as twisted as this strike again?

Reiger turned left onto El Camino.

He had to get Harrison off the streets. Now.

When he got to the station, he should call Harry Seltz, deputy district attorney. Reiger had assured Paul Adams that Harrison would be arrested if the gloves were a match. But it wasn't always that easy. If the evidence was too circumstantial, Seltz wouldn't go for the case.

He prayed the gloves would be enough.

Reiger's pager cut through his thoughts. He reached for his car phone and called the station.

The message from dispatch snapped him to attention.

He barked orders into the phone, then slapped a portable flashing light on top of his car. His siren keened as he skidded around a corner and flew toward the freeway.

~ ~ ~

Gavil's desperation sparked like a live wire. He paced back and forth, back and forth between the kitchen table and far counter, eyes fixed on Chelsea. Over and over, he recited his facts. Went to Atherton Tuesday night, went to work the next morning at 9:30, got to the office at 10:00. If she so much as batted an eyelash, he was in her face.

Chelsea prayed every time he ricocheted past the knives. Cold sweat beaded on her arm. "Please." She licked her lips. "I need some water."

Gavil's eyes glinted. "Stop your whining. I'll get you a drink."

She pointed to the cabinet that held glasses. Then watched, muscles tense, as he circled the center island. A band closed around her chest. This was her chance. Breath whooshed in her nostrils as she waited for him to take his eyes off her. A few seconds would do it. Chelsea saw herself lunging around the table, hitting the panic button. Her hands pressed against the chair, her thighs gathered to spring.

Gavil was two steps from the cabinet. Adrenaline puddled in her chest. Every gland in her mouth drained.

Don't throw up.

He opened the cabinet. His head disappeared behind its door.
Now!

Chelsea leapt from her seat and scrambled around the table, nearly falling over Gavil's chair. In peripheral vision, she saw his head snap around, his body roll into motion. He flew behind her, caught her around the waist, and yanked her away.

"Ungh!" Chelsea jabbed both elbows back, hitting him in the stomach. Air gushed from him. He staggered. She wrestled free, straining toward the alarm.

He swayed toward her again and grabbed her shirt. She brought down her left hand hard, sank nails into his wrist. Her right arm stretched before her like a limb on a torturer's rack. She was close, so close.

Her fingertips grazed the control pad.

"Stop!" Gavil yanked her hair. Chelsea's head jerked back, and the control panel fell away.

She lunged for it again.

Time jolted into slow motion as they struggled. Her fingers strained … strained … the panic buttons just out of reach. With a final push, she felt their smoothness. Then they melted away.

Gavil's arm crooked around her neck. "So this is it, huh, Chelsea." He pushed her to the floor. "You just want to *destroy* me."

Chelsea gulped air. She dared not look at his face.

~ ~ ~

Paul sliced the Lexus over two lanes to careen around cars, then skidded back to the fast lane. Both hands gripped the wheel. His eyes fixed on the road.

God, protect her. Please! I'll do anything.

He never should have gone to work. He would never forgive himself—or God—if anything happened to Chelsea.

An approaching wail. Paul's eyes flicked to the rearview mirror. A highway patrol car closed in behind. Yes!

He was ten miles from Woodside Road. Would his heart last that long? His car sucked up cement, but it wasn't fast enough. Every minute that passed, every second, filled him with dread.

A second highway patrol appeared, pulled even with his car. The one behind him strained closer. Paul sped up. They stayed with him. He sped up more. So did they.

Then he realized they weren't there to help. They were shielding him from other cars, trying to force him to the left shoulder near the grass median. He wouldn't make his exit.

"Stop! Get away!"

His voice reverberated inside the car.

Paul clutched the steering wheel with his left hand and groped for the cell phone again. Snatching it up, he punched the recall button.

"This is Paul Adams! Get the two highway patrols off me!"

Could the Haverlon station reach highway patrol headquarters in time for him to make the Woodside exit?

Paul eased off the accelerator a little. His speed dropped back to one hundred.

~ ~ ~

"You *will* say I didn't kill her!"

Chelsea shivered on the floor as Gavil ranted.

"You started all of this, you can end it. Now get up!"

Lord, help!

What would Gavil do to her now? He looked so *incensed*.

From nowhere, the faces of Michael and Scott flashed before her. How could they live if something happened to their mother? How could Paul live?

Righteous anger flooded her.

Gavil reached to pull her off the floor.

She drew away. "Don't *touch* me."

He started at her sudden vehemence.

"You're not going to touch me again."

Chelsea wrapped her hand around a chair and pulled to her feet. She teetered once, gripped the chair until she felt stable, then straightened. Raising her head, she looked Gavil in the eye.

In the distance, a siren whooped.

The sound swiveled Chelsea toward the cutlery block. She grabbed the first knife she could reach. Out *hissed* her wide-blade French chef knife. She grasped the handle with both hands and spun to face Gavil, an arm's length away. With a vengeance she had not known she possessed, she swung the knife in wide arcs. He jumped back and raised his arms. The blade nicked his shirt.

The wailing grew closer. More than one siren.

She swung again. "I've got two children!" *Swing.* "And they're not ..."

Swing!

"... going to grow up ..."

Swing!

"... without a mother!"

Gavil kept moving back, and she followed. When he hit the wall, she planted her feet apart and pointed the knife at him like a gun, daring him to move. Her hands shook.

"You're not going to touch me again. I'll kill you first."

They faced each other in a standoff, faces distorted. Then Gavil lashed out a foot and kicked the knife upward. It flew high out of her hands, tumbling once, twice through the air. Chelsea's brain pleaded for her to chase it, but her legs locked tight. The knife clattered to the floor.

Outside the house, squad cars shrieked.

"Help!" Chelsea turned and raced for the door.

~ ~ ~

Woodside Road was one exit away. Still the highway patrols blocked Paul. With two miles to go, he slowed down. His pursuers did the same. He lifted his foot more, dropping the speedometer to eighty-five.

He flipped on his right blinker. *Come on!*

Paul glanced at the car beside him. The policeman was reaching for his radio. Paul looked in the rearview mirror. The second cop was doing the same.

A large green sign, indicating Woodside Road a quarter mile ahead, flashed by.

The patrol to his right dropped back.

Paul slid in front of it. With no other cars in the way, he crossed all lanes and onto his exit.

The patrol cars followed.

He sped down Woodside and fishtailed onto Pennhill Lane. The winding road seemed eternal. Skidding onto his long driveway, he caught sight of his house, littered out front with squad cars and police. Paul's heart turned to ice. He screeched to a stop, spotting a detective he guessed to be Reiger running toward him.

"We've tried every door." Reiger's breath came in huffs. "All locked. Our megaphone hasn't gotten any response."

Paul hit his garage door opener, snatched his keys from the ignition, and fell out of the car. "Here!" he shoved the keys at Reiger. "Take the front door, I'll go through the garage."

He flew past the Range Rover parked in the garage toward the kitchen door. Two policemen beat him to it.

Locked.

Paul sped back out the garage and up the wide stone steps leading to his front porch. He shoved past Reiger and two backups as they threw open the door. "Stay outside!" Reiger yelled.

Paul burst across the threshold.

He slid to a halt.

The house was so still.

"There!"

Reiger's shout sent three heads swiveling. Paul saw Gavil Harrison leap over the family room couch and rush toward the library. In seconds the man was tackled and pinned to the floor.

"Chelseeeaa!" Paul raced to the kitchen and panned the room. Empty. Normal.

Then his eyes fell on the large knife lying in the middle of the hardwood floor.

"Oh, no."

He whirled around and spurted for the stairs. "Chelsea!" He leaped two steps at a time and ran to each bedroom, bellowing his wife's name. Nothing in Michael's room. Nothing in Scott's. Ahead danced the guest suite. He banged around the corner. Empty. He raced for the master suite and skidded to a stop. An overturned shelf and books littered the floor. His shoes were tossed at odd angles. A lamp lay on its side.

Paul sucked in air and listened to the quiet.

"Chelsea?"

He heard it from the dressing area around the corner—a muffled sob. Paul's energy drained away. What would he find?

Filled with dread, he propelled himself forward, blood pounding in his veins. His neck prickled as he looked past the doorway.

The floor was littered. A makeshift arsenal.

Paul raked his eyes over brushes, razors, a long shoehorn. The broken-off handle of a back scratcher. A fingernail file. A packet of needles.

And finally, Chelsea. Huddled against the far wall, clutching a pair of scissors as if her life depended on it.

"Oh, Chelsea."

Paul's throat closed. Tears stung his eyes as his heart tried to kick into gear. With one foot, he scuffed the self-defense pile aside and dropped to his knees, burying his face in his wife's red-gold hair.

Chapter 34

Gavil Mark Harrison was booked at 11:45 A.M. in San Mateo County jail. Alleged crimes: false imprisonment, penal code number 236 (the unlawful violation of the personal liberty of another); burglary; resisting arrest; plus an accompanying assortment of police jargon delineating the errors of his ways. False imprisonment was short of kidnapping, involving the unsolicited detainment rather than the unwanted transportation of another. It was known as a "wobbler," a crime that could be either a misdemeanor or a felony, depending on the circumstances. Because of the factors of violence and menace associated with Gavil's actions, the false imprisonment was bumped to a felony, resulting in the second charge of burglary—in this context, entering with intent to commit a felony.

Reiger led Gavil Harrison through the booking procedure, talking in curt sentences, his strong right hand clamped firmly around the man's arm. Harrison flinched when they took everything away from him except the clothes on his back. His watch, his money clip, some spare change, the hotel key, belt, shoelaces. His car keys. They gave him a receipt. He was fingerprinted and photographed, front and side. His face had turned an ashen gray.

Booking complete, Reiger walked with Harrison down the hall and led him to a cell. The jail door clanged, sealing the suspect off from society.

Reiger could not push Chelsea Adams' face from his mind. She had inched down the stairway of her home, clinging to her husband like a terrorized child. Reiger hoped later that night, when darkness fell and the half moon shone, she'd be able to sleep, knowing Gavil Harrison would be behind bars for a long time.

But the sergeant had his doubts.

Yes, Gavil's actions had warranted immediate arrest. But the charges weren't good for much. Bail for false imprisonment couldn't be very high—most likely peanuts for a successful salesman. With Harrison's clean record, he could be right back out on the street.

~ ~ ~

In the deputy D.A.'s hole-in-the-wall office, Reiger sat across from Harry Seltz's desk, holding his breath. Lining the office perimeter and piled as high as two feet were stacks of files from various cases, tattered and dog-eared. To Reiger's left hung a wanted poster of a slit-eyed white male with puffy cheeks and shaggy hair. Michael "Mickey" Howlinger, convicted murderer and prison escapee. According to scuttlebutt around the D.A.'s office, Howlinger had a contract out on Seltz's life, the result of an in-the-trenches prosecution Seltz had won against him.

Reiger knew Harold R. Seltz as a man of quiet, brilliant passion. His entire legal career had been in the district attorney's office, where he'd been dedicated to mopping society's slime off the streets. Seltz's face was hardened by the things he'd seen through the years, a mirror of the barriers he'd raised to protect his soul from the pain and filth. He stood a wiry five-foot-ten and moved with the grace of a gymnast, back straight, chin up. The deputy district attorney's blue eyes could take on the coldness of a frozen winter's night as he tore apart a witness. Or they could soften when he gently probed a victim or grief-stricken parent on the stand.

Seltz was recognized throughout the county as the best in his business. Judges, cops, and bailiffs knew his name. Reiger knew defense attorneys were never happy to go up against Harold Seltz.

"So this is The Case, huh." Seltz was looking through Reiger's notes. "Gavil." He chuckled. "Sounds like a name destined for the courts." Seltz read for another moment. "You have everything in this one. Even religion."

Reiger wanted to let it pass, but something inside wouldn't let him. "Well, I wouldn't call it 'religion,' Harry. I'd call it God's intervention."

Seltz shrugged. "Religion, God, they all go together."

"Not really. Religion is anything. Bowing to Buddha, chanting a mantra, dabbling in New Age. God is ... God. Our creator."

Seltz looked almost amused. "Well, Dan Reiger! Didn't know you were into that stuff."

A pang of guilt shot through Reiger. He'd known Harry Seltz for years, longer than he'd been going to church. He forced himself not to look away, gathering his courage. "I've been a Christian since I was thirty-five."

"Oh."

Reiger could not remember ever seeing Harry Seltz at a lack for words.

"That's ... good." The deputy D.A.'s eyes fell back to the file. "Well. You're going to need any help from Up There you can get on this one. Doesn't look good."

"What's the problem?"

"The evidence won't hold. It's too common."

The words hit Reiger like bullets.

"Look at it this way. Your own wife gardens, right? She's probably got a pair of gloves like the ones from Harrison. What gardener doesn't? She uses fertilizer too, maybe even the same kind that's in Harrison's house." Seltz chuckled. "Guess what, Reiger, *Edith* could have done it."

Terrific. "What do you expect me to do?"

Seltz shrugged. "You got no fingerprints, no palm prints, no footprints, no hair, no semen, nothing. You'll have to scrape up some more evidence, something that unequivocally ties your suspect to the victim. Something that's *not* found in all the gardeners' closets in the county."

Reiger's face drained.

"Look, I'm only doing my job. You know if you can't sell *me* on the case, you won't sell the judge at the preliminary hearing."

"I don't know how I can get anything else right now." Reiger's tone was grim. "The DNA's going to take another week at least, and that could just as well turn out to be from the victim. Tell you one thing, Seltz. I am *not* leaving your office until you figure out a way to keep Harrison behind bars."

Seltz sniffed. "All right. We'll figure out something."

Reiger knew the man wasn't eager to allow Gavil Harrison back on the streets either, not after he'd chased down a wife and mother in her own home. Seltz had a thing for mothers. He'd admitted to Reiger that his own had saved him from a pot of stew a few times.

The D.A. stared at the wall, thinking. Then he reached for the bail schedule on a gray metal bookcase behind him and shuffled through its pages. "Okay. False imprisonment—$5000. Plus the burglary. And we got felonies, which makes minimum bail $10,000 anyway." He shelved the book and faced Reiger. "That kind of money's going to be pretty easy for your perp, right? So you're going to get out of my office pronto and write an affidavit to set higher bail. Let's make it, say, half a million. That ought to park him for a while."

Reiger nodded.

"There's just one catch." Seltz looked hard at Reiger. "You've got to come up with something strong enough for a murder charge before arraignment."

A deep groan.

"Look, Reiger, it's the best I can do. If Harrison stands before a judge Wednesday afternoon on $500,000 bail for false imprisonment and burglary, my head's gonna roll. Before that time, you can bet I'll have Harrison's attorney all over my back." He pointed at the sergeant. "I'm telling you, forty-eight hours is the max. You give me something good, and I'll wear bells when I file a complaint charging Gavil Harrison with murder. But you bring me nothing, your guy'll post some property bond and bail himself out of there as fast as the judge can bang his gavel."

Chapter 35

Turnbow checked the clock in his car. Forty-six hours. So little time. At 11:00 A.M. Wednesday, Gavil Harrison would be arraigned in municipal court.

The detective pictured the proceedings as he drove toward Marian Baker's house. The courtroom would be full of people waiting to be arraigned. Those in custody would be brought in by twelves and seated in the jury box. As one completed the proceedings and left the courtroom, another would fill his place. Women would be seated separately. With such high bail, Harrison likely would be handcuffed and in leg irons. And his jumpsuit would be fire-engine red. Harry Seltz and Harrison's lawyer, whoever that was, would stand with him before the judge.

Harrison. Turnbow sneered. He hoped the scumbag's face would be white. Turnbow could see him inching in his leg irons to the front of the courtroom.

Turning onto Dapple, Turnbow rolled slowly toward visitor parking. He'd phoned Marian at her office earlier to request a meeting, but the receptionist said she'd called in sick. He then reached her at home. She sounded sick all right. Sick at heart.

He hated to put her through any more questions, but he had no choice. At least he was able to come alone. Reiger was busy going over the case with Chief Wilburn.

Turnbow knocked on Marian's door and heard her footsteps approach. She managed to give him a weary smile. "Hi."

Unlike the last time Turnbow had seen her, Marian wore makeup, and her hair was fixed. Had she done that for his sake?

She led him into her living room.

They sat on opposite ends of the couch. Marian's face filled with unasked questions, the fear of knowing. Turnbow had told her nothing over the phone. He was afraid, once she heard the news, that she'd be too upset to talk further, and his own questions would go unanswered.

"Marian, before I tell you what's going on, I need to ask a few things."

"Okay."

"First, the gloves. You kept them in that back closet, right?"

She nodded.

"Did anyone else have access to them? Did you loan them to a neighbor?"

"No. Just me. I always use them and put them right back."

"But they were in the house last Thursday night, remember? Reiger noticed them on your counter. Why were they there?"

Marian's eyes drifted upward. "I don't know."

"Okay. Let me lead you through it. Remember, it was Thursday, and you were just home from work. You went on a business trip Tuesday and returned Wednesday. Now think. Where were the gloves when you left for the trip?"

She stared blankly, as if ticking through events. For the first time, he noticed the flecks of gold in her eyes.

Marian blinked. "I left them on the front porch."

Oh, great. "Go on."

"I'd finished some garden work Monday evening." Marian's expression was far away. "Just then, the phone rang. I took off the gloves and left them on the porch before running to answer it. It was long distance from a friend, and by the time we finished talking, I forgot about the gloves. The next morning, I left early for my plane. I noticed them when I walked out the door but didn't take time to put them away."

Turnbow's heart sank. When Harrison got to trial—*if* he got to trial—his attorneys would have a field day would this.

"When I got home from my trip Wednesday, they were still there. I brought them into the house and tossed them on the counter. I had work to do at home that night and forgot about them. Thursday, you came to the door soon after I got home. Later that night, I put them in the closet."

Marian looked almost proud of herself. This could be her first coherent thinking since Saturday morning.

"Let me understand you. The gloves sat on your porch from Monday night to Wednesday night? Would Gavil let them sit there all that time?"

She lifted a hand. "Gavil is neat in the house, but he doesn't pay much attention to the garden or outside."

Present tense. For some reason it irked Turnbow.

"I wasn't surprised to see them lying right where I'd left them. I'm sure he walked by and never even noticed."

Turnbow tapped a thumb on his knee. How did this puzzle piece fit? He tried to picture Harrison taking the gloves off the porch, then dropping them in the same spot afterward. If he didn't get rid of them, why hadn't he at least put them away? Maybe because Marian would expect to see them still there?

Turnbow quizzed her more about the gloves. Marian answered his questions, but something about the way she fidgeted with a pillow, eyes averted, told him he was hitting a nerve. What was she not telling him?

They fell silent. Marian gazed at him, distrust flitting across her face.

"Please." Her voice was tight. "What happened this morning?"

He dreaded this. "Okay. I owe you that."

Gently, he told her most of what he knew. Her eyes widened as he admitted that the newscast about Chelsea Adams' vision was true. At the news about the fertilizer match and Meg's wearing the gloves, her face drained white. Finally, Turnbow told her

215

what Gavil had done to Chelsea Adams and of his arrest. Marian shrank like cellophane under heat.

"No, it's impossible, he wouldn't *do* that! I can't *believe* it! I won't believe *any* of it!" She tossed the pillow aside, raking a hand through her hair. "He can't be in jail. It's not true!" Tears filled her eyes. She turned away, shame etching her face.

Turnbow reached toward her, but she shuddered from his touch. He withdrew his hand, feeling her misery. "Marian, listen to me. Please." He moved nearer, reaching out again.

"No, just leave me *alone*."

He couldn't. Three times he touched her arm. Three times she pushed him away.

"Marian, I'm so sorry you're going through this."

"Just leave me."

But she wasn't getting up, fleeing the room. She *wanted* him to hold her, she just didn't know how to say it. How to grieve for one man in the arms of another?

Turnbow slid over until he was beside her. He laid both hands on her shoulders. Her skin felt cold beneath her cotton shirt. He rubbed gently, willing her not to pull away. Eased her close. At first Marian's body felt rigid. Then she leaned against his chest.

He let her cry it out.

"Listen to me, Marian. It's a terrible time to tell you this, but I've got to. Gavil may be out of jail in a few days, and I'm afraid for you. I want you to promise me you'll change the locks on your doors. Even though you think you've got all the keys."

Marian began crying again.

"I just don't want anything to happen to you."

Marian grew still. Then raised her head to gaze at him openly, as if seeing him for the first time.

She lowered her head once more to his chest.

The curls in her hair were soft beneath his fingers.

Tuesday, June 13

Chapter 36

He should have known Harry Seltz was behind this.

The whole case was a bubble off center, as far as William S. Tanley, Esq.—Bill, to his friends—was concerned. He'd almost not taken it. A prestigious Palo Alto lawyer like himself could choose his clients. What would he want with a piddling false imprisonment arrest—except that the alleged lawbreaker turned out to be Gavil M. Harrison, Silicon Valley salesman and possible suspect in the Trent Park homicide. At first, Tanley had decided to shelve the part about Gavil's being a murder suspect. Best to deal with the charges at hand. That was until he heard that his client's bail had been set at a whopping half a million. And that Harry Seltz was handling the case.

"Harry, this is William Tanley." Irritation coated the attorney's voice over the phone.

"Well, how are you, Bill? Haven't talked to you in quite a while." Seltz's tone was ever so friendly.

Two years and three months, as a matter of fact, thought Tanley. The climax of their last trial together. Seltz had mesmerized the jury with his closing remarks, and Tanley's client had been convicted for kidnapping and attempted murder. Tanley had disliked Seltz ever since. And Seltz's ingratiating way of calling him "Bill" didn't smooth any feathers.

"Seems we got a little problem here, Harry."

Seltz agreed that, sure enough, there was a minor problem with the Gavil Harrison case that had resulted in bail being set a little higher than usual.

"Half a million dollars, and all you can say is it's 'a little higher than usual'?"

"Well, we've got some extenuating circumstances. Nothing I can discuss at this time. That should all be resolved by tomorrow."

"Don't give me any of your runaround, Harry! I've already got reporters calling, assuming my client's gonna be charged with Trent Park. You have something solid on him, you'd better tell me about it! Otherwise, I don't want that murder even *mentioned* in court!"

"Sure, Bill, we'll see what happens. See you tomorrow."

The phone clicked in Tanley's ear.

He slammed down the receiver and cursed. He'd see Harold Seltz tomorrow in court, all right.

He'd see him *fry*.

~ ~ ~

Two days ago, Marian had placed it in one of those small clear plastic vials used for storing contacts. She hadn't had the nerve to look at it since.

Gathering her courage, she opened the door of her medicine cabinet and took out the vial. It felt smooth in her hand, almost weightless. She examined its contents, mouth twisting. Marian shut the cabinet door and glimpsed her image in the mirror. She looked terrible. Red eyes, puffy face, gray-white skin.

Marian turned away from the sight.

What should she do with this thing? Part of her wanted to bury it, flush it down the toilet, send it through the garbage disposal. Destroy the evidence, this dirty blotch, and Gavil might go free. Free to walk the streets, go back to work—if they'd still have him. Free to be with her. Turn over this piece of evidence to police, and Gavil would be charged with murder. There'd be a trial. Jail. Attorneys, judges, courtrooms.

How could she survive that? How could she live with herself knowing what she'd done to Gavil?

219

But *she* wouldn't be to blame, Gavil would.

Who *was* this man? Not the one she'd known.

Had she ever really known him?

Marian weighed the vial in her hand. *What* should she do? How many lives would be affected by her choice?

The plastic seemed hot in her fingers. For an instant, she imagined the thing sprouting legs and escaping like some hideous beetle.

Marian shuddered.

On impulse she yanked open the medicine cabinet, shoved the bottle onto a shelf, and slammed the door.

Spreading her hand against the white bathroom tile, she stared at herself in the mirror for a long time.

~ ~ ~

Not one new lead. Reiger could hear the click ticking.

He and Turnbow had spent the night playing scenarios off each other, an exercise in futility. When Tuesday dawned—the Bay Area's fifth day in a row with no fog—they began once more making the rounds, talking to neighbors, poring over notes. How many times could they ask the same questions, hit the same dead ends?

Their only hope seemed to lie in their new profile of Gavil Harrison—a purposeful, cunning killer with a fetish for gloves. They called all jurisdictions within a two-hundred-mile radius, looking for similar unsolved homicides. Turnbow had already checked with the jurisdiction in which Gavil had previously lived, but they tried again, hoping their newfound information would trigger something. Anything.

Two o'clock. Reiger trudged from a breezeless eighty-eight degrees into the cool lobby of the Haverlon police station, wiping sweat from his forehead—and met with promising news. Six months ago, Turnbow told him, a blonde woman, twenty-eight years old, had been found on a rural street two miles from her house in Fremont across the Bay, dead from a blow to the back of the head. A boyfriend had been the immediate suspect but was later cleared. Three important facts could possibly connect the murder with the Trent Park case. First, the woman had commuted to work in the Silicon Valley area. Second, six months ago, Gavil had lived alone in his San Jose condo, which would give him more opportunity to stalk and kill someone farther away from his own neighborhood. And third, the victim had been wearing gloves. At the time, the investigating officers had not found that suspicious, since the murder had occurred on a cold, rainy day in January.

With renewed energy, Reiger drove down the highway and across Dumbarton Bridge to review the homicide in more detail. Turnbow stayed behind to run down any information his partner might phone in. By the time Reiger reached Fremont it was 3:30. He checked his watch as he hurried through the police station doors. So little time. If this long shot were to yield any usable information, he'd have to gather it today. That would give him enough time the next morning to book Gavil for homicide, and for Seltz to issue a second complaint to add to his first for false imprisonment and burglary. Harrison could then be arraigned on all counts at the hearing.

Officer Tom Felder, a detective in the Crimes Against Persons Unit handling the homicide investigation, briefed Reiger on details of the Laura Jackson murder and offered autopsy and forensics reports. Laura had been killed sometime Thursday morning, January 10. Exactly where the crime had occurred was still unknown. The body had been dumped off the side of a little-used road and had lain undiscovered until that evening. The police had no fingerprints or witnesses, but they had lifted a shoeprint with some clear characteristic markings. Plus, they'd found a few foreign hairs on the victim's body.

Reiger listened to the details, masking his reaction. Evil in the world was such an ugly thing. Sometimes he wished he were anything but a policeman. "What was the victim like?"

"A career person, pretty bright. Worked in computer sales. Lived alone but had a steady boyfriend."

"How did she dress? Flirty, heavy makeup?"

Felder thought for a moment. "No, I wouldn't say that. In general she was the picture of a young all-American girl working hard to get ahead in life."

Reiger scratched his chin. "I don't have much time. I'll pick up a quick search warrant for the shoe, see if we can match your print. Then there's the hair."

Felder made a face. "Yeah, well, you know you can't get that easily. Your guy's attorney won't allow it."

"I know."

Reiger called Turnbow, asking him to check on Harrison's whereabouts at the time of Laura Jackson's death. No point in wasting energy on this if Gavil was meeting with a computer chip company in Japan that week.

The sergeant checked his watch again. Four-thirty. He shook hands with Felder. "Thanks a lot. Let's hope this works out."

~ ~ ~

As soon as Turnbow hung up from Reiger's call, he phoned Titan Electronics and asked for Gavil's secretary. The woman's tone cooled when Turnbow identified himself. He'd have to tread lightly.

"Ma'am, I need some information regarding Gavil Harrison's whereabouts on the morning of January tenth this year. Can you check his calendar for any meetings or appointments he may have had at that time?"

"I'm sorry, Mr. Harrison always keeps his own calendar and books his own meetings. All I do in that area is make travel arrangements." The calendar was a small black notebook, she said, probably in his briefcase.

Turnbow thanked her and hung up. Nothing was ever easy. One lousy piece of information, and it sat in the briefcase. Yesterday, a patrolman had cleaned out Harrison's rented room at the Welthing Hotel, taking his belongings back to Marian's house.

If, by chance, she'd stayed home from work again, she could look for the calendar. *If* Turnbow could persuade her.

He reached for the phone.

On the third ring, she answered.

"Hi. It's Pat Turnbow."

Awkward silence.

Turnbow knew he'd crossed a line yesterday, one that could get him in serious trouble. It was a common temptation between a vulnerable victim and officer, and so had been addressed within the culture of police work. Bottom line—*don't* do it.

"Marian, sorry to bother you again. I need some more information." He told her his request.

Marian balked. What was happening? Why did he need to know where Gavil was on that day?

Irritation washed through Turnbow. Why couldn't she just trust that it was important?

"Look, I just need your help right now. Later, when we have more time, I'll explain it to you."

She finally agreed. Gavil's black appointment book would be in his briefcase. She'd shoved all his belongings into his closet. "I can't stand to look at them."

The comment pleased Turnbow more than he cared to admit.

"I'll go through the briefcase and call you back."

"Thanks."

Turnbow hung up and stared out the window. Seemed like all of Haverlon had ground to a halt, waiting for him and Reiger to pull a miracle out of a bag. Gavil sitting in a jail cell, Marian crying in her townhouse. How would she feel after tomorrow's hearing? If Gavil was freed, would she be glad? Would she take him back?

Turnbow knew Paul Adams had also stayed home from work. Mrs. Adams was having a difficult time turning a corner in her house alone. Reiger had been in Turnbow's office when he remembered to check on her. Of course, Adams wanted to know what was happening with the case. Reiger had to warn him things were shaky, but they were doing their best. Adams was so relieved over Chelsea's safety, all he could do was thank Reiger. "I'm not worried," Reiger had reported his saying. "I know you'll get him."

Which, Turnbow sighed, laid more weight on their shoulders than if the man had yelled his head off.

The phone rang. Turnbow snatched it up.

Marian sounded all business. "I remember now after looking at his calendar. He left for a convention in Houston on Tuesday of that week and didn't return until Thursday evening."

Turnbow brought a hand to his eyes. "Are you sure?"

"Yes. The reason I remember is because Gavil took his car in for repair while he was gone. I picked him up at the San Jose airport Thursday, he stayed with me that night, and the next morning we got his car."

"Are you sure he went to the convention?"

Annoyance edged her voice. "Well, I know I called him at the hotel late Wednesday night. Late for him, anyway, there's a two-hour time difference."

"What hotel?"

"I think it was the Hyatt near the airport."

Could Harrison have had time to leave Houston, fly to San Jose, drive to Fremont, commit murder, then get back to Texas for his flight home? "When you picked him up at the airport, did you wait outside at the curb or meet him at the gate?"

"At the gate."

"So you saw him get off the plane."

224

"Yes."

"You're sure."

"Yes."

At the firmness in her voice, Turnbow understood. The unexpected smile, a welcoming kiss at the end of the plane ramp. It had been a romantic thing to do.

"What *is* it?" Marian asked. "What's going on?"

Turnbow would track down records, ensure that Harrison was at the convention and on the plane. But at this point it sounded like a dead end.

Disappointment lumped like cornstarch in his throat. "It's nothing."

~ ~ ~

Thirty minutes later, Reiger puffed in. "What'd you find out?"

Turnbow hated to tell him. His partner hadn't looked this energized since yesterday's arrest. Now it was all sliding away. "No dice." He related the news. "I called the hotel and they found the record. Harrison checked out Thursday morning."

Reiger's shoulders sagged. He fell into a chair opposite Turnbow and stared out the window.

A minute ticked by.

Reiger made a sound of defeat in his throat. He picked up the phone and punched in a number. Turnbow heard two rings.

"Mr. Adams, Sergeant Reiger here. I'm afraid I've got some bad news."

Turnbow could hear Paul Adams' voice drifting across his desk. The man didn't berate or yell, although at the moment, the detective felt they deserved it. Evidently, Adams had been thinking about what to do if Harrison was freed. Turnbow heard him say he'd pull his kids out of school year early and send them and their mother to Dallas, where Chelsea's parents lived.

And if Gavil came around the house again, Paul Adams promised, he'd deal with the man himself.

Wednesday, June 14

Chapter 37

Turnbow was running, running but couldn't gain on the suspect. In the distance, a vague figure reached out, called to him. From nowhere, an alarm jangled, then died, jangled, then died.

A rattle in his throat woke him.

Turnbow opened bleary eyes and tried to focus on the day lightening outside his office window. Sullen gray hung over the world. Fog. Birds chattered on the telephone line across the street.

Wednesday. Just hours before Gavil Harrison's arraignment.

The phone jangled again.

Turnbow struggled to raise his upper body off the desk. His neck ached something fierce. His left arm, stretched out, tingled down to his fingers. Turnbow pulled himself up and blinked. He and Reiger must have compared notes until 3:00 A.M. He couldn't even remember laying his head down to rest.

Where was his partner now?

Another jingle rattled Turnbow's ears. He fumbled to pick up the receiver. "Turnbow." His voice sounded rusty.

"It's Marian."

"Uh-huh." His mind wasn't working.

The voice in his ear hesitated. "I ... need to see you."

"Marian?" Turnbow rubbed a hand over his eyes. "What time is it?"

"Six. Look, I need to see you. It's important."

Turnbow straightened, wincing at the pain in his upper back. "Okay. When?"

"Are you all right?" Her tone mixed worry and impatience.

"I'm fine. I just didn't get much sleep last night."

Or the night before, for that matter.

"Well, wake up, I'll be there in ten minutes."

What was this? Not the Marian he knew.

"Okay." Turnbow extended his arm toward the phone base and rattled down the receiver.

Groaning, he pulled to his feet and stumbled into the hall. The station was quiet. He started to head for the bathroom, then backtracked toward Reiger's office.

The sergeant was sitting at his desk, going over his notes. Again. Probably hadn't slept at all.

"Morning."

Reiger's head came up slowly. "Morning." Dark bags hung under his eyes, and his mouth drooped.

Turnbow felt a pang. "You been there all night?"

"Since you cashed in your chips on me, yeah." Reiger didn't sound accusing, just bone tired. All the same, Turnbow could have kicked himself for falling asleep. It hadn't done him much good anyway.

"Marian Baker just called. She's on her way over here to see me."

"Right now?" Reiger's eyes wandered to his watch. "What for?"

"I don't know." Turnbow leaned against Reiger's doorway. His neck and back still throbbed. "She said it's important."

Reiger stared at his partner. Turnbow could almost hear the gears in his head. "You think maybe she lied yesterday? Maybe Harrison really was in town that Thursday?" Reiger was grasping at straws, and Turnbow knew he realized it. "Want me to talk to her?"

"*No.*" The answer sounded more harsh than Turnbow had intended. He lightened his voice. "I'll see her."

Reiger surveyed him. "Something going on between you two?"

"Oh, Reiger, put a lid on it."

Turnbow straightened with effort and ventured back into the hallway. "I'll let you know what she wants."

Reiger remained silent.

Turnbow stumbled into the bathroom to rinse his mouth and splash cold water on his face. He stood in front of the mirror, adjusted his clothes, then swept a comb through his hair. Just dapper. Sliding the comb into his pocket, he pushed through the door and toward his office.

Marian arrived a few minutes later, her eyes bloodshot. She slipped into the chair before Turnbow's desk, barely able to look him in the face. "First I want to say," her tone was stilted, "that I haven't known this for long. I really had no idea."

Turnbow studied her. He could hear morning greetings from other officers in the hall. "Okay."

"And I'm sorry. Really sorry for all the trouble I caused."

What *was* this?

"I hope that after all this is over …" Marian flicked her hand in the air as if to erase the thought. "Anyway, here's something for you." She reached into her purse and drew out a small object. She clutched it to her chest, then placed it firmly on Turnbow's desk with a little *tap*.

He frowned at it. A small, clear bottle. Turnbow picked it up, bringing it even with his face. His eyes saw the object, but his weary brain refused to comprehend.

Marian sat motionless as he rotated the vial.

Realization hit like lightning.

Turnbow's breath hitched. He flicked off the lid and dumped the contents onto his desk.

Out fell a soiled and broken red fingernail.

Turnbow ogled it, then jerked his gaze to Marian. In her gold-flecked eyes he saw the residue of an agonizing decision. Her stillness told him even more. This wasn't just a choice between right and wrong. She was offering him herself, giving up the final link to past loyalties.

Turnbow started to reach for her hand—then stopped.

Despite Marian's sacrifice, his priorities now lay elsewhere. In one mind-boggling moment, he and his partner had reversed course, were on their way to winning, and any intimacy with the woman who'd just become their star witness would be a stupid gamble.

Turnbow shoved the nail back in the vial. *"REIGERRR!!"* He jumped up and ran for the door.

Leaving Marian, frozen, shoulders sagging, in the chair before his desk.

PART III
JUDGMENT

Honest scales and balances are from the Lord;
all the weights in the bag are of his making.

Proverbs 16:11

Monday, September 18

Chapter 38

Testimony in William Tanley's biggest case to date, *The People v. Gavil Harrison,* was scheduled to begin at 9:00 A.M. Monday, September 16, in San Mateo County Superior Court, Department 25, Justice Robert L. Benelli presiding. Robert Lawrence Benelli had nearly twenty-two years as a San Mateo County judge under his belt. Recent years had seemed to mellow him, but Tanley could remember the judge as an irascible, animated character, pounding his gavel when he decided things were getting out of hand. "This is a courtroom, not a church social!" he would yell, glaring over his reading glasses.

Jury selection had been a long ordeal. The jury now consisted of seven women and five men—a nurse, an elementary school teacher, two homemakers, a college student, three in the computer field, a retired electrician, a telephone operator, an accountant, and an airline mechanic—plus two alternates. They ran the gamut of socioeconomic level, race, color, and creed.

Before *voir dire,* or jury selection, a flurry of pretrial motions had been filed. First, as was typical, Tanley had filed to exclude all witnesses from the courtroom. They would await their calls to the stand in the small witness room off the courtroom foyer. The room was a kind of purgatory, removed from the melee of reporters in the hallway. Witnesses scheduled for a particular day would be notified by counsel. They must show up on time, then wait—sometimes hours—to be called. In his motion, Tanley had offered two exclusions he knew the prosecution would request— Reiger and Turnbow. Reiger, as officer in charge of the case, would act as helpmeet and gofer to the deputy D.A. in addition to testifying. Turnbow would also take the stand and could watch proceedings if he wanted. But Tanley knew Turnbow would be playing double-duty at the station for himself and his partner during the trial.

Motion to exclude witnesses was granted.

Tanley's second motion, which ultimately led to the third, hadn't been so easy ...

~ ~ ~

"How's it going?"

The convenience of social niceties, Tanley thought as he eyed his client over a battered table. The cloying smell of sweat, smoke, and cage-fueled fear hung over the room. On the other side of the dingy gray wall were more small and windowless rooms just like this one where the accused met with their defenders, trading scrutiny, claims of innocence, and promises—often empty—of hope.

Gavil made a face. "Just great." He looked battle worn.

"Good. Look, we have to talk about something. The burglary and false imprisonment. We can't afford to have those charges mixed up with the murder charge. They're far too prejudicial. There's no denying these charges, and when the jury sees that, they're going to believe far more easily that you did the murder."

"So what do we do?"

Tanley spelled out the options. One—he could move to have the two charges "severed." Ask for a separate trial for them, thereby keeping all evidence of the two charges out of the murder trial.

"Then what's the problem?"

Tanley exhaled. "It's likely we'll lose. Most severance motions are denied." He shrugged. "Here's a likely scenario. Seltz and I go before the judge. I argue the prejudicial nature of the charges. Seltz will give some song-and-dance about how the evidence is cross-admissible—your being in the Adams' house had to do with the murder investigation—plus it shows consciousness of guilt. And the judge will most likely go for it. He'll cite judicial economy—same defendant, same attorneys, same witnesses—might as well do it all at once, save the taxpayers some money, etc., etc. And we're stuck with one trial."

Gavil rubbed his lip. "What's option two?"

The attorney leaned in. "I've thought about it a lot, Gavil. I've consulted some colleagues. I know it's extreme, but we've got little to lose."

"And?"

"We plead no contest to the burglary and false imprisonment."

Gavil's hand smacked the table. "No!"

"Look, Gavil, it's the best we can do. Like I said, there's no question you did those things. You're going to take the rap for it, our fighting won't do any good. But it could do a whole lot of bad. It could lead straight to a murder conviction."

Gavil lifted his hands. "So at the very least I get two, three years in a place like this!"

A wince. "Maybe six."

"Six years! No *way!*"

"Look. If it's a choice between six years or being Lwopped what are you going to choose?"

Gavil needed to understand. An Lwopp—life without possibility of parole—was a definite risk. Attached to his first degree murder charge was the "special circumstance" of "lying in wait." Lying in wait, Tanley explained, carried a broad definition, meaning little more than getting the drop on the victim, thanks to some ludicrous case law. Which meant it would be fairly easy for the prosecution to prove.

The good news was that Seltz had decided against seeking the death penalty, even though in California certain special circumstances, including lying in wait, could attach capital punishment. Tanley knew the decision probably had come from the district attorney, and Seltz was merely following orders. Gavil

236

Harrison was white and a successful businessman with no previous record, so the chances of winning the death penalty were minimal. Politically, it would not be a chance the D.A. would care to take.

"I won't do it!" Gavil's face hardened. "I will *not* stay in jail! You fight *every one* of these charges, understand? If you won't, I'll get another attorney!"

Voice rising, Tanley argued that Gavil was being impulsive, emotional, stupid.

Gavil wouldn't budge. Then or the next day. Or the next. Tanley filed the papers for severance.

And lost.

~ ~ ~

The loss on the motion for severance left Tanley on the horns of another dilemma, one he hadn't discussed with Gavil.

What to do about the so-called vision from God?

By law, such phenomena were inadmissible, and an obligatory motion would ensure that no witness could speak of Chelsea Adams' imponderable vision. Tanley's problem was this: *without* the psychic evidence—which was an oxymoron if he'd ever heard one—he couldn't rationalize why his client had decided to enter the Adams' house uninvited. True, the jury may remember the circumstances through the media's reporting. But that was long ago and would be easily overshadowed by current courtroom argument. Besides, they'd be taking an oath not to use information from the media in their deliberations.

A few weeks after losing the motion, Tanley had thought about the "vision from God" as he dressed in his spacious home in Palo Alto. He considered his problem while driving down El Camino to work, sipping coffee, taking calls, pushing files. With the trial only three weeks away, he *had* to figure out what to do. He made no decision that day as he worked on other aspects of the Harrison case, but was still noodling his options as he dragged home at ten that night, undressed, and fell into bed. As he dozed off, he imagined grilling Chelsea Adams about her vision, fingers twitching at the mere anticipation.

The following morning over breakfast he considered the wild card option of allowing the psychic aspect in. If he allowed it, he could paint the picture for what it really was—a witch-hunt against his client. The police had latched on to Gavil only because of Chelsea Adams. As for Mrs. Adams, Tanley could imagine numerous avenues of questioning that would make her look like a religious freak. All he'd need were a couple of rational accountant types on the jury. Even if she had known the place and the method, why should she be right about the perpetrator? There'd been holes. She hadn't known *who* the victim was, had she, or the time, or why.

Gavil's venture into Chelsea Adams' home could then be portrayed as an innocent man desperate to clear his name. Throw in enough reasonable doubt about the murder, and the prosecution's whole case could go in the tank. One holdout would hang the jury.

The idea was gutsy, and Tanley wasn't about to make any rash decisions. He let it simmer in the back of his mind.

What if he lost?

The following afternoon, Tanley sat at his computer reviewing case law for ineffectiveness of counsel. It was a relatively new concept—the two main common law cases dating back only to 1979—that allowed a defendant found guilty to allege that his attorney had committed serious errors in handling the case. In *People v. Pope* it was ruled that a defendant who proved this could be awarded a new trial, his guilty verdict set aside. In 1984 a U.S. Supreme Court case, *Strickland v. Washington,* declared that to prove a defense attorney's representation was deficient, the defendant had to show the errors were so serious that, had they not been committed, a high probability for acquittal existed.

These motions for new trial, as they were called, were rarely won. Tanley knew that. This was due mostly to the stringent nature of *Strickland*. If a defense attorney could show *any* reasonable foundation for his tactical decisions, he could not be found ineffective.

There lay the rub. Could allowing clearly inadmissible information like psychic mumbo jumbo to be introduced into court—what's more, playing it up—be considered "reasonable"?

Tanley pictured himself on the witness stand in his own defense, trying to explain his allowance of such evidence if Harrison was Lwopped. He could hear Gavil's new attorney now. "A *lifetime in jail*, Your Honor. All because Mr. Tanley was afraid Gavil Harrison might be convicted of lesser charges and spend a mere six years in prison!" Worse yet, he'd be expected to cooperate, offering up his own reputation for the sake of his former client, who ultimately could go free if the motion for new trial was won.

A malpractice suit would surely follow.

Shaking his head, Tanley closed the file.

~ ~ ~

Less than a week later, Tanley and Seltz stood before Benelli's gleaming cherry wood desk in the judge's chambers. Tanley flapped his hands as he talked. Seltz kept his shoved in his pockets. A court reporter sat in the corner, talking quietly into the cupped megaphone of her recording machine. Surrounding them on the walls were a collection of framed certificates, a letter from a previous California governor, and photos of Benelli's trips around the world with his family. A particular favorite of Benelli's, Tanley knew, was one of him and his wife on camels amid the wave-ribbed sands of the Sahara.

Seltz was giving Tanley a hard time about his motion to exclude all reference to the vision, as if the deputy D.A. didn't know it was inadmissible.

239

"Come on, Bill." Seltz made a face. "How am I supposed to explain to the jury what Chelsea Adams was doing in the middle of nowhere when she found the body?"

"She was hiking, Seltz," Tanley shot back. "Just hiking."

"And what about the false imprisonment and burglary? How do you expect to handle that?"

Judge Benelli drummed his fingers on the arms of his black leather swivel chair. Tanley's temper flared. Seltz had no doubt guessed his quandary over the issue and was now baiting him, much to Benelli's amusement.

"The vision is highly prejudicial and has not *one ounce* of probative value, Seltz, you know that! As for the burglary, I'll handle it just fine."

Seltz's mouth opened, but the judge cut him off. "Enough, both of you." He smacked a palm on his desk. "Motion granted."

"But, Your Honor — "

"That's all there is and there ain't no more, Harry." Benelli looked over his glasses at the deputy district attorney. "I'm not going to stand for any woo-woo carryings-on in my courtroom!" He gathered papers, then rose with an air of finality. "Next thing you'll want, is some witch doctor chanting spells in my witness stand. Now out, both of you!"

He pushed his hands at them, as if shoving rowdy children out the door.

~ ~ ~

With less than a week to go, Tanley finally found his case coming together.

Reiger and Turnbow might see this as an open-and-shut case for first-degree murder, but he knew that wasn't true. There was always something he could pick at, tear apart, pull down. And thanks to the American law system, the defense had the upper hand. All he had to do with each prosecution witness, and the case as a whole, was let loose a certain little bug in the minds of the jurors—reasonable doubt. The prosecution's job was to build a wall of evidence so high and wide that the jury would be convinced to a moral certainty of the defendant's guilt. Tanley's job was to crack the foundation of that wall—even one hairline fracture. He would have numerous opportunities.

One such opportunity was to expose Sonya Hocking for what she really was—a heartless liar who was willing to sacrifice her own lover to save her reputation. As if *she* hadn't been making enough noise, her husband had loudly decried Gavil Harrison for three months now, ever since word of Harrison's claimed affair with Sonya became public. Stuart Hocking even had the nerve to call Tanley, demanding that he go easy in questioning his poor, beleaguered wife, who, in light of her unflagging good works, deserved none of the sullying she'd endured because of Harrison. Tanley's response? "Call me again, and I'll tell the judge you're trying to interfere with judicial process."

Tanley's problem with the false imprisonment and burglary remained. He'd decided what to do, but it was chancy. Searching for a rational reason for Gavil's irrational behavior, he'd come up with little. So he chucked rationality altogether. Gavil's act was irrational, and he'd play it that way. Which would be very dangerous. Irrationality and violence went hand in hand.

Tanley would need to put it in perspective.

And Chelsea Adams was going to help him.

241

Chapter 39

"When you looked into the gully with your binoculars, what did you see?"

On the witness stand, Chelsea felt her stomach do a small flip. Harry Seltz, clad in a dark gray suit and maroon-striped tie, balanced on the balls of his feet, a hand cupping his chin. The courtroom's four long rows of seats were filled, reporters' pens scribbling. Chelsea had avoided looking at Gavil Harrison, who sat straight ahead of her at the defense table with his attorney. Detective Reiger sat at Seltz's counsel table. Below Chelsea and to her right were the desks of the court reporter and court clerk. The jury was on Chelsea's far left.

She took a deep breath. "I saw a body at the bottom of the gully. It was a woman."

"What clothes were on the body?"

"Yellow jogging shorts." Chelsea hesitated. "That's all I could tell."

"Don't remember what kind of shirt she wore?"

Chelsea expected Seltz to play this out. They'd gone over it. He wanted the jury to picture the victim.

She licked her lips. "No. The body … a lot of the upper part was gone."

A woman in the second row of spectators grimaced.

"Did you see something near the body?"

"Yes."

"What was that?"

"A coyote."

"What was it doing?"

Sickening memory rushed Chelsea. "His nose was buried in her stomach. What was left of it."

A muffled reaction wafted through the room.

"May I approach the witness?" Seltz asked.

Benelli was cleaning his glasses with a fold of his black robe. He grunted.

"Mrs. Adams, I'm sorry to have to put you through this." Seltz sounded empathetic. "We all know it's difficult for you, so take your time. I'm going to show you some pictures that were taken at the scene of the crime and ask if you recognize them." He walked over to his counsel table and picked up a manila envelope. Every eye in the room followed him. "Ready?"

Chelsea was aware of the stares, the breathless anticipation of her reaction to the full-color gore. It was a moment she'd dreaded. She'd spent the summer in much prayer for her own healing. Her nerves were frayed, and she carried lingering fears of being alone. She and the boys visited Dallas in June. Then in August their whole family flew to Maui for two weeks. Lying on the beach, hearing the hypnotic roll of the water, she finally felt God was putting the frazzled pieces of her mind back together.

Paul's deep love for her had shown in his patience and emotional support, even while his opinion of her Christianity remained as negative as ever. Why had this God of hers put her through all this? he demanded one day. Chelsea couldn't answer. Still, when they returned home, Paul told Chelsea he didn't mind if she went to church. "Only because I know you enjoy it so much." Defeat tinged his voice.

"Mrs. Adams?"

Chelsea focused on the manila envelope in Seltz's hand. "I'm ready."

Seltz slid an eight-by-ten out of the envelope and laid it before her. "Can you identify this picture?"

Her eyes fell to it, then raked away. "It's the body I saw in Trent Park."

Seltz took out another photo. "I need you to look at the other two pictures. Can you do that?"

Chelsea flipped through the crime scene photos. The last one was a close-up. "Yes, that's her." Chelsea's voice was thick.

"Okay. No more of that, I promise." Seltz picked up all three photos and handed them to the court clerk, who logged them, calling them people's exhibits 1A, 1B, and 1C. Judge Benelli made a note. Seltz took the photos from the court clerk and solemnly handed them to juror number one. "Please pass these down and I'll collect them."

The colored glossies began to shuffle through a dozen hands.

Seltz turned back to Chelsea. "What did you do after seeing the body?"

"I ran back up the trail to the main road."

"You ran the whole way? Are you a jogger?"

"No, I was just ... scared."

"Why?"

"Because of what I'd seen, and because I realized how alone I was. That girl had been there alone too, and she was dead."

It was the answer they'd practiced. Seltz nodded. Tanley opened his mouth as if to object, then shut it.

"When you got to the main road, what happened?"

"I ran into a county park ranger. Literally. He grabbed me and I started hitting him because I was so scared. And then I guess I fainted."

"Have you ever fainted before?"

"No."

"After you fainted, what happened?"

"When I woke up, I told him what I saw."

For the next half hour Chelsea answered questions about meeting Gavil Harrison at dinner, Seltz steering clear of her vision. The prosecutor then moved to the following Monday, when Gavil entered her house. To Chelsea, who'd experienced her vision so vividly, avoiding that fact during the questioning seemed out of sync. Seltz led her through the details of seeing Gavil, running from him, trying to fight him off.

Chelsea shivered as she related the times she'd tried to get away from Gavil, the futile reaches for the alarm button, and her knife-wielding. She couldn't look at Gavil but felt his eyes on her. Just being in the same room with him was frightening. She was glad Paul had taken the day off work to be in the courtroom.

"Why did you swing the knife?" Seltz remained to Chelsea's right, allowing a direct line of sight between her and the jury.

She searched to explain her transformation from terror to mad woman. "I was afraid he would kill me—"

"Objection!" Tanley said. "Assumes facts not in evidence."

Benelli looked like an annoyed parent whose child had just switched the channel from his favorite TV show. "Overruled." He looked to his left. "Jury will remember that the witness is merely relating her thoughts, that is all, and should not consider the statement for the truth of the matter." He nodded to Chelsea to continue.

She fiddled with the lace collar of her blouse. Seltz had approved the blouse, along with a simple navy skirt. She wore no jewelry save for her wedding ring and small gold earrings. "I just couldn't imagine leaving my two boys without a mother. They need me so much."

Seltz let her statement hang in the air. Every mother in the jury box—and there were five—would know exactly what she was saying.

"Then what did you do?"

"After I swung the knife one time, maybe two, it cut his shirt and he backed away. By then, we were hearing the sirens."

"What happened when you heard the sirens?"

"He backed into a corner, and I stood there pointing the knife at him, hoping to hold him off until the police got there. Then he kicked the knife out of my hand. It flew up in the air and landed on the floor. I turned and ran for the door."

"The front door?"

At the memory Chelsea's muscles tensed. "Yes. I wanted to get outside and run for the police. But then I remembered the door was locked, and I wouldn't have time to unbolt it."

"Where was the defendant?"

"Right behind me. He was running after me."

"Then what happened?"

Chelsea took a deep breath. "I veered upstairs, thinking if I could reach the bedroom, I'd lock the door and wait for the police." Heat flushed her face. "The only reason I got away was because he tripped on the carpet. But by the time I reached our bedroom, he was close again, and I couldn't stop to lock the door."

Her voice shook. Chelsea willed it to be strong. Seltz had told her crying was okay, even expected. Maybe for him, but not for her. The horror she'd experienced was not some spectacle for onlookers. Including the jury. Only half of Seltz seemed sorry for putting her through the memories. The other half relished her discomfort, hoping to draw the jury in. The women would shudder to imagine themselves in such a scary situation. The men would picture their own wives, mothers, daughters, fleeing for their lives.

"Your honor, I wholeheartedly object to this entire line of questioning." Tanley sounded indignant. "It's irrelevant and prejudicial."

"Overruled, Mr. Tanley."

The attorney stood up. "But Your Honor—"

"Sit. *Down.*" Benelli glared.

Seltz frowned at Tanley, as if the defense attorney was attacking the poor witness. Tanley caught the look. His expression smoothed.

Chelsea focused on her lap. So much of this was sheer dramatics. Would the jury see through all of it and just get to the truth?

Seltz adjusted his coat and turned to Chelsea. "Mrs. Adams, what happened when you reached your bedroom?"

She closed her eyes. "My mind is a little blurred. I remember turning over a bookshelf in front of him and throwing some books. One hit him in the head and slowed him down some, I think."

"Were the police there by this time?"

"I don't think so."

"Then what happened?"

"I ran into our dressing room area and started pulling out everything I could to defend myself. Razors, scissors, things like that. Then I realized Gavil wasn't there anymore. I heard him running down the stairs. I heard voices and shouting. I was still terrified. I couldn't tell what was happening."

"And what did you do?" Seltz's voice was low.

"I kept pulling out things I could use for defense. With all the noise downstairs, I wasn't sure who'd come back up to find me— Gavil or the police." Chelsea shuddered. "Then my legs gave out. I collapsed against the wall, holding a pair of scissors. I should have run into the bathroom and locked the door, but I just … couldn't move." Her eyes filled with tears.

Seltz gestured toward a box of tissues. She reached for one, clutching it in her hand.

"Who found you, Mrs. Adams?"

"My husband, Paul." A tear spilled on her cheek. "I heard him calling when he got to our bedroom. But I was so scared, I couldn't talk. I tried to answer, but …" She dabbed at her face. "So I sat there until he came around the corner. And then," her chin quivered, "I knew I was safe. Everything was going to be okay." She hung her head as more tears fell.

A long moment passed before Seltz spoke. His tone remained grim.

"Thank you, Mrs. Adams. I know this hasn't been easy." He looked to the judge. "Perhaps this would be a good time to recess."

Court broke for lunch.

~ ~ ~

Seltz had warned Chelsea about Tanley's cross-examination, that he'd try to pick her testimony apart in ways she would never suspect. She was to stay calm and answer without anger. If Tanley got too nasty, Seltz would object to break the rhythm. She was never to answer a question while an objection was pending before the judge. Seltz guessed Tanley wouldn't get too out of hand, since she was an empathetic witness.

"Good afternoon." Tanley gave Chelsea a tight smile. He was dressed in a dark blue pin-striped suit with a multi-colored tie. Even standing behind his counsel table, he was imposing—over six feet with broad shoulders. "Now, Mrs. Adams, we've heard you relate the details of some unfortunate incidents, and I see no need to put you through that again." He glanced meaningfully at Seltz. "I simply want to clarify a few details. You have identified this man, Gavil Harrison," he laid a hand on Gavil's shoulder, "as the person you first met Wednesday evening at Bayhill Restaurant, when you and your husband were interviewing him for a possible job with your husband's company. Not just any job, but the vice president of sales. Correct?"

"Yes." Another of Seltz's admonishments—answer only the question asked, nothing more.

"Would you say that the position in your husband's company is an important one?"

"Yes."

Stepping from behind the defense table, Tanley led her through a series of benign questions to establish the fact that Gavil had already been interviewed numerous times by Paul Adams, the main investor in the company, and other board members.

"And why did your husband also want you to meet potential applicants, Mrs. Adams?"

"I'm very interested in the company. And he trusts my judgment."

"He trusts your judgment." Tanley rotated a little toward the jury. "What does that mean?"

Chelsea hesitated. She couldn't talk about "intuition" for fear of treading too close to her vision. Seltz had warned her Tanley could cry mistrial if the judge's order about that was breached. "He respects my opinions about people."

"Do you think those opinions of yours are usually right?"

Chelsea flicked a look at Seltz. "Yes."

"I see. And what did you first think of Gavil Harrison?"

The path he was about to lead her down flashed into view. It would end short of the vision that had so changed her opinion.

"Objection. Irrelevant."

Seltz to the rescue. Tanley glanced at the deputy D.A., his face impassive, but Chelsea could see the hidden smirk. He spread his hands before the judge. "Your Honor, it goes to the witness's state of mind. Counsel spent a due amount of time on that, and I ask only for the same leeway."

Benelli thought a moment. "I'll allow it. But let's not go too far with this, Mr. Tanley."

"Yes, Your Honor." Tanley looked to Chelsea. "What did you first think of Gavil Harrison?"

She worked to keep her expression bland. "I liked him."

"You liked him. And regarding your husband, he was just about to hire Mr. Harrison at the time. Is that correct?"

"Yes."

"Did your husband appear to like Mr. Harrison?"

"Yes."

"Mrs. Adams, would you say that your husband is a good judge of character?"

Chelsea glanced at Paul, who smiled in encouragement. "Yes, he is."

"Both of you, then, were initially impressed with the defendant."

"Yes."

"And did you agree with your husband that he was a strong candidate for the position?"

"I thought he could have been."

"Could have been?"

"Yes."

"Well, was there something you could point to that made you think he was *not* a good candidate? Anything about his background, his person?"

Chelsea pictured Gavil's eyes, dark and deep, boring into her. "I ... guess not."

"So you did think of him as a good candidate?"

Chelsea fingered her skirt. "Yes. Initially." She placed emphasis on the last word.

Tanley steered her toward another topic—Gavil's "encounter" with her at her home in June. As he probed every detail of that event, a very different picture of the defendant began to emerge.

"I'm going to restate the events as I understand them," Tanley said after lengthy questioning. "Let me know if I'm wrong. You saw Gavil in your living room."

"Yes."

"You turned and ran, and he followed."

"Yes."

"Then you started hitting him. You punched him in the face."

Chelsea eyed Tanley. "Yes."

"He responded by trying to hold down your arms."

"Yes."

"Later you picked up a knife and started swinging it at him. He backed up. Eventually, he kicked the knife out of your hands. Are all these things true?"

"Yes."

"And am I also to understand that the very first thing the defendant said to you was 'I won't hurt you'? And that he said those words numerous times?

"Yes."

"The defendant was with you alone in your house and never once so much as hit you or threatened to do so."

Anger brewed in Chelsea's stomach. "He was in my own home, holding me against my will!"

"But did he ever hit you?"

She searched Tanley's face. "I was terrified of him! He grabbed me by my—"

"*Did* he ever hit you?" Tanley's words fell like stones. "Just answer the question, yes or no.

Chelsea dropped her eyes. "No."

"Did he verbally threaten to hurt you in any way?"

The anger burned her lungs. "No."

"And didn't he in fact say very clearly that he would not hurt you, that he just wanted to talk?"

Chelsea's face flushed. "That's a funny way to have a conversation."

Tanley pressed his thin lips. "Mrs. Adams, please just answer the question. Didn't he say he was not going to hurt you?"

"Yes. I guess."

"You guess?"

"Yes."

Tanley took a few steps toward the jury. "Mrs. Adams, surely you would agree that this kind of behavior does not fit the profile of someone who killed a young woman in cold blood."

"Objection!" Seltz sounded disgusted. "Motion to strike."

"Sustained." Benelli shook his jowls at Tanley.

Chelsea eyed the attorney. He'd planned that statement. So what if it was erased from the record? The jury couldn't really forget it. Would they start seeing her as some hysterical female?

"All right." Tanley focused on her. "Would you say that Mr. Harrison's behavior that day was rational or irrational?"

What was this?

"He was very irrational. He was calm one minute, then he would start screaming. I couldn't predict what he would do next."

Tanley let her embellishment pass. "And yet, five days earlier you and your husband had been so impressed with this man that your husband was considering offering him a very high position in his company."

Chelsea's jaw set. "That's true."

"Would you say, then, that Mr. Harrison behaved differently when he was in your home?"

"Completely differently."

Tanley rubbed his scalp. "Mrs. Adams, can you tell me, to the best of your knowledge, what happened to Gavil Harrison in that five-day period?"

"What do you mean?"

"Well, did you meet with the police regarding the body that you'd found?"

She hesitated.

"At any time during those five days?"

"Yes."

"And, to your recollection, did they tell you that Gavil Harrison had become a suspect in the murder of Meg Jessler during that time?"

"Yes."

Seltz remained quiet. Why wasn't he coming to her rescue?

"Did this change your opinion about wanting him to work for your husband?"

"Yes."

"So he had lost his chance for the job."

"Yes."

Tanley paused. "Anything else you know happened in those five days? What about the defendant's home life?"

"Well, I think his girlfriend asked him to leave her house, if that's what you mean."

"I see." Tanley paced a few steps. "So the defendant appeared normal to you on Wednesday, when you met him, correct?"

"Yes."

"In the next few days, the police started questioning him about a murder, correct?"

"I understand that to be the case, yes."

"As a result, Mr. Harrison lost the chance of a job at your husband's company and apparently also lost the woman he loved *and* the home in which he lived. Correct?"

"I guess so."

"I'd say that's a pretty busy five days." Tanley raised his eyebrows, as if testing her for agreement. "Then on Monday, when the defendant was in your home, you say he acted irrational." The defense attorney paused.

Seltz rose from his seat. "Your Honor, would counsel like to take the stand himself? He's testifying throughout this entire line of questioning."

"Mr. Tanley." Benelli's tone was disapproving, "Is there a question in there somewhere?"

Tanley lifted a hand. "Yes, Your Honor." He rested against the defense table, arms folded. "Mrs. Adams, what did you say happened when you ran, literally, into that county ranger in Trent Park?"

Chelsea mentally pivoted. "I said I fainted."

"No. Something before that."

"Oh." She thought a moment. "I hit him. Because I was scared and because, well, I didn't know who he was at first."

"I understand." Tanley smiled. "At that moment you felt you were defending yourself."

"Yes."

"And what did the ranger do to calm you?"

"He held my arms. And he talked to me."

"I see." Tanley studied her. "Mrs. Adams, would you say that you act more rationally or less rationally when you're frightened?"

She frowned. "I don't understand."

Through more questions, Tanley reminded her that she'd run toward the park's main road because she was afraid of being alone and wanted help. When she found the park ranger, she should have been glad, yet she'd hit him. Was that a rational response? Chelsea admitted it wasn't.

Back to Monday morning. Were her actions not the same? In her fright she tried to hit Gavil. In her fright she swung a knife at him, overturned a shelf on him, threw books at him. Gavil's only actions through it all had been to defend himself—holding down her arms, kicking away the knife. While she was pulling out weapons in the dressing room—including a deadly pair of scissors—he backed off and ran down the stairs. The defendant had never once given her any real reason to believe he would hurt her. His only concern had been to convince her of where he'd been the morning of the murder, as if clearing his name with her would somehow clear his name with the police.

Tanley was most agreeable, empathy spilling from him with every question. Chelsea half expected his blue suit to waterlog. She knew the picture he was painting—her fear of Gavil had been unnecessary, her opinion of him so tainted by police she wouldn't listen to reason. Despite Seltz's objections, Tanley couldn't be stopped from telling only half the story. Without her vision, both her actions and those of the detectives appeared unwarranted.

It was also understandable, Tanley continued, that she'd been scared of Gavil after hearing he was a murder suspect. Nobody was accusing her of doing anything wrong. Everyone sympathized. The ordeal that Monday morning had been traumatic. But her fright had caused her to do things she ordinarily wouldn't do. She didn't usually fight, did she? She'd never pulled a knife on anyone, never punched anyone, had she? She'd simply been overcome by her emotions.

Anger swirled through Chelsea. She didn't dare look at Paul. He was probably ready to strangle Tanley.

"You've mentioned that you tend to act differently when you're scared." Tanley, pacing slowly, pulled to a stop. "Did you ever stop to think, Mrs. Adams, that Gavil Harrison's behavior that Monday morning was due merely to the fact that, because of all the things he'd experienced in the previous five days, he was *just plain scared?*"

"Objection, leading the witness." Seltz tried to sound bored, as if the last forty-five minutes were beyond sensibility.

"Sustained."

Seltz had warned her. Chelsea no longer cared. She'd had enough. She glared at Tanley, then shot a daring glance in Gavil's direction. If the defense attorney could play games, so could she.

"Yes." She articulated each word. "I *have* thought that. He was 'just plain scared' of getting caught for killing that poor woman."

Reaction radiated through the courtroom. Tanley rose up on his toes. Seltz managed to hold a smile in check. Reiger wasn't so successful. Reporters scribbled. Jury members waited for the next move.

"Objection!" Tanley's cheeks flushed red. "Motion to strike!"

Benelli sustained, admonishing the jury to disregard the comment. "My dear young lady." He shot a stern look over his glasses at Chelsea. "You must refrain from making such statements. Especially when I have sustained an objection. Is that clear?"

Chelsea nodded, feigning meekness. Then turned back to Tanley with a defiant blink.

255

Thursday, September 21

Chapter 40

Marian flicked mascara on her lashes, enhancing her hazel eyes. A little blush and lipstick. A quick comb through her hair. She didn't have the energy for anything more. She stepped away from the full length mirror and studied herself. In the last three months she'd dropped fourteen pounds. Her face was thinner, with more cheekbones. She'd let her hair grow out of its perm. It now fell in soft waves around her face. She looked better than she ever had.

But this was still the worst day of her life.

Worse than the day her husband had left her for another woman. Worse than the day she'd discovered the broken fingernail in her garden glove. Worse than the long hours she'd spent agonizing over Gavil's guilt, his innocence. Worse, even, than the day she'd finally turned the fingernail over to police.

Today she would testify in court against the man she once loved.

Ironically, the day also marked her new beginning. When it was over, she could shut the door on this part of her life.

Marian had not seen Gavil since he walked out of the townhouse that Saturday morning in June. He'd called from jail, written, begged her to visit. She read his letters and cried and cried until she thought she'd used up every tear. But she couldn't bring herself to see him. Not in jail. She knew what he'd say anyway—the same words he had repeated over and over. "I didn't do it, Marian. Why can't you believe me?"

At first his insistence had tugged at the tiny hope in her heart. But not for long. Bad enough to do what he did. But to try to make *her* feel guilty for holding him accountable ...

Marian caught her own eyes in the mirror. How had she made it through the summer? Somehow she'd gone to work each day, her face a mask of calm. She threw what energy she had into extra intensity, adding seven new businesses to her client list. At night she was so exhausted she'd fall asleep on the couch after staring at the TV. With so many calls from reporters, she stopped answering the phone. Many times she forgot to eat. Other times she just didn't care.

After a few weeks, Marian found a therapist. She felt like she was being sucked down a hole. Without help, she'd never dig her way out. There were so many issues to work through. Her guilt over Meg's death, her shame at having lived with Gavil. How could she ever trust a man again? The therapist was good, but the sessions were grueling. To deal with her emotions, Marian had to relive all the events that had triggered them.

Pat Turnbow started calling a few weeks after Gavil's arraignment. At first Marian avoided his calls. She didn't know how she felt about him. But she was so lonely. Eventually she gave in, and they started talking. Soon it was every night. In time Pat let her know he wanted more—after the trial was over. Until then he couldn't see her. He was a detective on the case, she was a prosecution witness. The defense would have a heyday with news of any relationship between them. At best, her testimony would suffer. At worst, the defense attorney could suggest the two of them had planted that fingernail in order to get rid of Gavil.

How *sick*.

Sometimes Marian thought she'd go crazy spending another evening alone. But she'd probably run like a scared rabbit if Pat did try to come over. That trust issue again.

In July Marian surprised herself by starting to go to Haverlon Baptist Church. The first Sunday she was stunned to see Sergeant Reiger across the sanctuary. She ducked out fast after the service so he wouldn't notice her. Still, she went back the next week, and the next, drawn by the preaching and worship. The people there seemed grounded and strong, while she was tossed on a raging sea.

Marian wondered about Chelsea Adams. What kind of woman would hear God like that and be brave enough to tell the police? Marian asked Pat for details of the vision, and he told her. Amazing.

"So what do we do with it?" she asked him one night.

"What do you mean?"

"Well, here we are going about our lives. I don't know about you, but I pray now and then when I need help with something. I never hear much back. All of a sudden through this vision, God speaks—really loud. Things happen as a result in your life and Sergeant Reiger's and mine and other people's. So—don't you think God had a reason for doing this?"

"Haven't thought much about it. Weird things happen."

"This isn't just weird. This is ... God."

Silence for a moment. "So what do *you* think?"

Marian sighed. "I don't know. I'm going to church now. Trying to figure it all out. Maybe later you and I can go together some time."

"Maybe. " Pat hadn't sounded excited.

Marian took one last look at herself in the mirror. She shut her makeup drawer and snapped off the light.

One thing was certain. When Pat Turnbow saw her again, he'd be in for a surprise.

~ ~ ~

Brick by brick, Seltz was building his case. After calling Chelsea Adams to the stand, he went through county park rangers Jim Sykes and Troy Jenkins. Pathology and forensics followed. Hal Weiss explained the pieces of evidence taken from Meg Jessler's body and procedures he'd followed in matching the fibers, dirt, and fingernail. Not surprisingly, the blood and hairs taken from the rock were identified as belonging to her as well.

Jenkin Tommason's testimony, following that of Hal Weiss, established a narrow window for time of death. Turnbow's and Reiger's turns on the stand had eaten up most of Wednesday.

Now the time had come to question the most empathetic witness of all.

Seltz stood and addressed the judge. "Prosecution calls Marian Baker."

A bailiff left the courtroom to usher in Marian, who looked very different from when Seltz had first met her. As the entire courtroom watched the attractive woman walk stiffly toward the witness stand, Seltz mentally practiced his opening question.

~ ~ ~

Legs shaking, Marian raised her right hand to take the oath, then sat down. Now that the dreaded moment had come, she felt not quite present, as if she hovered up in a corner, watching herself. She folded her hands in her lap and planted her feet on the floor. All eyes in the courtroom were on her. She recognized Reiger and a few TV reporters, including Milt Waking. Mrs. Geary was there, and so was her neighbor, Jack Doniger, seated in the back row. He caught her gaze and nodded in encouragement.

Marian could feel Gavil's stare.

What was *he* feeling? Did he think she looked good? Was he sorry for what he'd lost?

Of their own will, her eyes strayed until they locked with Gavil's.

Her heart jolted. He stared at her with such an aching expression, she could hardly bear it.

And he was so pale.

She'd lost fourteen pounds, but he must have lost at least twenty. His cheeks were hollow, his eyes sunken into his face like dark wells. He sat straight, unmoving, like a wet rag dried to stiffness. If you bent that rag, it would crumble at your touch.

260

Life in jail must be beyond belief. What were his days like? Could he get out of his cell? Read? How had he been treated? Had he been sick?

Abused?

Marian dropped her gaze.

Seltz started his questioning, apologizing for what he would have to ask. For the next hour, he led Marian through all the events of the week Meg was murdered. She answered as they had practiced. Every answer was a brick in the road that would lead her out of the courtroom and to the beginning of a new life.

Seltz had warned her he would bring out the fact that she hadn't turned the fingernail over to police right away. Far better for the prosecution to offer this information than the defense. She was to be completely honest about her indecision.

"Let me understand you, then." Seltz was standing by the jury box. "You kept the fingernail in your medicine cabinet for two days, knowing how important it was?"

"Yes."

"And what caused you to turn it over to the police?"

Marian's eyes tugged back to Gavil. A lump formed in her throat. She pressed her lips and looked down. "I'm sorry."

"That's all right. Take your time."

When she raised her head, her vision blurred from tears. The courtroom was silent. "I couldn't deny what it was any longer. I didn't want to believe it. But I had to. I didn't sleep Tuesday night, and first thing Wednesday morning, I took it to the police."

Seltz nodded. "Ms. Baker, until today, have you seen the defendant since that time?"

"No."

"Do you live alone now?"

"Yes." Something made her go on. "I took all of Gavil's things and put them in storage. *Nothing* of his is in my house anymore."

Seltz allowed her statement to reverberate, then told the judge he had nothing further.

Tanley rose, all business. "Good afternoon, Ms. Baker."

Marian nodded, hiding her wariness. What might this man try to do to her?

The attorney moved out from behind the defense table. "Let's move to a topic that will be easier for you." He picked up an envelope and glanced at the judge. "May I?" Judge Benelli waved him on. Seltz asked to see what was in the envelope. The judge motioned both men up front, and the three of them huddled, talking in low tones.

Marian focused on her lap.

When they were through Seltz resumed his seat. Tanley walked toward Marian, holding the envelope and some photographs. He handed her the top one. "Do you recognize the building in this picture?"

She examined it. "Yes. That's the outside of my house."

"Where would you say the photo was taken from?"

"I guess ... somewhere beyond the sidewalk."

"Okay. Now, Ms. Baker, how far would you estimate the distance is between the street sidewalk and your front porch?"

She thought a moment. "Maybe nine or ten feet."

"And is this the porch on which you left your garden gloves?"

"Yes."

He indicated the photo. "Where exactly were they?"

"Near the front right edge of the porch, as you face the house." Marian pointed.

"I see. Would you say they would be easy to spot?"

"Yes."

"They weren't hidden by anything? Bushes? Flowers?"

"No."

Tanley laid down the photo and handed her a second one. "Would you identify this picture, please."

It was her porch again, this time taken from the other side of the street.

"Can you see anything on the porch?"

She stared at the picture. "A pair of gold garden gloves."

Someone had set up this picture without her knowing? The thought made her feel violated.

"And this picture?" He handed her a third.

"It's my house, taken from the side, about three doors down."

"Do you see anything on the porch?"

"Yes. The garden gloves again."

"Thank you." Tanley gathered the photos, went through the procedure of having them logged as exhibits, then gave them to the jury. Leaning against the counsel table, he crossed his arms. "Ms. Baker, do you agree that the garden gloves that sat on your porch the nights of June third and fourth could be seen from the street?"

"Yes."

"And from how far away would you guess they could be seen?"

Marian lifted her shoulders. "I'm not sure."

"Let's try it another way. Is the street narrow or wide?"

"It's pretty narrow."

"Narrow. And we've heard other testimony that the houses are all in a row. Right?"

"Yes."

"So if you stood on the sidewalk in front of your house, you could see the gloves, right?"

"Yes."

"And if you crossed the street and stood on the far sidewalk, do you think you could see the gloves then?" He glanced toward the jury, still passing around the photos, as if to remind Marian of his proof this was so.

"Yes."

"Okay." Tanley stood up straight. "And you've already identified a photograph in which you could see the gloves from three doors down."

"Yes."

"What if you went down four doors? Do you think your neighbors four doors down could see the gloves?"

"I don't know. Maybe."

Tanley walked over to the jury to pick up the pictures from juror number twelve. He fanned them like cards in his left hand. "But it is a fact, is it not, that a neighbor, *any* neighbor, who walked by your house on the sidewalk nearest you, in the street, or on the sidewalk across the street could see the gloves. Isn't that true?"

"Yes."

When Tanley was finally done, Seltz questioned Marian again. He tried to temper Tanley's point. It was the weakest link in his case, Marian knew, but one that made little difference to her. What she'd found inside the gloves was the fact that mattered.

By the time her testimony was complete and court had recessed for the day, Marian was more than ready for her final act of severance—walking out of the courtroom.

Leaving Gavil behind.

~ ~ ~

Turnbow found Marian's car parked a few blocks from the courthouse. He almost drove by it as he cruised the area. She'd told him she'd lost weight and changed her hair. He tried to imagine how she looked. It felt like years since they'd seen each other.

An hour earlier, Turnbow had been called to a residence to take a report on stolen jewelry. Driving away from the house, Pat found himself turning toward the courthouse in Redwood City. It was almost five. Court would be letting out. One thing about Benelli, he liked going home on time. Turnbow toyed with going inside the courthouse, catching Marian on the way out. Talking for a minute. But could he hide his feelings, seeing her like that in public? Could she?

Would she still be glad to see him—after seeing Harrison?

Then Turnbow saw her car. On a small side street.

How about that?

He slid into a spot near the end of the block and waited.

He really shouldn't be doing this. He should go.

Turnbow got out of his car and pocketed his keys. Wandered down to Marian's car and leaned against the hood.

He didn't have long to wait.

She came around the corner, holding a folded newspaper section. She'd probably used it to shield her face from cameras at the courthouse. Pat caught his breath. She looked stunning. He'd liked her short, curly hair, but this new cut was beautiful. An ache to be with her filled him.

Marian stopped to pitch the newspaper into a trash can, then fumbled in her purse for keys. Glancing up, she saw Turnbow— and his heart played a slow-motion beat.

She drew to a halt.

Reactions ruffled across her features—surprise ... pleasure ... apprehension. She glanced around. Then walked toward him, back straight. Guarded.

"Hi, Marian."

"Hi."

She passed him to step onto the street, car keys in hand.

He pushed away from the hood. "How did it go?"

She took a breath. "It was the hardest thing I've ever done."

He nodded. So her mind was on Gavil. "I believe it." The words hung between them.

What else could he say?

He placed two fingers beneath her chin. "You look incredible."

A current streamed between them. He knew she felt it too. Neither moved until a car turning the corner drew their attention. Turnbow dropped his hand. The driver continued down the street.

"What are you doing tonight?" The words were out before Turnbow could stop them.

Marian's eyes widened, then she turned away, resigned. The car key slid into its lock. "I'm going home."

She reached for the door handle, but he blocked it with an arm. She raised her eyes. "Pat, what are you doing?"

What *was* he doing?

"I'm coming to see you tonight, that's what. In fact," he tilted his head, "I'm coming for dinner."

"But the trial …"

"Your testimony is over. Not likely they'll call you back. And the trial only has a few more days. We've waited all summer, Marian."

He watched her absorb his words.

Pain flicked across her face. "Not tonight. You can't possibly understand what I went through in there. I should … I just want to be alone. Sort out my thoughts."

A pang shot through him. Sounded like the same fragile Marian. She would say no more, but her expression screamed her ambivalence. Did she think she *deserved* to go home and cry all night?

"Uh-uh." He shook his head. "I'm not letting you be alone tonight."

"But—"

He laid a finger on her lips. "I'm coming. In one hour. We'll have steak, baked potato, and salad. And chocolate cake. You have any cake?"

Marian shook her head.

"Then I'll buy one."

"Pat, really I can't."

She wanted him. She was just scared. "We've waited long enough, Marian."

She gazed at him.

Warmth flowed through his veins. "One hour."

~ ~ ~

The steak was wonderful.

With the sizzling of meat, the plop of sliced cucumbers into a salad bowl, Marian had felt herself loosening. She *was* glad for Pat's company. She'd be crying her eyes out if he hadn't come over. At the table they talked of anything and everything but the trial. Pat announced that rule before the steaks were done. He told her about other cases he'd been called out on—burglaries, drug deals, a recent suicide. Marian told him about her new clients.

Pat exuded energy as they talked, as if trying to pull her emotions along. Marian was grateful, but she still felt exhausted. He ate the last bite of his cake and pushed the plate away. "Let me ask you something." He leaned in. "Do you ever laugh?"

She gave him a look. "No, Pat, I don't believe in it."

"Come on, really."

Her eyes rolled. "Yes. If you must know, once or twice in my life I have laughed."

"You know." He touched her arm. "I've never heard you."

Marian held his gaze, then looked away. "There hasn't been much to laugh about lately."

"Agreed. But that's going to change tonight. Here's what we're going to do."

"Oh, no, not again."

"I'm going to drive down to the video store and rent the funniest movie I can find. We'll watch it and eat popcorn. You like popcorn?"

"Pat, you're crazy."

"Yeah." His gaze fell to her lips. Heat rose within her. He glanced at her plate. "Finish your cake. I bought it, you eat it."

She picked up her fork and made a point of shoving a large piece into her mouth.

"There ya go." He nodded. "While I'm gone, practice this." He placed a finger in each corner of her cake-filled mouth and pushed up.

Marian threw her napkin in his face.

~ ~ ~

Pat came back with *What's Up, Doc?* An old movie they'd both seen, but it didn't matter. That night it seemed funnier to Marian. They laughed and laughed and ate popcorn. Somewhere along the way Pat reached for her hand, and she slipped her fingers in his his. The touch radiated.

Pat grew quiet.

What now? Marian's heart scudded. She tried to focus on the screen.

Pat touched her cheek, urging her face toward his.

She followed his touch. "We'll miss the movie."

"No, we won't."

Eyes on her face, Pat groped for the remote control. A click of the button, and a red Chinese dragon froze midflight on a crowded Chinatown street.

"We won't miss a thing."

Saturday, September 23

Chapter 41

A vague sense of impending disaster had settled upon Chelsea as she left the courtroom five days ago. Paul hugged her tightly before starting the car, telling her how well she'd done. She knew he attributed her quietness to exhaustion. She didn't tell him otherwise. He'd been so patient all summer. He deserved to see her in better spirits.

What's going on, Lord?

She'd had trouble sleeping since then.

Initially, she told herself she was just backtracking a little. Emotional healing wasn't always a steady ascent. She prayed about it, asked Gladys to pray about it. But by Friday it hadn't lifted. Chelsea was having trouble being patient with the rowdy boys and could no longer hide it from Paul.

"What's wrong?" he asked as she sank into bed Friday night.

She laid a hand across her eyes. How could she explain her doubts when he was already so negative toward God? "I'm just tired, I guess. All the stress of waiting for the trial to be over."

That night, she tossed and turned.

Chelsea visited Gladys for coffee Saturday afternoon while Paul took the boys to a movie. "It came to me last night." Chelsea sighed. "I think I know what's wrong. It's so awful, I don't even want to say it. But I'm afraid Gavil's not going to be convicted."

Gladys waved a hand. "Oh, pshaw! With all that evidence?"

"I know, but you should have heard how that defense attorney tore me down. Gavil appears in my house, and *I'm* the bad guy." Chelsea shook her head. "I can't imagine what I'm going to do if he's set free."

"I really don't think that will happen."

"I wish I could believe you." Chelsea pushed at her coffee spoon. "I don't know, maybe it's not that at all. Maybe it's just that I don't feel close to God like I used to. This vision has seemed to cause nothing but trouble. I wish I'd never had it!"

Gladys nodded. "Well. If I were you, I'd probably be saying the same thing. But you know what, I'll bet the apostle John was terrified when he saw his vision—the one that's recorded in Revelation. In fact, the Bible says he fell to the ground like a dead man. And how about the apostle Paul's vision that led him to Macedonia? He was beaten and jailed as a result of his obedience. Bottom line, following God's will isn't always easy. But God doesn't make mistakes. He picked you for this task because he knew you could handle it."

"Yeah, well I wish he'd tell my husband that." Chelsea made a face. "Maybe I should call Sergeant Reiger. Just to see how the trial is going."

"Do. He'll probably tell you things are right on track."

When she arrived home, Chelsea phoned the Haverlon police station, asking if they would call Dan Reiger at home for her. He called back within minutes. At her questions, he assured her the trial was going well. It would take a major coup by the defense attorney for Gavil to go free, he declared. "Tanley's decided to let Harrison take the stand Monday. Just wait till Seltz gets hold of him."

If only Chelsea could share Reiger's certainty. Something still nagged at her.

"By the way," Reiger said, "you may be interested to know that Gavil's ex-girlfriend, Marian Baker, is coming to our church every week. She sits in the back, afraid to let me see her, I think. It's a big sanctuary. But I've taken to watching for her. Seems to me she's looking for some answers."

Empathy washed through Chelsea. She couldn't imagine the pain this woman must be facing. "Maybe you should talk to her."

"I've thought about it. But I don't think I'm the one. She'd probably feel uncomfortable with me. I've played a far different role in her life, after all."

A voice inside Chelsea responded. *You talk to her.* Chelsea blinked. The impression filled her mind again. She couldn't shake it. Sudden lightness released in her chest. Maybe this was the issue—God wanted her to reach out to Marian Baker. Her uneasiness all week had prompted her to call Sergeant Reiger.

"I should talk to her, then."

Reiger hesitated.

"Really, I should. I don't know what I'll say. Goodness knows what she thinks of me. But I think this is something God wants me to do."

"Well. Okay. If that's the case, I'm sure God will give you the words."

"Wait, though." Chelsea ran a hand through her hair. "Does she ... blame me?"

"I doubt that. If she thought you were the bad guy, she never would have brought us that evidence."

"Yeah. Guess you're right." Chelsea thought a moment. "Paul may still have Gavil's old home number. I don't suppose *you* could give it to me."

"I really can't." Reiger sounded sorry. "It's a privacy issue. But I do hope you find it."

That evening as Paul helped with dinner dishes, Chelsea told him about her conversation with Reiger, leaving out the part about Marian Baker's attending church. "Do you still have Gavil's home number, Paul? I'd like to call Marian."

Concern flicked over his face. "Why?"

"I just ... feel sorry for her. I imagine she could use some support."

"Chelsea." Paul placed the dirty dish in his hand on the counter. "*You* need support. *I* need support. I think we've got enough to do, just getting through this ourselves."

"But I'm only talking about—"

"One phone call, I know. And then what? Say she does need support. You'll think you're the one to give it."

"I need support." Paul's vulnerable statement echoed in Chelsea's mind. She wrapped her arms around his neck. "I'm sorry. I should realize more how hard this has been for you too. Plus you have all the problems at work to deal with. I'm really sorry, Paul. I love you."

He clung to her, breathing into her hair. "I love you too. So very, very much."

Later that night, Paul disappeared into the office and emerged with a piece of yellow paper in his hand. On it was Marian Baker's phone number. Chelsea looked at him, eyebrows raised. He shrugged. "Chelsea, I just … can't keep you from being you. Call her if you want. Do whatever you think is best. I just hope we won't be sorry."

Thank you, Lord, Chelsea prayed. *Now please continue to use the vision you sent me until all its work is done.*

Monday, September 25

Chapter 42

Multiple news vans glinted in the sun as Turnbow entered the courthouse. No reporter wanted to miss a defendant on the stand. They didn't get to see such a thing very often. In the hallway outside Department 25, the throng of camera crews, reporters, and spectators was being shushed by a bailiff in a helpless effort to keep the noise from other courtrooms. It was midmorning break. Turnbow spotted Reiger thirty feet over and waved. They maneuvered to a corner away from the crowd.

Turnbow kept his voice low. "How's Harrison doing?"

"Better than I expected, unfortunately. I'd wondered how Tanley could allow him to testify. Now I get it. He's done a lot of coaching. Plus, Harrison's the salesman."

All he'd have to do is convince one juror. They'd have a mistrial. Still, no question Seltz would try the man again.

"What'd they cover?"

Reiger leaned against the wall. "Harrison spent the time telling us all what a great guy and successful businessman he is, a little about his childhood, stuff like that. Tanley seemed to want to make the point that Harrison's parents were loving and supportive. Meaning, in other words, they couldn't have bred a killer. Then they talked about Wednesday morning, how Harrison was with Sonya Hocking, etc., etc."

It would be the first time the jury had heard this. "Any reaction?"

A bailiff opened the courtroom doors, and the camera crews wrapped up their filming. People surged forward.

"I gotta go back in." Reiger pushed away from the wall. "You busy at the station?"

Turnbow flicked the ring button on his pager over to vibrate. "Yeah. But I'm going to hang around a while."

~ ~ ~

Harrison's suit was a dark gray pinstripe, the shirt white, collar starched. They couldn't hide his pallid complexion.

All dressed up with no place to go. Seated in the second row, Turnbow imagined Marian with this man and felt sick.

"Where did you go after Ms. Baker asked you to leave her home?" Tanley was standing to the right of the defense table.

"To the Welthing Hotel in San Carlos."

"Did you speak with her that day or the next?"

"No. I left a message as to where I was. She didn't call back."

"And your ... friend, Sonya Hocking?" Tanley pronounced "friend" as if it left a bad taste in his mouth.

"She hung up on me again and again."

"Did you seek support from anyone during that weekend?"

"No. I had no one."

"I see." Tanley crossed his arms.

Turnbow flicked a look at the jury. They were too quiet, too rapt. He searched individual expressions, found nothing. Maybe a hint of cynicism from the middle-aged man in the front row.

"Let's talk about Monday morning. Why did you go to see Mrs. Adams?"

Turnbow made a face. *"See"* Mrs. Adams? He listened for the next half hour as Harrison spewed excuses. He'd had no one to turn to. He was afraid. All he wanted to do was talk. He never verbally threatened Mrs. Adams, never meant to hurt her, had never hurt anyone in his life. Around the courtroom, reporters scribbled. Spectators were unusually still, as was Judge Benelli. Harrison's voice undulated hypnotically, now pleading, now

276

indignant. Tanley drained the pathos from him, poured it back, drained it again.

I love you, Marian. Turnbow could imagine Gavil silking those words over his lies. The man had demeaned Marian, conned her. Just like he was conning the jury now.

Seltz stood to cross-examine, and Tanley's spell was broken. A spark flicked through the courtroom at the prosecutor's sarcastic tone.

"So you didn't want to hurt Mrs. Adams, is that right?" Seltz crossed his arms.

Harrison eyed the deputy D.A. with a practiced stare. "No, sir, I did not."

"According to Mrs. Adams, the moment she saw you in her house, you chased her. True?"

"Yes."

"You forced her down on her stairway. You fell on top of her and covered her mouth so she couldn't scream?"

"I didn't mean to hurt her."

"You didn't."

"No."

"Just as you 'didn't mean to hurt her' when you forced her again to the floor in her kitchen?"

"No. As I said, I just wanted to talk to her."

Seltz spread his hands. "Is this the way you usually talk to people?"

"No."

"Ever 'talk' this way to a coworker, a secretary?"

"No."

Seltz's voice dropped. "Ever talk this way to a man?"

"No."

"Only women."

Hesitation. "No."

"Chelsea Adams isn't a woman?"

Turnbow heard a faint titter.

"Yes. She is."

"So you only talk this way to women."

"No. Only to Chelsea Adams, that one time. Because I was desperate. I had never been in such a situation before."

Turnbow's feet and hands went hot. His shirt collar scratched his neck as he simmered. He couldn't help but imagine Harrison's voice cajoling Marian over the phone. *"Don't believe the police, Marian. Can't you see it's all a lie?"*

"Let's talk about your claimed lover, Sonya Hocking. The wife of your best friend and mentor."

Seltz now danced from subject to subject, throwing punches like a bantamweight boxer.

"You say you and Mrs. Hocking had an affair, do you not?"

Harrison appeared to shrink. "Yes."

"And that no one else knew about this."

"Yes."

"And that you were at her house from Tuesday night, June 4, until 9:30 A.M., Wednesday, June 5?"

"Yes."

"For purposes of a sexual nature."

"Yes. Among other things."

"Other things?"

"We had breakfast."

"Oh."

Another titter.

Seltz surveyed the ceiling as if calculating, then resumed pacing. "What—strike that. Why did you lie at first to the police?"

Harrison's eyes hooded. "I didn't want anyone to know."

"To know what? Where you'd *really* been?"

"Objection, leading the witness!" Tanley rose from his chair, irritation splaying his hands.

Benelli eyed Seltz. "Care to try again?"

278

"Yes, Your Honor." Seltz nodded. Tanley sat down. "Mr. Harrison. What didn't you want police to know?"

"I told you. About my relationship with Sonya."

"Ah, yes. And did Marian know?"

Harrison's face hardened. "I said she didn't."

Turnbow watched Tanley's back stiffen.

"You never told her about your relationship with Sonya Hocking, correct?"

"No."

"So you lied about that."

"Objection, Your Honor! Leading the witness."

"Overruled." Benelli nodded at Harrison. "You may answer the question."

"I ... well, I didn't really lie. I just never said anything about it."

"Well, did you lead Marian Baker to believe you were having sexual relations with no one but her?"

"Yes."

"Don't you consider that a lie?"

Harrison's eyes wandered. "I guess it is."

"You 'guess'?"

"Okay. Yes. It was a lie."

Seltz took his time. "Now, when you arrived at work the morning of Wednesday, June 5 ... you say it was about ten?"

"Yes."

"Did you see anybody when you came in?"

"Sure."

"Who did you see?"

"Like I said, the receptionist first, and I told my secretary I was in."

"Uh-huh." The question was casual. "Did you tell them where you'd been?"

No answer.

"Mr. Harrison?"

"Yes." Sullen.

"What did you tell them?"

Tanley was in motion again. "Objection, Your Honor. This is beyond the scope."

Benelli stroked his jaw. "No, Mr. Tanley, you brought up the subject in direct." He jutted his chin at the prosecutor. "Go ahead."

Tanley sank into his seat.

"What did you tell your receptionist about where you'd been, Mr. Harrison?" Seltz had stopped pacing to await the answer.

"I said I'd been home, working."

"Really. And why did you tell her that?"

"Because my relationship with Sonya was a secret."

Seltz didn't move. "And your secretary? What did you tell her?"

Harrison inclined his head. "The same thing."

"That you were home working."

"Yes."

"Mm." The pacing resumed. "So let me understand you. You lied to Marian Baker, the woman you say you loved." Seltz stopped, facing the jury. "You lied to the police about where you were that morning. You lied to your receptionist. Then you lied to your secretary. Correct?" He glanced over his shoulder at the defendant.

"Yes."

"Seems to me, Mr. Harrison, you do an awful lot of lying."

Silence. Turnbow looked for Tanley to rise, but saw only the tautness of his back.

Seltz turned to the witness stand. "Are you lying to us now, Mr. Harrison?"

"No."

Turnbow watched the jurors assess the interplay. Did they sense there was something more? Because of the hearsay rule, he and Reiger had been unable to testify about Harrison's claimed

280

alibi and Sonya Hocking's denials. Today, for the first time, the jury was hearing testimony of the alibi, but it was obvious the deputy D.A. wasn't buying it. They wouldn't be able to put it all together until Sonya Hocking testified.

Turnbow lingered in the courtroom, watching Seltz's dance-and-punch. Among other things, the prosecutor covered Harrison's relationship with Meg Jessler (he barely knew her, Harrison said) and the garden gloves on the porch (he didn't notice them).

As Judge Benelli called for recess at noon, cold vengeance surged through Turnbow's veins. One thing was certain. Gavil Harrison couldn't even lie well anymore.

~ ~ ~

"Hi." Jack Doniger greeted Marian from his sidewalk as she stepped outside her door after dinner on Monday. A small stack of mail lay in his hand. Marian's heart sank. She should have checked through the window before heading out to her own mailbox. She didn't feel like talking to any neighbors. "Everything okay with you?" Jack asked.

Marian managed a smile. "Sure. Everything's fine."

"Okay." Jack eyed her with concern, as if he wanted to say more. "Please let me know if I can do anything for you."

"I'll do that. Thanks." She nodded at him and smiled again. "Well. I'm pretty late looking at my mail today. Better get it." As she walked down her sidewalk, she heard his front door open and close.

When Marian returned with her mail, the phone was ringing. She hurried inside and snatched up the receiver. Maybe it would be Pat, with news of Gavil's testimony.

"Marian Baker?" a woman's voice said with hesitation. "This is Chelsea Adams."

Marian froze.

"I know it's kind of awkward, calling you. I have no idea if you even want to talk to me or not. But I just ... wanted to see how you're doing."

Marian's gaze drifted across her kitchen. A strangeness settled over her as she listened to the voice that had first accused Gavil. Yet the phone call seemed right somehow, as if their linking would open another door to her healing. After all, this was another woman that Gavil had wronged. "It's okay. There have been times I wanted to call you too. I've had ... so many questions."

The conversation remained stilted for a few minutes. But after a while Marian found herself speaking of her life with Gavil, of the pain she'd gone through since his arrest. Soon, she peppered Chelsea with questions. How had the vision come? When? Why? Before she realized it, Marian had drawn up a kitchen chair, soaking in the information. Chelsea Adams expressed such a powerful faith in God, yet she sounded so humble. She wasn't some religious, holier-than-thou person. She even admitted being overwhelmed at times with her own questions.

They talked for over an hour. Glancing at the clock, Marian suddenly remembered Pat. He'd probably been trying to call. "Oh, dear, I have to go."

"Me, too. But look ... would you like to come to church with me Sunday? Then come over for lunch? We could barbecue or something. I have a friend you'd really enjoy meeting. She's a lot more experienced about all this stuff than I am."

Marian hesitated. Talking on the phone was one thing. Visiting Chelsea and her husband was something else. Marian wasn't feeling very social these days. Still, the prospect of Sunday tugged at her heart. "I think ... okay. Thank you."

They made plans.

When Marian finally hung up, the phone rang again within minutes. It was Pat. An odd excitement knocked around in Marian. "Pat, you're not going to believe who just called me."

Wednesday, September 27

Chapter 43

Tanley's thoughts spun as he returned to the courtroom after lunch. It was his third day of calling witnesses. The week had gone fairly well. Gavil had been on the stand until midafternoon Tuesday, maintaining his composure amazingly well under Seltz's double-barreled cross-exam. Monday and Tuesday were sweat days. Once Gavil stepped down, the worst was over.

Tuesday afternoon and this morning, Tanley had called in half a dozen people to testify regarding their certainty of Gavil Harrison's inability to commit murder—Gavil's secretary, two other colleagues from work, and three friends. Seltz had done what he could to discredit their testimony. They knew Gavil Harrison well, correct? They were absolutely sure he could not commit murder, correct? Had any of them been aware of his claimed relationship with Sonya Hocking? No? Shocked, surprised? Well, then, either he was not exactly what he seemed, or he was lying. Which was it? Seltz also managed to pull from one Titan Electronics employee that Gavil had spent most of the day after the murder holed up in his office, hardly talking to anyone. Harrison's secretary, however, insisted he'd been busy crunching end-of-the-year numbers that day, and that his behavior was "not at all unusual."

All in all, Tanley believed his witnesses had made an impact, Seltz's gyrations notwithstanding. Today was the day to pull it all together.

"Defense calls Robert Naydeen."

Naydeen identified himself as a law enforcement consultant with an office in San Francisco—one of the few private agencies in the country from which detectives could be hired to help crack unsolved burglaries and homicides. Naydeen's specialty was serial murders. Notches in his belt included trailing some of the nation's most infamous killers, from California to Key West. Naydeen had a reputation for his ability to review details of a homicide, such as cause of death, position of the body, and surrounding circumstances, to determine a profile of the killer.

The two opposing counsels jockeyed back and forth in Naydeen's *voir dire*—the determination of the knowledge and experience that qualified him as an expert witness. *Voir dire* of a witness was in many ways as predictable as the calculated drama of the testimony itself. One attorney stacked the expert's credentials as if the person were God himself. The other side poked holes in them, nitpicking at the lack of a published article here, or continuing education course there, or the unfamiliarity with some narrow vein of expertise.

After half an hour, Seltz allowed Naydeen to be offered as an expert witness, and the questioning began. It would be a different kind of questioning from that of other witnesses, with both counsels expecting more lengthy, explanatory answers.

"You reviewed the photos and documents from the Trent Park murder, is that right?" Tanley asked.

"Yes, I did." Naydeen leaned forward, green eyes resting on Tanley. His dark hair was cut military style.

"Go through, if you will, the details you noticed, and your resulting profile of the person who killed Meg Jessler."

Naydeen cleared his throat. "Well, there are a number of things. First, of course, the murder took place in an isolated area off the main road of Trent Park. My immediate question was, 'How did the perpetrator get Ms. Jessler there?' It seemed at first as though she must have known the person who murdered her, and so hiked to the gully voluntarily. I've discovered since then, however, that the victim was sometimes, uh, impulsive. Friends called her 'flighty.'" He shrugged. "That's their word, not mine. With this type of personality, as opposed to an aggressive woman very certain of herself, she could have been scared enough by someone to allow herself to be forced down the trail. The perpetrator must have used some means to force her, however, such as a gun or knife."

"What makes you think that?"

"Well, it's somewhat unusual that a woman who jogs early in the morning, alone, wouldn't try to fight off an attacker. You tend to think of that kind of woman as assertive and disciplined. And typically, female joggers remain very aware of their surroundings in order to ward off potential trouble. Yet Meg Jessler didn't do that. She allowed herself to be pulled off the main road into a situation from which she would not get out alive. Two things must occur in order to convince me of that scenario. One, the woman scared easily and was apt to quickly fall apart at the moment of attack. From what I gather about her personality, I see that as highly probable. And two, the attacker must have had some weapon that scared her enough to force her into walking a mile or so. That's a long walk under such circumstances."

"Does this look like a stalker to you?"

Tanley knew it was a leading question, but Seltz let it pass.

Naydeen nodded. "Yes, I'd say so, especially given the early time of day. It appears to be the work of someone who watched the victim, who knew when she jogged and where, and lay in wait for her at the head of a trail. I'd say the murder was well planned."

"I see." Tanley retrieved the photo exhibits of the victim from the court clerk and showed them to Naydeen, who identified them. He had looked at numerous photos and all the autopsy information, he indicated, and had spoken with the coroner. Tanley strolled toward the jury. "And what did you notice about the body?"

Naydeen leaned back. "What interested me were these facts. First, she was beaten in the face. Second, the death blow was to the back of her head. In other words, from her neck down she was left untouched, as far as we can tell. At least we can be sure there was no rape."

"Do you find that unusual?"

"Well, murders run the gamut of variations, but overall, I would say, yes, this kind of killing often would involve rape. By 'kind' I refer again to the fact that they were out basically in the middle of nowhere. It took some time to get to the gully. This was not a murder that occurred spur-of-the-moment in someone's home."

"Anything else?"

"There's also the strange fact about the gloves. Why would anyone put a pair of gloves on a victim before killing her?"

"Then remove them afterwards."

Naydeen shook his head. "I don't see that as unusual. Once you've used gloves, if you've got any wits about you at all—and clearly this person did—you'd take the gloves off so they wouldn't be found as evidence. The question here is why use them in the first place? It could be symbolic."

From the corner of his eye, Tanley could see a courtroom artist sketching his profile and Naydeen on the stand—a drawing that would be taped onto the hallway walls during recess and filmed for the evening news.

Courtroom watchers would call this a day for the defense.

Tanley leaned against his table. "Could you give us your overall picture of the killer, explaining what you mean by symbolic?"

Naydeen ticked off the points on his fingers. "First, I'd say you've got someone who dislikes women, probably stemming from trouble with Mother as a young child. Abused, perhaps molested. This person likely could not keep a stable relationship with a woman. He may be good at surface friendships, enough to fool a lot of people. But a long-term successful relationship—I doubt it. Second, I'd say there's something about a woman's hands that bothers the perpetrator. This again could tie into trouble with Mom. He covered the victim's hands so she couldn't touch him. The very thought of her hands may bring revulsion. Take that one step further. If, in fact, Mom is the reason for the anger, then the victim could have been a stand-in for Mom. A child is beaten, abused in some way, and he can do nothing about it. But the anger rages. When he gets older, that anger turns toward other women. They become the scapegoat, the punching bag, if you will, for all the things he wanted to do to his mother. This could also explain the lack of rape."

Naydeen paused for a drink of water. Tanley waited.

"I'd say the wounds to the face and blows to the head again fit the picture. The perpetrator sees Mother. He hates the things she says, he hates her eyes on him. He hates the thoughts that rage through her head. So he covers the hands, then he beats that face and mouth, and bangs that head against a rock until all is still. And he's free. At least," Naydeen pressed his lips together, "for a while."

Tanley drew out a pause, reveling in the energy of doubt swirling around him. The discerning eyes of numerous jurors fell on Gavil Harrison. How could this man, who'd testified of a loving mother, possibly fit the profile of such a sick mind?

"Are you *through*, Mr. Tanley?" Benelli's voice rasped.

The defense attorney jumped. "Yes. Yes, Your Honor, I am."

He turned the witness over to the prosecution.

~ ~ ~

Seltz rose, adjusting his coat. He respected Robert Naydeen. Didn't know him personally, only through a colleague who had prosecuted a case in which Naydeen had been helpful. Handled appropriately, Naydeen could be helpful to the prosecution again.

"Mr. Naydeen. I'm most pleased to meet you. I've heard much about your work."

288

"Thank you." Naydeen's face remained impassive, but the slight shift in his posture betrayed his pleasure.

Conversationally, Seltz began asking questions about the case Naydeen had worked on the previous year. He laid the foundation that Naydeen's profile of the perpetrator had been "right on target," and that the case was ultimately solved and the murderer convicted.

Seltz was aware of Tanley's alertness at the defense table, his eyes darting from prosecutor to witness. Continuing his questions, Seltz established basic details of the case. The victim, forty-year-old Maude Victor, had been found stabbed to death in her car, with multiple cuts on her face. She'd been sitting upright, and all doors were locked.

"Objection!" Tanley lifted a hand. "This is irrelevant. What case are we trying here?"

"Your Honor," Seltz cut in, "there are similarities in these two cases. My colleague has brought to light Mr. Naydeen's expertise. I merely want to make use of that knowledge for the benefit of this trial."

Benelli glared first at Tanley, then at Seltz, as if annoyed by the interruption. "All right, Mr. Seltz, proceed." He pointed a bony finger. "I'll give you sixty seconds to get to the point!"

"Thank you, Your Honor." Seltz inclined his head before turning back to Naydeen. "As we were saying, the car doors were all locked. Is that true?"

"Yes, it is."

"You made one particular point regarding the fact that those doors were locked—a point which indeed proved correct. Could you relate that point for this court, please?"

"Sure." Naydeen paused. "The car was parked on a major city street. It belonged to Maude Victor. Inside, as indicated, was her body. But why would the car be locked? Someone stabs Ms. Victor a total of twenty-two times, then is thoughtful enough to lock her car door so the radio isn't stolen? It just didn't fit." He stopped for another drink of water. "After thinking about it for a while, I came to the conclusion that the locked doors spelled ownership. In other words, someone who would stop to lock the doors in that situation must be used to locking the doors on that particular car. Call it habit, or what you will. It was simply a rote response."

"But wasn't the victim herself owner of that car?"

"Yes, that's true. But," Naydeen held up an index finger, "someone close to her may have driven the car often and locked the doors on such occasions. That was my determination. Maude Victor was not murdered by a stranger, but by someone very close to her, someone who knew her well enough to be allowed to drive her car."

Seltz cast a quick glance at Benelli. He made no move to intercede. "And briefly, Mr. Naydeen, the outcome of that case?"

"Police immediately requestioned Ms. Victor's boyfriend, who had given an alibi that seemed solid at first. After further investigation, that alibi fell through. Ultimately he confessed to the crime and was convicted."

"So would you say that the boyfriend may have gotten away with the crime had you not hit upon your idea of ownership?"

Naydeen lowered his chin. "Well, I can't say for certain what the final outcome would have been. But, yes, the idea of ownership sent the police back to look again at the boyfriend."

"I see." Seltz turned toward the jury, gazing with such intensity at the upper corner of the courtroom that a few members glanced up to see what had caught his attention. He let out a breath, frowning. "Let's talk about the gloves in this case. What do you make of the fact that they were returned to the very spot from which they were taken?"

"Yes." Naydeen glanced at the defense attorney—a glance of recognition and, perhaps, apology. Naydeen's ego, Seltz knew, would not allow him to leave unexplained his concern about the gloves, lest anyone else think of it and find his observances wanting. "Yes, we have not discussed that."

"Does not the fact that they were returned so neatly denote again your idea of ownership?"

"Objection, leading the witness."

"Sustained." Benelli focused his eyes on the prosecuting attorney with an air of a tired parent. "Try again, Mr. Seltz."

"Your Honor," Tanley made a face, "this is going nowhere. I object, and I ask that you move counsel back to the case at hand."

One corner of Benelli's mouth rose. "Sounds to me like he's already come around." He waved a hand at the deputy D.A.

Seltz remained nonchalant. "Please tell us, in your opinion, what the returning of the gloves means."

"Well, it could denote ownership. This is only a theory. There may be another explanation we just can't know. Maybe it was done on impulse, or as an act of arrogance. But it also could be that, for some reason, it seems the perpetrator found it important that the gloves be returned unharmed to their owner."

"Okay. Since we know that the actual owner of these gloves is not implicated in this crime, are you saying that it could be someone close to that person?"

"*Objection!*" Tanley jumped up.

"Sit *down,* Mr. Tanley! I'll thank you not to yell in my courtroom again. I can hear you well enough!" Benelli pressed two fingers in the center of his forehead before motioning for Seltz to proceed. "Your question was leading, counsel. Try again."

Seltz rephrased.

"Well, within this theory," Naydeen said, "I believe it could be someone very close emotionally to the owner of the gloves. I would also guess that it is someone physically close. In other words, I can't imagine a murderer intent on returning from the scene of a crime going out of his way to place a pair of gloves back on someone's porch."

"So, let me see if I understand this. You have two opinions regarding the person who returned the gloves, and, as I understand, both factors are important, correct?"

"Yes, assuming this theory is true."

"First, the killer was emotionally close to the owner of those gloves, close enough to care that she got them back?"

"Yes."

"And second, he was close in proximity."

"Yes, I believe both those statements could be correct, again within the confines of this theory."

"Thank you, Mr. Naydeen." Seltz allowed himself a slight smile. "I have nothing further."

Seltz knew Tanley wouldn't leave it there. He came on strong in redirect, trying to repair the damage to his case. He gained back little ground.

During Tanley's questioning, Seltz rested an elbow on the table, cupping his chin. Poker face intact, in his head he danced over his victory. Rare in a trial were the moments he'd just catalyzed—the dissolving of an opposing expert witness into a chemical reaction that heated up one's own case. More often than not, the most an attorney could do was damage the credibility of the witness. But Seltz had to admit he'd been nothing short of brilliant. He knew it and was aware that the jury and spectators knew. Shoot, he'd stand up and take a bow if centuries of courtroom decorum did not preclude it. Reiger evidently was having a harder time appearing unaffected. One of his legs jiggled under the table, and the side of his mouth would not stay down.

Thursday, September 28

Chapter 44

Psychiatrist David Wagner took the stand Thursday morning. Reiger looked him over and raised an eyebrow. Six-foot-three and over 250 pounds. His large head was framed by a mass of gray hair and matching beard, which he stroked occasionally. All he needed was the couch.

Wagner's credentials were extensive. So what? Look far enough, interview enough, and any attorney—prosecuting or defense—could find a medical expert who'd support his theory, no matter how whacked-out it was. Just as Seltz had presented his own psychiatrist, a woman who'd testified that Gavil Harrison was a dual-minded man capable of hiding murderous tendencies, so Tanley's man was now spouting presumptions of innocence under the guise of psychiatric mumbo jumbo. That the defendant could not be the killer profiled by law enforcement consultant Robert Naydeen. That he was the only child of professional parents, both deceased. That he displayed innate tendencies to cheat on the women he loved, tendencies which he could not seem to repress, even though he'd tried.

Wagner's suppositions fell like fat drops of Chinese water torture. How was it affecting the jury? Reiger slid a look at the twelve. Half of them were taking notes, brows wrinkled.

Somewhere behind Reiger sat Meg Jessler's parents, as they'd been every day of the trial. What inner strength they had, subjecting themselves to hear all the testimony.

If Gavil was found innocent, how could Reiger ever look them in the eye?

Despair flashed through Reiger. It hadn't helped that preceding the psychiatrist was an expert in DNA who'd proved through numerous impressive graphs and charts that the tiny piece of skin taken from the rock matched neither the victim nor Harrison. It really shouldn't matter. The matching fingernail superseded all else. The DNA had merely proved to be an example of a not uncommon aspect of police work—something first thought to be highly significant turning out to be nothing at all. Through cross-examination, Seltz had made the point that the piece of skin could have been left by anybody who'd hiked out to the gully and sat on the rock to rest. Still, the testimony had not made Reiger happy.

Nor did the psychiatrist, now on the stand. Reiger took a deep breath, annoyed with his own doomsday theories. Shaking aside his thoughts with an effort, he forced himself to concentrate on the testimony.

~ ~ ~

The clock showed 1:30 p.m. The trial was winding down, and Seltz could feel the jury's tiredness. Defense had rested its case after Dr. Wagner's testimony. Seltz had the floor again, this time for rebuttal.

The jury was about to get a wake-up call.

"The people call Sonya Hocking."

The name sent a ripple through the courtroom.

In a blue silk suit and matching pumps, Sonya Hocking made her entrance down the aisle of the courtroom with a regal air. Her black hair was in a stylish chignon, her makeup flawless. The courtroom rustled as she took the stand, all eyes drawn to her as she smiled at her husband, whose confident presence in the third row assured the public of his support. As Seltz stepped around the end of the prosecution's table, Sonya Hocking inclined her head to Reiger. The sergeant nodded back.

"Good afternoon, Mrs. Hocking," Seltz said.

"Good afternoon."

Seltz glanced at the jury box. He could see on their faces their assessment of the woman. Beautiful, poised. Possessing an aura of quiet dignity amid the distasteful task she had been summoned to do.

"Ma'am, please tell us where you live."

"On Wenelle Street in Atherton, number six."

"And with whom do you live?"

"My husband, Stuart."

"No children?"

"No." Her voice was low, regretful. "His children are gone and I ... we have none."

Seltz lowered his chin to show his sadness at that fact. "Are you employed, Mrs. Hocking?"

"No."

"How then do you spend your time?"

For the next ten minutes Sonya Hocking passionately explained her role in various children's charities. During the last year she had focused on the Sonya Hocking Foundation, which she recently established for children suffering from cancer. Since she could have no children of her own, she said, and God had blessed her financially through her marriage to Stuart, she decided to devote her time to helping these unfortunates. From February through August of the current year, when she hadn't been raising money for a state-of-the-art oncology center in Sunnyvale dedicated to saving these "dear little ones," she'd been visiting the sick children and lending their parents emotional support. Now, finally, the funds were in and the center would soon be under way.

Seltz posed his questions delicately, nudging the information from her as though she were far too humble to expound on her virtues without his urging. He was aware of the attitude of listeners in the courtroom. They liked Sonya Hocking. They were soaking in her answers. He *had* them.

When he could stretch out the discussion of her charity no longer, Seltz indicated the defendant. "Mrs. Hocking." His voice inflection indicated that he was introducing an unwelcome but necessary topic. "Do you know this man?"

Expectation hung in the courtroom, played out in the dangling of pens over reporters' notepads, the flicking eyes of the jury. Except for juror number eight, the male college student, who was losing the fight to suppress a yawn.

Sonya Hocking allowed herself a sad glance at the man who'd once been her husband's friend. If she was shocked at Gavil's appearance, she gave no sign.

"Yes. Gavil Harrison and my husband were very close."

"Did you meet Mr. Harrison through your husband?"

"Yes. He was the best man at our wedding."

Seltz paused, allowing the piece of information to sink in. "How long has Mr. Hocking known him?"

She thought a moment. "Over ten years."

"And you said they were very close?"

"Yes. Stuart mentored Gavil. He made sure Gavil got the job at Titan Electronics."

"And what has your relationship with Mr. Harrison been like, Mrs. Hocking?"

Her eyes closed briefly. "We were friends. Stuart and I went to dinner fairly often with Gavil and Marian Baker, the woman Gavil said he wanted to marry. Sometimes I'd play golf with the men. Marian doesn't play. I respected Gavil." Her brow furrowed. "I liked him a lot. And I thought he respected me."

Seltz nodded. "Now, Mrs. Hocking, we must turn to the morning in question—Wednesday, June 5. Would you please tell this court where you were that morning?"

"Certainly." She took a breath. "I was home alone until about 10:30. At that time, Stuart came home, and we left together for a golf game at La Prima, our country club. Our tee time was around 11:15."

"Where was your husband before he came home?"

"On an overnight business trip to Portland. He had an early flight Wednesday morning so he could get home in time to play golf."

"I see. And what were you doing before he came home?"

She lifted a shoulder. "Working in my office, as I remember. I had lots of phoning to do in regard to raising the funds. Following up on contacts, things of that nature."

Seltz paused. "You are aware that the defendant claims he was with you that morning until 9:30?"

"I am." The words tinged with regret.

"And he was not?"

She looked Seltz squarely in the eye. "No. He was not."

"Mrs. Hocking." Seltz allowed the pitch of his voice to fall. He spread both hands, his head shaking in bafflement. "There's really no way to say this gracefully. The defendant claims he had a sexual relationship with you, and that he spent the night of Tuesday, June 4, with you in your home, staying until 9:30 on the morning of Wednesday, June 5. Is this true?"

Sonya Hocking pressed her lips together. "I am aware of his claims. They are false." Her eyes wandered to Gavil, then to her husband. Stuart nodded, encouraging her. She looked again to Seltz. "We were friends, as I told you. Friends, because he and my husband were friends. But not one word of that statement is true."

Seltz saw the question in juror number two's face, one which would be festering in the minds of many. Juror number two worked with computer data, and she was analyzing now.

"I must ask you something in order to clarify your answer, Mrs. Hocking. The defendant claims he was alone with you from about 10:00 Tuesday evening until 9:30 Wednesday morning, and indeed your husband *was* out of town Tuesday night and did not return until 10:30 Wednesday morning. How do you explain this coincidence?"

"It wasn't a coincidence." Sonya Hocking sighed. "Gavil knew I was home alone that night because I had told him a few days previously that Stuart would be out of town."

"And what prompted you to do that?"

"I'd been helping my husband set up a golf foursome for Wednesday. At Stuart's request, I called Gavil sometime the previous week, asking if he could join us. When I told Gavil our tee time, he wondered why it was so late. I explained that Stuart would be out of town the previous night and was catching an early flight Wednesday. Our tee time, 11:15, was the earliest Stuart and I could make it to the club."

"And what was Gavil Harrison's answer to your invitation?"

"He wanted to play, but said he just couldn't because he had so much work."

"I see." Seltz strolled toward the jury. "So when Mr. Harrison told the detectives he'd been with you from Tuesday night until Wednesday morning, he knew that you had been home alone during that time, correct?"

"Yes."

The deputy D.A. pressed his fingertips together. "After this phone call in which you invited the defendant to play golf, when did you next talk to him?"

"Not until Friday night, June 7. He called me at home."

"How did he sound?"

"Objection, Your Honor, calls for speculation." Tanley perched on his seat like an eagle scanning for a mouse.

"Your Honor, I'm not offering it for the truth of the—"

"Sustained." Benelli gestured with the back of his hand, like sweeping at a fly. "Continue, Mr. Seltz."

The deputy D.A. nodded. "Mrs. Hocking, what did the defendant say to you?"

"Objection, calls for hearsay."

Seltz spread his hands. "It goes to the defendant's state of mind, Your Honor."

Benelli considered, his head tilted. "Overruled."

Seltz let out a breath. "What did the defendant tell you during the phone call that night?"

Disbelief etched Sonya Hocking's face. "He said that two detectives probably were on their way to my house to question me. He said they suspected him of murdering the young woman found in Trent Park the day before."

Seltz could hear the reporters' pens. Juror number two had leaned back in her chair. "You were aware of that crime?"

"Yes. I'd heard about it on the news." She glanced at Reiger. "When Gavil called me about the detectives coming over, at the time I just couldn't believe they'd think Gavil had anything to do with it."

Reiger inclined his head, as if to say he understood. Seltz pretended not to notice the bit of planned interaction. "Did the defendant say anything else?"

Sonya Hocking brought a hand to her cheek.

"Your Honor," Tanley stood, "I object to this entire—May we approach?"

A sidebar ensued, Seltz arguing his position against a simmering Tanley. The hearsay rule should not apply. The jury had a right to know the total scope of the defendant's supposed "alibi." Benelli ruled in his favor.

Seltz repeated his question.

"Yes, he said other things," Sonya Hocking replied. "He said that he'd told the detectives he was with me from Tuesday evening around 10:00 until 9:30 Wednesday morning, and that he'd also told them we were having an affair." Her face pinched.

"*Were* you having an affair?"

"No, *never*." Sonya Hocking shook her head. "I would never do that to my husband. I love Stuart, and I've never looked at another man since he and I met. And neither would I do anything to jeopardize my good name, when the building of the oncology center rests upon the public's trust in me. Those children *need* me, Mr. Seltz." Her voice wavered. "If *I* don't build that center to save them, who will?"

Seltz suppressed the urge to wince. She'd gone too far in her indignation. Tanley could hang her by her thumbs.

"When the defendant told you this disturbing news, Mrs. Hocking, what did you do?"

"I just couldn't *believe* it. I asked him again and again, 'Why did you tell them that?' I couldn't see why he needed to say he'd been with me at all. I couldn't understand why he was doing that to me."

Seltz allowed the jury time to lock away Sonya Hocking's stricken expression. "So, if I understand you correctly, the defendant gave you details of an alibi he had stated to the police, correct?"

"Yes."

"What did he expect you to do, if anything?"

Sonya Hocking closed her eyes. "He wanted me to back up his story."

Seltz reacted. "Are you saying that he asked you to relate the exact details of his alibi to the detectives?"

"That's right." Her eyebrows raised. "He did. He absolutely *begged* me to stand by his story."

~ ~ ~

The slightest smirk played across Tanley's face as he watched Sonya Hocking draw herself up, preparing for cross. "Here we go, hold on to your seats," he whispered to Gavil, rapping the table with his knuckles. Gavil managed a wan smile.

Tanley approached the witness with a perceiving stare. He knew he had to play this just right. Come down too hard, and the jury would feel sorry for her, the big, bad defense attorney harassing the innocent witness. Come down not hard enough, and he'd lose the opportunity to score some very big points.

301

"Mrs. Hocking," he said with a lightness in his voice intended to fool no one, "may I remind you that you are in a court of law. That you have taken an oath to tell the truth. And that perjury is a criminal offense."

"Objection, Your Honor!" Seltz appeared offended. "That's clearly argumentative."

"Stable your horses, Mr. Seltz." Benelli peered over his glasses at the deputy D.A., then fixed Tanley with a glower. "Proceed, sir. Try asking a question this time."

"Very well." Tanley folded his arms. "Mrs. Hocking, I'd like to talk a little bit more about your fund-raising efforts for sick children."

"All right." She eyed him warily.

"You mentioned that when you're not raising funds for these children, you're visiting them. Where exactly *is* it that you visit them?"

Sonya Hocking's eyes told him she knew where he was headed. "Most of them are very sick, Mr. Tanley. They are in the hospital."

"In the hospital?" He feigned surprise. "Which hospital?"

"That varies, depending upon where the children live. But many times they're in the Palo Alto Children's Hospital."

"I see. That's the facility known for its excellent medical care, right? And, as I remember, that hospital—the *entire* hospital, not just a part of it—has been funded by a charitable foundation, has it not?"

Sonya Hocking's expression was impassive. "That's right."

"And the woman who established the foundation, Edith Dressell, isn't her name across the entrance to the building in large letters?"

Sonya shrugged. "I believe so. Yes."

"Uh-huh." Tanley thought a moment. "So evidently, this hospital, Palo Alto Children's, takes poor care of children with cancer?"

"I never said that."

Tanley assumed a confused expression. "Well, no. But when you were talking about your fund-raising efforts, you said, 'If I don't build that center to save them'—meaning the children—'who will?' Correct?"

"I guess. I don't remember exactly what I said."

"Would you like me to have the court reporter read it back to you?"

She surveyed him. "No, that won't be necessary."

"So you did say those words."

"I suppose I did."

Tanley pressed his lips. "Well, if the Palo Alto Children's Hospital, which bears Edith Dressell's name, is meeting the needs of these children, why do you think you need to 'save' them?" The word was tinged with sarcasm.

"Objection, Your Honor." Seltz sounded indignant. "He is *badgering* this witness!"

"Your Honor, I'm merely—"

Benelli held up a hand. "Enough, Mr. Tanley. I'll overrule for now. Just get to the point."

Tanley hid his irritation. Seltz had held his objection until the time when it would best interrupt his line of thought. "Do you remember the question, Mrs. Hocking?"

"I remember it very well, Mr. Tanley," she replied coldly. "And I'll be happy to explain my statement." Her tone fell to one of controlled patience, as if she was talking to an imbecile. "We are discussing the needs of children who are *dying,* sir. They need *every* bit of help they can get. All the hospitals in this geographic area, while very good, are more general in scope. *My* center will be dedicated solely to eradicating cancer—a horrible killer of children."

Tanley's mouth curved. "*Your* center? Don't you mean the center built and funded by the foundation you established?"

"Yes, of course that's what I mean."

"The foundation involves many more people than just *you,* right?"

"Yes." Her face was hardening.

Tanley's eyes narrowed. "Tell me this, Mrs. Hocking. Don't the plans for this oncology center call for *your* name to be across its entrance in large block letters?"

"Yes, I believe that's right."

"You *believe?* Didn't you in fact argue—quite angrily—with the architect of that building for the letters of your name to be far larger than what he'd planned?" Tanley was taking a calculated risk. He knew this to be true, and if she denied it, he would call the architect as a witness to impeach her.

Sonya observed him. "Oh, I do remember the issue of the letters now. And yes, I *discussed* them with the architect."

"Discussed. You didn't argue?"

She hesitated, eyes locked on him. Tanley had the distinct impression she was gauging how much he knew. "It was a heated discussion, that is true."

"I see. And exactly why did you have this 'heated discussion'?"

She sighed. "The letters were imbalanced with the rest of the building."

"'Imbalanced.'" Tanley considered this. "Meaning you thought your name wasn't prominent enough?"

"Meaning that the geometric images that I also wanted on the building overshadowed the letters to such an extent that I thought the design was poor."

Tanley nodded, considering his next move. He itched to take the subject of the letters further, but Seltz would object that he was badgering the witness again. Tanley didn't want to risk Benelli's sustaining it. The jury's sentiments might flow in Sonya Hocking's favor. Tanley inclined his head. "Well. Perhaps we'll come back to that." He cleared his throat. "By the way, do you remember telling Mr. Seltz you'd never do anything to jeopardize your good name?"

Sonya Hocking blinked. Tanley watched her grow still as the realization of what he could do with such a statement settled over her. A silent, deep breath raised her shoulders. "Yes."

Tanley nodded, then shrugged. "Well. Let's talk about your background for a moment."

Distrust shimmered from her unwavering gaze. Tanley knew she wasn't fooled by his temporary reprieve. *Don't worry, Mrs. Hocking, we'll come back to your slip of the tongue.*

Carefully and with initial empathy, Tanley began probing, pulling from Sonya Hocking the facts of her poverty-filled childhood. Her immigrant parents. The hand-me-down clothes, her dreams of rising above it all. Her hard work in high school, followed by landing a job as a bank teller. And fifteen years later, her first look into the eyes of Stuart Hocking when he entered the bank one day to make a substantial deposit into a savings account.

Then Tanley began turning the screws he'd placed with such precision. Sonya Hocking had risen far since marrying Stuart, hadn't she? She now lived in a huge house, enjoyed luxuries and the company of the wealthy. She enjoyed her reputation, the deference others gave her, first because of the man she'd married, and finally because of her own deeds. She was proud of all she'd become, wasn't she? Proud of her plans for the oncology center, yearning for the day to see it built? What a personal testament to her—that building with her name in large letters. And weren't some of her friends now encouraging her to enter politics? Wasn't she indeed considering running in a future election for state assembly? She had to admit, did she not, Tanley prodded, that her good standing in the community would be absolutely necessary to obtain votes? And that, in fact, her current project, the center, rested just as strongly upon her good name? She herself had stated that it did. And how did she know this was so? Wasn't it through her experience of seeing wealthy people pledge money because of their faith in her integrity? In fact, what had happened to pledges for the hospital wing when Gavil Harrison's claim of having an affair with her first became public? According to the foundation's accounting records, hadn't pledges declined drastically? And hadn't funds begun flowing again only after she'd spent countless hours assuring many individuals that Gavil Harrison's claim was false?

By this time, a faint sheen had spread across Sonya Hocking's perfectly powdered face. Her jaw was set, eyes hard, back ramrod straight. *How dare you treat me this way!* her countenance screamed. Seltz did his best to shore up her Rock-of-Gibraltar façade as the pebbles began to fall. He objected often and with disdain, seeking to upset Tanley's flow of questions. But Benelli was having none of it, repeatedly ruling that Sonya Hocking had opened up the entire line of questioning.

Onlookers appeared on edge, reporters' eyes darting from attorney to witness. The jury's expressions reflected their analyses of Sonya Hocking's motivations. Without turning around, Tanley could *feel* Stuart Hocking's hatred boring into his back. Maybe if he got lucky, the man would lose all control and lunge for him.

"Well," Tanley said, "obviously, your public life has been seriously affected by the defendant's alibi." He glanced at Gavil. "And what about your personal life? What might happen, say, if you were unable to convince your husband that you're telling the truth about not having an affair with his best friend?"

Sonya Hocking nearly trembled in her wrath. "I don't see the point of your question. He *does* believe me."

"I understand that." Tanley lifted both hands, palms out. "It's merely a hypothetical question."

The defense attorney plunged on, managing to paint a grim picture of what could happen to Sonya Hocking if her husband divorced her for infidelity. She probably would be left with a paltry settlement, correct? Wouldn't she lose the house, her social standing, her friends? Without money of her own, what would she do? Go back to being a *bank teller?*

"Who knows, Mr. Tanley?" Sonya's tone was chilling. "I haven't given these things a moment's thought because my husband *knows* that I have been and will always be faithful to him."

"Maybe so, Mrs. Hocking." Tanley gave an affected shrug. "Maybe so. But there's just one thing that bothers me." His words became precise, deliberate. "You told Mr. Seltz that you'd never do *anything* to jeopardize your good name. Right?"

Sonya Hocking's chin raised in defiance even as her throat clicked in a nervous swallow. "Yes."

Tanley did not move. *"Anything.* That was your word."

She glared at him. "Is that a question?"

"No, Mrs. Hocking. *This* is my question."

Fleetingly, Tanley imagined the jury's vociferous deliberation of the final point he would now make in *The People v. Gavil Harrison.* His heart was pounding, his throat tight. All the preparation, all the witnesses and examinations and cross-examinations. All the anxiety and lost sleep. The entire case now came down to one last question. He glanced at the jury. *Just one of you. All I need is one.* Tanley planted himself in front of the defense table, feet apart, arms crossed.

"*This* is my question, Mrs. Hocking. If you *did* have an affair with Gavil Harrison, and if he *was* with you the morning of Wednesday, June 5 ... in light of your admitted determination to protect your good name at all costs, *why should we expect you to tell us the truth?*"

Friday, September 29

Chapter 45

Reiger's stomach was acting up. He'd begun feeling it on Thursday, while Dr. Wagner was on the stand. Edith's dinner of pork chops and potatoes hadn't set well Thursday night. Now this morning he kept burping paprika. To make things worse, the trial would close today, leaving everyone hanging over the weekend for a verdict.

Digging in his pocket for an antacid, Reiger watched Judge Benelli scour some papers before him with a frown.

The judge's head came up. "All right then." He looked from one attorney to the other. "Good morning, all. Mr. Seltz, any more witnesses at this time?"

"No, Your Honor, I'm through."

"Mr. Tanley?"

The defense attorney shook his head. "We're done."

"Humph." Benelli scratched his nose. He checked the large courtroom clock. It was 9:15. "Okay, then. Let's move on to our housekeeping."

Reiger worked his mouth, tasting the slightly sweet chalk of antacid as the trial's conclusions began—the boring process of discussing which logged exhibits the attorneys wanted to be placed into evidence. Judge Benelli kept an eye on the clock, shortening the lunch hour when it finally arrived, wanting everyone back at 12:45 to leave enough time for closing arguments, wrap-up, then jury instructions before sending jurors off to deliberate. The way Benelli was gunning for conclusion, Reiger figured he must have weekend plans and wanted to beat the Friday traffic out of the Bay Area.

After lunch, Seltz offered his closing arguments. Tanley followed. By three, the defense attorney was wrapping up. Reiger's rear end was tired, and his stomach felt no better than it had that morning—an entire pack of antacids ago. Unfortunately, at the rate Benelli was moving things along, the chance for an afternoon break seemed bleak.

As Tanley spoke, the jury took notes, ears pricked and eyes alert, like horses heading for the stable. Reporters who'd sauntered in and out during the morning's more mundane moments, much to Benelli's displeasure, were now back in their seats. Milt Waking was scribbling. Camera crews roamed the hallway, ready to pounce on the attorneys for predictions of the outcome. Tanley and Seltz would respond diplomatically. They'd done their best and now it was "in the hands of the competent jurors," who'd worked so hard and been so attentive during the trial, etc., etc.

In the hands of the jury.

Reiger dared a lingering look at them. How were they leaning? Seltz was good at reading jury members, saying which ones he "had" and which were "problems." But even Seltz would qualify his statements by adding that in the end nobody knew what a jury would do. They were as changeable as chameleons in a crayon box.

Juror number six looked in his direction, and Reiger slid his eyes back to Tanley, who stood at a podium before the jury box, summing up his theories on the murder charge.

"And so, ladies and gentlemen, after all your deliberation, you may find Gavil Harrison guilty of Meg Jessler's murder. But that's if, and *only* if, you can determine logical explanations for all of the questions and coincidences I have raised over the last hour. And they are many. Let me reiterate them quickly."

He ticked off his fingers. "First, you must firmly believe that the fact that those gloves sat on the porch for two days has no significance. Those gloves that sat on a porch just a few feet from the street sidewalk, easily visible to all who walked by. Any person entering that complex could have picked up and returned those gloves. But you must deny that fact. The prosecution would lead you to reason that the chances of someone else using those gloves to murder a young girl and returning them are slim. *Slim.* They have never said it was impossible. Because you and I know it is not impossible. If you believe that it is impossible, how can you believe that the defendant *himself* picked up those gloves, committed murder, then put them back? Why would he not take them into the house and put them away? Certainly he would want to examine them, make sure no bloodstains or other evidence was present. Or why wouldn't he get rid of them altogether? Surely he'd expect to see police in the area once the victim's body was found. After all, she was a neighbor. Yet we are supposed to believe that he would casually toss those gloves back on his own front porch to sit in plain view. How much more likely that someone else used those gloves and returned them to their visible spot? What a splendid, cunning way to point the police in someone else's direction! And you and I know we are dealing with a very cunning and vicious killer."

Tanley allowed the point to hang in the air as he took a drink of water.

"Second, in order to find the defendant guilty, you must unequivocally believe that the DNA, matching neither the victim nor Gavil Harrison, came from an innocent hiker who rested on that particular rock. Further, you must believe that the tiny piece of skin recovered from that rock remained there—was not knocked aside—during an intense struggle in which the victim's head was smashed again and again on that rock. Third, you must discount the testimony of every friend and coworker who sat in this witness stand, under oath, and swore that they were absolutely certain that the defendant is incapable of such a heinous crime. You must rationalize that each one is either lying or is badly mistaken. Every. One.

"And fourth, you must also discount the testimony of two professionals who are highly esteemed in their fields. Robert Naydeen, law enforcement consultant, described his profile of Meg Jessler's killer. Someone with an abused childhood, someone who cannot maintain a relationship with a woman, someone who perhaps has killed before and will likely kill again. Now we know the defendant has not killed before. The arresting officer's own testimony of his background checks on Mr. Harrison established that fact. And Gavil Harrison lived with a woman whom he wanted very much to marry. I would certainly call that a long-term relationship. Look at all of these facts, ladies and gentlemen. This does not fit in any way the portrait of the killer that Robert Naydeen painted for us.

"In addition, to find Gavil Harrison guilty, you must ignore the opinion of Dr. David Wagner, a psychiatrist who examined the defendant on two separate occasions, and who strongly believes he is not capable of murder.

"And fifth, ladies and gentlemen, you would have to believe that Sonya Hocking is telling the truth when she says Gavil Harrison was not at her house the morning of Wednesday, June 5, and that she never had an affair with him. Let me remind you that this is a woman with *a lot to lose*. She herself admitted, on this very stand," Tanley gestured over his shoulder, "that she would never do anything to ruin her good name. *Anything*. That was the word *she* chose. Now I know she said that in context of denying the affair. But it's those slips of the tongue that are the most telling, wouldn't you agree? The comments that spill automatically from one's mouth when one hasn't had time to consider the consequences. *'I would never do anything to jeopardize my good name.'* Ladies and gentlemen, *that* probably is the most truthful statement Sonya Hocking has uttered in regard to this entire trial. She indeed would do anything to save her own reputation. *Anything*. Even *lie*. Even if it means an innocent man would go to jail. I ask you, after watching her performance on the stand, can you be *absolutely sure* she's telling the truth?"

Tanley leaned across the podium, his voice dropping. "So, what to do with all these considerations and incredible coincidences? You may be able to explain away one of them in a manner that seems rational and reasonable. But can you do so with *all* of them? Because that is what you must do in order to find Gavil Harrison guilty of murder. You must be absolutely certain of his guilt, leaving no room whatsoever for reasonable doubt. Not the slightest. For if you do have doubts about any of these questions, under the law of our land, you cannot find the defendant guilty. Beyond a reasonable doubt, ladies and gentlemen. The gloves—no doubts. The testimonies of Robert Naydeen and Dr. Wagner—no doubts that they both are wrong. The testimonies of so many friends and coworkers—no doubts they are wrong. The word of Sonya Hocking, a woman whose very way of life depends upon saving her reputation—no doubt that if she *did* have an affair with Gavil Harrison, she'd admit it to the world.

"Do you believe all those things? Can you, in the deepest regions of your conscience, clear away every doubt?" Tanley swept his gaze across the jury, catching the eyes of each member.

"I don't think you can."

He held his stance, breathing the force of his convictions. Then with a nod, he pivoted and returned to his seat beside the defendant. Gavil gave him a wan smile. Tanley patted him on the shoulder.

Coughs, clearing throats, the shuffling of papers throughout the courtroom.

Reiger extracted another antacid from his pocket and slid it into his mouth. He was halfway through his second roll.

Benelli looked to the deputy D.A. "Mr. Seltz?" With the burden of proof on the prosecution, Seltz was allowed a final rebuttal.

"Thank you, Your Honor."

He rose energetically, strode toward the podium, and gazed at the jury without a word. A long pause. He raised his hands in a shrug. "Mr. Tanley is right. To find Gavil Harrison guilty, you cannot retain any reasonable doubt. The key word, my friends, is *reasonable*. We've already discussed all the evidence that links Gavil Harrison to the brutal murder of Meg Jessler. The gold fibers under her nails that match the garden gloves in his home. The victim's broken fingernail found in one glove. The defendant's lack of an alibi for the time of the murder. These are key pieces of evidence, every one. And not one of them has been refuted by the defense to leave room for *reasonable* doubt.

"Let's look again at the garden gloves. Yes, they were on the porch the morning of the murder. Yes, they were visible from the street. But, in my mind, I can't get rid of the question, 'If Gavil Harrison didn't use those gloves, then who did?' The defense's scenario is that someone else picked them up, someone perhaps who lived in the complex, who could return them as well as steal them in the first place. But who? In their investigation, the police questioned every neighbor more than once. And not one individual gave them reason for suspicion—other than Gavil Harrison. Why? Because he was the only person in that complex who immediately, upon his very first encounter with police, lied about his whereabouts on the morning of June 5. Remember that before he ever came up with the story involving Sonya Hocking, he told the police he had been at work."

Seltz began to pace. "Now. To retain a reasonable doubt, we must believe that someone else did commit the murder of Meg Jessler. That is difficult enough, given the thoroughness of the detectives' investigation. In addition, we must believe that this someone else took the time, after committing such a vicious crime, to put the gloves back. Think of the incredible risk. Someone walking down his own front sidewalk may not be so noticeable, but that same person stopping to throw something on

314

a neighbor's doorstep—that's a more memorable action. Picture this person, looking furtively right and left, tossing down those gloves quickly in hopes that no one would notice. What for? Why take such a risk? We're talking about someone who had just murdered a young woman in cold blood, not a law-abiding citizen worried about whether some gardener gets her old, beat-up gloves back. No. The only person who would have good reason to return the gloves is Gavil Harrison. And why did he throw the gloves back on the porch instead of taking them inside to put them away?" Seltz emphasized each word of his answer. "Because the woman he lived with testified that's where she expected to see them. That he was not likely to bother with a pair of gloves lying on the porch. So he put them right back where he found them. And she picked them up when she returned home later that day. Just as she expected.

"Next, the defense would have you believe the testimonies of Gavil Harrison's friends and coworkers who say he is incapable of murder. I do not doubt that these people are sincere and are telling the truth, as far as they know it. But let me remind you of something. *You can be very sincere, and still be dead wrong.* True, not one of those friends believed Gavil could have killed Meg Jessler. But every one of them also had trouble believing he could be having an affair with his best friend's wife. And none of them would ever have thought Gavil Harrison would terrorize an innocent woman like Chelsea Adams in her own home. But he did. We have numerous witnesses regarding the incident with Mrs. Adams. Defense itself has not denied the facts regarding that crime. Which can only lead us to assume one thing—Gavil Harrison obviously isn't what he appeared to be, is he? Every friend who testified in this court ... Gavil Harrison had every one of them fooled.

"As for Robert Naydeen, who gave us his opinion regarding the profile of the killer, his profile may indeed be correct. Gavil Harrison could well fit that profile. Mr. Naydeen noted that the killer would not be able to hold a long-term relationship with a woman. Gavil Harrison, if you will remember, is over forty years old and has never married. He was trying to hold together a relationship with Marian Baker. Obviously, he did not succeed.

"Indeed, Mr. Naydeen gave one final piece of the killer's profile which defense has chosen to ignore—his concept of ownership regarding the garden gloves. That same issue of ownership proved true in one of Naydeen's former cases—true enough to send a man to prison for the murder of his girlfriend. Now we face the same issue here. Ownership. Again, who but Gavil Harrison would care what happened to those gloves after they had been used in a brutal murder? Who but Gavil Harrison would not want anything to be out of place when his girlfriend returned home?"

Seltz turned with a piercing look to the defendant. Gavil stared back.

"And the good psychiatrist, Dr. Wagner, who testified regarding his doubts that Gavil Harrison could commit murder. What did he also say under cross-examination? 'People are changeable.' I agree. People can change, even from one day to the next. And a person like Gavil Harrison can change. One minute he is playing the role of Mr. Businessman—the role his friends knew. The next, he's ditching work, sneaking into Chelsea Adams' home. Terrorizing her. Those facts are undisputed. And that's certainly change enough for me.

"Lastly, what do we do about the testimony of Sonya Hocking? She's a highly esteemed woman who's done many things for the less fortunate. For sick children. Despite Mr. Tanley's unabashed attack against her, Mrs. Hocking's testimony remains the same. She *never* had an affair with Gavil Harrison. He was *not* with her the morning of Wednesday, June 5. The fact is, much to Mr. Tanley's disappointment, he has been completely unable to refute Sonya Hocking's testimony. He has not found *one person* who could testify to knowledge of an affair between Gavil Harrison and Sonya Hocking. *Not one.*

"Now." Seltz took a deep breath. "Defense raises the issue of coincidence. Let's talk about coincidence. Meg Jessler's death occurs on a morning when the woman with whom Gavil Harrison lives just happens to be out of town. On a morning when Gavil Harrison's closest friend, Stuart Hocking, also happens to be out of town, leaving his wife at home by herself—a fact the defendant knew in advance. What perfect timing! Harrison is home alone and, if pressed, has an alibi almost impossible to prove or disprove. At best, his alibi sticks by him until the whole investigation blows over. At worst, the alibi denies it, but Harrison insists his story is true and that Sonya Hocking is lying. It's simply his word against hers, isn't it? It's better than no alibi. And what does he care if an innocent woman's reputation is ruined, as long as it plants the seed of reasonable doubt in the mind of one juror?

"My good men and women," Seltz came to rest against the podium, "what you have here, as defense has declared, is a very cunning killer. Someone cunning enough to plan exactly how to murder Meg Jessler and when. Someone smart enough to wait until just the right day. Someone with analytical and strategic thinking skills. Someone like Gavil Harrison."

He looked over his shoulder toward the defense table, then sauntered toward Gavil, hands in his pockets. "*This* cunning man made only one mistake. He didn't count on the tenacity of two detectives and one county criminalist. The men who discovered the irrefutable evidence that he, Gavil Harrison, and *only* he could have killed Meg Jessler. *This man,*" Seltz pointed at Gavil, "unmercifully beat young Meg Jessler. He bashed her head against a rock again and again until, in agony, she died. And then this man turned his unwanted and frightening attention on Chelsea Adams, the woman who in innocence happened upon the victim's body. Who knows what would have happened had not the same detectives arrived on the scene in the nick of time along with Mrs. Adams' panic-stricken husband?"

Seltz dropped his hand and returned to the jury. "Amidst all the evidence can you truly see justice done by proclaiming Gavil Harrison innocent? A man who lied to the police, a man who so viciously pursued wife and mother Chelsea Adams? Can you see a man like *that* free again to walk the streets? *Our* streets?" Seltz shook his head. "That would not be *justice,* my friends.

"That would be a *travesty.*"

Like Tanley, Seltz rested his eyes for a long time on the jury before resuming his seat.

Reiger could have sworn he heard someone drop a pin.

Saturday, September 30 – Thursday, October 5

Chapter 46

Saturday found Marian in her garden. No rain had fallen for months in the Bay Area. October typically began the rainy season, which lasted until around April. Summer months were dry. She scanned the grass, looking for brown spots, but saw none.

It had taken a number of months to get the backyard in shape again after she whirled through it like a banshee. The season for roses had passed. The bushes were now pruned, gathering strength for the following year. The orange trees had offered their summer fruit, much of which had gone uneaten. The oranges had been heaped in a bowl on the kitchen table until, one by one, she threw them out, brown and shriveled.

Thank goodness Pat had come along.

She couldn't have held out much longer, she told herself, as she pulled weeds by the back fence with a new pair of gloves. He'd been over twice more after the day she'd testified, and she'd reveled in his touch like a flower in the sun. And yet, after Pat would leave, Gavil would wash through her mind. Her first date with him ... the candlelit birthday dinner he'd made for her ... the day he'd moved in. Her emotions had been like feathers before a storm. When she was calm, it was with the placidity of a crater lake, hiding things in its cold depths she could not begin to fathom.

If only she could just *settle*. She wanted Pat in her life, could not imagine losing him now. And yet how dare she, even as Gavil awaited word of his fate? Her desires, so sweet as Pat had held her, now seemed selfish, her loyalties capricious. Pat's victory was Gavil's downfall, and Gavil's win, Pat's loss. All the same, she knew she could never go back to Gavil even if he were acquitted, for his release would not be due to his innocence. But what would he *do* if he was freed? Would he bother her? Come between her and Pat? The most selfish part of Marian wanted him behind bars for the sake of her own life, not because of the life he'd taken.

What a horrible thought.

Marian's future was out of her hands now, resting on the decision of twelve people who could not know, and would never see, the consequences of their choice.

She grasped a clump of weeds and pulled, wishing she could extract her ambivalence as easily. Tomorrow was church and the Adams' invitation. Would she even have the energy to go?

~ ~ ~

Reiger hated gardening. But Saturday afternoon, he found himself with Edith out in the backyard. The jury's short deliberation time Friday afternoon had given way to a weekend off, which made him feel powerless. The welfare of a family, an ex-girlfriend, grieving parents, the town of Haverlon, all hung in the balance while jurors were out shopping or taking naps. Reiger puttered around in the dirt for about an hour, trying to help, but managed to be more in the way than anything. Well aware of his anxieties, Edith tried to be patient. And she managed—until he inadvertently dug his feet into a flower bed when he stopped to pop an antacid in his mouth.

"Dan, isn't there a ball game or something on TV you can watch?"

He wandered off, too preoccupied for a response.

~ ~ ~

Turnbow played basketball Saturday, pounding out his anxieties in the high school gym. A childish "she loves me, she

321

loves me not" kept tripping through his head as he pivoted, faked, and shot. Every basket was in his favor, every miss, a "she-loves-me-not." He'd risked a lot to be with Marian before the trial was over, but he didn't regret that. Even for a while after the verdict they'd have to be careful lest news of their relationship sift back to his superiors. Or Reiger. Turnbow knew he'd disapprove.

He heaved a long shot and the ball *shooshed* through the net.

Turnbow knew the verdict would be guilty. The evil in Gavil's eyes was as certain as the unshirted bodies pounding the gymnasium floor. Turnbow's uncertainties lay not in Gavil's conviction, but in the fluctuating emotions of a woman who seemed lost at sea. If she would let him, he would rescue her.

He plunged forward for an easy shot.

The ball bounced off the rim.

~ ~ ~

Sunday afternoon Chelsea sat with Paul, Gladys, and Marian on the back deck, enjoying the sun and the smell of barbecuing ribs. The boys tossed a baseball at the far end of the lawn.

Marian had enjoyed church. She was now talking business with Paul and Gladys. Chelsea could see Paul was impressed with her. "Good thing you did call her," he whispered as they brought out drinks from the kitchen. "She'd make a great business manager for AP Systems."

How ironic.

Last month Paul had finally hired his V.P. of Sales for the company. *Without* Chelsea's help. Paul said she had enough on her mind.

Chelsea had prayed all week about Marian's visit. The minute they met at church, she sensed the woman's pain. Marian's grief had to be far worse than Chelsea's frayed nerves.

The trouble was, those frayed nerves had not disappeared. Last Monday, Chelsea felt better after reaching out to Marian, but that sense of doom soon returned. Even now, in the beautiful afternoon, a heaviness hung over her shoulders. Prayer hadn't helped. Something was wrong. Chelsea could no longer deny her fear of what it was.

Gavil was going to be acquitted.

Dressing for church that morning, Chelsea had finally voiced her worries to Paul.

"No way," he said. "Even if by some miracle the murder charge doesn't stick, they'd certainly convict him for what he did to you. *That* happened—no way around it."

"What if they feel sorry for him, if they believe what his attorney said—that Gavil was pushed beyond his limits?"

"Oh, get real. Stop worrying about it, Chels. No man is going to terrorize a woman in her own home and get away with it."

Paul had to be right.

So why did she feel this darkness?

Lord, please show me what's wrong. Is there something you want me to do?

"... grew up in church," Marian's voice caught Chelsea's attention. "So I know its traditions. But I never heard the things I've been hearing in church lately. Or what Chelsea said when we talked on the phone."

"Yeah." Gladys tilted her head. "But ... I do think there's a big difference between 'knowing church' and knowing Christ."

"What do you mean?" Marian asked.

Paul stood up. "Better check the ribs."

Soon he was tossing a baseball with the boys.

Chelsea listened as Gladys explained to Marian that through Jesus' death on the cross, all who accepted His forgiveness for their sins could draw near to Him and know Him personally. Marian asked a lot of questions. But after a while, Chelsea could see the conversation had played itself out. Time for a change of subject.

"Hey, Marian, want to know what this lady does for fun? Go ahead, Gladys, tell her."

Gladys' eyes sparkled. "Okay. What would you like to hear about first? My cross-country motorcycle trips, last year's African safari, or my New Year's resolution two years ago that I've kept more than a dozen times?"

Marian eyed her. "Wow. Uh ... what was your resolution?"

"To jump out of an airplane." Gladys grinned.

~ ~ ~

Monday dawned under blue skies. With the jury back in deliberation, Seltz and Tanley hung around the courthouse, playing at reviewing other files. There they would remain, as would Judge Benelli, in case the bailiff brought a question from the jury. Reiger tried hanging around for a few hours too, then left for the station, where he was greeted with many a thumbs-up. He'd been away from his office for two weeks. He spent the first hour or so wandering, talking to various officers about the case. He chatted with Monica in dispatch, who shared some home-baked chocolate chip cookies when lunchtime rolled around. He didn't feel like eating anything else. In the afternoon, he pushed paperwork, trying to help move the mountain off Turnbow's desk.

When the clock in his office read 5:00 p.m. he went home.

~ ~ ~

Tuesday.

Reiger told himself this would be it, at least by late afternoon. The day ticked by laboriously. Reiger was relieved to pull down a few other assignments. But his mind and stomach couldn't stay at ease for long. Three o'clock approached, then 4:00. Five o'clock came and went.

Seltz phoned at 5:15. "Benelli's antsy as a kid in summer school. You should see him. He's worse than Tanley and me put together."

Reiger leaned an elbow on his desk. "Did he poll 'em?"

"Yeah."

He straightened. "And?"

"It's ten–two."

"Ten–two." Reiger pictured the faces of the jurors. The nurse, the college student, the computer folks, the airline mechanic … "Who do you think it is?"

"Not sure." Seltz sighed. "Anyway, it's only two."

Reiger rubbed his forehead. "Two's one more than they need."

~ ~ ~

Wednesday seemed interminable.

By the afternoon, Seltz was sure the jury would remain hung. Tanley feared the same. Marian could not concentrate at work, dressing down three coworkers before she realized what she was doing. Chelsea didn't leave the house all day, even arranging for friends to pick up the boys from school. She couldn't chance missing the verdict. Reiger had promised to call when the jury was in.

Reiger was chewing two antacids at a time.

~ ~ ~

Thursday morning, 10:15. Reiger's phone rang. He was working at his desk, filling out a report on a break-in. He grabbed the receiver. It was Seltz.

"Jury's in."

His mind on automatic, Reiger called Chelsea. He thumped out of his office, then backtracked, pulling his spiral notebook from his pocket. He looked up Marian Baker's work number and called it.

"Where's Turnbow?" he called to Monica as he crossed the station lobby.

"Out on a call." She raised tweezed brows. "Is it time?"

"It's time."

He rolled toward the door like an expectant father.

325

Chapter 47

Reiger hurried past media vans and into the courthouse to find its hallways bristling with activity.

Reporters filmed the entrance of Meg Jessler's parents in a competitive scurry. Cameras turned on others then, gobbling up the tension, feasting on the drama. Only when the courtroom doors closed, Reiger knew, would they stop rolling and shut down the lights. Crews would then wait to record the verdict's aftermath in a glaring melee of shouted questions, attorney speeches, and reactions from the victim's family.

Reiger pushed through the crowd. He greeted Seltz in the sudden quiet of the courtroom, noting the reporters already present. The artist had claimed a seat on the front row's end and was pulling out her chalks. He and Seltz nodded to Tanley when he entered, then worked at small talk, guessing when the autumn rains would start. Reiger stepped back to shake Mr. Jessler's hand and nod at Mrs. Jessler. They thanked him, whatever the outcome. He dipped his head in reply.

~ ~ ~

Chelsea hurried in, flushed from running the gauntlet of reporters. Paul was at his office. She'd promised to call him afterward. She was so frightened of the verdict, she felt sick. What if Gavil was acquitted? He'd walk out a free man, right then and there. What would she do? *Please, God, please, let your will be done in this!* Tremulous, she flicked her gaze around the courtroom. A flash of a gold business suit in the doorway caught her eye. It was Marian, anxiety hovering about her like a dust cloud. Chelsea waved her over.

"How are you?" She squeezed Marian's hand.

Marian looked pale. "I don't know." She managed a weak smile. An older woman and a young dark-haired man in his twenties entered. Marian raised feeble fingers at them.

Chelsea stared. "Who are they?" She'd seen the woman in the audience when she testified. She could have sworn the man hadn't been there, yet he looked vaguely familiar.

Marian inhaled. "My neighbors. Mrs. Geary's our homeowners' association president this year. She's kind of a busybody. And that's Jack Doniger. He lives next to me. I don't know him well, but he's been very nice."

"How would they know to come?"

Another half smile. "Mrs. Geary knows everything. She's probably been hanging around the courthouse since Friday."

The old woman pulled Jack along, one hand fluttering. "How *are* you, dear," she gushed to Marian. "Now don't you worry, everything will be *fine*. I just know."

"Mrs. Geary," Jack tapped her on the shoulder, glancing apologetically at Marian. "Why don't we sit down? I see some empty seats."

"All right, all right." She rolled her eyes at Marian, as if to say, "Aren't kids brash these days?" They threaded through the knees of other spectators one row down and claimed their places a few seats to Chelsea's right.

Marian seemed relieved. "I want this over with," she whispered to Chelsea. "I just want to get on with my life."

Chelsea murmured her understanding, yet had only half heard. She was staring at the one-quarter profile of Jack Doniger. Where had she seen him?

The memory hit her.

A rustling up front snapped her eyes forward. Gavil was being led in. He sat beside his attorney, receiving a pat on the shoulder.

Marian sucked in a breath. The jury filed in and took their seats. Not one of them looked at Gavil. Was that a good sign? Four additional bailiffs lined the right wall, their presence intended to squelch any overt reactions to the verdict. The bailiff whose face had become familiar throughout the trial stood with them, hands clasped.

"All rise."

The hushed stir of clothes, papers, and bodies.

Judge Benelli entered, sweeping the courtroom with a discerning stare before sitting.

"You may be seated."

A settling down, notebooks shuffling, then a sudden, breath-holding stillness.

"Before we proceed," Benelli declared over his glasses, "I want one thing understood. There will be no outbursts in my courtroom." He searched out the reporters over his glasses. "And once the verdict is read, I expect everyone to remain seated while the jury is polled. No running for the doors, understand?" He checked the clock. "You all may have to scramble for the noon news, but you'll make it. Everybody with me?" A few heads nodded. "Counsel?"

"Yes, Your Honor," Seltz said.

Tanley bounced the palm of his hand against the table. "Ready, Your Honor."

Chelsea fought to concentrate. Something was wrong. Their voices were fading in and out like a distant radio station. Her vision began to blur.

Benelli swung his head toward the jury. "Have you reached a verdict?"

"We have, Your Honor." The foreman stood. His voice seeped in as if from a deep cave.

Then all sound ceased.

The courtroom darkened. Chelsea became enfolded, wrapped in a cocoon. A tunnel stretched before her, enveloped her. She felt herself swept inside, through it, beyond.

No, no!

The whisper of wind through sequoias blew in Chelsea's ears.

Please, Lord, help me!

Even as she realized what was happening, she fought it, sitting perfectly still, trying to return mentally to the courtroom. She could not bear to relive the nightmare of her vision again. But she couldn't stop it. She felt the seat stiffen into hard, cold ground. The aroma of eucalyptus trees filled her nostrils.

"I hate you!"

Chelsea screamed inside, bracing herself for the pain. She felt a fist slam into her mouth, her eyes. A pair of hands lifted her off the ground. "No!" she cried, her voice reverberating through the woods. The hands pushed her down. Her head smashed against the rock. They lifted her again, pushed her down again. Her hands flailed, hot and heavy in gloves. She was lifted a third time. Crashed a third time. She tried to speak, but her tongue would not form the words. Her blood thickened, her body struggled against its own shutting down. In her last conscious moment, the face above her focused into clarity. Her eyes flickered in startled recognition, then dulled.

The world went black.

Far, far away Chelsea began to hear the voices of the courtroom.

~ ~ ~

Marian's eyes locked on the jury. The foreman was juror number eleven. Who was he? The computer technician? The accountant? The teacher? Did it matter? She looked at Seltz for a clue, but his face remained impassive.

The bailiff walked toward the jury box, shoes squeaking through the quiet courtroom. The foreman waited. In his right hand was a folded piece of paper. The bailiff accepted it and headed toward the judge. The foreman resumed his seat. Benelli extended an arm. The piece of paper changed hands again. Benelli flipped open the paper, adjusted his glasses. Read it without expression. Folded it again. Gave it back. "Please give this to the clerk."

Marian existed on another plane. She dared not breathe, fearing she would hyperventilate. Her hands tingled, and she wiggled her fingers. Three steps to the clerk's desk. The bailiff offered the piece of paper, and the verdict moved once again to a new hand. Returning to the wall, the bailiff stood with his colleagues, all with feet spread, hands clasped.

The clerk rose from her chair. Marian saw Gavil's back stiffen. "Would the defendant please rise." He obeyed. Tanley stood with him, a hand under his left elbow. The clerk cleared her throat. "We, the jury, in Superior Court of the State of California, in the matter of *The People v. Gavil Harrison*, docket number ..."

Marian noticed Seltz leaning on his elbows, one hand cupping his jaw. Reiger's palms lay flat against the table. With a surge, Marian wished Pat was there, then realized that if he was, in her weakness she would give them both away.

"... in the charge of false imprisonment, pursuant to penal code section ..."

Marian's hands clenched.

"... we find the defendant guilty."

A murmur took flight and vanished. Reporter's pens scribbled.

Gavil lowered his head. Two jury members glanced at him, then looked away.

Marian's heart turned over, suspended.

In the front row, Mr. Jessler tightened his arm around his wife.

The clerk spoke again, addressing the burglary charge. The verdict: guilty.

More scribbling. A muffled gasp from Mrs. Jessler.

Five to six years, Marian thought. That's what Pat had told her. Gavil would be in jail at least that long. Relief—and devastation—flooded her. As if in a vacuum, the courtroom was sucked clear of sound once again. Here came the part everyone had waited for.

The clerk read the final charge of first-degree murder. "We, the jury, in Superior Court of the State of California, in the matter of *The People v. Gavil Harrison* ..." Marian's heart flailed like a leaf in a storm, then thudded against her ribs. Her mouth went dry. Both hands shook.

"... find the defendant guilty."

The word rang in her ears.

Guilty.

Marian could not move.

Would she ever move again?

One final strike remained and was delivered quickly by the clerk. The jury charged Gavil with the special circumstance of lying in wait.

Marian's head dropped. Gavil would never be free again.

Gavil folded into his seat, shoulders shrinking. The low murmurs in the room grew louder. Tears blurred Marian's eyes as she gazed at him. She was beyond feeling. Mrs. Jessler collapsed against her husband's chest, sobbing quietly.

Benelli banged his gavel, once, twice. The courtroom hushed. The jurors were polled as to each verdict. Marian sat like stone as "Yes" resounded from a dozen resolute mouths, four times each. Benelli thanked them magnanimously for fulfilling their duties.

Then, with a simple declaration—"Court is adjourned"— it was over.

The courtroom doors banged open, then the foyer doors beyond. "Get in here, it's guilty!" Milt Waking held open the outside door while his cameraman rushed in, followed by a herd of others. Bright light bathed the room. Equipment whirred.

Marian found herself in a barrage of reporters. She couldn't remember moving from her chair.

"Ms. Baker, what are your plans now?" Milt Waking closed in on her.

"Do you plan to visit Gavil Harrison in prison?"

"What do you think about his claimed alibi?"

Dazed, she looked left and right, searching for a way out. Someone grabbed her elbow, began pulling her to safety. "Come on, I'll get you out of here!" It was Jack Doniger. The group surged away from her toward the attorneys and Reiger.

"You're seeing the system at its best today," she heard Seltz declare behind her. "Justice was done, and for the sake of Meg Jessler and her family, I'm gratified ..."

With a sob, Marian escaped into the hallway.

~ ~ ~

Chelsea cowered in a corner of the courtroom, as yet unnoticed by the crowd. She didn't know how she'd gotten there. She didn't know how she'd get out. She didn't know how to take her next breath.

Her mind lay shattered, the puzzle pieces of Meg Jessler's murder having flown into a million shards in her brain, then back together in maniacal rewind.

But now the picture was different.

The truth was different.

Spots blackened Chelsea's vision. Her knees grew weak. This knowledge would choke the very life from her.

Gavil Harrison was innocent.

PART IV
TRUTH

"So is my word that goes out from my mouth:
It will not return to me empty,
but will accomplish what I desire
and achieve the purpose for which I sent it."

Isaiah 55:11

Thursday, October 5 –
Friday, October 6

Chapter 48

Chelsea had been kneeling in her bedroom for over an hour. Her legs had long since gone to sleep, throbbing with the sensation of a thousand biting ants. Tears were all cried out for now. Her eyes were red and swollen, her forehead hot. Groaning, she unbent her knees to lie on the carpet.

She couldn't face anyone.

Somehow, she'd fled the courtroom while the defense attorney pledged the rolling cameras a hard-fought appeal. Somehow, she'd gotten into her car, driven home. Somehow, she'd called Paul, leaving a one-word message with his secretary. *Guilty.* The word had stuck in her throat. She knew Paul had tried calling home. The phone had rung more than once. But she hadn't answered. He had to be wondering where she was. How could she tell him? How could she tell anyone? What had she *done?* She'd destroyed an innocent man's *life.* The guilt and shame and fear were almost more than she could bear.

God, why did you wait so long? Why have you done this to me?

As she'd prayed and sobbed, God answered her desperate question. She had not waited for Him. In her impatience and fear, she'd blurted Gavil's name to police even after God had warned her through Gladys not to. He had allowed things to go this far not to punish her, but to teach her. Lesson hard learned, she would never misuse her special gift again. Now if she would only obey Him and tell the police what she knew, in His mercy he would set things right.

But Chelsea could not obey.

What would people say? The detectives, after they'd worked so hard? After they'd saved her from Gavil's impulsiveness? What would folks in her church say? What about all those who heard the news story about her vision and had realized God's power? What about Marian, who was so close to making her own commitment to Christ? Not to mention Paul's reaction.

"God," she whispered, "I can't *do* it."

More minutes passed, a half hour, an hour, as Chelsea remained on the floor, pouring out her heart. Finally she dragged to her feet, eyes grazing the clock. Two-thirty. The boys were in basketball practice until five. She would have to pull herself together by then. In the meantime, she had to talk to *somebody*. Drawing a deep breath, she picked up the phone.

~ ~ ~

"You never confronted me about mentioning Gavil right away," Chelsea said after she and Gladys had spent a long time in prayer. They were in Gladys' family room, just as they'd been the day after her first vision of the murder. It seemed so long ago.

Gladys reflected. "At that point, I wanted to support you, not second guess you. And as things progressed, it looked like you were right."

"You don't think I'm crazy now?"

"No. I felt God speaking to me while we were praying. I do believe God has shown you the truth."

"Thank you." Gratitude surged through Chelsea. She needed so much for someone to understand. But—what now?

"What should I *do*, Gladys?" Her eyes pricked with fresh tears. "I can't go back to the police, not after everything that's happened. They'll never believe me. I know that sounds so selfish, with Gavil in jail, and the real murderer free to hurt someone else. Part of me can't *believe* I'm thinking of myself right now. But—I just *can't*."

Gladys nodded, her face grim. "I can't tell you what to do, Chelsea. I can only pray that God will help you do what he wants." She searched for words, shaking her head. "I do think, through all this ... mess ... that God will teach you some things, and in the end you'll be stronger for it. I know that's not much help now."

It had been such a long four months. Chelsea didn't *want* God to teach her anything else.

She just wanted the nightmare to end.

~ ~ ~

Somehow Chelsea got through the tasks of picking up the boys, making dinner, greeting Paul when he arrived home from work. She felt numb, removed from herself, exhausted.

"What's the matter, Mom?" Scott asked as he scooted his chair to the table at dinner. "Everything happened at the trial like you wanted, right?"

Chelsea managed a smile. "Yeah, honey. I'm just tired, that's all."

"You should go to bed early tonight," Michael declared with the wisdom of a twelve-year-old.

Paul eyed her. "Yup, let's make sure Mom gets an extra long sleep. She's had quite a day."

The day wasn't over. Chelsea knew what she had to do.

Later that evening in their bedroom, Chelsea, hesitant and trembling, faced her husband. "I have to tell you something."

She related the vision she'd experienced in court.

Paul stared at her, slack-jawed.

"Chelsea, you know this can't be. After the way Gavil threatened you, chased you? And now the trial's finally over. You can get on with your life now. Our life."

"But it's *not* over, that's just it. I thought it was, too. I wanted it to be. But it's not. And now I don't know what to *do*."

"What to do? You do *nothing*, that's what. Let this be, it's over."

Tears fell from Chelsea's eyes. "But I'm going crazy, don't you see? How can I just sit on this knowledge when an innocent man is in jail and the guilty one is free? I can't *live* with myself! But I'm so scared." Her words ended in a wail as she sank onto the bed. Paul pulled her into his arms.

"Maybe this is just the emotional aftermath," he said. "You know, sort of like a soldier with no more battles to fight? You'll calm down in a few days, get back to normal."

"How do you know?" she cried into his chest. "What makes you think I'm wrong now and not before?"

"Because look at all that's happened!" He lifted her chin to look into her eyes. "You were hardly the only one involved here. *Police* found evidence on Gavil. A *jury* found him guilty. Everything worked out, right in line with your feeling about him."

She wiped at a tear. "But you didn't believe me then, either. Not until things started to happen. It could be the same way again."

Apprehension flicked across Paul's face, then faded. "No, *nothing* else is going to happen. I want things to be normal again, Chelsea." His voice thickened. "I want you back. I just want my partner back."

"I'm so sorry, Paul. I never meant for all this to happen!" Chelsea sobbed into his shirt until she could cry no more. Finally spent, she allowed him to tuck her in bed.

"Let's see how you feel in the morning," he whispered. "I think it'll all be better tomorrow after you've slept. I really do." He gazed at her, begging for agreement.

~ ~ ~

But the morning brought Chelsea no relief. Only the renewed knowledge that God had shown her the truth. "Think about it some more," Paul said as he left for work. "I'll call you later."

339

Chelsea thought and prayed, begging God to give her a way out. "Let someone else find the truth somehow! Don't make me have to go to the police!"

But she knew in her heart what God wanted her to do. She just didn't know how she could go through with it.

Paul phoned later that morning to check on her. Dread filled Chelsea as she told him the truth. "I've been praying and praying. I can't continue like this. My insides are full of lead. I *have* to go see Detective Reiger. I'm scared to death, but I have to go."

Paul sighed. "I'm not going to talk you out of this, am I?" His voice sounded so weary.

Chelsea's eyes closed. How could she do this to him?

"I can't change what I know. I wish I could. But I can't."

She gripped the phone hard, waiting.

No reply.

"Paul? Please don't pull back from me now. I need you."

"Detective Reiger won't believe you, Chelsea. He'll think you're crazy."

"Then you have nothing to worry about." She swallowed, her throat tight. "Maybe I should just tell him and leave it in his hands. If it goes nowhere, then ... that's it."

"I want our lives back to normal," Paul said. "For us and the boys. The verdict was supposed to be the end of all this. I do *not* want you continually upset. *When* will it end?"

Paul was right. Her husband didn't deserve to be put through any more. Maybe she *could* forget this. Just ... force herself to go on with her life.

But how could she ever pray again? Sit in church? When she *knew* she'd purposely not listened to God's voice.

Chelsea hung her head. "It will end, Paul. After I do this. If I don't ... I can't live with myself."

"Fine." Paul's voice hardened. "Go ahead. But that's the end of it. Put it on Reiger, like you said—then walk away. There's no more evidence you can give. Nothing else you can do. When I come home tonight—it's *over*. We talk about this no more. We go on with our lives. You hear me? I mean it, Chelsea."

"Yes." Chelsea could barely talk. "I hear."

Chapter 49

Chelsea sat woodenly before Reiger's desk. She knew how much he was respected, particularly now. Even as he'd led her down the hall to his office, stopping to tell Pat Turnbow she'd arrived, he heard congratulations from colleagues. Right now both detectives had to be "Men of the Hour" around that station.

How could she ever make it up to them after this terrible mistake?

Turnbow entered the office and took a chair on Chelsea's right.

Here goes.

Heart fluttering, Chelsea told the two men about her second vision. Then steeled herself, awaiting their response.

Turnbow sat with legs apart and arms crossed, staring at her like she'd just landed from Mars. Reiger rocked in his chair, his expression a mixture of shock and disbelief. Chelsea searched for more words but found none. She'd explained it all, had practically gone on her knees before them.

Reiger cleared his throat. "Well. This is ... interesting."

Turnbow snorted. "Interesting? This is *insane!*" His eyes narrowed. "How can you do this now? Whatever would possess you to come in here *today,* one day after the verdict, and say something like this?"

Chelsea looked at her lap.

"Wait a minute, Turnbow, settle down." Reiger frowned at him. "You'll have to forgive my partner, Mrs. Adams. This is a lot to take in all at once."

She nodded, feeling about two feet high.

Reiger blew out air, his gaze roving the ceiling. "Okay. I know the story you've just told us isn't based on logic. But now that you've told it, let's look at the facts. It's all we can do."

"Yes. Okay."

"First. You said you recognized the guy as the maître d' who helped serve you that night at Bayhill—"

"Which is beyond belief right there." Turnbow leaned forward. "People don't 'recognize' a restaurant employee four months later. They hardly even pay attention to them during *dinner*."

"Pat, just hold *on* a minute!" Reiger looked to Chelsea. "Mrs. Adams, this doesn't make sense. If Doniger worked at Bayhill, he and Harrison would have recognized each other. They lived next door."

"I know. But Gavil hadn't lived there very long. Maybe with different schedules ... "

Turnbow shook his head hard. "We interviewed this guy. I even went back a second time and finished the interview when we were interrupted. I *knew* the significance of Bayhill Restaurant. If Doniger had said he worked at Bayhill, I'd have picked up on it. He doesn't work there. Period."

Reiger reached for the phone. "Let's just check it out right now."

Turnbow leaned back, shrugging.

Reiger dialed Information, asked for the number of Bayhill, then punched it in. "Hi." Chelsea marveled at the lightness of his voice. "Is Jack Doniger in by any chance?"

Both Chelsea's and Turnbow's eyes fixed on his face. Surprise flickered across his forehead. "Oh. Okay, thanks. By the way, he's worked there some time now, huh? How long has it been?"

Turnbow stilled.

"Right. Thanks." Reiger hung up and looked at each of them, eyebrows raised. "He's the evening maître d'. Been there six months."

343

"Oh, come *on!*" Turnbow jumped up. "That's impossible! I've had enough of this, I'm going to get my notes." He strode across the office and banged through the door.

~ ~ ~

Selfish religious hypocrite!

Turnbow yanked open his drawer containing the Trent Park murder book. They'd placed it in his office just yesterday since Reiger's filing cabinet was so overloaded. Who'd have ever guessed he'd need it one day later.

He smacked down into his chair, jerking early pages. There it was. Their first interview with Doniger. Turnbow's eyes flitted down the page. He remembered they'd been gunning for Harrison to show up, and as soon as he had, they'd cut the interview short. *Restaurant worker* was the note regarding Doniger's employment. Turnbow remembered that much, but it had to be mere coincidence. The Bay Area was full of restaurant staff. He sighed, flicking pages until he found the follow-up interview. Employment information had to be there. Place of business including address and phone were rote questions. Following along with his finger, Turnbow read his notes. Backed up and read them again.

No mention of where Doniger worked.

He read them a third time.

Nothing.

Sourness spread through his chest. How could he have done this? How could he have been so *stupid?* He checked one last time. It wasn't there.

Turnbow ran a hand through his hair, then sat motionless, thinking.

This *was* quite a coincidence.

Not that it mattered. Coincidence was all it was. So Doniger worked at Bayhill. So Turnbow had made a mistake interviewing

344

the guy. So *what?* In light of everything else, this was a flea against an elephant.

Turnbow slammed the notebook shut and filed it away.

Okay, so he'd have to admit his error. He still wasn't about to let this go any further. He'd waited too long for the trial to be over. Marian had waited too long. Imagine what gossip like this would do to her. To *them.*

No way.

Turnbow gathered himself to return to Reiger's office.

No way.

"Okay." He sat down hard in Reiger's office chair. "I have to admit—you're right. Somehow I neglected to ask Doniger where he worked. Don't know how, but I did." Turnbow shot a look to Reiger. "It still doesn't mean anything."

Reiger rubbed his forehead. "Oh, man. This is too much." He flopped back in his chair and raised his hands. "I'm not quite sure where to go next."

"Nowhere," Turnbow said. "Absolutely nowhere."

Chelsea Adams took a breath. "What if everything Gavil said in his defense is true? Somebody else *did* pick up the gloves. Gavil *was* with Sonya Hocking that morning."

"Yeah?" Turnbow pointed at her. "And who *really* chased you?"

Chelsea lowered her eyes.

He leaned forward. "Look, Reiger, all of this is ridiculous. We shouldn't give it the time of day. Can you imagine telling this to Chief Wilburn? He'd kick us both out of his office!"

Reiger fixed him with a look, indicating Chelsea with a tilt of his head. Turnbow counted to five.

"Mrs. Adams," Reiger's voice was calm, "sorry for the disagreement. It's just kind of a jolt, you understand. But to get back to the facts, even though Doniger served you dessert that night—"

"He didn't just 'serve us dessert,'" Chelsea said. "He was *right there* when I had that vision. Understand? He was standing by Gavil. I remember it so well. *His* presence was the evil I felt."

"Okay, okay. I know you believe this. And I have to admit there are some coincidences I can't explain. But you have to understand—the case is *over*. Harrison has been convicted."

Chelsea straightened. "You've got the DNA from the rock. Just check it. It'll match Jack Doniger."

Turnbow repressed a snort.

"We can't do that," Reiger said patiently. "We have no cause to ask Doniger for a sample. You have to understand that we play by lots of rules. *I* don't make them up. But I sure have to abide by them."

"So you're telling me there's *nothing* you can do? What if I *am* right? You want the wrong man sitting in jail? You want the *right* man still on the streets? He lives right next to Marian!"

That was too much for Turnbow. "Don't go saying *anything* about this to Marian. You've already filled her head with enough garbage—"

Turnbow caught himself. The words hung in the air.

Stupid, stupid!

Reiger's eyes narrowed.

Chelsea shifted in her chair. "I ... if you're referring to Sunday, I'm very sorry. I thought ... it seemed to me that Marian enjoyed it."

Reiger stared lasers at Turnbow. "What happened Sunday, Mrs. Adams?"

"She came to church with us. And to lunch afterward. That's all."

Silence. Chelsea looked questioningly from one man to the other.

"I see." Reiger gave her a slight smile. "No harm done there, I'm sure." His eyes drifted back to Turnbow. "Tell you what,

346

Mrs. Adams, I'm going to think about how to handle this, and I'll get back to you." He started to rise.

This was not going to be good after she left. Turnbow could feel it coming.

Chelsea Adams didn't budge. "Thank you. Like I told you on the phone, I spent hours in prayer before coming here. Still, I almost didn't come because I was so afraid. Before you make any decisions, please pray about it. I'll pray for you, too."

Turnbow surveyed Reiger. He was clearly looking for a response that would appease her without embarrassing himself in front of his partner. This was Turnbow's chance to bail Reiger out, and right now Turnbow needed all the good graces he could get.

"Mrs. Adams, a question." He spread his hands. "If God sent you that first vision and He's so infallible, then ...?"

Chelsea looked away. "He *is* infallible, Detective. And so are His words. Unfortunately I'm not." She swung her gaze back to him. "I've already explained where I went wrong. I hope you'll hear that. This is the hardest part of all for me, you know, thinking I may cause others to question. Please don't think this is God's fault. Put the blame on me, where it belongs."

How to respond to that? Remorse at his own harshness washed over Turnbow. Then disappeared.

He would not be swayed by her misplaced sincerity.

Chapter 50

"You want to tell me how you heard about Marian visiting the Adams house?"

Reiger had escorted Chelsea out of the station, instructing Turnbow to stay put. Both now stood like wary fighters in a ring, the door closed.

Turnbow looked like a defiant teenager. "Marian told me."

Reiger exhaled. He'd seen the signs. He just hadn't wanted to look at them. "You got something going with her?"

"That's none of your business."

Reiger saw red. "None of my—! During the *trial,* Turnbow? How could you *do* that, with everything at stake!"

"It wasn't 'during the trial,' all right? I waited all summer, so don't go preaching to me!"

"The trial was over *yesterday.*"

Turnbow crossed his arms. "Okay. So I saw her after she testified. Her part was over. I figured it couldn't do any harm."

"You're rationalizing and you know it. You could have done a *great deal* of harm."

"All right, all right. But that's over. Whatever happens now has nothing to do with you."

"You can't go running around town with her. What's it going to look like?"

"I *know* that. You think I'm *stupid* or something?"

Reiger gave him a look.

"We'll take it easy, okay? She's so mixed up in her feelings anyway. You have no idea what this has done to her." Turnbow brought a hand to his eyes. "And that's why I don't want any of this nonsense fed to her. She's been through enough."

"That really what you're worried about? Or are you more worried about her loyalties?"

Turnbow's back stiffened, a vein pulsing in his neck. "I don't have to listen to this!" He pivoted for the door.

"Pat!" Reiger's tone swung the younger man around. "You do what you want. I can't stop you. But understand this. You're *off* this case."

Turnbow's mouth curled. "*What* case?"

"I don't know. But whatever it is, you're off it!"

"No, no, no. You wait one minute." Turnbow stepped within inches of Reiger. "You don't go messing around with four months of our work and tell me I can't know what's going on."

"That's exactly what I'm telling you."

"Oh, no, you're not!"

"Yes, I *am,* Turnbow! Just look at yourself! Where's your focus? Where's your head? It's not in finding out the truth here. It's on your own wants. I can't have that."

Turnbow glared at his partner. "First of all," his voice was tight, "we've already found out the truth and there is *nothing more to be done.* And second, believe me, if I really thought Marian was in danger from that guy next door, I'd be the first to do something about it."

"You wouldn't see it even if it *was* true. Because you don't *want* to see it."

Turnbow cut his eyes to the window and visibly steeled himself. "Look, Dan. I'm asking you—nicely—to leave this alone. There's no *point* to it."

"My *point* will be to check this out a little further so I can lay it to rest. Since you're so sure there's nothing to it, you've got nothing to worry about."

"I've got Marian to worry about. And I won't have her hassled."

"Fine, Turnbow, fine." Reiger held up a hand.

"Listen, Reiger, you mess with this too much, I'm telling Wilburn."

"Oh? Like I've got nothing on *you?*" Reiger's jaw hardened. The kid was pushing way too far.

Turnbow tightened his mouth and swiveled for the door, slamming it on his way out.

~ ~ ~

Reiger leaned over the desk, head in his hands. Never before had he lost his temper with a partner. So many things were happening at once, he hardly knew where to focus.

Amazing to think that just twenty-four hours ago, he'd been on top of the world. Victorious.

Part of him still boiled with anger at Turnbow. He had every right to be angry. And under the circumstances, his decision to cut Turnbow out had been the only thing to do. All the same, he *needed* his partner right now, as much for emotional support as for his professional skills.

As for Chelsea Adams' latest vision, Reiger didn't know what to think. He believed her sincerity, admired her immensely for coming back. How much turmoil it must have caused her to tell them what she had! No amount of desire for more limelight could drive a person to do that. It was just too risky, too certain to result in humiliation. Besides, she wasn't that kind of person. She just plain thought she was right. And Reiger had to admit that the bit about Doniger was a heart stopper. But he'd spent so many weeks, as had Turnbow, believing in Harrison's guilt, that all the evidence in the world would barely turn him around. His brain needed more time to adjust to even the slightest possibility that this was true.

Reiger dug fingers into his scalp.

Worst of all was his own cowardliness. When Chelsea Adams asked him to pray, he'd left her hanging out to dry in front of

350

Turnbow. All because he was embarrassed to speak up for his own faith. For God himself.

"Oh, Lord, forgive me for my weakness."

Reiger did not know how much time passed as he sat holding his head, eyes closed. Thinking about his shortcomings, all the chances he'd been given over the years to speak up for God but had said nothing.

"No more, Lord," he whispered, "no more." If someone twenty years younger and a good eighty pounds lighter could speak up the way Chelsea Adams had, why couldn't he? "Give me more chances, God. I won't let You down next time. Show me how to share with others what You've done for me. Including Pat. Especially Pat."

Even then, Reiger could not lift his head. Remembering Chelsea Adam's admonition, he prayed for guidance. What should he do next? May God open or shut doors as needed.

He could only hope the doors would all shut. Fast.

Chapter 51

"Sorry I couldn't be here last night."

Turnbow sat with Marian on her couch, dishes from dinner in the sink. Marian had waved a hand at Pat's offer to help, saying she'd leave the job for later. She'd changed from her business suit to jeans and a T-shirt. Her bare feet were tucked under her as she leaned against Pat.

"Don't worry about it," she said. "I don't know what kind of company I'd have been. It was such a hard day. Too many emotions. That's why I just couldn't go back to work after court."

He lifted a strand of her hair and watched it fall. "You're doing better today."

"Yes, I am." Her tone was decisive. "It's done. Over with. I have to go on."

Turnbow's thoughts flitted to that morning.

"Anyway, I'm glad you're here now." She smiled at him, and his heart softened like wax in the sun.

"Me too." He kissed her, their lips lingering. She felt so right in his arms, He couldn't imagine letting her go. They both had wounds. His were just older than hers. If Marian thought she was the only one being cared for here, she was wrong.

She snuggled against his chest. "You going to church with me this Sunday? I really want to go back."

He felt a wall go up. "You know we can't. It's too soon. We'll still have to do some hiding out for a while."

"All right. I guess I just have to follow your lead on that. But that means when we *can* go out, you'll go. Right?"

He played with her hair. Amazing how even the best women could be so manipulative. "I suppose so."

"Good." She was silent for a moment. "You want to come over tomorrow and help me garden? That's 'hiding out.'"

"Must be a better way to do it than that."

"Well." She looked petulant. "The work needs to be done. I'll have to do it with or without you." She sighed. "Oh, never mind. Maybe at least Jack will keep me company over the fence."

Turnbow's hand stilled. "Jack?"

"You know, my young neighbor."

"What's he doing, hanging around?"

"He's not hanging around. He lives here."

"Well, why's he talking to you?"

Marian frowned. "It's not very often, Pat, only when he sees me gardening or getting the mail or something. Most of the time I never see him. What's the matter, you jealous?"

"No." He tried to sound bored. "I'm not jealous. I just ..." Apprehension fluttered down his spine. Second time today this guy's name had come up. He tried to shake it off, but it attached itself with spindly fingers.

"Just what?"

"I don't want you talking to him."

Marian drew back, eyeing him. "Why?"

"Because ... just because."

"Pat, come on, he's ten years younger than I am. I'm hardly interested."

"Why's he interested in you?"

She shrugged. "He's just being nice. Probably feels sorry for me. He almost acts protective, asking me where I work and wondering whether I'm ever alone in the building."

The spindly fingers squeezed. Pat's nerves tingled.

This couldn't mean anything. It couldn't.

"What did you tell him?"

"About what? Yes, I told him where I work. As far as being alone, I don't know. Sometimes I work late." Her gaze danced across Turnbow's face. "What's wrong with you?"

He forced a smile. "Too many years as a cop, that's all. You hardly know the guy. Now he knows where you work, some of your habits. You're being too open. You should know better."

She drew in her shoulders. "Really, he's harmless."

"That's what you thought about Gavil."

Marian froze, then turned away.

Turnbow rolled his eyes. What did he say *that* for?

"I'm *sorry*." He reached for her, urging her chin back toward him. She resisted. "Come on, Marian, I'm an idiot. Please." He nudged her face again until she followed his touch. Tears stood in her eyes. Turnbow pulled her head down to his chest as he'd done that day so long ago. A silent sob shuddered through Marian. He held her, gentling her hair.

This was going to be a long road.

Within seconds, his mind wandered back to Jack Doniger.

Saturday, October 7

Chapter 52

Reiger pocketed his keys, eyes grazing Dapple Street's townhouses. With luck Marian wouldn't spot him through her window. He saw no one outside. For a Saturday, it sure was quiet. Heading for number six, he glanced over his shoulder at Alice Geary's place. If anyone saw him, it would be Geary. He could imagine her rushing to her porch to yodel his name in greeting. So much for his clandestine call. But as he trod across the parking area, he heard only birds chirping and faint music in the distance.

His visit was a result of much prayer and ambivalent planning. He'd not slept well last night—which was nothing new. He tossed, thinking, *Do nothing, Reiger, let this go.* Then he turned, praying for God to show him the next step. By morning, he felt sure of what to do. But it would have to be on his own time, unofficially. Even then, it was no small gamble. If Wilburn caught wind of anything, Reiger would have a lot of answering to do.

He stepped onto Jack Doniger's sidewalk, eyes flitting to Marian's porch. The two porches *were* very close, not more than ten feet apart.

But he'd known that.

He rang the doorbell and waited, muscles tense. What was he going to say? And what could Doniger say that would settle his mind one way or another? All the same, this was nothing new. It was a fishing expedition, and he'd been on plenty of those in his career. Some went places, some didn't.

He heard a noise inside. Doniger was home.

He recognized Reiger, surprise flitting across his face. "Hi." His hand remained on the doorknob.

"Mr. Doniger." Reiger nodded. "Sorry to bother you on a beautiful day like this. But I was in the neighborhood and wondered if you could help me with some final cleanup of our case."

Doniger hesitated. "Okay. Um. You want to come in?"

"Thanks." Reiger stepped inside, gaze wandering. The place looked neat, sparse. Lots of brown and white, dotted by a few plants.

"So. I kind of figured you'd be out celebrating." Doniger waved Reiger to a small couch.

"Well, a detective's work is never done, I guess." He smiled. "Actually, this is work I just want to get out of the way. Tanley—Harrison's attorney—is bound to appeal the case, and I want to have a few extra facts straight so we can fight it." Reiger held Doniger's gaze, hoping the man knew little enough of the law to believe him.

"Okay."

Relief skidded across Reiger's stomach. "Good. I don't know how much of the trial you saw, but one of the issues was about the gloves being on the porch."

"Uh-huh."

"Did you ever notice them there? Or maybe lying around the yard at any other time?"

Doniger thought a moment. "No. To both questions."

"Okay. How about Gavil and Meg Jessler. Ever see them together?"

Doniger's lips thinned. "I can't remember that. But he must have known her pretty well."

"He hadn't lived here very long. You hadn't met him at all, had you?"

"No, but ... not until he came into the restaurant. Even then, I didn't know who he was."

Reiger kept a poker face. He hadn't expected Doniger to bring this up. "So you did see Harrison with Chelsea Adams and her husband that night."

"Yeah."

"Okay. I know we never really talked about this."

"No. But I didn't know about it until I heard about that woman's vision on the news and put two and two together. I had seen a lady kind of go into a trance at a table I was serving. At first I thought, nah, it can't be. But I guess curiosity got the best of me, and I went and checked the receipts from that night. A Paul Adams had signed the credit card bill."

Reiger sat very still, as if any motion might stop Doniger's flow. People could get themselves in trouble by yakking too much. Still, this meant nothing. So what if Doniger had figured this out?

"Why didn't you tell us this?"

Doniger lifted a shoulder. "What was to tell? Next thing I knew, you'd arrested your suspect. You and your partner never came to my door again. Besides, I didn't figure that stuff would go far in court."

"You're right about that." Reiger's mind raced. Where to go next? "They left the restaurant pretty soon after that, didn't they?"

"Yeah. The lady forgot her purse. When I noticed, I thought it was too late, but I took it outside just in case. She and her husband were sitting in their car. She looked like she was crying. I was kind of embarrassed to interrupt, but she needed her purse back, so I knocked on the window."

Fresh disquiet filtered through Reiger's veins. He'd never heard this before. Not that it made any difference. But after all this time on the case, nothing should be new to him.

He nodded, feeling almost displaced, as if he were watching himself from afar. "That was nice of you."

"I guess."

Doniger grew quiet, waiting. Reiger scrambled for something to say. "That vision—amazing story, isn't it."

"*Really* amazing. I'd never heard of such a thing. And to find out it was all true. Wouldn't want that woman for *my* neighbor."

Reiger smiled.

"But I've often wondered about it. I mean, you've been at your job a long time, right? You must have seen some things over the years. What did you do when that woman first came to you?"

Reiger considered the best answer. "I didn't really know what to think. 'Course, we didn't know we had a murder on our hands then."

"Oh, right. Then she found the body, right? Just where she said it would be?"

"Pretty much." A chill puddled in Reiger's chest.

Wasn't he just being too edgy? Anyone would be curious about this subject. But something about this man's curiosity seemed a little too driven.

"So she really *did* know everything."

"Uh-huh."

"Wow." Doniger shook his head. "Amazing."

Silence. The conversation would end if Reiger didn't think of something fast. There was a springboard here, something he was missing. His mind fled back to the day at his kitchen table, when the description of Meg's hands had bothered him so. *Help me, Lord, is there something here? It's my only chance.*

For no reason, his heart began to scud. Now he really was being ridiculous. A veteran detective worried over such a paltry interview? *The case is over, Reiger, get hold of yourself.* He sensed Doniger's eyes on him, wondering at his stalling. His heart beat harder. What was *wrong* with him? He should just leave right now.

"She even knew what he said as he killed her." Reiger heard his own voice. "Remember that?"

Doniger cocked his head. "Mm. Yeah, I think so. Actually, now that I think about it, that's kind of why I figured Harrison knew her pretty well."

Reiger's blood whooshed in his ears. "Sure. That makes sense."

The young man nodded. "Yeah. I mean, 'I hate you.' He must have had something going with her at one time, huh?"

Reiger swallowed the dirt clod in his throat. "That's what we guessed."

A knowing expression crossed Doniger's face. "She probably dumped him or something. Ticked him off. I mean, we've all been there. Right?"

"Sure." The sergeant's answer sounded distant to his own ears. "We certainly have."

~ ~ ~

"Hey, Reiger, what're you doing here?" the dispatch officer said as Reiger whooshed through the station door. "Haven't had enough of a week?"

He tried to smile but failed. "Just got a few things to look at."

In his office, he dug out the keys to the locked box of the Trent Park tapes, clacking through them for the one of Chelsea Adams. He shoved it into his tape player, preparing to put on earphones, then stopped. His eyes flicked toward the door. Putting down the earphones, he dialed out front. "I'm not here, by the way."

"No problem."

He locked his door, then perched in his chair, eyes darting as he listened. Fast-forward. Again. A third time. She was now talking about the tunnel at the beginning of her vision. His heart thumped as he sucked in her words. There it was. He closed his eyes, concentrating. Backed up the tape, listened again.

I hate you. I've always hated you.

Dread drew a fingernail down the back of his neck.

Reiger took off the earphones and stared out the window. He was almost positive no news story had ever included that information.

Could that be true?

In his head, he played and replayed the television and newspaper accounts. After Channel 7 aired the story, others had picked it up. Everybody milked the vision for all it was worth. But there'd been no new information after the exclusive. Once Chief Wilburn spun through the station in a rage, whoever had leaked the story apparently hadn't dared to tell any more. News reports had given Chelsea's name and details of the murder that were important as evidence. But other things they hadn't mentioned. Not the name of Bayhill Restaurant nor the surrounding circumstances of the vision. News time was tight. The stories had been edited for greatest titillation.

Had Milt Waking's break of the story included those words?

Reiger squeezed his eyes shut. What was he supposed to *do?* He couldn't call the station for a copy of the film. There'd be questions. Talk about tipping off the media. Who *else* would know? How could he be sure?

He tapped his desk, thinking. Then picked up the phone.

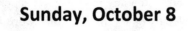

Sunday, October 8

Chapter 53

The sun had risen only to hide itself in fog. Reiger sat stiffly in his favorite armchair, its brown arms and headrest threadbare. Edith had threatened to replace the chair for years, but he couldn't bring himself to part with it.

His bleary eyes rested on the pendulum clock hanging above the television. It was after seven. His better half would be appearing soon, heading for the coffee he'd made a good two hours earlier. He hadn't been to bed all night.

This case had an odd way of circling back on itself.

Reiger's gaze dropped to the VCR with its power light still shining red. He reached for the remote and clicked off the machine, then stared at the blank television screen.

All last evening he'd watched news footage of the Trent Park case, courtesy of Alice Geary. Calls to the Adams' home and to a few close friends in town had gone nowhere as he'd sought his information. Then he'd thought of the townhouse association president. He hadn't wanted to call her, knowing she'd be full of questions. But she was his last resort. Sure enough, she had a notebook full of newspaper clippings and a videotape of every news story that existed on the case, going all the way through the trial. Apparently, she'd flipped between channels night after night, chasing stories, one reporter cutting abruptly to another. Reiger tried to convince himself he only needed to check the stories from the case's beginning, starting when the exclusive about Chelsea Adams aired. But he found himself watching the entire tape, scanning every newspaper story, just to be sure those three words had not slipped into some copy down the line. There was no room for error here.

Edith helped him. When they were through, they talked and prayed a long time. Finally, she went to bed.

Few nights in Reiger's life could compare to this last one. At first, left on his own, he made no headway. He could only raise his fist at God, struggle to assimilate, demand answers. He thought his head would burst. His whole line of thinking for the last four months had to be reprogrammed. Even after failing to find those three critical words in any news story, even while sensing deep within that he'd finally stumbled upon the truth, he still did not want to believe. In vain he searched for any other explanation. In vain he asked the Lord to take his gut feeling away if it was not on target. As the hours passed and his sense of foreboding strengthened, Reiger grew angry at God. *Why* had He allowed them all to be so wrong? Why had He blessed their thinking with a court victory? And why had He released the truth only now, when their hands were tied?

In the last hour before dawn, Reiger began moving toward acceptance. He still didn't know the answers to his questions and perhaps he never would. But in faith, he began asking the Lord for guidance. He would need help every step from here on out, for he was completely at a loss. Finally, he prayed for strength. And courage.

He sensed danger ahead.

With a loud sigh, Reiger released the footrest on his chair and pushed himself up. He needed to catch Turnbow early before the man headed out for the day. Probably doing something with Marian. Reiger rubbed his eyes at that thought. Maybe after talking to Turnbow, he could still make the late service at church. All the same, he'd tell Edith not to wait for him.

Only God knew what this day would bring.

Turnbow surveyed the fog from his kitchen table. His head was every bit as clouded. Reiger was on his way over with an "it-can't wait." A far cry from their victory song two days ago.

Which could only mean he'd found something.

Turnbow dreaded Reiger's knock on his condo door as much as a dentist's drill. Just when everything had settled down—the case, his ability to be with Marian, his peace of mind—the world threatened to go haywire. Maybe this was nothing, a mere blip on the screen. But the uneasiness from the weekend gnawed at his stomach. This business with Doniger kept raising its ugly head.

Turnbow had spent Saturday with Marian, even helped her garden for a few hours after lunch. They'd been quietly working, he by the fence shared with Doniger and she at the far corner, when Doniger called her name.

"Figured you'd be out here," he said.

Turnbow's hand stilled. He didn't care for the familiarity in the man's tone. He glanced up but could not see Doniger.

"Hi." Marian's gaze slid to Pat as if to gauge his reaction.

An awkward silence followed. Turnbow sensed Doniger's sizing her up, weighing her hesitation as his eyes followed hers. Slowly, Doniger's head arched into view. A sudden, irrational fear pierced Turnbow's chest as he imagined consequences from Doniger's knowledge of their relationship.

Their eyes met.

Doniger's stare bore into him, reactions moving across his face like blowing sand over stone. Recognition. Surprise. Righteous indignation. His brow knotted and his chin jerked. Then his eyes traveled back to Marian and hung there. His jaw tightened as he surveyed her.

Turnbow couldn't breathe.

Chin high, Doniger turned and disappeared.

They hadn't seen him since.

Turnbow fingered the handle of his coffee mug, remembering. There was no denying Doniger had acted like a man betrayed. Even Marian picked up on it.

"I don't like the way he looked at me," she said at dinner. They were in an Italian restaurant in San Francisco's North Beach.

Turnbow reached for her hand, struggling with how much to say. "Maybe you shouldn't talk to him anymore. His schedule's so different from yours, you probably won't run into him much anyway. But if you do and he makes you feel uncomfortable, I want to know about it."

This morning, not fifteen minutes before Reiger called, Turnbow had awakened suddenly, his mind wrapped around one thought. What if Marian went to church with the Adams—and Chelsea said something about her latest vision?

He jumped from bed and found the telephone book, dialing the Adams' number. Tell her *nothing,* he commanded a surprised Mrs. Adams, failing to keep the edge from his voice. Chelsea Adams agreed, tactfully avoiding personal questions. She only asked if he and Reiger had any new information.

"We're working on it," had been his curt reply.

A knock at the door brought Turnbow back to the present. Bracing himself, he let Reiger in, then poured coffee for them both. Neither said anything about their argument on Friday. Reiger's presence superseded any words.

He wasted no time launching into what he'd discovered.

Their coffee grew cold.

By the time Reiger was done, Turnbow's spine crawled with ants. "There's got to be an explanation."

Reiger closed bloodshot eyes. "I'd be mighty grateful if you found it."

This was too much. Turnbow groaned. He'd spent four months despising Harrison. He wished for time to think, yet was afraid to take it. What if it *was* true? His mind whirled, dread and disbelief entwining. He told Reiger of Marian's encounters with

366

Doniger, watching his partner's pallid face drain whiter. His own felt numb.

Turnbow's words ran out.

Silence.

He and Reiger looked at each other across the table.

"What do we do?" Turnbow felt like an orphan adrift. "We've got nothing. This is no evidence to take to Wilburn. It's truly *nothing*. Words from a vision matching words from an interview. So what?" He jumped up from his chair and started pacing. "The whole thing's crazy."

"Pat." Reiger's voice weighted with fatigue. "I *know*. I've been up all night with this. But tell me. What do we do with this match? Nothing that Chelsea Adams actually saw or heard in her vision has proven false. *How could Doniger know?*"

"I don't know!"

"Then tell me something else." Reiger leaned across the table. "Can you drop this right now and have no doubts about Marian's safety?"

Turnbow stopped his pacing.

"After what you saw in Doniger's face yesterday?"

Turnbow relived the moment. Something clunked within him, like a critical machine part sliding into place.

"No."

The answer hung in the air.

"Neither can I."

Turnbow dropped into his chair. "You think he had something going with Meg Jessler at one time? Maybe she told him to get lost?"

"Sounds like it."

"Her friends didn't know about it."

"Her friends knew about the guy in Chicago. Maybe she kept her disloyalties to herself."

Turnbow rubbed his temple. "We can't do anything. I'm not telling Wilburn this. He'll put us both in the nuthouse."

"I know."

The coffee in Turnbow's stomach turned sour. He pushed his cup away. "Marian shouldn't stay in her home. Even if it's a small risk, it's not one I want to take."

"How's she going to take the news?"

Turnbow didn't want to think about it. "Probably fall apart."

What if this all turned out to be true? Would her guilt over Harrison turn her back to him? Turnbow calculated her reactions to the mere *possibility* of Harrison's innocence, feeling sick at his selfishness.

"On second thought," Turnbow said, avoiding his partner's eyes, "I won't tell her the whole story. I just can't. I'll tell her we've found something on Doniger, that's all."

A new thought sped through Turnbow's brain. He examined it, wondering at the irony. Then gave a sarcastic laugh. "Just occurred to me we're finally where Chelsea Adams would want us. All we've got is her vision. Relying on nothing but 'the word of God.'"

Reiger's eyes flared like a match in darkness. The fatigue lines in his forehead unraveled as he processed the statement.

Turnbow eyed his partner. What in the world was so profound about that cynical comment?

~ ~ ~

"Hurry, boys, go get dressed. Your mom will want you out the door in fifteen minutes." Paul picked up the breakfast plates and headed toward the sink as his sons left the kitchen. Sunday morning routine—the only time Paul did dishes. Chelsea was already upstairs getting ready for church.

The phone rang. Paul picked it up. "Hello."

"Mr. Adams? Sergeant Reiger."

Paul stilled. "Oh. Hi."

"I told Mrs. Adams I'd get back to her regarding ... her concerns."

"Right." Oh, boy, here it was. How would Chelsea react when she heard her new vision had gone nowhere? "She's kind of busy right now. I can give her a message."

"All right." Reiger paused. "Well, Mr. Adams, I'd like to lay your wife's concerns to rest, but I'm afraid I can't do that yet. We're going to have to do a bit more investigating. Very quietly, mind you."

Paul's insides gelled. He leaned against the counter. "What's happening?"

Five minutes later he hung up the phone and stared at his feet, the sergeant's words roiling in his head. *The man described a detail of the crime he shouldn't know ... of utmost importance that you two tell no one ...*

Paul could not *believe* this.

Surely this would come to nothing. They all *knew* Gavil was guilty.

Well, at least the cops didn't think Chelsea was crazy.

But this was worse. Much worse.

Paul trudged up the stairs. He found Chelsea in the dressing room. "That was Sergeant Reiger on the phone."

Anxiety slackened her expression. "What did he say?"

Paul tried to speak, but no words came. He gazed at his wife—the beautiful woman he loved more each day, even as her amazing ability caused him to understand her less.

"Paul! *What?*"

What if she was *right?* Of course, she couldn't be. But what if ...?

Throat tightening, Paul took Chelsea in his arms, protectiveness surging within him. "It looks like we're not quite out of the woods yet."

Chapter 54

Marian sat with Chelsea and Gladys in the sanctuary, nerves humming. Had the pastor written this sermon just for her? He was talking about Psalm 22. Marian had never heard this psalm even though it was right before the most famous one of all. But she clung to King David's cries of distress. *I've felt like that too.* A new awareness built inside her as the pastor explained that the text mirrored Jesus' death on the cross. Eyes riveted on the pastor, Marian felt his words flow through her, streaming with hope and *life.*

Was this what Chelsea had tried to tell her? That God could renew her hope, grant her strength to face the messiness of her circumstances? The thought of such a possibility gave way to another one, sharper yet, like a dart in her chest. Could God be using the tragic events in her life to bring her to these questions?

Deep within Marian, something shimmered with the promise of renewal.

The sermon over, everyone stood for a final praise chorus. The song filled the sanctuary and reverberated within Marian, its lyrics speaking of darkness turned to light, hopelessness to joy. Marian's throat closed, tears pricking her eyes. Something was happening, something in her soul. Truth rose before her, gleaming like a sunrise through a dirty window. If she could only wash that window and see the truth, know it completely!

Tears slid down Marian's cheeks. She didn't bother to wipe them away.

Chelsea slipped her a tissue.

Marian thanked her with a faint smile and glimpsed understanding in Chelsea's eyes. Marian's tears flowed harder.

"If you do not know Jesus personally," the pastor said in closing, "I invite you to pray this prayer with me now, silently, right where you stand. It's a prayer of salvation and the start of a new life."

I want that. I want a new life!

The words of the prayer rained down on Marian, and she drank in their meaning and promise. Then all the emotions within her quieted.

In their place—peace.

After the service, Marian couldn't leave. She longed to meet the pastor, tell him what she had experienced. "Do you think I could talk to him?" she asked Chelsea.

"He'd love to meet you."

Chelsea led Marian down to the front and introduced her to the pastor. "I prayed the prayer with you," she told him. "I just ... knew it was right."

Long after the sanctuary emptied, Marian sat in a pew with Chelsea and Gladys, talking, asking questions. What to do next? Every once in a while, Michael or Scott bounced in with an are-we-*ever*-going-to-get-out-of-here look on their faces.

Gladys grinned at Marian's mounting intensity. "You're just like me when I became a Christian. All business, wanting to know what was next on my checklist. It didn't take long to realize there's little you have to *do* in the world's sense of the word. Jesus has already done it for you. But I found myself longing to study the Bible and pray. And to spend time with other Christians."

"What about Paul?" Marian turned to Chelsea. "Doesn't he ever come to church?"

Chelsea gave her a rueful smile. "We're working on him."

Marian nodded. Would Pat be the same way? He hadn't seemed very open to the idea.

What if she lost him over this? What if she had to choose between him and God? Marian's heart seized. That wouldn't happen. She needed Pat too much.

All she could do was pray. Maybe God would show her what to do. Although Marian had no idea how that worked.

~ ~ ~

Turnbow's gaze roved over townhouse number six as he rang Marian's doorbell. No Doniger in sight.

Marian answered the door expectantly, her face radiant. She hugged him before he was even inside, then pulled him to the couch, where she told him about the church service, what she'd felt, that she'd become a Christian. On and on she went. Turnbow tried to take it all in.

Her words pierced him in ways he didn't understand.

Something was different about her. Turnbow couldn't deny that. She seemed alive, energetic, filled with purpose. He leaned against a pillow and watched her in wonder. How could anyone change this drastically in one morning? He thought of Friday, when a slip of his tongue had sent her into an hour's crying jag. Of last night after dinner, when she'd been exhausted after an uneventful day.

"Pat." She squeezed his fingers. "Please don't shut this out immediately. At first I was afraid to tell you, but I just *had* to."

What in the world to say?

"I'm glad for you. Really. I can see this means a lot. So why shouldn't I listen? I just …. I'm not looking for this for myself right now."

Marian nodded. Even the gesture was different, not one of meekness or fear. It was a knowing nod, as if she understood what was best for him and would pray that he realize it.

Irritation plinked down Turnbow's spine. He didn't need a woman telling him what he lacked. Matter of fact, he'd had enough of the subject of God for the moment. Or any time in the near future. When he thought about it, he was surrounded—Chelsea Adams, Reiger, now Marian.

Plus now this problem about Doniger.

Was God trying to zap him or something?

And just what would happen to Marian's bubbling new faith in God if Turnbow told her everything about Doniger? That would probably take the fizz out in a hurry.

"Look, Marian. We'll talk more about this later. I promise. But I've got something important I need to tell you too."

She smiled, as if news of a national disaster wouldn't shake her. "What is it?"

He had practiced this a dozen times. "Reiger came to my condo this morning. He found out about us."

Marian's eyes widened.

"No, it's okay. That's not the point. Thing is, he's been following up on some reports about Jack Doniger. We're still checking things out, but we have reason to believe Doniger could be dangerous. Now we're both real concerned because Doniger's been paying attention to you. And you live within feet of him. So I think it would be best if you stayed with someone for a while until we can get to the bottom of this. I need to know you're safe."

He watched the news shift across her face. It was a moment before she spoke. "This is *weird*. First Gavil and now Jack? What *is* it about me? I must be some kind of strange *magnet*."

Turnbow braced himself. A day ago, this kind of thought would have sent her reeling.

"What did he do?" Her eyes remained large.

"I can't tell you that right now. You're just going to have to trust me."

A stillness came over her. "It couldn't possibly have anything to do with Meg's murder. Right?"

It was the question Turnbow had hoped she wouldn't ask.

He hesitated. He couldn't bear to tell her the truth. What if it drove her back to Gavil?

"No."

She nodded.

Remorse pinged through Turnbow. She was so trusting.

Marian sighed. "Are you sure I have to go? I don't *want* to. I'm comfortable here."

"Yeah, you do." He fingered her hair. "I know it's hard. But if anything ever happened to you ..."

She searched his face, then smiled. "Haven't we been here before?"

The comment knocked around Turnbow's stomach. "Yeah."

What if he *had* been wrong about Gavil? Think of all he'd put Marian through. The urge to protect her, make it all right for her no matter the cost, surged through Turnbow. "But now it's different. Now I love you."

The words smoothed her expression, soaked into her. "I love you too."

A statement Turnbow had not heard in a long time. It shimmered in his chest.

"And I'll go somewhere, if you think I need to," she said.

If only she could stay with him. But that was far too risky. "Somewhere close, I hope. I don't want to let you out of my sight."

An idea lit her face. "I'll bet the Adams have an extra room. Plus, that would give me more chances to talk to Chelsea."

Oh. Very bad idea. What if Chelsea Adams talked about Doniger? "You sure you'd want to be there? Wouldn't that be too much a reminder of ... everything?"

"No."

Turnbow shook his head. "I just ... I don't know."

"Why?"

"I ..."

Marian surveyed him. "You tell me I have to leave my own home. Now you're telling me where I should stay?"

"No. Just ... where you shouldn't."

"You have a good reason for that?"

Pat looked away. *Why* was nothing going right all of a sudden? "No."

"Fine then. I'll call Chelsea."

Monday, October 23

Chapter 55

Turnbow hung up from talking to Marian and smacked his desk. Everybody was so testy these days. Marian was testy because she'd been away from home for two weeks. Chelsea Adams was testy because he and Reiger hadn't done anything to catch her new "killer." Reiger was testy because their hands were tied, and Doniger hadn't done one thing to warrant them being on his back. And Turnbow was testy because he, too, was tired of Marian's staying with Chelsea Adams, getting deeper and deeper into this new Christianity kick. *And* he was tired of this case. All of their sweat and sleepless nights, and he felt like he had back in June when they couldn't trip up Gavil Harrison.

With all this "vision from God" stuff, it should have been the case from heaven, not hell.

Not to mention the tangle of their personal lives. Thanks to Turnbow's phone call to Chelsea Adams, she'd figured out his relationship with Marian. Chelsea had promised to say nothing to Marian about Doniger, but the two of them were probably talking a blue streak about Turnbow. Praying a blue streak too. And Marian was becoming more insistent that he go to church with her. As for Turnbow and Reiger, two things kept coming between them. First, Reiger's lingering disapproval of Turnbow's seeing Marian during the trial. And now Reiger's mouth burbled as it never had about God and what the Lord had done in his life. It was as if somebody had unglued it all of a sudden. Now even *Reiger* was pushing Turnbow to go to church with Marian.

"I thought you didn't like us being together," Turnbow had retorted yesterday.

"I don't like that you *lied* to me. You *know* you were wrong. But going to church with her now that the trial's over? I wouldn't want to be a barrier to that."

Yeah, sure. Chelsea had told Reiger all about Marian's conversion. They were all partying over it. Probably figuring Marian would do poor old Turnbow nothing but good.

He felt like a fifth wheel.

Turnbow pushed back from his desk with a sigh. Thank goodness the day was almost over. Marian was coming to his house for dinner after work. Even when they'd gone out somewhere, he'd refused to pick her up at the Adamses. It would be too uncomfortable. He hadn't seen Chelsea Adams since he lit into her in Reiger's office after the trial. He knew he should apologize, and the truth was he was grateful for her help to Marian—and for upholding her promise to keep silent about Doniger. But somehow Turnbow couldn't bring himself to do it. He pictured her, piously forgiving and understanding. He didn't need it.

Stacking some files, Turnbow prepared to leave.

Would Marian press him with more questions tonight? She seemed to sense he was holding something back, and it irked her. Every time he told her he had no answers about Doniger, she acted like she didn't believe him.

Unfortunately, that *was* true. The only thing he and Reiger could do was keep an eye on Doniger, see if he made any kind of move. What great police work. You wanted a suspect, he had to try to kill somebody first. At least now his target wouldn't be Marian. But what if Doniger *did* go after somebody else? What if he succeeded?

What if he didn't, and they were caught in this holding tank forever?

What if? What if?

Turnbow smacked the desk again.

He was *sick* of this case.

378

~ ~ ~

Chelsea stirred jasmine rice into boiling water, turned down the burner and covered the pan. All was quiet. The boys were in their bedrooms doing homework, Marian was out for the evening, and Paul hadn't arrived home yet. Thank goodness for some time alone. So much whirled in Chelsea's head, sometimes she didn't think she could sort it all out.

Marian's stay had been a blessing. Every day Chelsea thanked God for her friend's newfound faith and for this chance to help with her new beginning. Still, the relationship with Marian was so draining. Forced to hold back what she knew about the case, Chelsea felt so hypocritical, particularly when they prayed together for Gavil. He had been sentenced to life without parole the previous week and was on his way to San Quentin—*forever*—unless God intervened.

Lord, please do something soon!

Chelsea's thoughts wandered to Detective Turnbow. Marian was obviously in love, and Chelsea was glad for her happiness. Marian's influence upon him could be strong. She prayed often for his salvation. Chelsea prayed along with Marian, keeping her reservations about the relationship to herself. Being a new Christian with an unbelieving partner was difficult. Chelsea knew that all too well. Would Pat Turnbow end up turning Marian away from God?

As for Chelsea and Paul, their days went up and down. They needed to keep a strong front for Marian, but Paul still struggled with Chelsea's last vision. After Reiger's discovery, he no longer doubted the truth of it. But he couldn't understand how a "supposedly loving" God would allow things to go so wrong. Regardless of Chelsea's explanations of her own shortcomings, Paul refused to see her mistake in not waiting for God's further guidance. As far as Paul was concerned, it was God's fault for sending her a vision with holes in it. Chelsea had come up with the best interpretation she could. And if it was the wrong one, why hadn't God just zapped her with the truth right then and there?

I don't know, I don't know! Chelsea wanted to shout as she popped green beans. Why did everyone think she had the answers when she'd proved the frailest of them all? Sometimes she didn't think she could take another day of upholding Paul and Marian and now even Sergeant Reiger. He'd apologized to her for not standing up for his faith in front of his partner. He told her how much he admired her courage, and how he was now finding his own. Chelsea praised God for that, but she didn't want to be his model. She didn't deserve it, and she wasn't strong enough.

She popped the last green bean and put them in a covered bowl for last-minute steaming in the microwave. She would not be eating them. Or the rice. Or the chicken in the oven. This was her second day of fasting and praying for God in His mercy to break through this mess. Today, Gladys was fasting with her. They both sensed that the break would come soon. All the same, Chelsea felt like she was just waiting for the other shoe to drop.

~ ~ ~

Yearning streaked through Marian as she turned into her townhouse complex. If only she could come home for good. Staying with Paul and Chelsea had been wonderful, but it had gone so long. She'd begun to feel like a foster child. Her mail was being held at the post office, where she picked it up occasionally. And her poor houseplants had been relegated to the edge of the back patio, where they were watered by errant drops from the sprinkler system. She'd even had to promise Pat not to go into her house alone to check on things. He was adamant that her being near Jack Doniger could be dangerous.

Pat's attitude had placed in Marian a fear of her young neighbor, although she couldn't understand the reasons. At any rate, she was about to break her promise, just this once. She would soon need more clothes. Plus her car was long overdue for servicing and was scheduled to go into the dealership later that week. Chelsea would have to drive her to and from work while the car sat in the shop. So Marian would take this opportunity to pick up a few things from home before heading to Pat's house. It didn't matter anyway. Jack Doniger worked evenings.

What was going on about him?

Many times lately, Marian had felt vaguely misplaced, like an actor on the wrong stage. There was something about the tone of Pat's voice when he spoke of Jack, the veil that would fall over Chelsea's face at odd moments, even Paul's occasional piercing glances. Marian wondered about these things, turning them over in her mind.

Maybe they were nothing. She was still fragile, in the healing process. And so much in her life right now was new. She needed to get over her sensitivity.

But then again …

The parking area was full. Marian sighed. Too many people with second cars. Circling the small lot, she drove back the short distance to her townhouse. Residents weren't supposed to park on the narrow street, but it was raining and she'd only be there five minutes. She pulled as close to the curb as possible and ducked through the rain to her porch. A note was folded and taped to her door. She dropped her keys in her purse and pulled it off.

Hope you're doing well. Haven't seen you lately, and I've been worried. Give me a call and let me know you're all right. Alice Geary. P.S. Your boyfriend's partner wouldn't tell me what he was looking for when he borrowed all my stuff from the trial. Maybe you know?

Marian blinked and read the last part again. "Your boyfriend's partner." She shook her head. She should have known Mrs. Geary would monitor Pat's comings and goings. The whole complex and half the town probably knew about their relationship by now. But Reiger borrowing her "stuff from the trial?" And looking for a secret something? Marian hunched over the note, frowning. Why hadn't Pat told her? Did he not know himself?

"Hello, Marian."

She jumped. Swung around—and bumped into Jack Doniger. Marian gasped.

"Whoa!" He caught her arms. "Sorry I scared you."

She stared at him, feeling his hands on her skin. What to say? Her throat wouldn't open.

They looked at each other.

Marian pulled away. "That's okay. I was just ..." She shoved the note into her purse, scrambling for her house key. "Coming to get some things."

"Where've you been?"

"Staying with friends." Was her voice shaking?

Get a grip.

"Oh." He gave her a long smile. "I've missed you."

The words pulsed with meaning. Marian forced her lips to curve. "Aren't you working today?"

"It's Monday. The restaurant's closed."

"Oh, of course." Why hadn't she thought of that? "Well." She turned toward the door, key in hand. "I'm just here for a minute. Got to get some clothes and run." She fumbled her key toward the lock and dropped it.

Jack picked it up.

"Here." Easing her aside, he unlocked the door, swung it open, and stepped inside. He slid the key out of the lock and held it out to her. She looked at him helplessly. "Well, come on in. This *is* your house, isn't it?"

Marian stepped over the threshold, legs shaking, and took the key. Put it in her purse. "Thank you. Good to see you, Jack. I'm going to have to hurry now."

He made no move to leave, smiling again, showing perfect teeth. With a flick of his wrist, he pushed the door closed.

Marian's veins iced over. "What are you doing?"

"I just wanted to talk to you for a few minutes, that's all. You used to enjoy our conversations."

Marian emitted an odd little laugh. "I'm sure I still would, but I really have to be going."

His brown eyes roved over her living room. "Nice place. Decorated a lot better than mine."

"Jack."

"Hm?"

"I *really* do need to go."

"Okay. Go get your things. I'll help you carry them out."

"I don't need any help."

"I'll do it anyway."

"I don't *need* your help!"

He drew his head back. "What's the matter with you? I'm just trying to be neighborly."

"I appreciate that." She tried to swallow. "But my car's on the street. It shouldn't stay there long."

"Oh, sure." He shrugged. "So let me help you get your stuff."

Her heart beat too hard. She feared giving herself away, as if the dropping of pretense would open a dreaded door. "I really would prefer you wouldn't."

"Why?" He brushed a hair off her cheek.

She flinched.

"Are you still seeing that cop?" His tone was almost accusing.

Which answer would make him leave? Yes or no?

Jack's head tilted. "Ah. I see. That who you're staying with?"

How did he dare bother her, knowing a detective was watching out for her?

Then again, what had Jack done?

Jack's expression hardened. "His partner, that Reiger guy, came to see me after the trial, you know."

Marian's mind blanked. She fought to keep the surprise from her face.

Jack watched her. "Didn't know that, did you?"

She shook her head. Anxiety linked with her fear of Jack, dragged the chain across her stomach.

"You can bet your *friend* does."

Marian couldn't help herself. "What did he say?"

"That he needed more information for Gavil's appeal. I talked to him, of course. I've got nothing to hide. But I've asked a couple lawyer friends since then, and they said it sounds fishy. So I'm wondering now. What did he *really* want?"

Alice's crumpled note in Marian's purse weighed on her shoulder. Why all this activity *after* the trial? It made no sense. And why would Pat hide it from her? She *knew* he was trustworthy. She *believed* in him.

But she'd trusted her husband. Then Gavil.

Marian felt color drain from her cheeks. Suddenly, she felt oddly aligned with Jack, as if they were both targets of an unknown conspiracy.

"Would you tell me exactly what Reiger asked you?"

"Sure." Jack related questions about the gloves and his knowledge of Meg Jessler.

Nothing new. "Is that it?"

He shrugged. "I was curious about that woman's vision. He told me a little more about it. Then he left."

"I see. Well." Marian's smile felt like wax. "I'm sure it must be ... what he said it was. Nothing more."

Jack's lips thinned. "Yeah. Sure." Derision wafted from him like heat from asphalt.

Fresh fear rose in Marian. This guy was weird. "I should get my things now."

"Where you going in such a hurry?"

Should she tell him?

"You're going to see *him,* aren't you." Jack's voice lowered. "Your *friend.*"

What was wrong with this man?

Was this what it was like for Gavil? Trapped in prison with unpredictable men?

Marian shuddered.

"Yes. He's expecting me now."

Jack drew himself up. "Well, then. Wouldn't want to *detain* you."

"Thank you."

His eyebrows raised. "So let's get your things."

This wasn't happening. She should never, *ever* have let him in the house. *Lord, help me.* "Jack." She spoke distinctly, like a mother to a child. "I don't want your help. I will do it myself. I just want you to go now. Please."

Marian opened the door.

His eyes darkened to bitter chocolate. "You didn't used to be like this. You used to be nice. *I'm* being nice. I don't understand what your problem is. I've given you every chance. You're no better than the rest. But I'll go." He raised an indignant hand. "I'll go."

He strode out and slammed the door behind him.

Marian's knees weakened. She collapsed against the door and bolted it with a loud *click,* cringing at his imagined reaction to the sound.

Chapter 56

"I can't *believe* this!" Turnbow paced his living room. Marian had barely put her purse down before spilling her story. Horrified, he'd questioned her in detail, his fear churning more into anger with each answer. "How *could* you let him in? You wouldn't even let Reiger and me in the first time you saw us! I've warned you about him. You're hiding out from him, and you *let him in your house?*"

"I told you I didn't *let* him, he just walked in!"

"And you followed. Followed him inside, where you'd be alone!"

"What was I supposed to do? I couldn't let him know I'm scared of him. I'd have looked stupid, refusing to walk into my own house."

"Marian." Turnbow strode back to tower over her. "Who cares what you *look* like. How do you think women lose their lives? They tell themselves they're just being stupid, when their gut tells them otherwise. And you never should have been there in the first place. I *told* you not to do that!"

Marian's mouth hardened, tears filling her eyes. "I'm sorry, okay? I never thought he'd be there. And I don't need you yelling at me. It wasn't fun. I was scared. So just leave me alone!" She swiped at her face. "And besides that, you've got some answering to do yourself."

He glared at her. "What are you talking about?"

"I'm *talking* about your partner asking Jack questions after the trial and borrowing all of Alice Geary's clippings and tapes. She

386

left me a note, wondering what it was all about. I called her before I left my house, and she said Reiger borrowed them *two days after the verdict*. I want to know why!"

Turnbow's insides went cold.

"You *did* know, it's all over your face! You better tell me what's going on, Pat. I thought I could trust you!"

"You can trust me."

"Then why the guilty expression?"

"Marian, I … it's police work. Sometimes I can't tell you everything."

Betrayal etched her forehead. "I don't believe you. It's something more than that." She waited, breathing hard. "Chelsea knows, doesn't she? *And* her husband."

"What makes you—"

"*Everybody* knows but me!"

"Marian."

"*Tell* me! It's something to do with Gavil, isn't it? Something about the case. And Jack's mixed up in it. You told me Jack had nothing to do with it. And yet the only thing Reiger questioned him about was Meg's murder."

Turnbow gripped her shoulders. "Marian, stop. Believe me, please. I love you. I wouldn't do anything to hurt you. If there are things I haven't told you, it's for a good reason."

Marian slapped his hands away. "Don't touch me! You're not touching me again until you tell me. Something's wrong and I know it! You *lied* to me!" She locked eyes with him until he looked away. "And if you won't tell me, Chelsea will. You've made her keep quiet, haven't you? I swear if you don't tell me the truth, I'll never talk to you again!"

"Marian, calm down! You're acting like a child."

"I am *not* acting like a child! I'm acting like someone who's been lied to time after time! It's taken a lot to trust you, and now *you're* lying. I don't have the strength to be lied to anymore, Pat.

Or the willingness. I've been through too much. I'm just … so tired."

Marian dropped onto the couch, sobbing into her hands.

Turnbow's shoulders slumped. Now what to do?

He sat beside her, easing an arm around her shoulders. "Come on, Marian, it'll be all right."

"No." Her voice muffled through her fingers. "It's not 'all right.' Don't think you can get out of this just because I'm crying."

He couldn't keep up the pretense. She refused to believe him. He told her to let it be, that he'd reveal more when he knew the whole story. He'd always planned on doing that. She wouldn't budge. He pleaded with her, told her he loved her. She insisted. He'd never seen her so strong. This was far from the Marian he'd met or even the Marian of three weeks ago.

She stopped crying and pressed back against the couch, arms folded.

"This is it, Pat. I'm tired of arguing. You've got one minute, or I'm going to Chelsea. *She* won't lie to me."

Turnbow's eyes closed. "Marian, you are your own worst enemy."

"Tell me."

"You're not ready to hear it."

"Yes, I *am*."

He took her hand. "Will you be as strong as you're acting right now?"

"Yes."

"Promise?"

"Stop patronizing me!"

"Okay, okay."

He told her.

~ ~ ~

388

Fire in his heels, Jack paced his bedroom long after he'd watched Marian drive away. The burning began in his chest, sizzled down his arms, his legs, over his face. How *dare* she treat him like that! How *dare* she run off to *him,* when he'd given her every chance! Those hazel eyes of hers, that hair, her body, now so slim. He could still feel her skin captured in his hands. For two weeks he'd watched for her every day, longing, *needing* to be with her. Waiting for the opportunity to make a move. She was hurt, lonely. It should have been so easy.

"Aaah!"

He flung out a hand, crashing the clock radio by his bed to the carpet. For *this* he had waited. For *this* he had filled his head with dreams of her. She'd led him on all summer, chatting with him over the fence. So sweet, so sensitive. His lip curled. So *false.* Even Meg had given him two nights, cooing, "Oh, we really *can't,*" while every move of her body begged for it.

Jack's anger had threatened to burn him alive until he let it have its way. Then, peace. Blessed peace.

Now here he was again, heart aflame, kicked aside like a mangy dog.

Meg's taunts echoed in his head. "*My* man lives in Chicago … Chicago … Chicago …"

Just like his mother. "Come here, baby, hug your mommy. Come here, baby …"

"Shut *up!*"

Jack snatched up the radio and hurled it at his dresser. It smashed into the mirror with a loud *crack.* The glass shattered in jagged lines like ground in an earthquake, then fell into a hundred tinkling pieces.

He stared at them, shocked.

He stared a long time. Until dread calm settled over him.

Jack raised his chin.

No more of this. What did she want—for him to destroy his whole house? Who did she think she was?

A betrayer, that's who.

No better than Meg. No better than his own mother. Marian Baker was nothing but a traitor. She'd even sent her own *lover* to jail. Then skinnied herself up to attract the detective who'd put him there.

No more. She *would* be his. Just like Meg had once been.

A smirk twisted Jack's lips. Imagine what Marian would do upon hearing she'd gotten the wrong man convicted.

He thought that over. Shuffled to his bed, sank down on it to think some more.

Thought ... imagined ... dreamed ...

Planned.

Fleetingly, he considered the risk. But he'd managed to get away with it before. Once again, he'd wait. Watch for the best time.

Just once more, and his soul could be at rest.

Just once more.

Friday, October 27

Chapter 57

At day's end, Reiger stacked reports on his desk, mentally ticking off his "to-do's" for Monday morning. The week had been a long one. Crimes included a couple of kids spraying graffiti across a building, radios stolen from two cars (probably kids again), a domestic assault and battery, even a 7-11 holdup down on El Camino. But these were not the reason for Reiger's exhaustion. The business with Jack Doniger had dragged on for three weeks now, blanketing Reiger with anxiety. He was waiting for something—but what?

Chelsea Adams kept telling him to hang in there. God would not let this stand. She'd even talked to him about fasting, and he tried it for half a day on Tuesday. He'd never fasted before in his life and assured himself, as his stomach rumbled, that if he could muster that kind of discipline, surely God would do *something*.

On his way out, Reiger stuck his head in Turnbow's office. His partner was bent over reports. "Isn't it about time you got out of here?"

Turnbow glanced at the clock and shrugged. "I'll put in a few more hours. Nothing else to do."

"Marian still not talking to you?"

"No."

Reiger ambled in and dropped into a chair. "She'll come out of it. It's just a shock, you can understand that."

Turnbow shook his head. "I don't know. She's still questioning my 'intentions.' You know, me versus Gavil. Frankly, I think she's talking more about her *own* loyalties."

"Could be." Reiger tapped the arm of his chair.

"Why is this all *my* fault? Why isn't it Chelsea Adams' fault? Or yours? Why not *God's?*"

Reiger looked at his partner. "You tell her that?"

"Well, so what." Turnbow shoved at a file. "I was mad."

"No wonder she's not talking to you."

"Oh, come off it, Reiger, I don't need it from you too."

"Okay, okay." He held up a hand. "But you know what I think?"

Turnbow gave him a look. "I have a feeling you're about to tell me."

"I think what you're really mad at is yourself. Marian has changed—drastically. You can't deny that. She didn't crumble at the news. She's standing up for herself. That strength comes from her new faith."

"Are you going to preach at me again?" Turnbow lowered his head in his hands.

"No. Sorry." Reiger stood. "It's just that, as you said, seems like all we've got now is God. Looks to me like you're missing out."

"Reiger. Go home."

"Yeah, yeah." He made for the door. "Edith and I are going over to some friends' house for dinner. Otherwise I'd invite you over, try to get your mind off things. You look like you'd be such great company."

Turnbow grimaced. Reiger flashed a grin, then disappeared through the door.

~ ~ ~

Seven-fifteen. Darkness had fallen. Marian gazed out her third-story office window, mind still on her work. The parking lot lights had flickered on, bathing the cement with a yellow-orange glow. Marian had another fifteen minutes to work, but could have used two hours. Her car was being serviced at the dealership, so

Chelsea had offered to pick her up tonight, then drive her to Redwood City to retrieve her car tomorrow.

Twice Marian had picked up the phone to ask Pat to come instead. The police station was less than a mile away, and she'd even shown Pat her office one night after hours. Chelsea was unfamiliar with the area and lived a good twenty minutes away.

Twice Marian had put the phone back down.

She yearned for Pat, missed him terribly. But she needed time. Since Monday, her thoughts had circled with no place to land. Was the second vision true? Could Gavil really be innocent? Was he telling the truth about Sonya? What if he *was* innocent, sitting there in that horrible jail? And what Marian had done to put him there! By Tuesday morning, she had been too nauseated to pull herself from bed and called in sick to work. Which had backed up her projects even more. Chelsea continued to be supportive, listening, praying with her, trying to answer questions. And Marian had certainly been full of them. Once in anger and frustration, she'd even accused Chelsea, berating her for having the visions in the first place.

What a coward I am. Too afraid to yell at God.

Sighing, Marian turned back to her computer. A couple more emails, and she would shut it down. She'd promised herself not to take work with her this weekend. She had too much thinking to do.

"Hello, Marian."

The voice was honey over ice.

Her eyes froze on her computer screen. Pinpricks nettled her arms. Slowly, as if in a dream, she turned her head.

He was leaning against her doorway, smiling a twisted smile. "I've missed you."

Marian's heart stopped. Turned over. She couldn't move from her seat.

Jack stepped inside, reached out an index finger, and pushed the door closed. Locked it. "Working mighty late, aren't you?"

No sound would form in her throat.

"You know you're the only one here?" He eased toward her, eyes holding hers. "Shouldn't do that. Could be dangerous."

"What do you want?"

His teeth were so perfect. He lifted a shoulder. "Just wanted to talk."

"You could have called."

"Something tells me you'd have hung up on me."

He stopped before her desk. She swallowed. "I don't want to talk."

"Too *late* for what *you* want." His tone sharpened. "It's too late for many things."

Dear Lord, protect me!

He surveyed her sardonically, eyes falling to her throat. "Get up."

"Jack, stop it."

"Get *up!*" He jumped around her desk, shoved back her chair. "I'm tired of you not listening to me. *She* wouldn't listen either. Now *get up!*"

Marian pushed herself from the chair, legs shaking.

Somebody else must be in the building.

What would Jack do if she screamed?

"Good." He reached into his pocket. "Now you're going to do exactly as I tell you."

~ ~ ~

Chelsea drove slowly down Ashley Way in Haverlon, checking street numbers. A three-story building with lots of glass, Marian had said. Surrounded by trees and backed up to a creek. Chelsea had her cell phone on the passenger seat in case she couldn't find the building. But there it was—number 815. Spotting the large white numbers, she turned into the parking lot, rolled to a stop, and put the car in park. Seven-thirty on the dot. Marian should be right out.

Chelsea glanced around. No other car in the lot. Apprehension trailed through her stomach. This wasn't smart. No woman should be alone in a building after dark.

Chelsea locked her car doors.

A minute ticked by.

Two.

So quiet. *Too* quiet.

She turned on the radio.

Her gaze circled the parking lot, checked the rearview mirror. Very few times since that day in June had she been out alone after dark.

Two more minutes passed.

Chelsea leaned against the headrest, looking up at the third-floor offices. They all were lit.

Which one was Marian's?

The radio offered nothing but commercials. She fiddled with stations.

~ ~ ~

Jack sat beside Marian on the two-seater couch in her office. He'd watched her face crumble as he detailed the things he'd done to Meg. Things Marian had put her own lover in jail for. His hand now rested on her knee. It felt warm beneath his touch, silk and fire. Her hands were in black kid-leather gloves, butter soft. Gripped in her lap. The use of gloves for Meg had been unplanned, a last-minute, serendipitous discovery that had kept her hands from touching him. Even so, the garden gloves—rough, dirty, and cheap—had befitted her. Marian's gloves, however, had been chosen with care. They were refined, as she was. Soft, as she'd first appeared. Black, as her betraying heart had proven to be.

Jack reached out, raked fingers through her hair. She flinched. "Know what?" he whispered in his throat. "Amazing, but you're still Marian." He traced a nail down her cheek. "Even with the gloves on."

A frown flickered across her brow. She would not raise her eyes. His lip curled. It was beyond her to understand. With effort, he forced the anger down.

It wasn't time yet.

"Believe me, you *want* to stay Marian. For as long as possible." He encircled the back of her neck with his fingers. "Come here."

She braced herself.

He pulled her forward.

~ ~ ~

Chelsea rubbed the steering wheel. She toyed with going to find Marian, but didn't want to leave her car for a strange building. Her eyes veered to the clock. Seven-forty. This was taking too long. She needed to get back home, put dinner on the table.

She picked up her phone to call Marian's office. The cell slipped through her fingers and dropped near her feet.

Great.

She leaned forward, fumbling for it—and managed to hit the horn. The blare resounded through the night.

Chelsea jerked back.

Well. At least Marian must have heard the sound. Chelsea's eyes searched the top-floor windows.

~ ~ ~

Turnbow stretched in his chair, gratified at the popping down his back. Seven-forty. All his reports were done. Time to go home. To an empty house. It hadn't been long since he'd done that every day, yet it seemed forever ago. He'd become so used to being with Marian.

He made a face. What was he going to do with this weekend? If she didn't lighten up soon, he'd go crazy.

He tossed his completed reports in a pile and pushed away from his desk.

~ ~ ~

A horn blew somewhere outside.

Jack froze. He twisted his head toward the window.

Marian pulled back from him, mind racing. She couldn't see anything but the street, but the sound had come from the parking lot.

Chelsea.

Marian tore herself from Jack and leaped from the couch. Raced toward the window.

Jack jumped after her. His fingers scrabbled at her back.

"Chelseeeaa!" Marian lunged for the window and waved her arms. Jack grabbed her collar, yanked her backward. Her cry choked. Spittle flew from her mouth.

Marian jabbed back with her elbows. Caught him in the ribs.

"Ooof!"

Jack's grip relaxed.

She lurched again toward the window, screaming.

He grabbed the side of her neck.

With all her might Marian pulled him forward, arms flailing. His fingers inched around her throat and pressed.

Marian's screams fell to a growl. Black spots danced before her eyes. The window undulated like a desert mirage. Jack pressed harder. Her jaw dropped open, eyes bulging as she struggled for air. Jack spewed curses into her ear. His other hand found her throat and dug in. Hissing filled the room. Marian's gloved hands clawed the air.

"You've done it now," Jack spat. "I'm going to watch you *die.* Just like Meg."

His fingers closed tighter.

Marian gurgled. She felt herself sucked out of her body. She flowed to the ceiling and hung there, looking down in horror as her own knees buckled, her arms fell away ...

~ ~ ~

Chelsea's gaze glued to the third-floor window on the far end of the building. What *was* that?

Looked like two people. Fighting for their lives.

Marian. That was *Marian*.

And Jack Doniger.

Chelsea's heart stuttered. *Dear Jesus.* She scrabbled for her phone on the floor, snatched it up with shaking fingers. Punched in 9-1-1.

"9-1-1, what is your emergency?"

"I — " Chelsea's throat closed. Her eyes raked the third-floor window.

Jack slid a hand around Marian's throat.

"What is your emergency?"

The words tumbled out. "Office building at 815 Ashley Way in Haverlon. A woman's being strangled! Call Detectives Reiger and Turnbow. Tell them it's Marian and Jack. I'm going up there."

"Stay where you are, ma'am, stay on the line. We'll send—"

Chelsea threw down the phone and flung herself out of the car.

Chapter 58

Turnbow shrugged into his jacket, flicked off the office light. If only he had somewhere to go other than home.

"Hey, Pat, late night, huh," a colleague teased as he trudged down the hall.

"Yeah."

Maybe he should go to the Adams' home and pound on the door until Marian would talk to him. What could she do about it —call the cops?

Turnbow crossed the lobby, frowning, and pushed open the glass door.

"Okay, wait, he's still here. Turnbow! *Turnbow!*"

Dispatch's call brought him up short. He turned impatiently. "What?"

"We've got a 9-1-1, two cars on the way. Someone reported a woman being strangled at the office building at 815 Ashley Way. She said to tell you and Reiger. Something about Jack and Marian?"

A trapdoor opened in Turnbow's stomach.

Marian!

"Page Reiger. I'm going!"

Turnbow shoved through the station door.

~ ~ ~

The rolls were mouthwatering. Reiger had already downed three. He was reaching for a fourth when Edith squeezed his knee. He pulled back his hand.

"Oh, come on, she's a *lousy* actress."

They sat at their friends' dining room table along with two other couples who were bantering about the latest romance movie.

"Yeah, well, I don't think she was hired for her acting."

Reiger's pager went off. Edith eyed him with an oh-no-not-tonight expression. He pushed away from the table. "May I use your phone?"

He lumbered to the kitchen extension, still clutching his napkin. Prime rib sat heavily in his stomach. "Reiger here."

He absorbed the words with growing horror. "On my way." He smashed down the phone.

"Gotta go!" he shouted toward the dining room, then raced to his car.

~ ~ ~

Chelsea's footsteps echoed as she threw herself up the final stairway. She burst through a door, veered left, and raced down the hall.

What to do when she got to the end?

The office seemed an eternity away. Her legs wobbled like a colt's. The picture of those fingers around Marian's throat, her flailing arms, pushed Chelsea forward.

"Marian!" She hit the door, grabbed the knob. Wouldn't budge. *"Marian!"* She twisted the knob.

"Jaaack!"

Chelsea pounded on the door, kicked it, shook the knob with both hands. "Jack! Stop! Police are coming!" Tears flooded her eyes as she beat at the wood. "Open the door! Open the door! *Open the door!!"*

~ ~ ~

Marian's throat rattled beneath Jack's fingers. Still she fought. Gloved hands snatched at him, grabbed for his pants, his shirt. Even as he felt her knees give way and her body fold in on itself, those detested hands still clutched at him.

Cold hatred frosted Jack's veins. How *dare* she, after all his planning? After his "sick" days off work, watching, waiting. Before he could wrap tight arms around her while she was still Marian and make her his own.

Now all he could see in her was his mother.

"Marian!" A scream wafted through the door. Followed by pounding. "Jack!"

His fingers unhinged from Marian's throat, his nerves tingling. Marian crumpled to the floor.

"Jack! Stop! Police are coming! Open the door!"

He ducked away from the window and skittered across the office. Breathing heavily, he leaned against the door. Where could he hide?

A siren shrieked in the distance. Another followed. Their highs and lows intertwined, weaving confusion in his brain. His head swiveled back to Marian. To the door. To Marian.

What was he going to *do?*

The sirens wailed closer.

Jack yanked open the door.

~ ~ ~

Again Chelsea flung herself forward—and the door opened. She floated, midair, then crashed into Jack. Knocked him to the floor. Dazed, she scrambled to her hands and knees, tried to push away. Strong hands grabbed her shoulders. Threw her back.

"Ungh!" Her eyes squeezed shut. She couldn't get her breath.

He pinned her to the floor.

Those hands. She knew the feel of them.

Time split in two as she hurtled into the forest of her vision. How well she remembered the ground beneath her, the smells, his hateful words.

"No!" she cried, her voice joining Meg's.

Chelsea's eyelids fluttered open and Jack's murderous face materialized. She clawed at it. Her nails sank into his skin, dredged gullies across both cheeks.

"Aaaahh!" Jack jerked back and snapped both hands to his face. Blood sprang into the wounds.

Sirens screamed closer.

Panic filled his eyes. He fell back on his heels, then leaped for the door. His hand smacked against the frame as he plunged through, leaving a bloody print.

He was gone.

A stairwell door clicked open. Slammed shut.

Chelsea burst into sobs. Rolling to her side, she searched the office.

Marian lay near the window. Not moving.

Chelsea crawled toward her.

~ ~ ~

Turnbow carved to a stop in the parking lot.

The sirens were close.

He threw himself out of the car, nearly falling. Then pounded into the building, gun drawn.

He headed for the far right stairs.

At the stairwell door, he stopped, head cocked. Was that a sound from the stairwell? He readied his gun, snatched open the door, and burst through.

Nothing.

He listened again.

Silence.

He took the stairs two at a time.

~ ~ ~

She lay in a heap, her back to Chelsea.

"Marian." Chelsea rolled her over. Bruises covered Marian's throat.

God, help!

Chelsea felt for a pulse on her neck.

Nothing.

Felt again.

"No, *please*."

Marian's hands were gloved. Chelsea slid off one of the gloves and tugged at the sleeve of her lifeless arm, laying fingers against her wrist.

"*Please,* God, don't let her die."

The hallway door slammed open and shut. Chelsea couldn't move. So what if Jack returned? Didn't matter anymore. Look at what he'd done. What her tragic mistake had caused.

He might as well kill her too.

Sirens wailed to a stop out front. Chelsea hung her head over Marian, tears dropping onto her friend's pallid face.

~ ~ ~

Police lights flashed red across the cement as Reiger skidded into the lot. Turnbow's unmarked car sat near the building's entrance. Reiger bounded from his car and slid out his gun. He knew the building backed up to an area of dense sequoia trees, brush, and a creek.

If Jack could fade into that forest, they could lose him.

Movement flickered in the shadowed left corner of the parking lot. Reiger peered into the semidarkness.

A figure moved into the light, slinking toward the street.

"Stop! Police!"

The man pivoted and disappeared around the corner toward the forest.

"*Stop!*"

Reiger's eyes raked the building windows. Where were the other officers? He'd have no backup.

Gun ready, he ran after his suspect.

~ ~ ~

404

Turnbow burst into Marian's office—and saw Chelsea Adams kneeling over her body.

His blood ran cold.

He rushed toward them and pushed Chelsea aside. Purple marks circled Marian's neck. Turnbow groaned.

"Marian!" His voice broke as he lifted her up, pressing an ear to her chest, listening, *listening.* He forgot all training and experience. His mind screamed that she was gone, he was too late. Grief bubbled up his throat. He clutched her, rattling out a sob.

Chelsea Adams appeared beside him on her knees. "Jesus," she choked, "please save her."

God, please let her live. I'll do anything.

The prayer faded—and Turnbow's training kicked in.

He laid Marian on the floor and reached for his radio, calling for an ambulance. Then he nudged Marian's chin up, careful of her wounded neck. He looked to Chelsea. "I'm going to breathe for her. You need to pump the heart, understand?"

Chelsea lifted a tear-stained face and nodded. He hustled to Marian's other side, giving Chelsea room to work.

A minute later two officers ran into the room, guns drawn. Turnbow barely looked up. "Ambulance is coming." His teeth clenched. "Go find Doniger."

~ ~ ~

Gun in hand, Reiger glided through the darkness, following the sounds of Jack's flight. He stepped over a fallen log, nerves humming. Worries crowded his mind, endangering his focus. Turnbow and his two backups must be in the building with Marian and Chelsea Adams. He could hear an ambulance keening its approach.

God, let those women be alive.

A shadow moved behind a massive redwood trunk thirty feet away.

"Doniger, stop! *Now!* I got a gun on you."

"Leave me alone!" The voice sounded desperate. "I haven't done anything!"

"Come on out, Jack. You won't be hurt."

"You're *lying*. You lied to me before."

Reiger eased forward. "I'm not lying to you, Jack. There's nothing else you can do."

Silence.

"Come on, Jack, talk to me. I don't want to hurt you. Raise your hands where I can see them. Come on out."

Silence

Reiger stopped, flicked his eyes over the trees.

Deathly quiet.

Where was Jack? Was he armed?

Reiger slid behind a tree, muscles tense, weapon up.

He could hear his own breathing.

A small *crack* sounded to his left. Reiger jerked his head, struggling to pierce the darkness.

He was in a forested area with Doniger, just like Meg.

Another sound. He stared harder, saw nothing. Then a third sound, bigger, like a rock falling. Reiger aimed into the darkness, trigger ready. He crouched forward, easing each footfall onto the ground.

A whistle through the air behind him. Reiger spun. Doniger smashed a piece of wood against Reiger's right hand. His gun sailed into the air and landed a few feet away.

Pain shot up to his shoulder.

Reiger swung with his left arm, hit Doniger's stomach. The man fell back. Reiger dropped to the ground and scrabbled in the darkness. Where was the gun?

An ambulance siren wailed from the front of the building, then died.

Doniger lurched. Reiger swiveled to the side, grabbed Doniger's waist, and yanked him down. Doniger pummeled with both fists. He caught Reiger in the shoulder, the jaw. The sergeant gritted his teeth and pushed himself on top of Doniger, for once glad of his weight. The man thrashed and bucked until Reiger nearly slid off. Right hand dangling, Reiger squeezed Doniger's body with his knees, leaned forward, and shoved an arm against his throat. Doniger's hands flew up, then fell to the ground, fingers scuttling.

From the corner of his eye, Reiger saw Doniger's fingers find something, close upon it.

His own gun barrel rose to meet him.

~ ~ ~

"Come on, Marian, come on." Turnbow forced air into her mouth again.

Chelsea pumped the heart until she thought her arms would melt.

An ambulance siren wailed into the parking lot. Two doors slammed. Chelsea jumped up and waved furiously at the medics through the window. They gestured to her as they pulled out a gurney. She dropped again to her task.

Turnbow continued to breathe for Marian.

Wait. What was that?

Chelsea's eyes flew to Turnbow.

There it was again. A faint, guttural breath. Groaning low in Marian's throat.

Turnbow's eyes riveted to Marian's face.

Lord, please! Chelsea's hands hovered over her friend's chest.

Another groan.

The barest of pinks tinged Marian's cheeks, then faded.

They waited.

Nothing more.

"Keep at it!" Turnbow leaned down again. Chelsea pressed palm to back of hand and pumped.

~ ~ ~

Time flattened out, stretched between dark forest and sky. Reiger saw Doniger's finger slide across the trigger. His thoughts sped through memories and regrets, then dissolved in disbelief.

The finger jerked as Reiger lurched forward. The gun exploded by his head, battering his eardrum. He braced for pain but felt only Doniger's screaming jaws trapped under his rib cage.

A crash sounded in the woods behind them. Voices called. Reiger's left hand flew to Doniger's wrist and dug into tendons. The gun wobbled in the young man's fingers.

"Police! Put the gun down!" a voice shouted.

A second shot exploded.

This time Reiger's ears didn't ring.

Doniger convulsed beneath him, then lay still. Reiger's gun thudded to the dirt.

Seconds passed.

Reiger sucked air into his lungs. He could not loosen his knees from Doniger's sides. Then the muscles in his legs melted. He collapsed to one side and rolled off.

~ ~ ~

"Pat, get back!" the medic commanded. Turnbow couldn't loosen his fingers from Marian.

The young man slapped his hands on the detective's shoulders and pulled.

Turnbow fell away.

The two medics surrounded Marian, checking, pumping, feeding oxygen. Chelsea grabbed Turnbow's hand, forcing his frightened gaze to her face. "Pray. It's all we can do now."

She held on to him and prayed aloud.

Marian groaned again. The medics halted, checking.

"We have a heartbeat."

"*Yes.*" Turnbow clenched a fist.

For an eternity they watched as the medics worked.

"Come on," Chelsea begged. "Please, Jesus!"

Marian inhaled a ragged, deep breath. Then another.

A third.

Her blue-white pallor eased. Slow color appeared in her cheeks.

A medic looked up and nodded. "Turnbow. She's going to make it."

Epilogue

Chelsea clung to Paul's protective arm as he ushered her through the teeming courthouse hallway, waving Milt Waking and other reporters aside. As they entered the courtroom, she steeled herself, pushing away memories of the trial. They nodded to Reiger and Seltz but didn't speak, then claimed their seats.

Paul put an arm around Chelsea's shoulders and squeezed. "I love you."

She managed a smile. "I love you too. I'm so glad you're here."

"Wouldn't want to be anywhere else."

Gavil entered with his attorney, clad in suit and tie, looking like the businessman he once had been, although noticeably thinner. Word was that he relied on heavy doses of antidepressants but was improving. His cheeks were hollowed.

His mouth set as his eyes surveyed the crowd, finally landing on Chelsea. Her heart hung over a beat as they looked at each other. His face was stone. He took in Paul, Reiger, Seltz, then lowered himself into his chair at the defense table, vindication arching his shoulders.

Lord, please reach him. Don't let my weakness and terrible mistakes be used to harden his heart forever.

Through Reiger, Chelsea knew Gavil had barely settled into a routine at San Quentin before receiving word from his attorney about Jack Doniger. After Jack's detailed description to Marian of how he had killed Meg, police checked the DNA of the skin fragment from Meg's murder scene against Jack's. The DNA matched.

Sonya Hocking had continued her denials of Gavil's alibi. But the media soon began digging into her private life, uncovering a previous affair. A man who worked for Sonya's husband decided to put his guilty conscience about Gavil's fate to rest by confessing his own affair with Sonya Hocking the previous year. The man told authorities she had contacted him after her denial of Gavil's alibi became public, threatening that he would "lose everything" if he went to the police. After this man's confession, Sonya Hocking finally caved. On advice of her attorney, she pleaded guilty to perjury, hoping for a lighter punishment. She was to be sentenced by the end of the week.

Two days after Sonya's guilty plea, her brokenhearted husband held a press conference, insisting he'd known nothing of her affairs, and announced he was filing for divorce. He vowed that, for the sake of children valiantly fighting cancer, he would continue her work on the cancer center in Sunnyvale. The foundation Sonya had established would be renamed, and, of course, the building would not bear her name.

Chelsea half listened as the judge intoned his decisions. The hearing was mere formality at this point. Everyone knew the outcome. Gavil's conviction for first-degree murder was overturned. In light of the circumstances and partly due to Chelsea's personal pleas, his sentence for burglary and false imprisonment was reduced from six years to four with a high possibility of parole in three.

Chelsea thought of Marian and Pat. Where would they be in three years? Would they be married? Parents? She knew Marian longed to settle down. She and Pat had been almost inseparable during Marian's hospital stay and after she'd returned to Chelsea and Paul's home to recover. Love flowed between them. Watching that was a joy. But Pat remained hardened toward Christianity, and God was already impressing upon Marian the importance of a lifelong partner who knows Christ. At least Pat had gone with Marian to church last Sunday. A first step, even if

411

Pat had merely been trying to appease Marian. Chelsea and Marian could only pray that over time, his heart would be opened.

Miraculously, Paul, too, had been at that service. The four had sat together. He still resisted God's call, but Chelsea rested in the assurance that God would continue to work in his heart.

As for Chelsea, her swirling emotions over all that had happened still threatened tears at odd moments. Her gratitude to God for saving Marian's life and her own had sent her to her knees many times. Yet the relief that it was finally over mixed with the guilt that still fought to envelop her. Gladys had prayed with her numerous times that God would not allow her guilt over the past to tarnish the future He had planned for her.

The judge banged his gavel—and the hearing was over. Reporters descended. Ignoring them, Paul cupped Chelsea's chin. "You sure you don't want me to go with you?"

She nodded. "I'm sure."

A bailiff escorted Gavil out a side door. Chelsea looked to Tanley. He nodded.

She followed a second bailiff through the same door into a short hall, vaguely registering the shouted questions from reporters and Tanley's victorious statements. "Justice was finally done today ..." The door closed behind her, swallowing the voices, the sounds. Now there was only an echoing silence. Her knees weakened. The bailiff tilted his head toward a door at the end of the hall. "You've only got a few minutes."

She nodded. At least Reiger had managed to get her that much.

At the door Chelsea stopped, wiping moist hands on her skirt. She took a deep breath and opened the door to the small room. Gavil stood waiting, a hand in his pocket, chin held high. A bailiff watched from the corner.

"Hello, Gavil." Chelsea could hear her heart beat.

"Hello." His eyes were cold.

412

"Thank you for seeing me. I just ..." She forced herself to continue looking at him, memories of her terror from those eyes washing over her. Still they frightened her, even though the terror need never have been. "I want you to know how sorry I am. I know that sounds so ... paltry in light of all that's happened to you. But I had to see you face-to-face and apologize for my part."

No response. His expression mixed hatred and scorn.

"I know this may be hard for you to understand. My vision was accurate. But I didn't wait long enough for God to tell me the rest of it. I jumped out on my own rather than turning to Him. It's only because of Him that, at the end of the trial, the truth came out. I want you to know that. God *is* reaching out to you."

Gavil's lip twisted. "Yeah? Well, He could have done it a little sooner."

She nodded. "I know it—"

"You don't know anything! You're still living at home! With your family. I have *nothing*. No job. No home. Even the woman I loved is now with the cop who put me here. I bet you like that just fine." Gavil made a face. "She spouts this God stuff in her letters as much as you. *Now's* a fine time to write. Where was she before, when I was insisting I was innocent? Where was God?" He snorted.

"I'm so sorry." Tears bit Chelsea's eyes. She'd prayed so hard for the right words to say, and now none of them seemed to matter.

No way would she cry in front of this man. She turned to leave.

"Wait. You don't have to go just yet."

What was left to say?

Chelsea forced herself to face him again. If he wanted to let loose on her, that was his due. At least she could walk out of there free when he was done.

"Why didn't Marian come?" The raw edge had been sanded from Gavil's tone.

"She told you why. It would just be too hard. On both of you."

He glared at her, mouth tight.

Something inside Chelsea shifted. Suddenly she saw his expression, his stance, for what they were—puny defenses against a pain too deep to imagine. An ache for him filled her chest. *Lord, is there anything I can say to show him how badly I feel?*

"Do you want me to tell Marian something for you?"

Gavil didn't move.

Chelsea waited. Finally she dropped her eyes, then turned toward the door. Reached for the knob.

"Yeah."

Her fingers rested on the cool metal, waiting.

"Tell her I'm sorry for hiding Sonya from her." Gavil's words sounded so bitter. "Turns out, she was hardly worth it."

Tears welled in Chelsea's eyes once more.

"As for that chaplain she sent, tell her not to bother. I'm not about to listen to all that God stuff. My life—*our* lives—were *just fine* before all this started."

The tears spilled down Chelsea's cheeks. Gavil's hard heart formed such a wall between them. Part of her wanted to grovel for his forgiveness, then force his eyes open to God's healing power. But she knew he wouldn't listen. Not to her, not to God. The only thing left was to pray that eventually God would reach him.

"I'll tell her."

Chelsea opened the door and left him.

She followed the bailiff back down the hall on shaky legs, remorse surging over her. *God, I need Your strength now more than ever."*

As Chelsea stepped through the courtroom door to rejoin her husband, the wise counsel of Gladys rose in her mind. "Any time that guilt raises its ugly head you just tell it to go on back to the one who sent it. God has allowed you to go through all this for a reason, Chelsea. *Believe* it. He's going to use your spiritual gift in many new ways. You just have to keep your eyes focused on Him.

"Every minute."

Acknowledgments

My thanks to these professionals who granted me their time and expertise:

Benny Del Re, director of the Santa Clara County Crime Laboratory;

Bob Morse, former San Mateo County inspector for the district attorney and Sheriff's Department homicide detective;

Ron Martinelli, criminologist and law enforcement consultant;

Charles Constantinides, Santa Clara County deputy district attorney;

Kathy Jacomb, Redwood City defense attorney

These folks represent the best in law enforcement, the courts, and forensics in their counties. If you spot any errors, *mea culpa*.

Read the sequel, *Dread Champion*

Chelsea Adams has visions. But they have no place in a courtroom. As a juror for a murder trial, Chelsea must rely only on the evidence. And this circumstantial evidence is strong—Darren Welk killed his wife.

Or did he?

The trial is a nightmare for Chelsea. Other jurors belittle her Christian faith. As testimony unfolds, truth and secrets blur. Chelsea's visiting niece stumbles into peril surrounding the case, and Chelsea can't protect her. God sends visions, frightening and vivid. But what do they mean? Even as Chelsea finds out, what can she do? She is helpless, and danger is closing in.

Masterfully crafted, *Dread Champion* is a novel in which appearances can deceive and the unknown can transform the meaning of known facts. One man's guilt or innocence is just a single link in a chain of hidden evil ... and God uses the unlikeliest of people to accomplish His purposes.

Dread Champion

Chelsea Adams Series Book 2

BRANDILYN COLLINS

Dread Champion
Prologue

After twenty years of midnights among the dead, Victor Mendoza did not spook easily.

The graveyard shift at the graveyard. His superstitious mother had shaken her head when he first took the job. Victor didn't care. You want to talk fear, he told her, fear was the night he was four years old, clinging to his papa's bony back as they scuttled like rats across the U.S. border.

His mother's eyes widened. "But the *dead*."

"They don't scare me half as bad as the living."

Brothers Memorial Cemetery was oddly shaped at its rear, one corner crooking like an arthritic finger around the edge of Darren Welk's sprawling backyard. A single line of ancient gravestones formed that finger, an add-on years before the Salinas Valley sprang to life with ranches and crops. Victor didn't typically patrol the crook. No need to. Whoever once tended those graves had long passed on. His job was to protect the graves of those whose loved ones still visited Brothers Memorial. Folks whose money greened the cemetery and surrounding valley. Rich folks like Darren Welk, whose parents were buried on the eastern hill.

But that night something caught Victor Mendoza's eye, and he ventured in for a look.

Chilly air wafted around Victor as he drew near the edge of the crook, his breath puffing in fog. A crescent moon slung itself against a hazy sky, stingy with its light. He hunched, fists curling, about three feet from the rusty barbed wire fence running the perimeter of the cemetery.

There. A shadow.

Tall and skinny, a warped silhouette spilling across the entire driveway leading into the Welks' garage. The aberration moved in steady rhythm, spindly arms stretching, pulling back, stretching, pulling back. Victor stopped breathing and tilted his head, listening. A vague sound rolled toward him, then sharpened into pattern. *Crunch, hiss. Crunch, hiss.* In beat with the shadow's movement.

Victor's eyes followed the shadow's extremities to its bent shoulders, along its narrow torso, down a stick-figure leg. There it connected with a stocky man on the far side of the driveway, feet wide apart, shovel in his hands. Digging. He extended his muscular arms, and the skinny silhouette arms slid across cement. *Crunch.* The shovel connected with ground. He arced the shovel back and to the side, shadow arms mocking. *Hiss.* Dirt and tiny rocks flowed off onto a growing pile. A large potted bush, similar to others already planted along the driveway, sat a few feet away. Victor's eyes fell on a blazing lantern on the ground behind the man, the cause of his shadow. The light illuminated the man's trousers, haloing his back, fading into an umbra behind his head.

But Victor Mendoza saw just enough of the features to recognize him. Anyone in the valley would know this man.

Goose bumps popped down Victor's arms. His neck warmed with sweat. A man with money to spare for gardeners—planting a bush at 4:20 a.m.? But it was more than that. Something about the man's posture seemed depressed, heavy. Victor forced himself to pay attention, record. One of the man's feet was turned in slightly. Was that a shifting of weight or a half stagger?

Crunch. The man threw his weight behind the shovel, his shadow dancing.

Hiss. He swung his arms, dirt sliding.

He did not raise his head. His shoulders curved inward, neck bent.

Victor stepped back and twigs crackled beneath his boot. He froze.

The man's head pulled up and hung there, adrift.

Spiders crawled down Victor's spine. He remained unmoving, willing the night to blanket him.

Seconds ticked by.

The head lowered. Digging resumed.

Crunch.

Hiss.

Victor Mendoza let out his breath and faded into darkness, creeping around ancient gravestones. He could not shake his uneasiness. When morning dawned hours later, his back muscles still twitched. As he crawled into his warm bed at 8:30 a.m., work shift over, the *crunch hiss* still reverberated in his head.

Two days later Victor heard the news. Darren Welk's fancy wife was missing.

~ ~ ~

Harsh light spilled from the naked bulb, lancing Darren Welk's eyes. He winced.

"Sorry to bring you in here, Mr. Welk, but this holding cell's the quietest place at the moment." Detective Draker stepped aside as his partner, Les Kelly, took a seat at the table on Darren's right. "We had a little altercation in here a few days ago. Haven't gotten around to replacing the fixture yet." Draker settled his bulky frame in a chair opposite Darren. His thinning blond hair was clipped short, a matching mustache bristling under an oversized nose.

"No problem." Darren's response sounded hollow to his own ears. What hadn't been a problem the last two and a half days? He grasped for his last ounce of energy, willing his face and body into placidity while every muscle tensed. He could swear noises were louder. The creak of the door shutting, of clothes rustling,

iii

resounded in his ears. And the expressions! Every glance between Draker and his partner twanged with meaning. Could they see the truth in his eyes? In the twitch of his hands, the exaggerated rise and fall of his chest? Darren spread his fingers on the table. Did they look too stiff? He brought them together. He could barely control his breathing. He was on the edge, and the chasm ran deep.

"Can we get you some coffee?" Draker indicated his own cup. It looked black, bitter, like Darren's soul. His stomach turned over.

"No, thanks."

Les Kelly leaned forward, lacing his fingers on top of the worn wood, his narrow shoulders military straight. Kelly wasn't a tall man but his presence screamed authority. Darren glanced at the man's hands, wondering at his own. At what they'd done.

"What's happening with my house?" He forced the words to be chopped, forceful, like those of the Darren Welk he used to know. *The* Darren Welk of Salinas Valley, who could fill an employee with fear with a mere glance.

Draker cleared his throat. "Don't worry, your house will be fine."

Darren met the man's eyes. They were brown and deep-set, unfathomable. "Which means?"

The Monterey County sheriff's detective shrugged. "Look, I'm sure we can get this all cleared up quickly. That's why we brought you down here. But before we can talk, I just need to tell you that you have the right to remain silent. Any statement you make may be used against you in a court of law …"

Darren stared at the detective's wide face, his skin pebbling. How had he come to this? "I watch those crime shows, too." He tried to laugh, but it sounded more like a choke.

He forced himself to lean back in his chair.

Draker's lips curved at the little joke. A knowing smile.

Darren pressed his heels against the floor, resisting the urge to check Kelly's reaction. Shifty eyes he didn't need.

"Okay," Draker said. "We need you to tell us about the blouse."

Darren closed his eyes. The white blouse with gold buttons. Long-sleeved, expensive silk. She'd worn it out to dinner before they ended up on the beach. When Draker pulled it from beneath the newly planted bush, clods of dirt clung to it like bugs. Darren nearly retched at the sight. His son, Brett, hovered nearby, his face turning pasty white. *"No, Dad——"*

Darren steeled himself, the panic in his son's voice still echoing in his mind. "Shawna cut her head."

"After you hit her, right?"

Darren gave him a hard look. He could feel Les Kelly watching him. "I told you, I'd never hit her before. She just got me mad, that was all. And I was drunk. I didn't even hit her that hard. But she stumbled and fell. Her forehead hit a piece of metal or something in the sand. She got up right away. It wasn't a very big cut, but you know how a head can bleed."

"So the blood got on her blouse?"

"Look at what you've done! How dare you!" Shawna's scream of rage echoed through Darren's alcohol-laden brain. *"Hit me again and I'll have you in jail!"*

Darren vaguely remembered her fumbling with the buttons. "Yeah. That's when she took it off."

"Right there on the beach?"

Darren tilted his head. "It was one o'clock in the morning. Nobody else was around. The Browards had already left. Shawna saw she was getting blood on it and took it down to the water to wash it. She didn't like messes, you can ask anyone that."

The detective stared at him. "Why didn't she have a jacket? Even for an unseasonably warm night, this is still February."

"She got hot sitting near the fire and took it off. I guess Tracey brought it home."

Draker nodded. Darren's heart skipped a beat. Shawna's daughter had been spouting her mouth in the past two days to anybody who'd listen.

"So. When did the Browards leave?"

"I don't know exactly. I told you, I was drunk." Darren caught Les Kelly's slow blink. So the man was weary of hearing that, was he? Too bad, it happened to be true.

"Mr. Welk"—Draker leaned forward—"what did you do when Shawna went to wash the blouse?"

Darren's insides stilled. He made himself look Draker in the eye as he tried to remember.

Icy water on his ankles. Shawna whirling on him in fury. "What are you going to do now, Mr. Do-Anything-I-Please? Drown me?" His utter disgust with her, the fire in his belly, his fist pulled back ...

"I was *drunk.* I passed out on the sand by the fire. Next thing I knew, Tracey was kicking me awake, screaming that her mother was gone."

"You don't remember anything?"

"No."

Draker surveyed him. "Where do you think your wife is, Mr. Welk?"

Darren's gaze raked the ceiling. "How should I know? Probably ran off with some boyfriend. She had 'em all along, you know."

"Mm." The detective rubbed his chin. "She was a very pretty woman."

Words formed on Darren's tongue, but he made no comment.

Les Kelly shifted in his chair. "You saying she just ran off into the dark without her blouse?"

"I told you she had a jacket."

"You said Tracey brought the jacket home."

"Well, who knows? Maybe she didn't. Why don't you ask her?"

"We did. She brought it home."

Darren's throat ran dry.

"Don't you think," Draker said, "that if your wife was going to run off, she'd at least have put the blouse back on?"

"Look, I don't know, okay?" Darren's nerves tingled. "I *don't know*! The blouse was wet and cold and still had blood on it. She wouldn't have wanted to put it back on."

"Okay, Mr. Welk." Draker held up a hand. "All right. But *why* did you bring the blouse home and *bury it*?"

How to answer that so they'd be satisfied?

"Look. I know it sounds crazy. I brought the blouse home, thinking I'd get it cleaned. Thinking that when Shawna showed up, she'd be happy to see I'd taken care of it. I figured it would smooth things over, you know. But by the time I got home, I was mad all over again. Mad that she'd taken off. And I had that one bush in the backyard that the gardeners hadn't yet planted, and I thought, 'I'll show her. I'll stick that blouse where she won't ever find it. Serves her right.'"

Les Kelly spread his hands. "Why didn't you tell us this when we first asked you?"

"I was embarrassed. Sounds like such a childish thing to do."

Draker massaged his bottom lip with a finger. "Your wife is *missing*, and you lie to detectives because you're *embarrassed?*"

His words hung in the claustrophobic air.

Draker's eyes bored into Darren. "Perhaps we should talk to your son again. Maybe he'll remember some things you don't."

"No!" Darren's response was too quick. He worked to lighten his tone. "What would a twenty-two-year-old know anyway?"

"Well." Draker eased back in his chair. "Doesn't matter. We'll know more when our folks finish searching your house."

Apprehension pinged across Darren's shoulders. He sat very still.

"You did ask about that." Draker raised his eyebrows. "Sorry, we should have answered your question sooner. While you waited in our car to come down here, I froze your house. Meaning it's now under our control. No one comes in or goes out without our okay. We'll have a search warrant in a few hours. Then the criminalist will go over every square inch of your place, right down to the shower drains. Of course, that's only part of the investigation. They'll also search your car and rope off the beach where you were that night. They'll look for anything unusual that could point to where your wife could have gone. Anything washed up on shore, things like that."

Darren's thoughts spun.

Tracey slapping him. "What have you done to my mom?!" Stumbling across the beach, holding his aching head. Blood drops on the sand.

Draker still stared at him. So did Kelly. He could feel their gazes snake through his head. "Something washed up on shore? Just because Shawna's missing?"

The detective's smile chilled. "Are you aware, Mr. Welk"— his words dropped like stones—"that both you and I have referred to Mrs. Welk in the *past tense?*"

"When did I do that? I'd have no reason!"

"Your wife washed her blouse because she *didn't* like messes?"

Darren's body drained cold.

In that worst possible moment, Brett's anxious voice filtered through the battered door.